# Killing the Viper

## By: Col. Lee Martin

From:

**The McGowan Collection Series, Book 4**

If you think the only thing to fear is fear itself, you haven't met Bruce McGowan.

ISBN: 979-8-9886604-4-6 (ebk)

ISBN: 979-8-9886604-3-9 (pbk)

Printed in the United States of America

Edited and Produced by
I.E.R. Media

**Also by Col. Lee Martin**

- Wolf Laurel
- Provocation: Return of the Weatherman
- A Hateful Wind
- The Justice Club
- The Third Moon is Blue
- Starbright
- The Six Mile Inn
- The Valiant
- Ten Minutes till Midnight
- Southern Psalms
- Palisades

I hope that you have also read the highly-touted, *Wolf Laurel, Provocation* and *A Hateful Wind*, featuring the brash and bold counter-terrorist operative, Bruce McGowan, and *The Justice Club*, which introduced the deadly and calculating hit man, Atticus Steed. If so, you will be pleased to find that both characters among others resurface in *Killing the Viper*. Each of the above exciting novels is readily available on Amazon.com, Kindle E-Book.com, Barnes and Nobe.com and Audible.com.

———————————————————————-

NLM-

# CONTENTS

# Killing the Viper

- - - - - - - - - - - - - - - - - - - - - - - - - - - - - - - - - - - - - - -

## Foreword

Sometimes on those gloomy, rainy, nothing-going-on days when I can't get out in the yard to tend the flower garden or am not over in Lexington teaching some of America's finest young men and women at the Virginia Military Institute, I might just pull up a rocker on the veranda to watch and listen to it pour. Maybe I'll also lay my head back against the chair, breathe deeply, and take into my lungs the musty aroma of the moist earth. Love the rain. Unless it's a thirty-five-degree bone-chilling rain. But if it's a warm, humid day and I'm out there on the big porch lounging around in an old tee shirt and a pair of Bermudas, for sure an ice-cold Heineken will be sitting on the wicker table beside me.

I'm retired now. From the action game, that is. So, I often find myself getting a little bored. Sometimes I don't know whether it's Tuesday or Friday. The only days I know for sure are Wednesday, when I stand before the cadets filling their ears with my dose of the dub-yas...wit, wisdom and warfighting, and Sunday, when I accompany my pure-hearted, deeply spiritual wife to church.

And then sometimes when I'm sitting out there on one of those ground-soaking days listening to nature's symphony...the murmur of the wind blowing the branches and leaves around, the chorus of the red-eyed tree frogs, and the rain drumming on the tin roof...I might then unconsciously tune Mother Nature out and spiral into deep thought, reminiscing, musing, and meditating on those thirty-five years I spent in the action game. I promised myself years ago I wasn't going to do that...become a misty-eyed old dude in a rocker in his waning years, his body has betrayed him, bemoaning his lost youth, and feeling valueless and empty. Yeah, I might be sitting out there in a rocker, but I'm not wrapped up in a shawl with my wife feeding me my breakfast and oatmeal falling out of my mouth. Not there quite yet.

I do, however, miss the me I used to be. A man in demand by our government. A man hooked on that exhilarating narcotic called danger. I welcomed it. Lived for it. Lived for its lust and stimulation. The day after I retired, was the day I think I started going into the D.T.s. You just can't go cold-turkey all at once after doing the things I did all those years. Fortunately, I had weaned myself off that drug by working with the team on a part-time basis my last year on the job. It was a compromise...fully necessary to salvage my marriage. But, one day later I did hang up my spurs. Did so by choice...the day we buried Lionel.

I guess the experiences that ultimately defined me as Action Man, Bruce McGowan, were those final years I spent in government service as a counterterrorist operative that only few people knew about...a few of whom are dead now. I have been and still remain to this day under oath to never convey to others the particulars of that duty. And although the woman I share my life with has learned more about what I used to do than I have ever wanted her to know, there are things I still would never tell her.

Adriana and I were married a little more than five years ago after one of those later-in-life romances. As I had been raised in the southeastern quadrant of West Virginia, I had often returned to Greenbrier County in the late '90s and early 2000s for a little rest and relaxation. And it was on one of those trips back to the homeland to see my brother and his family that Adriana and I had an occasion to re-connect after thirty-some years. When I had left for college in the late sixties, she was only ten. That was the last time I had seen her.

But as my brother and I were standing one evening on the front porch of the old homestead back, he, smoking a nasty Marsh Wheeling, and I, nursing a glass of Merlot, he just happened to mention sweet little Adriana Randolph and how she was all grown up and pretty like. Her last name was now Wolf, and she was running the stately Bed and Breakfast out in the countryside a few miles away. He said I ought to drop by and get reacquainted with her. I would like what I saw. So, I went to see her. And yes, he was dead-on. I did like what I saw.

But R & R aside, I was actually also in the area on business. Government business. A young Middle eastern man was killed by a big brown delivery truck on a downtown street. In his possession was an alarming schematic of the inside of a factory, pin-pointing silos of rocket fuel and what appeared to be a collateral damage radius. All indications were that he was planning some kind of terrorist attack. And that's where I came in.

However, my intentions to go see the lovely Adriana and her charming country inn were not purely coincidental. My investigation had actually led me to her doorstep. Here's the thing. Not only was our country about to experience the most heinous terrorist attack in its history, but on that same day a nest of young terrorists living right there in good ol' Greenbrier County were postured to carry out one of their own ninety miles away. And it was one of those young lions of terrorism who was ironically staying at Adriana's B & B.

I merely told her I was a government investigator and was following up on some information about one of her boarders. However, it was probably when she later started seeing me in action as an 'investigator' that she began figuring out I wasn't just a run-of-the-mill G-Man. After I had learned that her boarder was one of three Islamofascist students, and who under the command of their leader, a junior college professor, had concocted plans to bomb a rocket and munitions factory down the valley in Charleston, she watched with wary eyes under her own roof as I began setting my own plan into motion. And that's when she found out who I really was...when I made the terrorist bastards suddenly come to their tragic ends.

After that little episode, as Adriana and I became closer over the next few months, she then began to realize that danger was not only a part of my life, but there were times I would actively seek it. And if on occasion I didn't, it would still find me. It was just two months later that my sweet daughter, Caroline, a newly appointed FBI Special

Agent, was kidnapped out in the Denver area by a revenge-seeking retro-terrorist of the Weather Underground persuasion. I tracked him down and although suffering a bit of pain, thanks to a bullet in my back, I was still able to rescue her from the mad man. But unfortunately, that story likewise came to a climax on the grounds of the B & B on our wedding day, nearly costing my beautiful new wife her life. Because I had now become part of Adriana's life, danger had also found her.

And then finally, there was that hateful day of horror a few years later when I returned to my headquarters following a mission to find that my entire team had been wiped out. Their blood was splattered everywhere...on the walls, the carpet, their desks and even the window glass. Only one of the victims was alive...but only for a few minutes. Spurting blood from his lips along with the name of his killer, the most brilliant G-Man and trusted friend I ever knew, Lionel Byrd, died in my arms.

It was a mass murder ordered by a United States congressman who by the way just happened to be a presidential candidate. I didn't divulge to the Bureau his name or that of the actual killer, who by the way was one of our own. I knew the bastards would somehow skate. So, I instead retaliated by dealing out my own brand of justice. And because of the way I responded, I look every day for someone to put the pieces together and send men with guns to pick me up. It would no doubt end with me facing Federal indictment and imprisonment for the rest of my life. You see, the day after the murders I went on my own killing spree to avenge my teammates' deaths. A ruthless and merciless response, yes...but nonetheless absolutely warranted. My involvement was never proved by the Bureau or Secret Service. However, in the aftermath of the killings, as the investigation lingered on, I finally knew it was time. Time that I ended my short career with our elite and highly classified counterterrorist team...Team Zulu.

But then scarcely three months after my retirement from Federal service, just as I was beginning to adjust to my new sedentary lifestyle, the government came calling...again. Seems I had been given yet one more opportunity to keep an act of terrorism from America's doorstep.

# CHAPTER 1

In was in mid-summer of that year on a Friday morning about 8:30 when Stoney Richardson called. I knew from the get-go that it was not a social call. There was nothing at all social about him. It had been just under four months since I last saw him...since I last saw any faces from the old Black Ops teams...Teams Omega, Delta, and India. It was at Lionel Byrd's funeral. The man who was my boss, mentor and friend was gone. And my team, Team Zulu, was gone as well. But, as I conveyed previously, in less than twenty-four hours after their murders, their killers were also dead. By my hand. One of them was my traitorous teammate. And when I was satisfied, they were all dead, their employer, the congressman, merely sneered at me. He bragged of his importance and that he was untouchable. But not to me. Without a second thought, even though he was unarmed, I then placed a bullet in his head. And I still have no remorse about that.

It took me a while for the shock of my teammates' tragedy to wane. The shock may be gone, but the bitterness, the anger, the sorrow, and the emptiness still remain. So, maybe I'm not over it all. Quite frankly, it killed me inside. Killed my will to continue. That's why the day I took justice into my own hands was the day I left government service for good. And it was a couple days later following Byrd's funeral when I turned down the President's offer to assume responsibility as overall team director...even after he practically begged me. The position then went to Richardson, the lead counter-terrorist operative on our Los Angeles team. Me? I took up a new position...full time husband and professional piddler.

As I stood in the upper bedroom of our historic Bed and Breakfast, cellphone to my ear and gazing through the window at Adriana's lovely late-blooming camellias, that old familiar shot of adrenaline fired through my arteries. Talking with any of my old cronies from days gone by...days of the Army Special Forces, the FBI, and again, Team Zulu...always tended to recharge my batteries. To my vexation, you see, my lifestyle had quickly become complacent, even dormant, ever since I finally, and once and for all, succumbed to this life of domestication. Part of that, of course, was because I was still under the enchanting spell of the beautiful Adriana...loving wife, sexual partner and co-owner of one of West Virginia's premier inns, Wolf Laurel. Having ambushed me back there in 2001 with her stunning beauty, her captivating blitheness, and her sultry Southern brogue, she had done much to tame me. But, as she had also been after me these years to give up the action game, it ultimately took seeing my team lying in pools of their own blood to finally convince me it was time to get out.

It was just the idea that somebody in the game still remembered this FAG (Former Action Guy) whether there was any further use for a washed-up has-been late of both the Justice System and the Department of State. Even though I had hung up my spurs and promised Adriana that I would forever and amen devote my time to her and the management of the inn, my brain had often flirted with the thought of grabbing just one more gig. One more for the old red, white, and blue. And maybe there was somebody still out there who needed a guy with my knowledge, skills, and abilities...the full package of attributes that few, if any, of my kind had.

It's never been about recognition and veneration. No awards and medals in shadow boxes, no Certificates of Appreciation, and no photos of a young, studly man of yesteryear taken with dignitaries gracing the walls of my den like many of my action buddies did, because that's not what I'm about. Nor have such accolades ever been important to me. All that junk is buried in an old steamer trunk in my workshop. I do, however, keep somewhere in the abyss of my brain the memory of all my experiences and atta-boys, especially a comment my friend and mentor Lionel Byrd said to me a few weeks before he was murdered. "Bruce, you're the best operative I have ever worked with. That's why the President expressly asked for you on this mission...the one man task force that you are." Although it's just not in me to draw attention to myself or bask in the glow of compliments, I did value that one. Because it came from him. It was genuine, as was anything that came out of his mouth. And that meant more than anything anyone's ever told me... except of course that day Adriana first told me she loved me.

I spent four years with Team Zulu in the Department of State. We were so clandestine as a team that even the State Department, which paid my salary, didn't have a clue as to who we were or what we did. Our four counterterrorist teams, based in New York, Washington, Chicago and L.A., answered only to Lionel Byrd, an ex-Cold War CIA Chief. And he answered only to the President. Even the Secretary of State thought Byrd supervised a bunch of foreign affairs officers located somewhere in Strategic Counterterrorism Communications, most making about $60K a year. Supposedly, we were paper shufflers and profilers working in support of intra-agency operatives with the tasks of reviewing the Visas of foreign nationals coming into the U.S., as well as any association they may have had with terrorist factions throughout the world. The Intel would come from sources like Interpol, the CIA, the NSA and FBI. We would in essence review and assess the information and then re-feed our analysis back to the requesting agencies for appropriate action. In other words, we were data people. So everyone thought.

However, in actuality, we fed nothing to no one. Once we gained the intelligence, we generally advised these alphabet agencies a realistic threat or terrorist connection was yet to be determined; then after quickly devising a calculated plan, we took out the terrorist threat ourselves with swift and violent execution. During my tenure, we eliminated a significant number of Islamofascist cells operating abroad as well as inside the U.S. borders. But, as I earlier conveyed, on one occasion I actually took out a domestic threat where a member of the 70s radical organization called the Weather Underground had resurfaced. He still wanted to blow up government buildings.

Anyway, I've spent these months of retirement trying to put all this action behind me. All I have left are the memories. We will soon have a newly elected President and he won't know anything about me. It's just as well. If I would not be at his beck and call, then there would be no opportunity for me to be tempted.

"Who are you talking with?" Adriana called from the kitchen.

"Nobody," I yelled back.

"Nobody?" Stoney shouted at me. "That must have been your wife I heard in the background. So, is that who I am now? Nobody?"

"I thought you always were, Richardson," I replied, smiling. "So, why are you calling from out of the blue? Miss me?"

"Just checking on you, that's all."

"I know better. You don't have a caring bone in your body. You want something."

"Ah, the great Bruce McGowan...code name Scorpion. I suppose I caught you wearing an apron and washing dishes...or did I catch you getting ready to do the dirty nasty with the Mrs. Is that why she's calling you? I can call back when you're done...in about thirty seconds."

I laughed. "Spoken by a man who wets his pants if a beautiful woman even asks him what time it is. Are you still living with your mum?"

Stoney Richardson was quippy like me. But not as funny as me. Socially inept, he didn't like hanging out with the team when work was done. But, he was good at his work. As he had been the lead operative when we were all up in New York, Lionel Byrd was nearly as high on him as he was me. Nearly. Now Stoney was in charge. Not only of the rebuilt Team Zulu but of all the teams. However, he was no Byrd. He wasn't as polished, nor did he have a stellar history with the CIA as did Byrd. Before the towers came down, we had all been in the New York operation. But then afterward, we were split up to form teams in strategic locations around the country, basically in the larger cities. And only days after 9-11, Byrd, three others and I moved down to Washington. Lionel then brought in a slew of new operatives...all from either the FBI or CIA. He had offered me that New York team; but I chose to stay with him in D.C.

I continued. "So, since I know you didn't call here to talk about my sex life, what do you want?"

"Do you remember Preston Johns?"

"Yeah, of course. Why?"

"He's now the President's new National Security Advisor."

"Good for him. It was obvious to me when we were both at the Bureau, he was a fast tracker. Number one graduate in his class at Howard University and number one graduate in our FBI class at Quantico." I had also heard that he made the list of the 50 most influential Black Men in America. Barely thirty when he was made Special Agent in Charge. Then three years later, he was working for the Director in Washington, DC. It didn't surprise me he went to a post like this.

"So, what about him?"

"He called me at the President's request this past Monday, wanting to know if you're not only still alive, but vertical."

"And he's interested why?" I asked.

"Johns wants me to set up a meeting between you and him. Says he will come to you."

"He wants to come here? For what reason?"

"He wasn't specific," Stoney replied.

"He just said he wants to engage you in something. I was a little taken aback that whatever deal he had in mind, he didn't choose me or any of my operatives, choosing instead a dinosaur like you who's been out of action a while."

"Jealous?"

"No. More like mystified."

"Maybe something's come up on one of my old cases...one where the book has yet to be closed. For weeks after Congressman Randall was killed, along with one of our own who betrayed our unit, killing everyone on our team, the Bureau was all over me. Like, what did I know about it? They wondered why I was the only person in my office to survive. And then they started digging into what we did. Of course, the President shut them down in a hurry."

Stoney said, "I took a little heat myself from the heavies in the State Department when I assumed leadership of the team. They had become suspicious that our office was not just about analyzing information and profiling subversives. And I've been doing my best to keep Zulu in defilade. But as far as I know, in regard to the team's massacre, Bruce, I think the Bureau's book is now finally closed."

"Let's get back to Johns. What specifically did he tell you?"

"To just set up the meeting. No elaboration. Again, he said he'd come to you. Whatever he wants from you, apparently, I'm out of it."

"When does he want to meet?"

"He says he has time on his calendar for Sunday afternoon...the day after tomorrow."

"Then tell him I'll be here. The afternoon is good. My wife and I will be back from church about one o'clock."

Stoney laughed. "You? Attend church? You've got so much blood on your hands, how the hell do you ever expect to make it through the Pearly Gates?"

"They were all righteous kills, pal. My conscience is clean."

"Maybe it's clean because you never used it." He laughed again.

"Good one, Stoney. You win the round. Tell Johns I'll be waiting."

"Good talking with you again, Scorpion."

"Tell your mother hello for me. You still taking her to bingo and out dancing at the American Legion Hall?"

"Ha, ha!" he said sarcastically. "I still like you, Bruce. As a matter of fact, it's common knowledge that nobody's ever had a higher opinion of you than me...and I think you're an asshole."

"Goodbye, Stoney."

# CHAPTER 2

While Adriana was still in our upstairs kitchen in her robe clearing away the breakfast dishes, I plopped my bones into the cushy leather chair I call my Big Easy, closed my eyes, and then began contemplating just what it was that Preston Johns could want with me. I had served with him briefly when we were both with the Bureau in Atlanta. During that short period of time, we became friends. However, sometimes working as a duo taking down mostly white-collar perps, we also on occasion hung out for a beer after hours. My first wife, Darlene, and his lady, Juliette, had become close friends as well, doing their own thing while we were chasing bad guys. For a few years after he left Atlanta and then went on to high visibility assignments, we stayed in contact. However, as his soaring upper mobility was putting him in the Justice Department limelight, we eventually lost touch.

And then I began to ponder how he would have known anything about me after my tenure with the Bureau. If in fact he had singled me out for some assignment that only a couple of people like me could do, how would he have known what my last tour of duty was? Again, Team Zulu, the most covert counterterrorist operation in the business, was known by only the one person...the President. At least that's what Byrd had told me. If Johns was engaging me in something, based on his knowledge of me during our

Bureau assignment together, I can't remember anything I did that might have impressed him. So, how would he know that I was touted as the most estimable and skillful of all terrorist hunters...smart, ruthless, calculating, and intrepid, not to mention modest and humble? Whatever Johns wanted; I was pretty damn sure he wasn't just coming by to meet the new Mrs. McGowan.

Speaking of my lovely wife finally came out of the kitchen to ask me who 'nobody' was. "Just an old friend from the L.A. team."

"The Lakers or the Dodgers?"

"Funny. Stoney's from the Los Angeles team that did the same thing I did in Washington.   He actually is the guy who replaced Lionel Byrd."

"He didn't call to drag you back into any counterterrorist thingy, did he?" Her tone was unusually curt. "Those days are over, Mr. McGowan."

I snagged her by the belt of her robe as she was passing by me, which toppled her onto my lap.

"How long has it been?" I asked.

"Since the day you quit the government? You..."

"No. Since I last made love to you."

She smiled and slapped me on the thigh.

"If you don't remember anything about last night, then my dear, you obviously chugged down too much of the grape."

"Hmm. It is all a bit fuzzy now that you mention it. How about a little more of that action to refresh my memory?" Always in scoring position.

She then pinched my nose between her thumb and forefinger. "Forget it, bad boy. I have to shower. Remember, we have that Florida couple coming in this afternoon and I have to get their room ready."

"A shower, huh? Well. I might as well join you since we're trying to conserve utilities around here. Did you see our water bill last month?"

"Since I take care of the bills, you know I did. And I know you didn't. You're just using that as a reason to get frisky. Sorry, Skippy." She then pulled herself up and sashayed off, teasing me along the way by dropping her robe so that I could get an eyeful of one of the most tantalizing bodies on this side of the Garden of Good and Evil.

"You don't play fair, Mrs. McGowan!" I yelled after her.

When she entered the bathroom, she smiled and gave me a little finger wave, then closed the door behind her.

I still couldn't imagine what was so compelling that would make Johns want to 'engage' me...and then come all the way down to my place to talk to me about it, the aging, retired public servant that I was. There was a hell of a lot younger, better trained, highly technical government operatives out there that made me look like a 58 Edsel in comparison. True, they may not be as well-seasoned and lethally efficient as good ol' dependable me, but my day had passed. If Johns wanted me to just do the behind-the-desk profile and assessment thing, the CIA, FBI, and NSA had battalions of people that could do that without missing a beat. So, obviously, he wanted something out of me he knew did not exist in any of these agencies, or even in Team Zulu. But I guess because they all had to play by the rules...well, there you are.

On the other hand, I can be had, if the opportunity is right. One can't live for nearly forty years as a highly energized action figure and then just retire with a pulse that doesn't rise above 68. However, I do raise mine once in the morning for about forty-five minutes when I'm out jogging...which happens religiously...and again most nights for another forty-five minutes when I am engaged in the act of coitus maximus with the Lady Adriana. Okay, I might have exaggerated ever so slightly on that last thing. However, if I didn't keep myself physically, cognitively, and sexually fit, I could very easily drop into the Big Easy every night and become a two-hundred fifty-pound sloth like nearly two-thirds of my age group. But I refuse to do that. I refuse to surrender to complacency and lethargy, sitting nearly comatose in front of the TV with a bag of chips or a pound of fudge. I do, however, stay away from a lot of the so-called health foods. At my age, I need all the preservatives I can get.

Yeah, it wouldn't take much for me to answer the call once again. Of course, I'd have to convince Mrs. McGowan once again there was absolutely no danger in the deal and that there was no one in the entire Justice System that had the skills, the brains, and the stones to get the job done. And then she would have to be convinced that the end of the world would be at stake if I didn't agree to do my part. But who am I kidding? No way in hell would she ever again let me hang out my shingle...the one that read Bruce McGowan Terrorist Hunter. Open for Business.

In less than a half hour Adriana was out of the bathroom and searching for something to wear. Looking very much like a Victoria's Secret model in her shimmering pink underwear, she finally pulled from the closet a blouse and some slacks. I just happened to be standing nearby salivating like Pavlov's dog.

"Yowser, Mrs. McGowan."

"Put your eyes back in your head, before they fall out on the floor, bad boy."

That's when I made a ground-breaking observation. "You know, I've always wondered why people say 'a pair of slacks, a pair of hose, a pair of shoes, a pair of underwear;' but then a bra is just a bra. Isn't that also a pair of something?"

She shook her head slowly and pursed her lips into a smirk.

"You obviously have nothing else to think about if you just sit there making comments about my underwear," she chided. "Isn't there a crossword or Sudoku puzzle lying around that you could use to re-fire the neurons in that brain of yours?"

"Hey, just wait a minute. I'm not only retired, but am present for duty being your husband instead of out taking down bad guys. Isn't that what you wanted...me being twice as much husband for half the income?

She just smiled and shook her head. "Don't you have a shower that needs to be taken?"

"Yeah, I suppose. Scrub my back?"

"Not a chance. I can't trust being around you with your clothes off."

"You can't trust me or yourself?"

She sighed. "I'm going downstairs."

It had been an unusually slow spring and early summer for our business. Maybe something to do with the economy. We probably had not had more than a half dozen guests since the first of May, and here it was August. Any other year, we might have rented twice the number of rooms by now. I shouldn't say our business. It's always been Adriana's. And she has managed it quite well since her first husband died some ten years ago. His name was Mason Wolf and Wolf Laurel had been in his family since long before he met Adriana. She and her long-time maid, Juanita, a plump, jovial Mexican lady, cook the breakfasts, change the bedding in the four guest rooms, and keep the place running like a top. Wolf Laurel continues to be quite popular on the List of Country Inns, and as it sits majestically off the beaten path in Greenbrier County, West Virginia, at the base of the glorious Alleghenies, it is always touted as one of America's most pleasing and picturesque B&Bs.

As serene and peaceful a place as it is, Wolf Laurel unfortunately had been the venue of two acts of terrorism, thanks indirectly to me. Again, the first, back in 2001, involved that young al-Qaeda jihadist who was staying at Adriana's inn, who was connected to the 9-11 terrorist faction and who plotted the attack on the Charleston area factory that was partly owned by an Israeli company. When I ended up putting bullets in him and his cohorts, his superior, out of revenge, decided to use Adriana, my brother, and a guest as bait to draw me into his trap. It was only right that I'd end up killing him as well. And then, that second time danger came to our B&B was when the Weather Underground terrorist, who had a grudge against me, checked into the inn while I was away and posed as a writer for a Country Inn magazine. On both occasions, Adriana almost lost her life at the hands of these terrorists. And that was when she began gaining a deeper knowledge of what my job was all about with Team Zulu. And that was why she wanted me out of the danger business.

But I love where I am now as co-host of Wolf Laurel, although I contribute very little to the operation, by design of course. Mostly, I'm off teaching Criminal Justice and Infantry Tactics at VMI over in Virginia or I might be found playing golf at the country club with a couple of my State Police buddies. I do mend a few structural things from time to time, take out the trash, and actually do a little gardening. I've become quite the horticulturalist and small-time farmer with the tending of perennials and the planting of colorful summer annuals. I also raise Mortgage Lifter tomatoes, some squash and onions, and have a small row of corn. Just that little bit of activity has kept me from going bonkers in this rather sedentary life I have agreed to live. But I do what I can to keep the woman I love happy. She's a complete one-eighty from my first wife. You see, what I did this time was not merely marry a woman that I thought maybe I could live with; I married a woman I knew I couldn't live without.

We do, however, have our spats from time to time. It was mostly in our first year of marriage that we argued about my traipsing off on missions with Zulu Team, flirting at every turn with danger and death, and then sometimes coming home with holes in my body from angry 9 millimeters. One thing I learned from those arguments with her, however, was to be a good loser.

I'm usually up at 5:30 or so, and like I said, as soon as twilight begins, I'm pounding the pavement on a five-mile run across the beautiful Greenbrier Valley countrysidee. Just taking that fresh morning mountain air into my pure lungs, that have never drawn in the smoke of a cigarette, is almost as invigorating as experiencing a night of hour-long, sensational sex. Almost. Jogging cranks up my morning like nothing else. I've always lived by the old adage; the early bird gets the worm. Whoever coined that saying, maybe Ben Franklin, considered too much the good luck of the early bird and not enough the bad luck of the early worm. But, I guess that's what Adriana meant by my thinking about worthless things. Maybe she's right...I do need to recharge this sponge of mine.

I had managed to temporarily sidestep Adriana's question about why an old friend was on the phone. However, she would soon find out what the call was about when Preston Johns was to show up at our place on Sunday afternoon. So, I thought it best to go ahead and tell her to expect a visitor from my old days with the FBI. But that didn't mean he was coming here to draw me into another gig after all this time. However, it was obvious he wanted me to do something for the flag, whether or not it had anything to do with bullets.

In short order, I showered, put on a splash of Bvlgari and donned a freshly starched oxford shirt and khakis, all of which would serve to tantalize Mrs. McGowan's sensual side. Any other day when we were not expecting guests, she might then drop what she was doing and lead me back upstairs to have her way with me. All right, maybe I am too much the dreamer.

The Florida couple arrived just before noon, having driven from where they stopped for the night in Charlotte. Both were in their upper seventies, perpetually tanned and covered in wrinkles. Seeing their crinkled skin made me want to go back upstairs and iron something. They were Jim and Jackie Barstow from one of the Sun City check-out generation developments. Adriana asked them if they knew her parents, Bill and Gloria Randolph, who lived in the same-name community near Jacksonville. They weren't sure. Adriana said they'd be sure to recognize her father with his wide, red suspenders, even hooking them up to his Bermudas, the GQ guy that he was. They said that accounted for 'probably half of the fellas.' Anyway, after they were settled in and struck back out to tour the

Greenbrier, Adriana and I sat basking in the delight of the warm afternoon sun that finally revealed its radiance on the west side of the veranda. The birds were singing out in yon trees and occasionally, thanks to a slight breeze, the intoxicating aroma of Wolf Laurel's gardenias filled our nostrils. It seemed like an opportune time to tell her that my former FBI compadre, Preston Johns, would be stopping by for a visit on Sunday afternoon.

"That's nice," she said. "Didn't I meet him at Mr. Byrd's funeral?"

"Hmmm, I don't think so or at least I didn't see him there. He's the National Security Advisor now. A big cheese in the President's cabinet. I served with him in the Bureau."

"So, he's just passing through? Or does he have another agenda...like wanting you to hunt down some terrorists for him?"

I smiled and placed my hand on hers. "My, don't we have a suspicious mind? I'm not sure why he's coming by. Maybe he has some business in the area and remembered that I retired here."

Adriana fixed her eyes to mine and her mouth formed a wry, even snide smile. "Maybe. But maybe he's coming by because he wants you for something." She then looked away toward the errant vine of the climbing roses off the edge of the banister. "We've talked about this, Skip. You've already given your pound of flesh to the government...literally." Referring to the times that slugs had to be cut out of me and pieces cut off of me.

"Adriana, I promise you I don't know why Preston's coming by. If he does want me to do something for him, maybe it's to just perform a little research."

"And there would be no one in any of the government's agencies who could do that...not the FBI, CIA or any other of those James Bond outfits."

I then patted her hand. "Before we jump to any conclusions, let's just let him get here and we'll see."

She nodded, but her eyes were sullen.

"Yes. Let's just see."

# CHAPTER 3

It was now Sunday. Adriana hadn't in the least forgotten about Preston John's looming visit in the afternoon. In fact, we had a couple of words about it on our way to the Methodist church. But once inside, she was cheerful and filled with bliss as usual. And me...I was on my best behavior, singing hymns in my off-key voice right along with everyone else. While the minister was making his points, I was nodding in agreement to every sentence. At least that's what Adriana thought I was doing until she caught me checking my eyelids for pinholes during a rather lengthy nod. She only had to dig into my thigh twice with her razor-like nails to keep me attentive. I think what gave her a clue that I was dozing was when the pastor made a very loud and emphatic point to which I responded with an *amen*. I had no idea what he was preaching about. It just somehow *sounded* like it needed an amen. Unfortunately, he was telling about seeing one of the parishioners coming out of the liquor store last night as he was driving by. Of course, every eye in the church turned toward me after my amen, especially Adriana's. Only *her* eyes remained on me for a more lengthy, rather uncomfortable duration.

We both had a healthy, baked chicken dinner at The General Lewis Inn on the way back from church as Adriana conversed with a couple of her old girlfriends sitting at an adjacent table. What's up with that? *I'm* not allowed to talk with *my* old girlfriends.

Winding around the curves on Route 60 in my sweet little Austin Healey 3000 with the loveliest of God's creatures in the passenger seat beside me...well, life just doesn't get any better than that. However, soon I downshifted into third and then into second to turn off the highway and onto the rough asphalt road that led to Wolf Laurel. The pungent smell of the rich, green earth and cow do-do was nature's perfume to me. Top-down, eighty degrees, our windshield cutting through the air, was the kind of religious experience I always want to have...on a bonny Sunday or any other day of the week. There's something about nature that gets me closer to God than anything else. And how better to enjoy such an experience than taking your little British sports car and your beautiful wife out for a spin.

No sooner had I pulled the Healey into the gravel driveway and brought it to a stop, I spied a black Lincoln limo with blacked-out windows sitting off to the northeast edge of our parking lot. It was difficult to determine whether anyone was inside the car or had gotten out to go look for me inside the inn. I immediately saw that it had Federal license plates and assumed, of course, it belonged to Johns.

"My guess is that this is the company you were expecting," remarked Adriana.

"Looks like it." I then pulled the hand brake and killed the engine.

"I think I'll go on inside, "she said. "Shall I prepare some snacks and something to drink?"

"I'd wait. He may not even come in."

"I can't imagine he'd drive all this way from Washington, DC just to chat for a few minutes," she said.

"Go ahead, then, while I go over to meet him."

Adriana swung her legs out of the car, glanced back again at the long limo, and then trekked up the front steps.

I am always wary when I approach large black units with blacked-out windows, especially when someone who came to meet me is not getting out of the car. I touched my fingers on the grip of my Glock beneath my sports coat. Yes, I'm *always* packing...even in church. Much to Adriana's displeasure.

I'd have thought Johns would jump on out when he saw me, then place a bear hug on me for old times' sake. However, it appeared he was waiting for me to come to *him*. But I have learned to trust *no* one; it's my only defense against betrayal. I learned that the hard way. And I guess that went for Johns as well, no matter how close we were at one time. I placed my hand fully around the grip of my weapon as I moved in toward the car. That's when the passenger side glass dropped, and the face of Preston Johns appeared. I then cast my eyes on his driver who raised his hand slightly in greeting. So far so good. I stopped within five feet of the limo, my right hand ready to pull.

"Hello, Bruce. Long time, my friend." he said.

"Preston Johns. Moving up in the food chain I see."

"Life's been good. Get in."

"Who's your driver?"

"This is Jerry Hayen, Secret Service, assigned to me by the President. Hop in and chat for a few minutes."

"Surely you didn't drive this distance just for me to sit in the car with you. Why don't you two come inside and rest up? Sit a spell." I spoke.

"I'd rather not, Bruce. What we need to talk about is a matter of strict confidence. I saw your bride go in and since there are three other vehicles in the lot, you obviously have guests." He then glanced at my 3000.

"Nice sports car. You must be doing well."

"The Suburban is mine and the van is my wife's. The Accord belongs to boarders from Florida. We have a parlor room with a door we can close. It's not available to guests."

"If it's all the same to you, Bruce, I'd like you to take a ride with me."

Now when someone in the professional ranks tells me to get into a black car and take a ride with him, my antenna goes up every time. I don't care if he *is* the number one guy in National Security Agency. But then again, I knew Preston. We put down a number of bad guys together after which we hit the bars and put down a number of steins. Of course, I had done the same with teammate Chuck Robinson who sold out Byrd, the team *and* me for a scant half mil, God rest his soul.

Johns apparently sensed my apprehension, so he then opened his door and got out. "You're acting a little strange, my friend, not to mention cradling your firearm as you are. But I guess I can't blame you, considering what went down with your team."

"And what do you think you know about that?"

"Remember who my boss is," he replied. "Maybe I too would be mistrusting of a government type who showed up at my house out of the blue. But it's me, Bruce. You *know* me. And yes, this is going to be about business." He then paused and looked me up and down.

"Retirement looks good on you. Somehow, you look younger...even in better shape."

"I married a young wife. She's taken ten years off me."

He smiled a genuine smile. Tall, lean, and broad across the eyes, he hadn't changed much either since our days in Atlanta.

My consternation now gone, I took my hand off the Glock and thrust it out to greet him. "See? No piece."

Johns laughed and shook my hand.

"Always the cautious one."

"Always," I echoed.

"Why don't we ride and talk. Anyway, I want to see some of this marvelous countryside. Maybe you can show me around."

"All right. Let me tell the wife I'm going out. I also need to give her the tag number of your limo *and* your description in case somebody finds me lying in a ditch somewhere."

He laughed again, which compelled his driver to force out a chuckle as well. I *would* be keeping my gun at bay.

"Here. Give her my card, my cell number and anything else you can think of. Tell her we'll be back in an hour or so...*and* that we're not going out to meet women."

I smiled at that and then went in to give Adriana the message.

"That's it. Go off and play," she said. "I guess I'll just go check on our guests to see if they need anything and then I'm going to read a spell."

I gave her a peck on the lips and pat her on her rear cheeks. In short order, I would then find out what it was that the National Security Advisor of the United States wanted with me.

# CHAPTER 4

Johns opened the right rear door for me, exposing the cavernous passenger compartment that contained two sets of seats, each facing the other. When I stuck my head in, preparing to enter, I immediately saw we were not alone. In the rear seat sat a well-dressed man and woman, both obviously in their low 30s and both wearing bright, eager sets of eyes.

"Bruce, meet FBI Special Agents Maggie Larsen and John Hickcock."

I stalled for a moment but then climbed into the middle seat that faced them. Johns slid in beside me. "FBI? I'm not understanding," I said.

Johns ignored my comment. "Let's move out, Jerry. Where's a nice scenic route to take on this fine-looking day, Bruce?"

"Okay, Feds, what the hell? Am I being taken out into the country to be whacked and left for the crows?"

"Come on, Bruce. It's *me*. Why all the paranoia?"

I glanced warily at Johns and the two agents and then said, "All right then. Turn left out of here, go to the end of the road, and in about a half mile, take a left onto Route 60 west. We'll go down through Lewisburg and then out into some farm country. If you go over the mountains and hit Charleston, then I've officially been kidnapped."

"Still got that sense of humor, eh pal? I do miss the old days down in Atlanta," Johns said.

"Let's cut through the chase, Preston. What is it you want and why is the FBI sitting in the back seat of this car with the National Security Advisor?"

"May I, sir?" said Hickcock.

Johns nodded.

"Go ahead, agent. I'll tag team along with you."

John Hickcock was a good-looking dude with thick, dark hair and Matt Damon looks. Kind of reminded me of *me* a hundred years ago. His partner, Larsen, was pretty enough with her pent-up, dark auburn hair and perky ta-tas. With a little make-up, I'm convinced she would have been a knockout. If I was not married, and two or three years younger, I'd have been knocking on her door.

Hickcock began. "Maggie and I were recently assigned to the FBI's Counterterrorist Division up in Washington, DC, mainly performing strategic assessment on radical fundamentalists here in the United States. More specifically, we focus on al-Qaeda terrorist activity, regionally, but also other groups which have found their way into our borders...such as the Palestinian Rejectionist Group, Hezbollah, and other terrorist elements from Syria and Libya. Are you with me so far?"

I nodded. "Yeah, Junior," I said under my breath.

He continued. "Al-Qaeda has been dealt several blows over the past few years that not only has left them relatively disorganized but shattered to a degree. However, recently, we have seen a strong *re*organization of al-Qaeda and a re-emergence of its presence throughout the world. Their leadership is historically very patient, and we knew it was just a matter of time."

I might have rolled my eyes once. "Splendid. You came here with Preston to give a retired government man an update on al-Qaeda?"

"Just stay with me, sir. Mr. Johns, who oversees all counterterrorism collaboration among the agencies, has received from both the NSA and the National Counterterrorism Center intercepted, encrypted transmissions, via a TACLANE unit, between a man who presents as the most imminent threat to our country's national security, named Asahif al-Massoud, and one Sheikh Mubarek Gilani. Al-Massoud has forged ahead of Osama bin Laden as *the* most dangerous terrorist in the world. Gilani, the leader of an American-based group called Jamaat ul-Fuqua, operates more than thirty-five jihadist training camps in about eighteen states."

"The group is also known as The Soldiers of Allah," interjected Johns.

"I know about them," I said. "But for the most part, they're not perceived as a real threat with the exception of the ul-Fuqra headquarters in Hancock, New York, and perhaps York, South Carolina."

"Right," commented Larsen. "But Gilani's recent communique to his Soldiers of Allah, issued in the form of a manifesto, outlines how a newly built training camp not far from here in the mountains of Virginia, west of Lexington, will form a jihad unlike anything that has been unleashed to date on American soil, surpassing the casualties of 9-11. The compound, which is located about seven miles outside of the Town of Goshen, houses about a hundred men with another seventy-five Arab-looking people, according to the locals, living in and around the town. Day students, you could call them."

Hickcock continued. "Last fall a couple of hunters stumbled into the Goshen camp. Before they were escorted out with AKs shoved in their backs, they observed from a distance training going on in combative, explosives, marksmanship and even how to separate a man's head from his body with a K bar. Also, hardware and feed store owners in the area have reported an unusual increase in the sale of bags of fertilizer, ammonium nitrate and diesel fuel. If it were just the fertilizer and fuel, which is used consistently by the farmers, perhaps eyebrows wouldn't be raised. But ammonium nitrate is another story. In essence, it seems to reinforce that an Oklahoma City type bomb or bombs are being planned to take out some very important targets."

"This is all very interesting," I said. "But why are you telling *me* this? I'd think it would be big news for one of your alphabet ATTF teams. Just go on in the camp and blow the shit out of them."

Johns shook his head. "Can't do that, Bruce. The land is owned by American citizens and protected by the court system, both federal and state. Our teams invaded a couple of these camps suspected of having WMDs and found nothing. The Muslim Brotherhood, American Defense League, ACLU and CAIR filed companion suits against the government, claiming profiling, discrimination and violation of human and property rights as protected under the constitution. The government's hands are currently tied. The President does not want to fight this battle with the courts, the ACLU, *or* congressional panels, especially in case we take this camp down and we're wrong. He wants the battle fought covertly. And as to how you fit in, we'll get to that in a moment. Go ahead Agent Hickcock."

"Thank you, sir. Al-Massoud, one of the new, emerging young lions of al-Qaeda, calls himself the Sand Viper. He now appears to be *the* great influence in the terrorist world, receiving praise and allegiance from al-Qaeda, Hezbollah, Hamas and a dozen other jihadist factions. He is directing Gilani, the man allegedly responsible for the murder of Daniel Pearl, to recruit more than 3000 followers in American prisons, blacks, and whites alike, convert them to Islam, and upon release, bring them into these camps for intense training. They have been placed in compounds all over the United States."

"Compounds?" I restated."Yes. The training camps I mentioned. Let me read from this list." Hickcock then opened his valise and pulled out a notebook. "Camps are located in Marion, Alabama; Commerce and Macon, Georgia; Talihina, Oklahoma; Falls Church and Meherrin, Virginia; three other camps in New York State besides Hancock; and locations in Colorado, Texas, California, Maryland, here in West Virginia, Florida, Washington State and Pennsylvania. As you can see, they've blanketed the entire continental United States. And these are only the ones we know about. Gilani's recruiting video along with al-Massoud's manifesto, proclaim that there exists an organized secret jihadist army that has battalions in each of these training camps capable, when summoned collectively, of bringing down America's infrastructure and national monuments, dealing a sweeping blow to the morale and security of America's citizens. Al-Massoud, in a separate intercepted communique, promises that Americans will be fleeing in fear in masses from its cities to the mountains and valleys. They will no longer have confidence in their government and its military to protect them. Gilani's video further proclaims, and I quote,

"We are fighting to destroy the enemy. We are dealing with evil at its roots and its roots are in America." He goes on to boast of operating the most advanced training camps in Islamic military warfare. He tells his people to "Live with the infidels. Act like you are his friend and then kill him." Is all that specific enough?"

I settled my head back against the seat and looked at each of them. Then I looked out my window and saw we were as far as Rainelle.

"Suggest we turn back now or we'll be in the mountains and curves. As Jerry here seems to have a lead foot, I don't want you people throwing up on me."

Hickcock and Larsen stared at me a moment and then looked at each other. It was a look that said, "What *is* it with this guy?"

"Yes, turn around, Jerry," said Johns.

"Okay, Bruce, we're almost done anyway. Here's the thing about al-Massoud, Bruce. UBL is still revered like royalty, especially considering his heinous terrorist plot he pulled off on 9-11, but he's a fading figurehead, now more myth and legend than effective al-Qaeda leader. But, this Sand Viper, as he likes to be called, is a different, more progressive breed. He is aggressive, fast moving and the most venomous of all of the Islamofascist leaders. And like the Saw Scale Viper, he has no distinct markings...meaning nobody has actually ID'd him. A master of disguise, he is touted in the Islamofascist community as the ultimate clandestine warrior."

"What's his nationality," I asked.

"Iraqi. And get this...he's Saddam's first cousin. As such, he is even more committed to bringing fire and brimstone down on America to vindicate Saddam's death. Besides turning out some of these camps against our cities, he has also targeted our President, several former U.S. generals, and the field commander whose unit captured his cousin. Already at his direction, his jihadists made an attempt on the life of the Secretary of State when he was visiting the troops in Afghanistan. And just a month ago, anthrax somehow made its way into the Pentagon and the Senate building; but most alarming, it was also found in the White House kitchen. Al-Massoud has long arms. So, you see, we have an imminent security crisis on our hands."

I felt myself frowning. "I never heard about those incidents. It never made the news."

"The government went to great lengths counseling with everyone in proximity to quell the information. After the CDC confirmed the presence of anthrax, we shut the information channels down so there would be no mass panic. Unfortunately, there were some deaths associated with exposure to that powder." Johns then winced. "We also counseled with the doctors and hospital staff. The deaths were recorded as heart attacks or some other illness. I can't tell you how complicated it was to see that all this was covered up."

I glared at Johns. "I can't believe that you and the administration did that to these people's loved ones. It's not only a callous deception of the American people, it's criminal. You *all* could face a congressional panel...or worse, go to prison."

"No, Bruce. It's humane. We kept Americans from fear and trepidation. Such knowledge would not only shut commerce down, but stores, banks, schools...everything. It was a decision made in the national interest, and I'm not apologizing for it. That's why I'm confiding in you. I know I can trust you. You're not the kind who would ever let this out."

I settled back in my seat again and closed my eyes. What had we become in the name of national security? For a long time no one said anything. All that could be heard was the purr of the Lincoln's engine and the sound of its tires on the asphalt. I then let out an audible sigh. "All right, I've got the picture. What do you want from me?"

"We want you to go to Antigua, Mr. McGowan," Hickcock said.

"What? What's Antigua got to do with anything?"

"That's only part of it, sir."

"And what's the other part?"

"A Black Bag covert mission, code name Operation Firestorm, that only the people in this car will know about...except one other person. A celebrated hitman whose name is Atticus Steed. An ex-Marine sniper who became a CIA operative, but who is now a fugitive from justice. You will go to where he is located in Antigua, bring him back here to the U.S., and together devise a plan to intercept al-Massoud once he enters one of two jihadist camps, which according to an intercepted communique, he plans to do. And before he personally sets the Jamaat ul-Fuqra plan of attack in motion to kill Americans, you two will kill *him*.

# CHAPTER 5

My furrowed forehead probably said it all.

"Sorry, Preston, I'm not very fluent in *idiot*. What on God's green earth would make you think I'd buy into an insane mercenary deal like this? You've got a thousand government operatives in five different covert agencies on the payroll who could pull off such a mission."

Johns took in a deep breath and let it out slowly.

"I have spent hours with the President on this, Bruce. He told me a lot of things about you...things these agents don't even know and will *not* know. You are the one person above anyone else who could make this plan happen. We need you. We have to stop this terrorist and..."

"And you want me to come out of my nice, comfy retirement and become a government-sanctioned assassin. Well, good luck with that."

Johns took a moment to respond and then nodded. "I won't put it that way. I don't like using the word 'assassin.' But *capture* is not an option, Bruce. The Viper has to die. It would also be your job to not only ramrod Operation Firestorm but to keep Mr. Steed in check...controlling his actions. You are *the* one man, according to the President, who above anyone else could execute this mission and head off The Viper's plan to attack American cities."

"*Execute* being the operative word. Hey, Jerry, how about picking up the pace a little and get me home? I've got a little Sunday afternoon gardening to do, and later, a hot wife to make love to."

Johns looked at me and shook his head. "Well, agents, that's Mr. McGowan. The last of his breed...noble, honorable and idealistic."

"Let me add incorruptible, legalistic and I play by the rules," I said.

"For the most part, anyway. But *this*?"

"Something told me you wouldn't go for it. My guess is you've become too...shall I say, domesticated. Gotten old, Bruce. Soft. Lost your edge. Well, disappointing to say the least. Drive on, Jerry."

"Nice try, Preston. Trying to shame me into the deal with a little indignant mockery. Old and soft, eh? You *know* I could take out any one of you in this car with a single crushing blow."

Johns tried to stifle a smile. "I *thought* I could get a rise out of you."

I didn't respond. Instead, I just looked out my window at the green, picture-postcard landscape whipping by. It was quiet again in the Lincoln for perhaps another long mile. I watched the young FBI couple with one another. Although they put on the best facade they could, I could tell they were involved with one another. *People assessment* is something I'm very good at. A finger touch here and there and the looks. They were not *partner* looks. They were the kind of looks that Adriana and I exchange with one another.

And then, as everything was quiet, a vision attacked my brain. I saw in my mind other young couples in love just like them. Maybe there were children sitting close by, listening to mom and dad reading them a story by the fire. And then suddenly the serene scenario was interrupted by explosions. Buildings were falling down around them. Innocent lives are suddenly being torn apart. Death in the streets. But it could all be stopped if the agencies put their people to work. Like I asked Johns, 'How many skilled counterterrorist operatives were out there that could do the job?' And a couple might even succeed.

As I sat there without a word, allowing the faces in the car along with their silence to send pangs of guilt through my arteries, I argued with myself as to the real reason I was inclined to refuse the task. In another time I would have jumped at a deal like this. But try as I did, I couldn't deny to myself that the *only* reason I would turn it down was Adriana. I had promised her after leaving the counterterrorist team that I would never accept any such work again. Action Guy was retired. My life needed no more danger in it. It's not because I had cheated death so many times. I'm *still* not afraid of death; I just don't want to be there when it happens. But the thing was, I just couldn't place myself in a situation where Adriana would lose yet another husband.

While I sat there beating myself up, I began thinking...what if I *did* agree to the mission? How would I tell her I was going ahead with it? Of course, I wouldn't tell her *everything*. But here's the thing; the way I saw it, all I'd be doing was finding this hit man in Antigua and then set him up to do the dirty work. I'd be instrumental in getting him in a position to where *he* would nail al-Massoud. There'd be no real danger in that. As I was sure Johns had arranged a little financial remuneration for me, I'd even make some extra bucks. Most importantly, I would also be saving a hell of a lot of American lives; and in helping to take down this al-Qaeda kingpin, I'd be setting this ul-Fuqra brotherhood back months or even years in their planning.

And that's how my brain works. Given a little time, I can talk myself into or out of anything. In *this* case, however, would I be getting myself into something that might put me before a congressional panel? I came close to that on my last venture. "So, tell me, Preston, what is it about this hit man that would put the U.S. Government in bed with a fugitive from justice? And doesn't the U.S. and Antigua have extradition agreements between them? The Antiguan authorities could find him and return him here, plopping him right into your lap. So why don't you arrange it? And then, why *him* in the first place? Doesn't the CIA have assassin teams anymore?"

Maggie Larsen then stepped in. "A lot of questions there but let me see if I can answer them all in one sweep. Steed is unquestionably the most guile and cunning of any hitman alive. He can also make shots that even a Navy Seal might not be able to do. Besides being deadly with a .308, he can filet you like a catfish with his K bar. And he was at one time the government's choice as a CIA international assassin."

"Okay, then, if his hits were government-sanctioned, why is he a fugitive?"

"Long story," she replied. "The Reader's Digest version is that he was coerced by a couple of high-ranking Justice Department employees to take down people who had literally gotten away with murder...people whose rights may have been violated at the time of their arrest. Or maybe liberal judges and juries let off."

"Like the movie...The Star Chamber, I think it was called. Michael Douglas and Hal Holbrook."

"Very similar. The people directing his hits, which we referred to as The Justice Club, were holding his past over his head. Before the Marines and the CIA, he was a mob hitman and they had tons of evidence against him. They paid him, but they *owned* him."

"Sounds like a complicated guy. And the Bureau didn't catch him?" I commented.

"Hickcock and I worked the case," Larsen added.

"We weren't able to take him down, the slippery eel that he was but, he did otherwise cooperate with us by helping us nail the bad guys in the justice system hierarchy, who by the way were a Deputy Director of the FBI and the Assistant Attorney General of the United States."

I let out a low whistle. "Intriguing. So, you know Steed is in Antigua, but don't know where? How did you find this out?"

"A money trail. We traced payments made to him by the money man in the Justice Club that went into a Swiss bank account. All that we've been able to get the Antiguan government to do is to allow us to freeze his account. But even though *they* might know where he is...they're not telling us."

"Why?"

"We think they're protecting him for some reason. Maybe he's paying them off."

"It sounds to me that you still have enough to go get him. I suppose you're not doing so because you don't want to get our government's hands dirty by picking him up and then carrying out this plan yourselves. Then you folks would be *directly* involved. What if he doesn't buy in? He won't work for free. Or will you, like this Justice Club, threaten to put him behind bars for the rest of his life?"

The agents looked at one another and then back at me. Hickcock said,

"Our hands are tied on this, Mr. McGowan. Legally, we can't directly collaborate with this man to hatch the plot."

"But, *illegally,* I can."

Johns then stepped in. "Bruce, you know that I am the President's advisor on America's security. But,,there are intricate details he *doesn't* need to know about. He's aware of the threat, but he's leaving the matter entirely in my hands. I'm taking the lead and coordinating the operation. I alone will answer anything that goes down on the matter. The only people who will answer to me are the two people sitting across from us...and you, if you decide that you're in."

We were now approaching the road leading down to Wolf Laurel and having jammed all this information into my brain, my head started to hurt. Maybe the hurting was from the fact that if I did take the gig, I had to find a smooth way to break the news to Adriana. And then I could only imagine what her reaction would be.

"All right. Say that I *did* agree to find this hit man and then help him to nail this al-Massoud; I'm no longer on the State Department's payroll. What would you do...tack a Christmas bonus onto my retirement check? Or would I simply be doing this for truth, justice and the American way?"

"You would see a *healthy* bonus, Bruce," replied Johns. "We're prepared to pay you and Mr. Atticus Steed a cool million each."

I let out a huge puff of air and again settled back in my seat just as the stately turrets of Wolf Laurel came into view.

"Nice chunk of change for us. Hmmm. Atticus Steed. Interesting name, by the way."

"The name brings back memories of months of headaches for Hickcock and me," remarked Larsen.

"You wouldn't believe the time we put in trying to nail this guy. He was good. Very good."

"*And* very elusive," added Hickcock.

I then looked over at Johns who seemed to be waiting for my answer, now that I had digested the information...and now that a million dollar carrot had been dangled in my face. I replied

"Who's to say this Steed will agree to it? And what other incentive would he have? He wouldn't be able to spend his mil in jail."

Johns nodded.

"Correct. We would not only unfreeze his assets, but we would take his name off the *most wanted* list and offer him a full pardon for all crimes known and unknown."

"I suppose you'll put that in writing to him."

"It'll be a kind of contract, yes. A rather covert one, however.

" He then shuffled his position and turned toward me. Bearing down on me with his pressing eyes, he said,

"Okay, Bruce, we have to get back to Washington, DC. What's your answer?"

I stroked my chin reflectively and gave it one more shot of consideration.

"I'd have to smooth this whole thing out with my wife. We've almost made a blood pact that I wouldn't ever again run off to play government games. My marriage is a hell of a lot more important than a mere million dollars."

"*Mere million*? You wouldn't be trying to squeeze me for more money, would you?" Johns asked.

I shook my head.

"If you really know me, Preston, you know that's not the case. And I won't even ask you where the money's coming from."

"Good."

"So, let me get this straight. I fly down to Antigua, on your nickel of course, marry up with this criminal, bring him in, hatch a plan, and together locate the deadliest terrorist since OBL, then I watch Steed blow the head off this desert snake. After that, I kick back while al-Massoud's ul-Fuqra followers, who are enjoying fun and games in these summer camps, become disorganized and fade back into the last century."

"Hmmm. That's part of it."

"*Part of it?* You mean there's more?"

"We have learned that al-Massoud will go to three places once he sets foot here in the U.S...a mosque in Detroit, the Fuqra headquarters in Hancock and then the

Goshen, Virginia compound. When he makes that third stop, you, Bruce, will then lead a highly-skilled, highly covert CIRG commando team into that Virginia camp and destroy it."

My face had to say it all. "*What*?"

"That's Part Two of Firestorm."

"Not going to happen, Preston. The wife will have a conniption if she gets wind of that. Get your *own* commander to lead that element into the compound."

"Here's the deal, Bruce. The task force *will* have its own commander. But you will be serving as kind of a pathfinder to collaborate with the element and be available somewhere in defilade inside that compound to bring them in. *You* know how to set that up. And by the way, I never told *my* wife everything my job entailed, and I know you didn't with the *first* Mrs. McGowan."

"Yeah, but I like the *second* Mrs. McGowan better."

"Uh huh. I know you were married to your current wife for a couple of years when you were with Zulu. And I'm pretty damn sure you didn't tell her about *all* of your assignments...especially the ones that put you in danger."

"That was then...this is now. And by the way, what the hell do you know about Zulu?"

"Not much, except what the President told me. And he didn't tell me everything, I'm sure. So, are you in, Bruce?"

"All I have is your vision on the mission. When would we talk about details?"

"When you give me your answer, and then I'll give you a couple more days to mull it over. If you're still in, I'll need you to meet with Hickcock here who will give you everything you need to get your plan rolling. He, with Larsen's assistance, will be your mission director and your only contact. I'm out of the picture from here on. But there's yet one more thing, Bruce."

"Yeah, okay. What?"

"You would need to make that flight almost immediately. All Intel points toward al-Massoud landing here in the U.S. in early September, maybe three weeks from now. We believe he's planning for this attack, wherever it will be, to coincide with the anniversary of 9-11. But, we don't know for sure. It's something that you need to somehow nail down. We're pretty sure the staging of that attack will come from the Goshen, Virginia compound. That's where *he'll* be and that's where *you'll* need to be well in advance."

"To do a recon and then to set up for the kill."

"Yes."

We had been sitting in the parking lot for about ten minutes talking things out, when Adriana came out onto the veranda. She looked down at the car and smiled. I guess she was wondering if we'd continue just sitting in the car or come on inside.

"She *is* very attractive, Mr. McGowan," commented Larsen.

"A woman I would never want to lose."

"I do have to get back, Bruce," Johns said.

"A three-and-a-half-hour drive at least. But you know that. Give her my regards and apologies for not going to meet her." He then paused.

"I'll be waiting to hear from you."

"All right. I'll need to talk it over with her. And of course, I won't tell her much. After I sleep on it, I'll have my answer for you by tomorrow evening."

"Good then. If you come in with us, these two agents will be at your beck and call for any and all Intel on al-Massoud, his movements and in particular, his planned return to the U.S." He then shoved out his hand.

"I'm counting on you, old friend."

I shook his hand and those of the agents as well. They gave me their cards and then I stepped out of the limo.

"Next time you come by, Preston, make it a social visit. Bring Juliette."

"I'd like that. See you soon, Bruce."

# CHAPTER 6

After the Lincoln pulled away, I looked up to Adriana who was still standing on the veranda...and still smiling. As soon as I climbed the four steps and set foot on the porch, she gave me a quick kiss, which always said to me that she was happy. When the queen is happy, there is peace in the kingdom. But how long would *that* last?

"What was the visit all about?" she asked. The question I was waiting for.

As Johns and company had only been gone a matter of seconds, I hadn't had an opportunity to prepare an explanation, a speech or a big, fat lie. But one thing for sure, I wasn't going to lie to her. Maybe white-wash my story a little, doing my best to soft-sell Preston John's proposition. And a husband always begins a conversation like this by telling her how bright and perceptive she is.

"Well, you were right, as always."

"About?"

"About my ex-FBI friend...and get this...who is now *the* National Security Advisor. He wants me to help out on a project."

The smile was still there, but I couldn't tell if it was a good smile or a 'tell me the whole story and then you will see the sun go quickly behind the clouds' smile. "What kind of project...to do a little government work behind the desk here at home or go off to Afghanistan or Libya and kill somebody?"

I had to laugh, but I think she detected it was a kind of nervous laugh. "No, no. Definitely not the latter. He merely wants me to fly down to Antigua to talk with a former government employee and then we together will locate and profile a man hardly anyone knows anything about...somebody who may be considered a threat to the U.S."

She then took me by the hand and led me over to one of the veranda rockers. "Let's sit." This said to me, the queen may in fact *not* be all that happy anymore. "Now, husband dear, can you be just a little less vague and evasive? I'm not recognizing that tune to which you're tap-dancing."

"No, really. That's what he's asking me to do. I'll make a good bit of money as well."

"Uh-huh. And how bad *is* this guy you and Mr. Antigua will be looking for and how dead are you supposed to kill him?"

"Who said anything about making him dead?"

"With all the agents and analysts Washington has on its payroll at its disposal, why would someone drive all the way down here and offer you an opportunity to just do some profiling?"

"It sounds all crazy when you put it like that," I said.

"And they know you can do it all...from analysis to annihilation. Look, Skip. I know you've been pretty bored around here the past few months and I appreciate how this has affected you. Then somebody from the government...excuse me, The National Security Advisor...suddenly shows up and offers you some kind of opportunity and you probably went ahead and jumped at it."

"Actually, I didn't. I told him I'd have to think about it and above all, talk to you."

"I know what you used to do in the 'action game' as you call it. I also know that you were always exposed to danger. But I married you anyway for three reasons: I love you, of course, but you had also promised you would be retiring from government service. *And*, I envisioned having you around until we both died natural deaths." She then gripped my hand a little tighter. "So, tell me all of it, Skip. Tell me this isn't something that could get you shot up."

I squeezed her hand back and searched her eyes with mine.

"I can't imagine anything like that could ever happen on this deal. As a matter of fact, after the gentleman, whom I will be contacting, and I do the research on this subject, and if we find out that he and other subversive elements need to be taken out, a separate joint task force will do the danger work." That, of course, was all pretty much the truth. I just conveniently left out the part where I will be there when that last thing happens.

"Which says that somewhere in this thing you might get caught up in a bit of danger."

"We're in a bit of danger every time we go out on the highway." A stupid thing to say, but I said it anyway.

She studied my eyes for a few moments and then diverted them to the climbing rosebush with its errant vine.

"I guess I need to do a little pruning before our prickly friend takes over the veranda." She released her hand from mine, stood, and then looked down at me with her dazzling but firm eyes. "Do what you think you need to do, Skip." Which meant all doubt was removed; the queen was *definitely* no longer happy.

I stood up and put my arms around her. "If I agree to do this project, I want *you* to be good with it, or I won't do it at all."

She then laid her forehead on my chest and said in a soft voice...the voice that gets me every time,

"And I want you to promise that you will not involve yourself in any business that will take you away from me."

"I promise," I replied in almost a whisper. "But, I still want to sleep on it before I commit to it. I want you to be happy. It's really all I *ever* want."

Adriana then pasted her lips on mine. She kissed me like we were sixteen-year-old kids who were tasting love for the very first time. And that is what this All-American beauty made me feel like just being around her every day of our marriage. Sixteen again.

I did sleep on Preston Johns' offer...an offer that would once again put me back in the game. Just how deeply in the game remained to be seen. For perhaps an hour, though, I laid awake fretting about it, mulling over the fact that I would in essence become something of a mercenary for our own government...a contractor who would receive a hefty sum of money for services rendered. I may not send the bullet into The Viper's brain, but I'd be part of the killing team. Lying there, I rationalized that it *would* be a righteous kill. I had killed many times in self-defense and because I in essence was saving the lives of American citizens. But only recently, I committed murder. It wasn't anything else *but* that. It was out of revenge to make the man who was responsible for the killing of my team pay for his own life. I didn't give him the choice of living or dying. He was unarmed, but he taunted me, daring me to do it. Without any remorse, I put a bullet in his head. But what continues to bother me even to this day is that the man was a United States congressman.

I was also lying there thinking about just who *was* this Atticus Steed, anyway. And why would I want to create an unholy alliance with a fugitive on the run? But, then my brain suddenly switched gears, the cognitive manic that I am. I began reveling in the fact that I was once again in demand and not just an aging, washed-up icon. The money was tempting, but in comparison, it really didn't matter that much.

Then again, the hell it *didn't*.

Once my feet hit the floor and I performed my bathroom functions, I noted that Adriana was already downstairs making a breakfast of sweet rolls, fruit and coffee for our guests. The aroma of the coffee permeated throughout the entire inn. When I finally dressed and went downstairs to grab my mug of java, I kissed her and said, "Morning, hon." She smiled, but I could tell she was not her usual jovial self; however, neither was she cold to me.

"It's going to be a beautiful day," I said. "Did you see that sunrise coming through our bedroom window?"

"Yes, lovely."

"So, what are your plans today," I asked. "Anything important going on?"

"No, not really." No elaboration.

"What's wrong?" I asked her.

"Nothing," she replied with a smile.

Which actually meant *something*.

"You're not worried about what we discussed yesterday, are you?"

She turned and poured the steaming coffee into my mug, then set the urn down.

"A little, I suppose. I worry about you even when you travel over to Lexington to teach your class."

I placed my fingertips under her chin and lifted her head.

"And I love you for worrying about me. But you don't have to. I don't plan to get into any shootout with somebody over road rage, and I'm not going to have an accident. So do me a favor and stop worrying."

"That's like saying that old sun out there to not set this evening."

"I'll be all right, this thing I'm doing. It's just a little contract work."

"I *knew* you would decide to go through with it," she said.

"Like I told you, I had to really think about it. There are so many things I need to do around here, I..."

"Don't give me that, Skip McGowan," she chided, grinning. "I know what you do...or don't do. When will you be leaving?"

"I don't know just yet. My understanding was that he wanted me to fly down to Antigua as soon as possible."

"And again, what was that for?"

"For a little needed tropical vacation." I then winked at her.

"No, seriously, I'm just supposed to meet up with some guy named Steed to strategize about how we need to find a man whose plan it is to commit an act of jihad."

"And again, when you locate him, what will you do with him?"

"I won't do anything with him except bring him back to the States." Which was true. Steed would return with me and then he'd kill the guy. In ending The Viper's life, we would hopefully upset a good piece of the al-Qaeda apple cart for a very long time.

"I know you're mincing words with me," she said. "Trying to tone down any element of danger associated with your *project* as you call it. That *is* what you're doing, isn't it?"

"Again, my dear, I do not see any degree of imminent danger in anything I'll be doing." Somehow, I needed to get her off the subject, although I knew there would be both words exchanged and worries on her part until the mission was all over. And I knew just how to end our conversation once and for all. "Let's talk about something more important...like when we're going to lunch and if we can maybe sneak in a little afternoon delight."

"How many times a day is it you think about sex? Aren't you just a little too old to be carrying around that big libido of yours?"

"I'll *produce* my big libido if you've got five extra minutes this morning."

"Get out of my kitchen and go sweep the veranda or whatever else you do around here."

I gave her a peck on the cheek. Works every time. All I have to do to get her off something I don't want to talk about is threaten sex.

# CHAPTER 7

Mid-morning that Monday, I called Special Agent John Hickcock's number. I got a menu with a laundry list of numbers to punch in: Press 1 for the Counterterrorism Division, which I did; if you know the name of the party with whom you need to speak, press pound, which I did; then I had to listen through the first part of the alphabet, beginning with Special Agent Andrews and et cetera, until I got to the H's; for Special Agent Hickcock, press 12, which I did. When the line clicked in, a woman with a smoker's voice answered. "Special Agent Hickcock's office." I think I let go with an "Arrrgh." In my days with the Bureau, I answered my own damn phone without the dial-by-number hassle that took ten minutes to get through.

"May I speak to him, please? My name is Bruce McGowan."

"Is he expecting your call?"

"Yes."

"Does he know what this is about?"

*"Yes, he does, now would you please get me to him?"* My tone was ugly.

"I'll check to see if he's in." *Her* tone was shitty.

There was a long moment of elevator music and then Ms. Snot Nose was back on the phone. "He's on another line, please hold."

"Sure. I guess I have nothing else to do, but would you please shut off the Muzak? I haven't had my nap yet today and it's not time. I want to be awake when he comes on the line."

I always speak my mind in cases like these because it hurts when I bite my tongue. And I guess I pissed her off royally because she was gone without another word and Yanni was back.

In about two minutes, Hickcock came on. "Mr. McGowan. I didn't expect to hear from you this soon. Obviously, you've thought it I'm sure he heard me let out a sigh. "I guess you can count me in."

"Excellent, sir."

"When do we begin?"

"In a few days. Maggie...Agent Larsen and I need to give you a complete brief at which time we'll discuss the timeline, more particulars about Steed, and recent communiques received on al-Massoud...the whole gamut."

"When do you want to meet?"

"As soon as possible, sir."

"Do I come to you?"

"It would work better if you did...that is if you don't mind. Here we have the photos and films on Massoud and the training compounds, the latest Intel on al-Qaeda communications, movements, threats and activities. Yes, *here* is better. I look forward to working with you, Mr. McGowan."

"When do you want me there?"

"How about Friday, say 1000 hours?"

"I can arrange that."

"Great. When you get here to the Hoover Building and clear security, take the elevator to the 5th floor, Suite 512. Leave your gun in the car so that I don't have to come downstairs and get you out of detention."

"I know the drill. I spent a little time in your building, remember?"

"Right. Well, I'm looking forward to having you aboard, sir. See you Friday."

"One thing, John. The Intel brief on al-Massoud, the communiques and the information about a tentative terrorist strike...that would be classified. I'm sure you realized when we all chatted in the limo that I no longer have a clearance. I'd say you and Johns committed a bit of a snafu."

"Not exactly, Mr. McGowan. We researched your latest clearance. Apparently, the last job you had with the government, whatever Black Ops deal that was, elevated from your Top Secret Clearance to TS/SCI, Top Secret/ Sensitive Compartmented Information, which of course is granted by the Director of Intelligence. You have to be in a 'read-in' status to get that. Not very many people in the government are in that category."

"Yeah, so?"

"Mr. Johns took the liberty of renewing your TS/SCI clearance before we talked."

"You people were that sure I'd bite, huh?"

"Neither Larsen nor I knew you, of course, but Mr. Johns was convinced you'd come in with us. And with the remote possibility you wouldn't, he would have revoked it immediately upon your refusal."

"He thinks I'm that predictable."

"He knows you to be a government man...but beyond that, a *patriot*."

"Then I guess I'll have to one day throw him a curve ball and do something *un*predictable."

"Just be predictable where it comes to this mission, sir. That's all we ask."

"Right. I guess I'll see you on Friday."

"You guess?"

I didn't want the young agent to get all panicky and wet himself, so I added, "I'll be there, don't worry about it, kid.

But hey, John, do the outside world a favor and get rid of that freaking phone menu system you people got up there."

He laughed. "Annoying, isn't it?"

"Also, get some Eagles or Earth, Wind, and Fire on your wait-line, for God's sake. And quit calling me *sir*.'""

He laughed again. "Got it, sir."

*****

My brother, Joey, who runs our family mortuary business, came by the inn on Tuesday, finding me washing the old Suburban. I have a lot in common with my nine-year-old piece of tin---prone to having mechanical failure, filled with bullet holes, although mine have healed, and occasionally a piece might fall off.

"Hey, bro," he greeted. "I see you're washing that old pile of junk."

"Not really," I replied. "I'm just watering it to see if it'll grow into a bus."

"You're funny, Skippy," I got that endearing handle long ago when i played junior high basketball. When I'd go in for a lay-up, it wasn't the ref who blew the whistle because I walked; the girls whistled because they said it looked like I was skipping to the basket. It's only Adriana and Joey who I let call me that.

"What brings you by, little brother?"

"I thought maybe you'd like to go down to the camp..." *Our family shack on the Greenbrier.* "...and do some fishing, kick back, have a few beers and maybe get a little drunk. Fish have really been biting lately, I hear."

"You mean go today?"

"No, I'm draining old man Gallagher's carcass today. His funeral's tomorrow. I'm thinking at first light on Friday."

"No can do, Joey. I have to be in Washington, DC on Friday."

"You *have* to be? Got business up there, do you? I thought you were done with the government, seeing as how you got old and retired."

"They still knock on my door every once in a while."

"Well, maybe some other time, then."

"For sure."

"I see you have guests." He noticed the Honda.

"Yeah. We haven't had much business this spring and summer. The inn might be long-paid for, but we still need revenue to keep it afloat...and eat. How's *your* business?"

"People keep dying. I just buried a lady your age. Had a heart attack and dropped dead. Of course, she weighed over three hundred pounds and obviously never met a pizza she didn't like."

"That's why I try to keep it going," I said. "I'm still running every day and Adriana keeps making me salads. She claims she wants me to stick around...survival of the fittest, she says."

"Yeah, I want you to stick around, too. Of course, as to the *rest* of the people, I don't believe in the survival of *anybody*. I'm a mortician, remember?"

I had to laugh. "Well, I guess I need to finish up with the old beast here. Adriana wants me to take her to lunch. Another salad place, I reckon. Yawn. Why don't you and Cora join us?"

"Like to, but the last I checked, old Gallagher was getting a little gamey. Better go pump some formaldehyde in him. But anyway, let's find a day we can *all* go down to the river."

"I'll have my people call your people," I said.

After lunch, I turned on the computer and went to the internet to perform some of my own research on this homespun Jamaat ul-Fuqra outfit. It's translation was literally 'Community of the Impoverished.' There was a good bit of information on these extremists as well as Gilani and his al-Qaeda training compounds, but little if anything on al-Massoud. Either the media didn't know much about him or our government had decided to keep all Intel on him in its secret files.

There was a ton of information on the net about the many denominations of perilous radical groups situated all over the world; but I was more so concentrating on those groups that had established inside the walls of our country a terrorist platform that could strike anywhere at any time. It was primarily al-Qaeda and the Taliban that had integrated into the ul-Fuqra organization and placed members inside several of its jihadist training camps. And it was Hezbollah that had established itself deep inside the North Carolina camp. Gilani and the ul-Fuqra headquarters in Islamberg (Hancock), New York, were linked to the 1993 World Trade Center bombing. Still, as Johns and Hickcock told me, the State Department does not list the element as a Foreign Terrorist organization. The lands on which these 35 or more compounds are located are privately owned and therefore protected under the U.S. Constitution. Moreover, state legislatures have failed to pass bills that allow searches of their properties. The media chooses to ignore the camps and the ACLU is the primary watchdog organization that jumps all over any attempts to call ul-Fuqra operations terrorist activities. Islamofascist Muslims who had been featured in investigative reports by the local media had filed lawsuits to shut down the reports as well as defamation suits against complaining neighbors. The courts had in nearly every case sided with the radicals.

Madrassas, or Islamic schooling of Muslim youth in America, were now full-blown. Imams, clerics, and Mullahs throughout the country were implanting in their young minds the value of jihad and a need to return to the Caliphate...the quest for a one-world nation under Allah that would not only make Islam a super-religion, but the *only* religion for all people. Even in their pre-teen years, children should be thinking in terms of personal sacrifice...giving up their lives if necessary for Allah as they exploded improvised devices that would kill masses of Infidels. The Madrassas further teach that Islam's primary goal in America is to destabilize our government, weaken the country's resolve, and incite enough fear to a point where America's citizens will even be afraid to venture into the streets. In other words, destroy our way of life.

Several passages form the Koran had made their way into the literature that supported a massive ul-Fuqra attack on American targets. Gilani especially quoted from Koran 8:59, *"The Infidels should not think they can get away from us. Prepare against them whatever arms and weaponry you can muster so that you may terrorize them. They are your enemy and Allah's enemy."* And *"Fight and kill disbelievers whenever you find them, take them captive, beleaguer them and lie in wait and ambush them using every stratagem of war."* Koran 9:5.

Just as Johns had conveyed, the Muslim Brotherhood tenaciously backs the ul-Fuqra training camps, both financially and through massive propagandizing in America's prisons. *Muslims of America*, a tax-exempt organization, whose members use aliases and who recruit converted Islamic prisoners, is financially supported by wealthy Pakistani, Kashmir *and* American citizens. They also provide monies for the recruits to attend paramilitary training camps in Pakistan. Amazingly, these home-grown breeding grounds for terror are known not only to the alphabet agencies, but local and state law enforcement, and even some well-informed American citizens; yet, the camps go unchecked and basically ignored. My guess was that the government was not taking any chances on experiencing another Wounded Knee incident.

Settling back in my chair, I was now allowing my tired brain to digest all of this information. As I had now convinced myself to accept Johns' invitation to the big dance, as of tomorrow morning my hat would be officially in the ring. Maybe it took that invitation and this internet refresher course in Terrorism 101 to get my head out of the sand and back in the game. But as recharged as I was, I still wasn't that sure about collaborating on the mission with the notorious hitman on the run, one Atticus Steed.

# CHAPTER 8

Having told Adriana that I would likely be staying the night in Washington because of a probable day-long meeting, I kissed her goodbye a few minutes past five-thirty on Friday morning, then shoved off for D.C. Still, four hours should be enough time to navigate through the Shenandoah, fight what was left of the Friday morning Beltway traffic and arrive at my destination in time for my meeting with the Bureau youngsters at ten. However, Murphy and his law got me again as I must have picked up a nail on I-81 just south of Lexington and with the time it took me to change my tire, I found myself a half hour behind schedule. None of the NASCAR teams would be asking me to join their pit crews anytime soon.

So, I decided to pick up the pace a little. Unfortunately, I had picked it up just a little too much. Near one of the Harrisonburg exits, a county Mounty's blue lights suddenly appeared in my rearview mirror. I then pulled off onto the shoulder and waited yet another five minutes for the deputy to call in my tag number to determine if I had stolen ol' Diablo. Finally, he dragged his fat ass out of his Charger and banged on the side of the Suburban with his knuckles. "Drop your window glass, please." I complied and then he came alongside my door, fingertips now on the butt of his Beretta. "License and registration, please," he said with a bit of an attitude.

I pulled them out and handed them to him. After perusing them as though he were studying for an exam, Deputy M. Seibert finally barked, "Do you know why I pulled you over?" And he didn't say that nicely.

I was already in a foul mood, but one of these days my sharp-ass tongue is going to be my demise. "You thought I had donuts?" I replied.

He wasn't amused. "Get out of the car and follow me back to the cruiser."

I did as ordered and then slid in on the passenger side. Before he had an opportunity to begin chiding me, I said, "I suppose you're going to ask me something brilliant like 'Where's the fire?', but I need to tell you I'm going to be late for a meeting up in Washington, DC with the FBI."

I thought trying to bedazzle him with my importance in the law enforcement community while flashing my retired FBI credentials would render him awe-struck and all apologetic for stopping me. But apparently, my snotty attitude had already done me in. After taking an impossible amount of time scratching out my speeding ticket, he then looked over at me and smiled.

"Have a nice day, Mr. McGowan, and oh yes, please drive carefully."

I think I fumed all the way into the city, so I wasn't in the best of moods when I stepped into Hickcock's office at three minutes till ten. First, however, I had to get through his girl Friday who was the same woman with the raspy smoker's voice I talked with on the phone. "You can go in now," she said, punctuating her words with a cough that sounded like a dog hacking up a bone.

Once through Hickcock's door, the first face I saw belonged to the lovely Maggie Larsen who was sitting in an armchair in front of his desk. Hickcock then rose from behind the desk to greet me, extending his hand.

"Very prompt," he said. "Did you have a good trip up this morning?"

I wanted to growl but realizing that this was just meaningless small talk on his part, I nodded and put on my best face. "It's a glorious morning out there today." I can be pleasant when I really put my heart into it.

There was more small talk and then he offered me a cup of coffee...or some bottled water, whatever my pleasure. I respectfully declined and gave him the impression I just wanted to get down to it.

One thing I learned right off the bat with John Hickcock was that he is pretty much all business...a no-nonsense Joe Friday kind of guy. And Larsen, I deduced, could be a bit of a wildcat if need be...fiery, green eyes, fierce expression, and a lean tautly toned frame. The kind of shrew a man would love to try taming.

"Well, why don't we go down the hall and get this started," Hickcock said. "You sure you don't want any coffee?"

"No thanks. I'm fine," I repeated. I then followed them into a medium-sized conference room three doors down where the duo had already set up a video system. When I sat down at the table, I found lying before me a stack of files, two of which contained the familiar stamp, *Classified.* On the wall was a large screen on which was displayed the seal of the Federal Bureau of Investigation.

Hickcock settled back in a leather chair just to the right of the screen. "Normally, on any kind of strategic briefing such as this, the room would be filled with a battery of agents from various arenas, especially our Anti-terrorist Department. Not so with this matter, of course. Not even our boss knows what we're doing. He does know; however, we're doing some kind of special project for the National Security Advisor."

"And when you leave the office to travel on this deal, how will you account for your expenses?" I asked.

"Everything will be charged to our other assigned cases."

"So, you're misappropriating government funds, eh? Negligible as that is, it can be hazardous to your career health."

Hickcock smiled. "All a means to an end, Mr. McGowan. Even misdirecting money on an expense account. All right, let's get to it. Let me first tell you about the man you will locate in Antigua...Atticus Steed." He then flashed upon his screen a grainy photo of a man in a hat and glasses who appeared to be entering a restaurant. "This obviously was a disguise. We know he doesn't wear glasses." A second photo was of his Georgia driver's license. "These are basically the only reasonably current pictures we have of him. Here are a couple of other photos of when he was a bit younger...this one from his CIA file and here's another as a twenty-eight-year-old Marine recruit. And just who was he before he disappeared? Nothing but a celebrated assassin. But make no mistake, he's the best shooter in the world...a former Marine sniper who was recruited by the Agency for covert kills. Not only a top shot, but a master in dealing the death blow a hundred different other ways."

"And I'm supposed to partner with him and place him into action."

Hickcock continued. "Maggie and I came face to face with him...actually on two occasions. I won't go into any great detail, but aside from what we've told you, we actually found him to have a rather disarming personality."

"Let me add," injected Larsen, "that he did manage to save our bacon when he found out his employer had placed Hickcock and me on his hit list at the point where we were inches from solving the case. I won't elaborate, however, for the sake of moving on."

"Sounds like a story to be heard over a couple of Heinekens," I said.

Hickcock continued. "We want you to leave as soon as you can, Mr. McGowan. You'll be flown down to Antigua on one of our Bureau jets."

"Why is he in Antigua?"

"His money is there, although he can't touch it. But our Intel is that he is tight with someone high up in the government. I imagine that *someone* is also wanting to get his hands on a little of Steed's money once it is no longer frozen."

"Do we assume Mr. Steed no longer kills people?"

"There hasn't been a peep out of him these months that we can tell. We assume he's enjoying retirement," commented Larsen. "Much like you."

"Except I'm not a retired hit man."

"And by the way, Mr. McGowan," added Hickcock, "We did a little homework on *you*. Army captain, Special Forces, Vietnam Vet, Ranger, awarded the Silver Star, recruited by the Bureau, served your twenty and then spent four plus years with the Department of State as an analyst. There's where our research ended. Your duties with the State Department were rather non-descript. Mr. Johns apparently knows some of what you did. We assume you were some kind of covert operator. I'm also surmising it had something to do with anti-terrorism or you wouldn't have been selected to carry out this mission. And I'm sure there are more credentials out there than we found in your Bureau file."

"First of all, John, you two can call me Bruce. And secondly, you need not be concerned about what I did for the State Department. I'd hate like hell to have to kill you." Old quip that every covert G man uses.

They sat there staring at me for a few moments and then I winked and smiled. "Just kiddin,'" I said. But, they did *not* need to find out anything about my work with Team Zulu, the most clandestine counterterrorist group in the government, unknown to any of the alphabet agencies...*and* still operating.

Hickcock showed himself more at ease by returning the smile, but Larsen remained stoic. If we were going to be friends, her tight ass was going to have to loosen up.

"Okay, Bruce, so you'll reel in Steed and convince him to join you on the mission by explaining that all his past goes away. As Mr. Johns said, we will unfreeze his money, take him off the most wanted list and the President will issue him a full pardon. But, it doesn't happen until the mission is complete...when al-Massoud goes down and the perceived ul-Fuqra threat is removed."

I then leaned back in my chair and scratched my head. "And just how am I supposed to convince a man like Steed that you'll live up to your end of the bargain?"

"That's for you to figure out," replied Hickcock. "However, here's a sealed handwritten letter I've prepared for you to put in his hands. In case it accidentally falls into someone else's hands, I have not spelled out the details of the mission. That's for *you* to convey to him personally. It will merely be a kind of promissory note explaining that if he accomplishes the task, his history will be purged. He'll trust *me*, I assure you."

"And how do you know that?"

Larsen then spoke up, "Because he and Hickcock had a little *mutual admiration* thing going."Hickcock glanced at her and scowled. "Ignore her, Bruce. Back to the letter. Once he reads and digests it, destroy it."

"Then he will have no insurance policy. The Justice Department could in essence renege."

"No it won't. He'll have Maggie, you *and* me to testify if that ever occurred. Anyway, we're the Justice Department. You know, I learned from my father a long time ago the one thing that is better to keep than to give."

"What's that?"

"Your *word.* And he'll believe me when you lay my word *on* him."

"That being the case, he must think pretty highly of his pursuers, namely you and Maggie."

"Let's just say we understand one another."

"And why did you convince Johns that Atticus Steed was the man to perform the kill?"

Hickcock turned his head away for a moment and then looked back at me. "Maybe we owe him. It was an opportunity to pay him back for not only helping us nail two justice system chiefs but taking out the people who had Maggie and me in their sights. Johns was reluctant to agree to him at first; but after he came to our division to talk out the mission and then got to know us, he trusted our judgment. As he already had *your* name, he suggested that you contact Steed and close the deal. Apparently, you're well thought of as not only a mission planner, but somebody who could ride herd on a guy like Steed."

"What happens if he won't agree to come back here with me and drop the dime on this Viper?"

Hickcock smiled. "Then I can envision a big damn fight ensuing between the two of you that you *will* win. But seriously, he stays on the most wanted list and sooner or later goes down."

For the last hour of the morning, the subject was al-Massoud. The agents had placed a pile of information on him in front of me; but the most important set of documents included the recent communique intercepted by Israeli intelligence that spelled out al-Massoud's plan to incite ul-Fuqra leadership and direct their attack on American targets. The NCTC and Department of Homeland Security had continuously been analyzing the communique and other intercepted documents.

"If you will pull out the green folder, Bruce, which I believe is the second file...yes, that's the one. You'll see that al-Massoud is writing Abdullah Jemaah in the Hancock headquarters location and Tahir Maslama who conducts training and operations in the Goshen, Virginia compound. I'll give you an opportunity to read it. While you're doing so, I'm going to step out for another cup of coffee."

"I think I now need a cup myself," I said.

"Good. I'll get it for you and then I'll also have my assistant order out for some sandwiches. Looks like we'll be here much of the day. What do you like?"

"A tuna salad on wheat would be good...and a bottle of water. No chips. Thanks, John."

"Maggie, what do you want?" Hickcock asked her.

"The same...and a Diet Pepsi, okay? I'll stick here with Bruce in case he has any questions."

When Hickcock left to attend to our lunch, I began digging into al-Massoud's communique:

*"Praise be to Allah and the prophet Mohammed. I send to you Allah's blessings and his peace. As I have placed all jihadist cells on alert to attack many targets in the Great Satan, we will coordinate these attacks through the Quds Force in the Iranian Interests Section of Washington. Our people now work from the mosques, safe houses and from the compounds in Islamberg, Reston and Goshen. It is Goshen where we have most of our weapons and much explosives stored. Our operational commanders at these sites will summon our brave brothers from the compounds and those living among the Americans. We have brought into America this year many of our brothers through the Mexican borders into Arizona and Texas with the assistance of the Venezuelan government, arranging their migration into many parts of the United States through our Mexican brotherhood. We are satisfied they are now settled into our many camps where they have been training for jihad.*

*"On the day of our attack the world will see a jihad by our people that has never been cast before against the Zionists. We have selected targets in fourteen United States cities in the eastern states and Washington DC which comprise of bridges, subways, government buildings and monuments. All transportation, power sources and commerce in these cities will cease to operate. When Washington is destroyed, the American government will be in shock. The people will see that its government can no longer protect them and there will be insurgency in all areas.*

*"As you have stored much of the explosives in the Goshen underground bunker, Maslama, your compound will be the communication point and apex of the mission. I will meet you on the 7th to coordinate with you what will be the beginning of the end for America. We will need only those four days for all elements to reach their destinations. Be ready, my brothers, and make ready the Army of Allah. Many of you will die as shuhada (martyrs). We will strike the blow that will be the death knell for the Great Satan. I will then stand beholding our victory like every successful general of his army. I will stand on the bank of the Potomac at Mount Vernon, the home of their revered first president and watch in the distance as smoke billows over their capital city, taking its burning stench into my lungs with much pleasure. Praise be to Allah."*

Hickcock came back into the room just as I was digesting the last few lines. "You read the reference to the date of the 7th. We believe that is September 7th, four days before the 9-11 anniversary. Obviously, the attack is intended as a celebratory event on that day. But we can't be sure. The Goshen compound will apparently be the apex of the operation. What will likely happen is that a number of trucks and vans will load up explosives from the bunker and depart at staggered times not to arouse suspicion. They will then be driven to various cities we believe to be New York, Washington as indicated, Atlanta, Miami, Boston and maybe even smaller cities like Richmond, Newport News, Providence and Charlotte. I imagine most of the targets will be in Washington and New York. They will try to knock out power stations, buildings of commerce, such as on Wall Street, the Brooklyn Bridge, and as many of Washington's monuments and government buildings as they can, simultaneously. It will have to be a precise, well-planned, coordinated attack on a single command. If it's done at different times, they know that our police and military will stop every truck and divert vehicles away from our infrastructure and national buildings. Some of the drivers, if not all, will be suicide bombers."

Larsen added, "Al-Massoud compares himself to bin-Laden. He has an ego, but he doesn't display it for everyone to see. It is he himself who coined the name the Sand Viper. We do know that through a series of aliases and disguises, he has slipped in and out of the United States. Word is that he has boasted visiting all U.S. jihadist training compounds."

"Right," said Hickcock.

"We don't have any really good photos of him because like the Chameleon he is, he changes his looks nearly every week. Many faces and many identities." Hickcock then flashed up on the screen several photos. "We believe these are of him. Our analysts are 90% sure these are all of the same man after applying the facial recognition algorithm."

"Then how can we be sure we have the right man in our sight? I'm not intending to stereotype Middle Eastern people, but with adding facial hair and changing the hairstyle, a lot of these yahoos look alike," I said.

"Therein lies our dilemma," Larsen remarked.

"Where is al-Massoud supposedly holed up now?"

Hickcock replied, "Interpol believes he is currently in the North African country of Mali, the former French colony. It is also well-known as a sanctuary for the al-Qaeda hierarchy."

"So, how does he manage to slip in and out of the U.S. so easily?"

"With a variety of passports and disguises, as I said, but also with the help of the American al-Qaeda network, which our government allows to operate. The network protects The Viper by arranging his travel, accommodations and funding. We think organizations like CAIR are the primary backers. A lot of inside people in their network."

"Incredible, isn't it?" I remarked.

"He's a ghost, Bruce, a phantom. Al-Massoud is believed to be behind more bombings and assassinations throughout the world than bin-Ladin or any of his followers. His assassination victims include Britain's MI6 director, the Israeli ambassador to the U.N. and a member of the Canadian cabinet. He has ordered the deaths of both our Secretaries of State and Defense, and was responsible for the bombings of one of the American compounds in Afghanistan where nineteen service members were killed. And we believe all of that is only a drop in the bucket. It's up to you, Bruce, to get the plan rolling. In my opinion, considering we don't know if and when al-Massoud will visit the Detroit mosque or Hancock, that your best shot at him will be inside the Goshen compound as soon as he arrives. You and Steed will need to be waiting on him. Maggie and I would like more than anything to be part of this on the ground, but our orders are to remain in a *laissez-faire* capacity. Other than the commando team going in, the government is officially mandated to neither harass nor enter these compounds unless we have indisputable, on-site, active intelligence that will prove an attack is being planned. This communique is just a piece of paper...an unproven threat as far as the Justice and State Departments are concerned. It all needs to be verified first hand. It's up to you to figure out how to do that."

"Wait a minute. I would think coverts like the spooks, or a military Special Ops team would be in place turning over every stone to nail him there where he's holed up. Is that not happening?"

Hickcock shook his head. "He is as elusive and highly protected as bin Laden ever was...maybe more. Our people have been all over that country's landscape, from the northern rocks to the southern Sahara. Every tribal contact we have in the plains and in the towns are either clamming up or purposely leading us down the wrong path. That includes the people the CIA is paying for information. We know he's there or been there, but lips are apparently sealed by fear. Every time we think there's a positive lead, it either turns out to be bogus or just someone who fits his description."

"Terrific. What else do you know about al-Massoud?" I asked.

"Well, although we don't have a lot on this serpent, we do know he is comparatively younger than most of the ideological Islamic jihadist types, far and away from looking like a Bedouin tribesman, who are relatively unintelligent and unsophisticated. Al-Massoud is bright and well-educated...we understand The University of Paris...and largely-touted among the al-Qaeda groups as the perfect terrorist leader. Someone who has a good head where it comes to Islamic politics and who possesses a warrior ethos...although he has never led an armed force against an enemy. Basically, he leaves the ambushes, bombings and murders of politicians, tourists and other civilians up to his subordinates. But make no mistake...he is now directly behind most all acts of terror in the U.S. and globally."

"Sounds like a unique breed of terrorist, all right. Someone greatly different from the towel head pricks I was used to pursuing."

Hickcock nodded and grinned. "And again, you must one day come clean about the kind of work you used to do *and* fill us in on some of the interesting experiences you had, Agent McGowan."

"Sure, Hickcock. It's starting to snow in Hell, too."

He smiled briefly but then posted a more solemn expression.

"Time is of the essence, Bruce. When can you leave?"

I laid Steed's and al-Massoud's photos aside and settled back in my chair. "It's mid-August now and you believe this Viper's plan begins going down in two or three weeks. For sure I need to get on my horse and go find Mr. Steed. But first, I need to check with the home front. I told my wife I anticipate having to leave in the next few days anyway. And she reminded me that my chores we agreed on were to paint the outside of the house before the fall, take her to Atlantic City to blow some of our guests' money, and catch way up on servicing her. Right now she needs her oil changed and a front end alignment."

"Well, I tell you what, Bruce," Larsen said. "Why don't you get a whole month of that 'business with the Mrs.' out of the way in the next couple of nights and then get your satiated ass on that plane to Antigua?"

I had to laugh. Curt, obtuse and opinionated, I liked her. A lot. On one hand, there was that svelte, feminine aura; but in a tomboyish kind of way, she was as tough as beef jerky. All combined, that equaled out to a healthy sense of androgyny. *And* I found out the hard-ass little vixen had a sense of humor after all.

# CHAPTER 9

For the remainder of the afternoon, I sat alone in the conference room again walking through the files on Steed as well as those on the man he would kill, al-Massoud, The Viper. And again, I reviewed photos and films, especially a few of the jihadist training compounds. Some of the training the ul-Fuqra types were doing looked a little lame, like performing body take-downs, firing Aks, and setting off explosives. I almost laughed out loud at some of their techniques and results. However, the still pictures I studied of al-Qaeda extremists taking machete-looking knives and separating heads from necks were quite chilling. I had seen such photos before, when I was with the counterterrorist unit, and it never gets any less ghastly. With some of these devils who I knew had committed such heinous acts, I took great pleasure sending their brutal asses to the boneyard.

Some of the narrated tapes were converted by interpreters to English complete with closed-captioned words at the bottom. One of the films provided a dialogue about how to kidnap U.S. politicians and businessmen abroad. And just as Johns had mentioned, there was a film of Fuqra types firing an RPG into an old, retired school bus that was sitting in a compound near Denver. From that, I assumed these radicals were not above attacking busloads of our school children. Another film revealed that mosques in the U.S. were teaching jihad ideology and nearly 500 radical

Islam centers were preaching extreme versions of Islamic doctrine...that all Americans are not only infidels but were their enemy as well. Small arms weapons were being stockpiled in a few compounds along with rocket launchers, det cord, C4, fertilizer and diesel fuel...even anti-aircraft weapons. Other activities in the films showed ul-Fuqra and al-Qaeda leaders studying U.S. city maps and photos of American icons such as the Empire State Building, the White House, and the Lincoln Memorial. Another photo captured men in turbans and skull caps standing and taking pictures of thousands of people in Times Square on New Year's Eve. There were actually two faces I recognized on film...two people who had received training in ul-Fuqra camps...Richard Reed, the shoe bomber, and John Mohammed, the Beltway Sniper.

I also read a piece put out by the *Center for Policing Terrorism* that Jamaat ul-Fuqra may be the best-positioned group to launch an attack on the United States, or more likely, help al-Qaeda do so.

Finally, I viewed a couple of propaganda films praising Pakistan as the epicenter of Islamic terrorism, showing scenes of the tribal badlands that had become havens for al-Qaeda Jamaat ul-Fuqra trainers. Among their recruits had been Faisal Shazad and Adnan Shukrijuman who were acclaimed as heroes for their terrorist acts on various New York infrastructure.

I sat long past five o'clock intrigued by what I was reading and watching. Some of the material I had seen before, perhaps a couple years ago. But seeing it again, and more, served to rekindle the ire in my brain, causing the blood in my arteries to boil like molten lava. But then, tiring a bit, I ultimately put the visual aids away and dialed Hickcock's extension to see if he was still around. He would need to retrieve everything in the room to be sure it would be put back under lock and key.

The agents *had* stuck around, waiting until I was through for the afternoon. I told them I would be pleased to buy them a drink and maybe some dinner after I checked into a hotel. I had thought about returning to Wolf Laurel and my understanding wife, but as the Friday afternoon traffic on the Beltway would be impossible, I was staying over. Larsen was trying to beg off, but Hickcock wanted to have more dialogue with me...whether it was business or not. Finally, Maggie succumbed to the idea, and we arranged to meet at one of their favorite haunts.

Failing to find a vacancy at a Holiday Inn Express or a Super 8, I checked into a fleabag called Marvin's just outside of the city. As it had a bed, a shower, and a mini-bar, I couldn't care less about having a room with a view or fancy soap in the bathroom. But, I had just enough time to check in, freshen up a little and change into a golf shirt and jeans before heading for the watering hole.

After putting the name *O'Malley's* and the bar's address into my GPS, I found that I was only about ten minutes away. When I arrived around six-forty, I spied the agents who were already seated at a high-top table with high-back chairs deep in a section of the bar near four pool tables where some rough-looking biker types, both men and women, were swigging beer and laying some pretty coarse language on one another. Of all the swanky bars in the D.C. area, I wondered why they had chosen O'Malley's.

"The beer is cold and half-price on Fridays before seven," said Hickcock. "And they have the best wings in town."

"You forgot to mention loud!" I yelled.

"And the floor ankle-deep in peanut shells!"

"We can go someplace else," Larsen offered. Sounded to me like she wanted to. I could tell she was either in one of those monthly moods or pissed off about something. So, I decided to refrain from any direct dialogue with her.

But I said, "I'm good here. I'm reasonably sure I won't end up with botulism or Legionnaire's disease."

Hickcock smiled and winked at Larsen. We each had a mug of cold beer in front of us as well as a couple of bowls of peanuts. We also ordered a platter of twenty wings which I was sure wouldn't be enough for the three of us.

"I read more of your Bureau file while you were in the conference room," Hickcock said. "I must say, you were quite a cop... decorated twice, wounded twice, a dozen written commendations and stellar evaluations. I hope *my* shield will look half as good as yours by the time I retire. So, now that you've put down a couple of beers, will you tell us exactly what it was you did for the Department of State? The file on you provided by Preston Johns indicated that you were some kind of analyst, but there was no job description or work history on you. It's a bit difficult to fathom that an ex-Green Beret and a retired FBI Special Agent with your history would settle for being a profiler and sit behind a desk from nine till five."

I took another swig of beer and replied, "One would think."

"And for you to receive a mission like this is going to be, there're obviously some pages missing in your book."

"Remember that I served in the same field office as Johns. He knows who I am *and* my capabilities."

"Yeah, but I'm not sure why you got singled out for *this* duty. Not only because there are hundreds of covert agency operatives out there, but you are..." He didn't finish his sentence.

"Go ahead and say it...*old*."

"Well, I wouldn't say old, but..."

"Vintage, then."

Hickcock grinned. "Vintage," he repeated.

"What's Zulu, anyway? Mr. Johns made reference to that."

I shook my head and didn't reply.

"You're never going to tell us, are you?"

"Well, like I said, I'm held to an official code of silence by someone who used to be very high up in the government."

"Used to be?"

"He's dead now."

"Oh, sorry. But it sounds like whatever you did up until your retirement, you might have been America's, James Bond."

And then that got me to thinking again about my friend, Virginia, the Birdman's trusted assistant who was murdered right along with him and the rest of the team. It was she who always referred to me as 007. A great lady. And I do miss her.

"It's an involved story. I won't tell it to you sometime." I then took another drink of my beer.

"I'd rather you told me about yourselves, like where you're from, went to college, choosing the FBI."

"Hold that thought, Bruce," replied Maggie.

"This beer is going through me like a fountain. I need to hit the restroom" She then hopped off her stool; but before she could take a step, she slipped on some shells and her foot just happened to trip a young woman passing by...who in turn lost *her* balance and spilled her stein of beer onto one of the gamers at the nearest pool table, causing him to scratch on the 8 ball. A rather unfortunate chain reaction.

"*What the hell*!" the guy shouted. "You just cost me the game, bitch."

"It was her who tripped me," the girl said, pointing at Maggie.

"Well, somebody's coughin' up twenty bucks."

The girl, who was in her early twenties, was large set and painted up in goth with black lipstick and fingernails. There also didn't appear to be a part of her skin that didn't have metal sticking on it, including her tongue.

"Well, don't just stand there, prom queen. Give the prick his money and me another beer."

"I'm sorry," Maggie said. "I slipped."

The girl then got in Maggie's face and squared off. "Are you gettin' me another beer or what?"

Maggie's face then suddenly took on a new attitude...from one of apology to one of piss and vinegar.

"That's a lovely shade of bitch you're wearing, butterball. Now before you get hurt, get out of my face."

'Uh oh,' I said to myself.

"Maybe you want to take this up a notch, huh red?"

"Does this look like a face of concern?" Maggie said to the girl.

"It will after I'm through smashing it."

Good one, Goth Girl, I thought.

Hickcock and I looked at one another and I shook my head. The spat was definitely escalating far beyond what it should have. And the big girl was asking for something she didn't want.

John quickly stepped in and announced that they were federal agents and "this doesn't need to happen. I'll buy you another beer, all right?"

"Don't fight my battles for me, Hickcock," Maggie admonished.

He then said into her ear with a low voice, "Maggie, stop it. We can't expose ourselves like this."

Ignoring him, the Irish was coming out in her in full force. However, she glanced at John and me, sighed and then turned back to her adversary.    "All right. Just sit the hell down. I'll get you your beer."

Unfortunately, that wasn't the end of it all. The jerk at the pool table was still out his money and accosted both women.

"Okay, which one of you two bitches are gonna pay me my twenty bucks?"

Hickcock, who was still on his feet between the women, answered him.

"No need to be disrespectful, sir. I'll..."

"Nobody asked you, sweetheart. Stay out of this unless you're comin' out of pocket for your girlfriend here."

It was then I saw Hickcock turn a deep scarlet.

"You don't have a clue as to who you're talking to, cowboy. I suggest you go back to your game."

All the while, I was nursing my beer and enjoying the fracas with great bemusement. I was also about to suggest the girls and the biker go mud wrestle in a big metal tub when a very large man, who I believed to be the bartender as well as the bouncer, came to the accident scene. Because the mouthing off between all the parties had elevated beyond the peak of normal bar atmosphere decibels and a small crowd had formed to watch and listen, it all must have attracted his attention.

"All right, you people. I don't know what's goin' on here but take this shit outside."

"That's a hell of a good idea," said the biker. He then turned to Hickcock. "Come on, prickface, out back."

Hickcock then tried to further de-escalate the situation himself and replied,    "Look, nobody's going outside. I'll give you your twenty and then I'll ask you to apologize to these ladies for your language."

"You know somethin', asshole? I ain't even wantin' the money, now. I'd rather take it out of your hide! Now, outside or are you just scared shitless?"

Hickcock looked at me and shook his head.

"Guess I'll need to go with this prick, Bruce. How about holding our table."

I was a little surprised that Hickcock was actually *going* outside with the brute, considering he was Bureau; but perhaps he was just trying to move the argument away from the restaurant and crowd.

Biker guy was certainly big enough...maybe six-three, two seventy-five, and a flaming red beard resembling Hagar the Horrible. On his head was a nappy rag containing images of skulls and crossbones. Hickcock, however, was nearly as tall, but wearing a hundred less pounds on his frame. I suspected it might have been an even fight, considering the size of the brute and Hickcock's FBI martial arts training, had it not been for the two huge biker buddies that followed.

Since I wasn't going to let Hickcock face these dudes alone, I walked out behind them. So did about twenty other curiosity seekers. The pool player then turned and saw me as he was exiting the back door. "You want some of this too, granddaddy?"

"I just want to be sure this fight that doesn't need to happen is one-on-one."

The man laughed and then stepped into the alley. Just as I suspected, the scene behind the building was set much like something out of West Side Story. A dumpster and large trash can sit just outside the door and a lone streetlight was set high up on a utility pole. It did appear that the rumble would be three against one. And that was not going to happen. I stood ready to assure him it didn't. Behind me stood Maggie and the ever-increasing number of onlookers.

Hickcock then said, "Look, mister. I only came out here to try reasoning with you. I don't know if you heard me inside, but I'm an agent with the FBI and the Bureau will not condone its agents participating in a back-alley brawl. What say we forget about all this and go home?"

"Hear that, fellas? Man's chicken-shit, just like I thought. I have another suggestion, asshole; if you don't wanna fight, what say you get down on your knees and suck..."

The straight punch came so fast from Hickcock's fist, the jerk wasn't able to complete his lewd sentence. Hagar hit the pavement like a rock. That's when pool guys two and three charged at Hickcock. When the first of the two men grabbed him by the neck, he reached under the man's left arm, turned, and bent, and sent his assailant over his right shoulder onto the asphalt. The man's face hit first, which put him out cold in a split second. When the other biker charged at Hickcock to take advantage of his back being turned, I stepped in and fired a punch of my own into the man's Adam's apple and finished him off with a knife-hand across the bridge of his nose. As he was gagging from the blood flowing into his nasal passages and trying to get his breath because of his crushed windpipe, I eased him to the ground and turned his head to one side so that he wouldn't choke on his blood.

But then the guy who started it all picked himself up and pulled out a six-inch blade, ready to run me through. That's when Maggie stepped up and placed the muzzle of her 9mm against his forehead.

"Drop the knife or the alley rats will be scarfing up your brains."

The man just glared at her and kept the knife in thrust position. She then cocked the hammer and said, "Go ahead...give me a reason."

I think the click of her gun caused him to piss in his jeans. He quickly let go of the knife and in a hardly audible voice, said "Okay, okay."

I then walked over to where Maggie now had the man on his knees and winked at her. To the biker I said, "Granddaddy here suggests you pick up your two ugly pals and de-ass the area...*now!*"

"Yes, sir. We're goin,' Sorry for the misunderstanding'."

Maggie then removed her pistol from the man's forehead and shoved it into her holster. The girl with whom she had the altercation slowly backed away as Maggie passed by her. In a tiny voice, she said, "Forget about the beer, okay?"

"No, I'll buy you that beer. Let's go back inside."

I almost laughed out loud. I was proud of both of these kids. Their poise, their style, and by God, their ability to bring it.

Our buffalo wings were waiting on us, although no longer hot. We returned to our table as though nothing had ever happened. A few eyes were still on us, but *our* eyes did not acknowledge their stares. Nothing really needed to be said about the forty-five-second fight, but we all knew we made a hell of a team out there.

Since the voices in the bar were still deafening to our ears, no one around us would understand or even care what we were talking about. So, we continued our conversation.

"When *can* you leave for Antigua, Bruce?" Hickcock asked.

"Give me the rest of the weekend at home. I'd say on Monday."

"Good. The clock is ticking, so the sooner the better. Let me know for sure and I'll have the Bureau's jet waiting for you at the Greenbrier Valley Airport."

I nodded. "If Steed agrees to come back with me, where do you want him stashed?"

"Can you bunk him in at your place?"

"Hey, I'm not sure I want this killer in the same house with my wife, John."

"He'll be no threat, Bruce. He's a contract man, not a psychopath. He's never killed anyone just to kill. He didn't kill Maggie and me when he had the chance. He needed to find out why we were on the hit list, and when he did, he refused the hit."

"Okay, what happens if he comes here and doesn't like the deal...goes back to Antigua?"

"Then he'll continue to be fair game."

"I guess when he and I get back we'll need to sit down with you again and put together the plan of action from there."

"That's fine, Bruce, but Maggie and I are going to stay out of the planning game. You know how to do this. You'll call all the shots. But we *will* be talking...and you *will* be keeping us informed."

"I understand."

"Do you have all the pieces of information on Steed locked in?" asked Larsen.

I tapped the side of my head.    "It's all in here."

"Good."

"By the way, I know the Bureau is a vast network of people, but I'm wondering if you ever met my daughter. She's a Special Agent out in Denver."

"You mean Caroline?" said Larsen.

I grinned.

"You *know* her."

"No. Remember, I read your file cover to cover. And we did a thorough background check before signing on with you. We know everything about you, Bruce."

I smiled and winked. "Not *everything*, Maggie."

# CHAPTER 10

I was back home by eleven on Saturday morning and greeted as always after an over-nighter by the sweet lips of the proprietress of Wolf Laurel. We had talked on the phone earlier when I was creeping down I-81 near Harrisonburg at a snail's pace. The lady was so happy I hadn't decided to stay for more than a day, she made up a special lunch for me. A salmon salad. Yech. She told me that eating like this will keep me looking young. I've got news for my lovely bride...the secret to looking young is *being* young.

Our guests from Florida had already departed, but a new couple from Massachusetts was bunking with us for about four days...Jan and Sue, lady life partners who looked to be in their upper 50s. They had chosen us over the Greenbrier, which made Adriana feel rather special. Of course, she also realized there was a difference of about three hundred dollars a night that was configured in their decision.

Joey had been back the evening before asking Adriana if I'd be good with us couples spending the day on Sunday at the cabin on the river fishing and grilling. I was fine with that as long as we were back by dark on Sunday night to ensure I had everything ready to roll out on Monday. It was after I had spoken with Adriana on my way home, I called Hickcock and told him that Monday would be a good day to fly south. He said he would have the jet at our airport by nine. But what I *hadn't* told Adriana was that if all went well, I would be bringing back with me another guest. For how long, I didn't know. I thought I would wait until I was sure Steed was returning with me before I told her.

She and I talked a little more about my Antigua trip which would happen in two days. She asked, "How long do you think you'll be gone?"

"I'm not sure, sweetheart. I'd surmise about two- or three-days max. What actual business I have with the man shouldn't take more than a day."

"So, you're just going down there for a meeting with him and not to...make him disappear, as you've been known to do."

*I think she seriously meant that.* I chuckled and then replied, "Do you actually think that *all* the business I have done for the government involves putting people in the ground?"

"It must be a McGowan trait. Joey does the same thing."

And then I really laughed. "Well, you've got me there. But, no, darling. Just a meeting this time. No gunplay."

*****

Joey and his wife, Cora, came by the inn around eight on Sunday morning and enjoyed breakfast of ham, eggs, and fluffy country biscuits with our two guests and us. It was probably the first time in a year that Adriana was going to miss church. However, considering I was going to be away a few days, she felt she needed a good day of fishing with me. And she had proven to be a whale of a fisherman...or is that a fisher*person?* I want to be politically correct in this day and time.

After breakfast, we loaded our fishing gear and cooler of steaks and beer into the back of Joey's van. It had been a long time since we were all together...I think maybe Christmas. I had no real friends. Maybe a couple of aforementioned police officers with whom I played a little golf, but otherwise we didn't hang out. In my former business, one didn't cultivate friends. The job didn't warrant close alliances. I couldn't even call my team members in our counterterrorist group 'friends.' *Business associates* would be more like it. The *killing* business. The one guy that even came close to being my friend and drinking buddy had betrayed me. Betrayed all of us. So, there you go. I haven't been close to anyone since. Except my brother Joey. And, oh, the lovely Adriana of course...my *best* friend.

Joey and I had had a lot of laughs throughout the years...mostly about crap we did, but also about times we had as kids being raised by *very* understanding parents, God rest their souls. We aren't that far apart in age; therefore, sometimes I felt back then that we were best buds rather than brothers. We fished a lot together, double-dated, and sometimes brought a pack of trouble down on our heads together. Like the time when I bought my first muscle car. I think I was seventeen and Joey, fifteen. Although I worked a little at Kroger's Grocery, I could hardly make enough to put gas in the thirsty beast. One night we slipped into the old school yard where they parked the buses and siphoned out a tank load of 105 octane of bus fuel. Unfortunately, in the process I accidentally swallowed a mouthful of it. I think it was the sound of me spitting, sputtering and heaving that might have awakened old lady Barrett whose house was just on the other side of the schoolyard fence. She then called Chief Merriman who promptly came to the scene and found me lying against the fender of my Plymouth with a kind of green, iridescent glow covering my face.

"Well, boy, I won't run you in out of respect for your old man; but if I catch you back down here doing something like this again, you're going to Pruntytown," which of course was West Virginia's famous boy's reform school. But I know he didn't arrest me for another reason. Punchy Merriman must have been eighty with one foot in the grave. And as he was soon to be one of our undertaker dad's clients, the chief wanted to be sure that when Dad laid him to rest in the coffin, he didn't make him up to look like Elmer Fudd or Howdy Doody.

While we were all down at the river that Sunday sitting on the bank of the Greenbrier River with our lines in the cool, flowing waters, Joey and I actually had more laughs visiting the gasoline incident yet another time. Adriana, who hadn't heard that yarn, laughed like I had never seen her...so loud in fact that Joey and I were afraid she would frighten away that mammoth trout we were looking for.

It was a nice late summer day filled with warm, glorious sunshine, music of birds warbling in the trees and sweet family moments. The steaks were juicy and tender and the Heinekens were ice cold. But alas, Adriana, whose mouth had been watering for some succulent trout, was resigned to eating one of the steaks. As perfect as that Sunday was, the fish were not cooperating.

*****

At 9:40 on Monday morning, I parked my car in the lot at the Greenbrier Valley Airport and dragged my bag inside. Although Hickcock had the day before made arrangements with the TSA for me to go through security with my firearm, I still had a bit of a problem when I took off my jacket and displayed my .380 in its shoulder holster. Two very large TSA agents with concerned looks and large fingers wanted to take my weapon and then do a body cavity search. One of them, who I thought had a wicked kind of smile on his face, was already snapping on his latex gloves. I was afraid he might tell me I had a purr-ty mouth. However, after I asked them to check with their highers, wherever they were, one of the agents finally made the phone call that allowed me to keep my weapon...and my dignity.

Greeting me on the tarmac at the bottom steps leading up to the Learjet 28 was the co-pilot who shook my hand and asked me to follow him. It would just be him, plus the pilot, who had remained seated in the captain's seat, and me on this four-and-a-half-hour flight. The Bureau was obviously treating me like a king on this trip. After we had become airborne, an hour or so later, as we were passing over the tobacco fields of North Carolina, the co-pilot brought me back a sandwich, a bag of chips and a Coke.

Then, much later, when I saw the snaking tail-end of the Florida Keys disappearing off our right wing, he gave me a mini-package of I believe thirteen peanuts and a small bottle of water. That was all well and good, but I'd have to speak with Hickcock later about other comforts. Where was the government flight attendant with the face and svelte body of a Beyonce or Catherine Zeta-Jones? And where were the mini bottles of Dewars or Captain Morgan?

While glancing down occasionally upon the wisps of clouds that lay over the blue-green waters of the Caribbean, I continued skimming through my notes on Steed. He was a pro all right, but a guy with a deeply troubled past. Born Billy Joe Cavanaugh, this Louisiana boy was orphaned early on, and as he had no one to take him in, he found himself on the street. It was then that he fell in with the Dixie mob in New Orleans. At first a runner for the don, he was suddenly performing hits...how many, was unknown. But at age twenty-eight, he pleaded for his release so that he could join the Marines. Because the mob boss liked Billy Joe and as he himself had been a Marine, he gave him his blessing. Not long after starting boot camp in Parris Island, Billy was recognized and touted as the best shot in his unit. Small wonder, considering his history. That's when he was sent to sniper school.

It was on his tour of duty in Iraq during Desert Storm in 1991 that his life took a different turn. Lance Corporal Cavanaugh was riding shotgun in a Humvee with a CIA operative in the rear seat when the vehicle came under enemy fire. After their driver was killed and the Humvee crashed off the side of the road, Billy pulled the operative out and placed him on the opposite side of the vehicle from the gunfire. He then set up his sniper rifle on the vehicle's hood and at a distance of over 500 yards picked off all four enemy gunmen, even though they were partially concealed behind rocks. Immensely impressed, the operative subsequently reported the feat to his superiors and suddenly after a two year hitch in the Marines, Billy Joe found himself on the covert side of the CIA as a government-sanctioned assassin.

Unfortunately, a few years later, the FBI showed up at his door and arrested him for a mob crime that ironically he did not commit. Seems an informant who had it in for Billy turned him over and that's when the Justice Department began digging into his bloody past. After Billy did a year in Sing Sing, a high-ranking member of that same Justice Department offered him an out. In exchange for his release, Billy Joe would agree to perform hits, no questions asked, on people who had obviously committed murder, but due to some technicality, either escaped prosecution or skated because of a liberal judge's or jury's decision. That was when Billy Joe Cavanaugh became Atticus Steed. Four co-conspirators made up this Justice Club, the head of which informed *and* warned Steed that he *would* carry out the hits to the letter. Any reluctance or refusal on his part would land him back in prison with no chance of parole.

Where the hit train finally derailed was when Steed found out his next mark was a young FBI agent and female partner, two straight-up kids who were getting too close to learning the identities of all of the conspirators. When Steed refused the hits, *he* then became The Justice Club's next target. Finally, when four newly hired, thugs were then dispatched to kill the agents, ultimately trapping them on the grounds of an abandoned service station, the agents found that Steed had their back, subsequently ripping the heads off two of the would-be assassins with his .308 while the agents took out the remaining two.

I could now better understand why Hickcock and Larsen had become rather enamored with him. As they had met him face to face and found him both engaging and charming, they also saw through his savagery an element of integrity, even right-heartedness. However, regardless of any good or righteous qualities Atticus Steed may have had, in my book he was still a cold, calculating and deadly killer.

Somehow in all my reading I came up with a stiff neck, so I laid Steed's folder aside, checked my watch and then saw we still had another hour of air time. As my eyes were tired from reading and my brain desperately wanted to sign off, I pushed my seat back and quickly fell asleep. An hour later the sudden jolt of the wheels touching down woke me. It felt like I had only been out a couple of minutes. After we had taxied down the short runway to almost the very end, we circled back in until the terminal sign atop the modest building came into view. *Welcome to St. John's.* It would be a long day for my aviators. A bite to eat at the terminal and some JP4, and then they would be off again...back home to Andrews.

An airport agent was kind enough to give me directions to the Antiguan Royal Police Force headquarters, so after I cleared customs, I rented an Explorer with a GPS and began driving. As I had never been to the island before, I found its rocky shores and pristine beaches on my drive to the station to be quite picturesque. In reading up on Antigua a couple days before, I found that about 90% of its inhabitants were either pure Africans or Mulattoes. For centuries it had been British territory, however. It was also an island home for a number of movie stars and celebrity musicians, most of whose estates were strung out all along its 360 degrees of beaches.

I arrived at the station about three-fifteen and told the desk sergeant that I needed to speak with Chief Jacques Reynolds, with whom Hickcock had set up a meeting. Within a couple of minutes, a large-set African male in a beige uniform came down the hall, then reached out to shake my hand.

"Ah, Mr. McGowan," the chief greeted in a very fine British brogue. I've been expecting you. Won't you come back to my office?"

"Of course. Thank you," I replied politely.

I then followed him back down the hallway and into a corner office that gave me a magnificent view of a lush meadow with scores of miniature palmettos, beyond which was a glassy, blue lagoon. On his walls were plaques, photos and framed certificates that clearly reflected he was not only some kind of hero in Her Majesty's eyes, but the recipient of a ton of atta-boys from an appreciative populace. There was also a shadow box among the wall hangings that contained a dozen or so combat medals. The last time I checked, Antigua had not been in a war with *anyone*, so it set me to wonder.

We enjoyed some small talk, which included a short history of the island and its attractions. I learned that the entire police force numbered about seven hundred, whereas the Antiguan-Barbuda Royal Defense Force (the military) had less than two fifty. If Antigua *did* fight a war, I hoped they picked on somebody their own size.

Reynolds then began asking me some questions about *me*, fully getting the impression that I was FBI. I didn't tell him any different and he didn't ask to see a badge. I assumed Hickcock's phone call to him had sufficiently introduced me.

"So, my American friend, I understand you came to our country to interview someone...another American?"

"Yes. I need to find a man by the name of Atticus Steed. He supposedly owns a bar somewhere on one of the beaches."

"I know most of the proprietors of American businesses and have been to all the beaches, but his name is not familiar to me. I will see what I can find." He then buzzed his civilian assistant on the intercom. "Mano, please see if you can find information on an American resident named Atticus Steed."

We made some small talk a few more minutes and then Mano returned with a piece of paper in his hand. Reynolds ran his eyes over it and then looked up.

"Mr. McGowan, in checking on this man, I find something very concerning."

I shuffled to a different position in my chair. "And what would that be?"

"We find an official request from your Justice Department that had apparently either slipped through the crack, buried in our files, or just ignored by our government. It's an extradition request. Atticus Steed also has over two million U.S. dollars in one of our Swiss banks and your government has frozen it. He is an American fugitive, sir. I assume you know that, however, and are here to take him into custody."

"My understanding is that there has been a temporary stay on that extradition request until such time I speak with him. I intend to ask him a series of questions to secure information and if he doesn't answer them to my satisfaction, our government will follow up on that request."

"If he is a fugitive from justice, why is there a delay? And if he is a criminal, he would not be the type of person we would want in our country. But, when he is sent back to America, it is probable that our government will confiscate his assets...to include, of course, his bank funds."

I could see the dollar signs coming out of his eyes and ears the very moment he discovered Steed was a criminal and had beaucoup dineros in one of his country's banks. It meant less to him that there was a fugitive living on Antiguan soil than the fact that he had the chance to get his paws on Steed's assets.

"Do you have his address?" I asked.

For a moment, I thought he was going to stall me so that he could think about his best course of action. Maybe the police would just go pick him up, make a phony case of their own, then tell our government they could have Steed in exchange for his assets. But he knew that would be breaking the 1996 extradition agreement between the two countries. I could sense the wheels turning in his head.

"Chief Reynolds?"

Finally, he leaned forward in his chair and scribbled the address on a piece of scrap paper, then handed it to me.

"The location is south of here in St. Paul's. If you wish, I can have two of my officers take you there."

I then stood and put the scrap of paper in my pocket.

"That won't be necessary. I have my rental outside. Just for your own information, I do not expect there will be any trouble from him. I will offer him a chance to go back with me, peacefully, before our government takes further action."

"What matters will you be talking with him about if or you just intend to take him back with you?"

"It's official business, Chief. I'm not at liberty to say."

"Any business in this country, official or not, is *my* business as well, Mr. McGowan."

"It is *not*, sir."

"Then, perhaps I will not permit you to go there."

"I think our conversation is now over, Chief. Thanks for the information."

"You are not excused to leave," he said sternly. Our meeting had suddenly and unnecessarily turned ugly.

"And I don't think you will try to stop me. Goodbye, Chief." I turned and walked toward the door.

"Mr. McGowan!" Reynolds called after me.

I stopped at the door and turned back around. But I didn't answer him.

He glared at me for a moment and then said, "You are advised to watch yourself while you are here."

I smiled but didn't respond. It was not worth asking him if that was a threat. I then turned again and closed the door behind me. Our conversation had quickly gone from cordial to contentious. And there was no doubt in my mind Chief Reynolds was going to try every angle he could to get Steed extradited and then confiscate his money. If Steed just voluntarily returned with me and ultimately ceased to become a fugitive, the money could never be touched by the Antiguan government. Anyway, it was the United States that froze the money, and only *it* could *un*freeze it.

I hadn't been in the country more than an hour and already I had not only pissed off its police chief but with my obstinate attitude, probably became an enemy of the state as well. I think *my* country was not going to like that. So, I thought maybe I needed to back off my attitude a little and not alienate one of our principal allies.

After turning onto Queen's Highway south toward St. Paul's, I put the address on the piece of paper into my GPS. I hadn't gone two blocks until I picked up a tail...a white Subaru with a bar of red and blue lights on its roof. However, I saw that the police unit was keeping its distance something like five hundred feet back. I had no reason to try losing it and certainly was going to stay within the posted speed limit. I did figure once I arrived at Steed's location, they might decide to go ahead and pick him up. That's when I would get Hickcock on the line.

"Just hang onto my ass all you want, boys," I said aloud, checking my mirror once again.

"You're wasting a damn fine afternoon on me."

# CHAPTER 11

The voice on my GPS took me toward the beach and into the gates of a very nice resort called *Jalousie*. True, I was on the Bureau's expense account, and although Hickcock knew I was going to be spending a couple of nights *somewhere*, I doubt he counted on me staying at a place that would equal a month of his salary. But first, just to be sure this was where Steed was living, I parked in a temporary spot so that I could go in and find out for sure. If he was staying there, either his bar business was really paying off or he had some money stored away somewhere that *wasn't* frozen.

After exiting my rental, I saw out of the corner of my eye that the police unit had pulled into a parking space two rows back from mine. The idiots in the cruiser couldn't really think they were so inconspicuous that I hadn't noticed them...or could they?

The native beauty at the desk in the colorful island blouse had a catchy little greeting,

"How can I make your day, sir?"

I tried to stifle a chuckle. I wanted to say, "*I've* got an idea." But I'm thinking the woman I left at home wouldn't exactly like it. "I'm looking for a friend of mine who I think may be staying here...one Atticus Steed."

"Sir, we have a policy not to give out any information on our guests. However, I *will* tell you that Mr. Steed is *not* staying here."

My heart sank.

"But I had this place as his address."

"Perhaps he gave you Jalousie as his *business* address, but his bar is on the back side of our resort on the beach. If you follow the beach to the west a few hundred feet, you'll then see his bungalow. It's the only pink house in that area."

I breathed a sigh of relief.

"Ah, perfect. Well, I do need a place to stay for a couple of days. Do you have any vacancy?"

"Yes. You hit it right. But Thursday we have a group coming in for a convention and all our rooms are reserved."

"I'll certainly be out of here by then. How much is your rate per night?"

"Three twenty-five, sir." Gulp.

"That's fine."

But it wouldn't be fine with Hickcock.

"Then, welcome to Jalousie."

I finished checking in, then re-parked my car and hauled my bag inside. On the way into the lobby, I turned to see if the cops were still there. They were and I'm sure they saw me. So that they could see that I was aware of their presence, I gave them a finger wave.

My Learjet ham sandwich now long gone; I was starved. After hanging up my clothes and washing my hands, I went downstairs to Jalousie's restaurant and enjoyed a nice grouper dinner. Then as it was approaching six-thirty and the sun had dipped below the palms, I took a stroll out along the boardwalk until it ended in the sand at a shack with a thatched roof, slightly sturdier than a lean-to. *The Last Chance Bar*. Perhaps it was aptly and metaphorically named by Steed himself. His last chance at life after all his years of bringing death. Maybe he would at last find peace, honor and meaning in his life.

The bar wasn't much, but it had a great collection of international beers as well as the usual hard stuff. And there were also a couple of skimpily clad vixens behind the bar that would give one of those conventioneers coming in later in the week a case of amnesia about being married.

After kicking off my loafers to allow the white, velvet sand to massage my tired feet, I stepped up to a bar stool and ordered a Merlot. Other than having a yen for a glass of wine, I was actually there searching for a face that might resemble the man I was looking for...someone in his early 40s, dark hair, square jaw, and what Hickcock had described as having steely eyes. However, all I found were the two ladies behind the bar, a blonde, Caucasian woman and a Mulatto chick with braided hair, and then a couple of white haired ladies in their low seventies on my side of the bar checking me out.

So, I struck up a conversation with the bar lasses.

"Great little bar," I said. And a great spot. Do you all own it?"

"Oh, no sir," replied the blonde. "A gentleman down the beach does."

"I've been thinking about buying something like this in my retirement. I guess the old guy is pretty well off, huh?"

"I suppose he does all right. But he's not an *old* guy. He's probably in his forties."

"Is he around? Maybe he can give me some pointers on setting a business like this up. I *need* a little financial advice."

"Well, you just missed him. He went home for the evening. Are you staying at Jalousie?"

"I am."

"He'll be here after one tomorrow if you want to talk with him."

"Okay. Maybe I'll come back then, although it might be a little too early in the day for me to wet my whistle."

"Well, we'll see you then. I hope you're having a good vacation. That *is* why you're here, isn't it?"

"A little business...a little pleasure."

"You have a good evening, sir."

I gave her a smile and nodded, put something in the tip jar and then took a final sip of the biting wine. It was a nice evening for a little walk on the beach, so I started walking west. The sun finally dropped below the water and a slight, warm tropical breeze then picked up, fanning the palm leaves over my head. It made me wish Adriana was with me, although I knew it wasn't possible to bring her. In the brief years of our marriage, we had yet to take a nice beach vacation, except for a few days at Myrtle. That sort of didn't count compared to a place like this.

Speaking of my lady, as I was walking along, filling my senses with the sights, smells and sounds of the seashore, I called her to let her know I had arrived safely. I gave her the name of the hotel and then told her I should be home sometime Thursday afternoon if all went well. She said she already missed me...as I did her.

Tuesday morning was probably just another day in paradise to the Antiguans; but to me, it's what I imagined Heaven would be like. Hopefully, I wouldn't have any trouble getting in. After putting down a protein bar and a bottled water, I set out on a run, this time along the shoreline toward the east. Running in sneakers in the thick sand which was sandwiched between the waves and the sea oats probably gave me two more miles worth of calorie burning than what I was used to. After checking my watch, I saw that I had been running about fifteen minutes longer than usual. One thing about running in the soft sand...the legs and feet love it and they tell my body it can go even further. But, as daylight was burning and the mid-morning sun was baking, I made my turn and headed back. Then I showered and had a banana for an early lunch. I figured since my vacation on the Bureau was costing three twenty-five a day, I needed to give them a break on the meals.

I would be sure to make my way down to a beach chair near the bar sometime after one o'clock, but in the meantime, I decided to piddle a while and watch TV. However, my gurgling stomach told me I had burned off a little too many calories on the run. Just before noon, I broke down and ordered room service. So that I would be true to my wife while on assignment, I selected a grilled chicken salad with fat-free dressing. Now my conscience would be clear and I wouldn't have to divulge that I had an affair with a 1200 calorie cheeseburger.

Sharply at one, I donned the Panama Jack hat and Hawaiian-style shirt I brought with me along with a tank top, over which the shirt hung open and loose, and a pair of Bermuda shorts. The shirt readily concealed my .380 in its shoulder holster. It was a small enough weapon to remain hidden, but powerful enough to blow the brains out of a skull. Either it or my Glock is always with me, depending on my attire. One must be conscious of his wardrobe in order to look GQ.

At one-fifteen, I found my chair, a large turquoise Adirondack situated halfway between the beach and the bar. After sliding on my pair of military Ray-Bans to take the glare off, I waited.

One-thirty came and went. So did one forty-five. Could the bar girl have been mistaken about today or had Steed changed his routine? I was just getting ready to get up and go to the bar for a cold beer, when a man about six-one with jet black hair, lean, tanned, and wearing a loose white shirt and green trunks, walked slowly up the beach in my direction. With a sense of dignified authority, he passed by me and made his way toward the bar. I thought it *might* be Steed but couldn't be sure. This man had a short, cropped goatee of a beard. And then instead of plopping down on a bar stool, he went directly *behind* the bar. It had to be Steed.

*Now* wasn't the time to approach him. Instead, I would wait the bulk of the afternoon and evening if necessary to follow him back down the beach to his bungalow. I needed to get him alone.

Watching him serve drinks with his girls and converse with his customers, casting smiles their way, I found him to be rather enigmatic. The smile and friendly demeanor were genuine; yet, the man was a killer, bold and cold. With the charm of a George Clooney, or further back, a Cary Grant, I could see how a gal like Maggie Larsen could be enamored with him...although it was her partner she accused of being captivated. I had seen older photos of him as well as the grainy ones more recently taken by surveillance cameras. And now I had seen him in person.

Steed had hardly been behind the bar more than twenty minutes when a lovely, dark-haired Latina-looking woman walked toward him with all the grace of a runway model and the body of the Sofia Vergara persuasion. If I wasn't in love already, it wouldn't take me long to get that way with the likes of her. What was interesting, though, was that they immediately began conversing as though they knew one another. Intimately. I watched them for nearly ten minutes, smiling and touching hands. Then he stepped around the bar and walked with her just a few feet until he took her by the hand and eased her into an Adirondack under a pair of palmettos within thirty feet of where I was sitting. He then took the chair beside her. Immediately from his pocket he pulled out a small black box and opened it. Even from where I was sitting, I caught the glint off the diamond ring that lay in it. After taking the ring out of the box, he placed it gingerly on her finger. They had a few soft words between them, which I could not hear, and then she began to cry. Tears of joy, obviously, because that led to a long, passionate kiss.

After a moment, he helped her to her feet and then they began walking slowly down the beach, passing close by me on their way. I pretended to be asleep, but as they couldn't see my eyes behind the lenses of my flight glasses, I continued to watch them. When they were perhaps twenty yards beyond me, I pulled out my cell phone and called Hickcock.

"I'm here, John. A man of Steed's description just passed by me."

"So, what do you think, Bruce? *Is* it him?"

I continued with my eyes locked onto the couple as they slowly walked further down the beach, arms around one another, like the lovers in paradise that they were. "It's him."

# CHAPTER 12

"You're sure."

"Yes," I replied. "I'm sitting just yards from his bar and this is the address the police gave me."

"Good. And now you go to work."

"A couple of minor complications, though."

"What?"

"Steed has a girlfriend...actually a fiancée. I watched him put an engagement ring on her finger."

"I see. Might be somebody who'll get in the way. You said a *couple* of complications. What's the other?"

"The police chief, Reynolds, could be a problem. He didn't know that Steed was on the 'most wanted' list as his department had let a U.S. extradition request slip by them unanswered. Since Steed has a couple of million in assets, I think Reynolds is going to try pulling some punches to get his hands on the money. If he takes Steed into custody and ships him back to the States, he'll try to get the money confiscated."

"He might try, but the U.S. has control of Steed's assets."

"But if he does pick Steed up and hold him for any length of time, our man will then be out of the equation. You'll have to go to Plan B."

"Yeah, I see what you mean. I'll get the Justice Department to block any attempt Reynolds and the Antiguan government make to put a move on him."

"Fine. I need to go, though. I still have my eyes on him and am going to follow him back to his house. Will let you know what happens."

"So, you're going to move on him today."

"One way or the other."

"All right. I'll be waiting to hear from you."

Steed and his new fiancée were now well down the beach, still close enough for me to keep my eyes on him, yet far enough away so that he wouldn't become suspicious about the man in the Panama Jack hat behind him. I did need to pick up the pace a little because he might be turning left into a yard at any time, and from my vantage point ,I wouldn't be able to tell which place. The girl at the check-in desk did tell me it was a pink bungalow, however.

After I had moved in on him within a hundred yards, he and his lady turned in. There were a number of smallish beach bungalows back off the beach under a cluster of palms and *three* of them were actually pink in color. The girl at the hotel desk had been wrong. One good thing about the sand, however, until the tide comes in, footprints will generally keep their shape. As the woman had on sandals and Steed was barefoot, I was able to track their prints directly to a gate behind which sat a small, stucco house with a cedar shake roof. So far so good.

I wasn't sure what I would do at this point. The woman complicated things. If she had not been with him, I would simply go up to his door and knock. If I approached him right away and told him I was an American agent for hire, he might go off on me...and she might get hurt. Even if that didn't happen, our government's proposal was not to be for her ears.

I stood for a long minute looking over the place, but then turned around and walked out to a point where the surf was crashing onto the beach. What to do? I could wait and catch him alone...maybe on his way back to the bar...if he in fact decided to go back later in the afternoon. But as he had just given her the ring, I suspected they might at this moment be in their bedroom sealing the deal. And who knows how long that would take? The virile man that *I* am, it might go on all night.

Turning briefly to take another look at the bungalow, I captured a photo of the place on my cell phone. I then must have stood there on the beach thinking and looking out over the aqua waters for a full ten minutes, when I had one of those experiences where the hair on the back of my neck starts to crawl. It was then I heard the click of the hammer. Slowly, I placed my hand inside of my shirt and wrapped my fingers around my .380. Then quickly, I pulled it from its holster and wheeled around, finding myself looking into the barrel of a Smith and Wesson and the searing eyes of Atticus Steed. For what seemed like an impossible minute, we stood with the muzzles of our pistols aimed at each others' heads, not saying a word.

Finally, I said, "Atticus Steed."

"Who are you and what do you want?" he replied.

"Put your gun down and we'll talk."

"You put *yours* down," he said.

It was a standoff. A very uncomfortable one at that. I continued my stare down but did not reply.

And he still didn't blink.

"Are you here to kill me or arrest me?"

Slowly, I then lowered my gun. The fact that he didn't put a bullet in the back of my head after sneaking up on me, reinforced my understanding that this was a man who did not kill for no reason. And he wasn't going to kill me.

My pistol now down at my side, I said,

"There are some people down the beach walking this way. Lower your gun, Steed, and we'll talk."

Steed glanced quickly to his right and then back to me to assure that I wasn't trying to trick him, then lowered his gun as well.

"I'll ask you again...what do you want and why were you following me?"

I could now see how perceptive this man was.

"Your girlfriend is inside. Let's not alarm her. Take a walk with me."

"Why should I?"

"I'm not here to arrest you *or* to kill you, Steed, or I would have already stormed your bungalow with the local SWAT. I'm not a cop and I'm not a hit man like you."

I holstered my .380 and that prompted him to shove his pistol down the back of his trunks. Then I turned and began walking. With some noticeable reluctance, he followed suit.

"My name's Bruce McGowan. I *was* FBI, but then I was hired on with the Department of State doing work as a counterterrorist operative. Since then, however, I have recently struck up a business relationship with a couple of old friends of yours...John Hickcock and Maggie Larsen."

Steed cocked his head and widened his eyes at my mention of their names.

"And they sent you here to pick me up."

"Not like you might think. I'm here to make you an offer, Mr. Steed."

He stopped.

"What kind of offer?"

I stopped as well and faced him.

"I'm staying down at the Jalousie. In my room, I have a letter addressed to you signed by Agent Hickcock. He and Larsen are now with the Counterterrorist Division of the FBI."

"I don't think I'm considered a terrorist, McGowan."

'Hear me out, Steed. As regards the letter, I haven't read it because it's sealed. But it supposedly extends an offer to you from the FBI that if you perform a little mission for them, any charges currently against you will go away. *And* you will receive a full pardon for all crimes, known or unknown, from the Justice Department."

Steed bore down on me with his eyes.

"The rational man would believe that this is some kind of trick to get me to turn myself in."

"It's no trick, Steed." I squatted down and picked up a large seashell, then ran my fingers over its smooth fuselage.

"Before I get into it, let me ask you something that is kind of bugging me. Why didn't you change your name after you got here? It's an unusual name and a seven-year-old kid on Facebook would have no trouble finding you. And then you settle in a country that has an extradition agreement established with the United States."

He turned his head and looked far out in the Caribbean, scanning the waters from one end of the beach to the other.

"I like this place. Always have. And I like the name I chose. I also knew it was inevitable. Someday someone would find me and I would go down. That woman in there, the love of my life, left me a few months ago, the day I came clean with her what I did for a living. When she walked out, my world didn't matter anymore. If someone came for me, I wouldn't put up a fight. All I wanted was a little peace for a while...and a little fun doing this bar thing. And now, ironically on the same afternoon you came for me, she walks back into my life. Is that funny or what?"

"Look, Steed, I don't like what I know about you. You've killed a hell of a lot of people for every reason in the world. If it were up to me, I'd do this mission alone and let them come get you."

"What mission? What in the hell are you talking about?" he asked.

"I'll lay it out for you in a condensed mouthful. The Bureau wants you to come back to the States and work with me on taking down an international terrorist. You would be firing the shot to kill the terrorist who will be in an al-Qaeda-linked jihadist training camp planning a massive attack on a number of government buildings and national treasures. Does that in any way intrigue you?"

"That's a compelling story, McGowan. Why should I believe you?"

"Actually, I personally don't give a damn if you believe me or not. I'm just relaying to you what Hickcock and the Justice Department is offering you."

He laughed. "The Justice Department. If you know anything about me, you know what my last experience was with them."

"I know about it. But I also know while you were getting screwed by those people and facing a hit yourself, Hickcock and Larsen were protecting your ass by going after them. Yeah, I realize you had their back as well, and that's why they want to engage you. And they're giving you an out here. I personally think the government is going beyond its authority in offering to make your past go away, but I have also had a dialogue with the man who has the President's ear...and vice versa. Believe me, the offer's out there. Hickcock chose you for the mission to give you an opportunity to do something for your country while also earning yourself a pardon."

"Nice try, McGowan. I go back to the States with you and waiting at the airport will be federal agents to take me into custody."

"What do you have to lose? If you don't go back with me, people will know where you are and you'll be fair game, anyway. And by the way, the Antiguan police are prepared to arrest you and turn you over to the United States as we speak."

"Won't happen, McGowan. I have a couple of friends in high places."

So, he *was* protected by someone big there, I thought.

We had walked about five hundred feet while talking, but then I turned us back around toward his bungalow.

Steed then began rubbing his forehead.

"So, what you're telling me is I'm damned nonetheless if I don't take the risk. Look, McGowan, the most important person in the world to me is in that house over there. She was with me for two years and then she left me. She knows I am a fugitive and can't go back to the U.S. If I go, that'll be the end of us." He then stopped, folded his arms and looked down into the sand.

"She came back to me today and said she forgives me for everything I've done...that she now wants to spend the rest of her life with me. I could flee with her tonight and go someplace where no one will ever find us. But, either decision on my part would probably destroy her."

We continued to walk without further word until we arrived back at the beach entrance to his bungalow. And it was at that moment when we returned that she appeared on the opposite side of the gate.

"Atticus, I wondered where you went."

Steed then went to her, opened the gate and led her out by the hand.

"Maria, this is Mr. Bruce McGowan who I just met. Ironically, he knows a couple of people that I know back in Washington. DC"

"Hello, Mr. McGowan." She extended her hand, and I took it. With my left hand, I removed my hat.

"It's a pleasure, Maria. Are you enjoying Antigua?"

She looked at Steed and smiled.

"More than you know." And then she held up her left hand to display her diamond. "I'm newly engaged as you can see. It's the happiest day of my life."

"Ahhh, congratulations. By the way, you can call me Bruce, Maria."

She smiled again and nodded. Her afternoon of bliss had obviously not yet waned as there were tears of happiness in her eyes. Steed and I looked at one another and then he turned his eyes back onto her.

"Well, Atticus," I said.

"I need to get back to the room. When you go back to the bar this afternoon, maybe I'll stop by for a drink and we can swap some more stories. How about around six?"

He nodded his head 'yes' and then we exchanged handshakes. "Okay."

I looked back at Maria. "A real pleasure, ma'am."

"I enjoyed meeting you, Mr. McGow...uh Bruce. Perhaps I'll see you again before you leave. How long will you be here?"

"Until my business is done...maybe a couple more days."

"Well, I hope your business is successful."

I then looked back at Steed.

"Thank you. I hope so, too."

# CHAPTER 13

A few minutes past six, I sat in the same chair as I did earlier in the day which was located about thirty feet from *The Last Chance*. Then at six-fifteen, I recognized Steed's form coming up the beach straight out of the sunset. The fact that he showed up showed promise. However, he could have just as well decided to tell me in person to go to hell.

But then he strolled right on by me and went to the bar. For a couple of minutes, he conversed with the young Mulatto girl, then after he turned around, I saw that he had two drinks in his hand and was walking toward me. Another good sign.

"I've become partial to Margaritas," he said.

"Here's one for you...on the house."

"Thanks," I replied.

"And I have something for you." I handed him the envelope from Hickcock.

After taking out a small pocket knife, he sliced the envelope open carefully like a surgeon with a scalpel. It made me think about what I read on the plane...about where he had sliced up a couple of his marks with a blade just a wee bit larger than that pocketknife. He then began reading the letter which took him no more than a minute to digest. Finally, he folded it back up and handed it to me.

"Just as you said."

"Do you have all the information you need out of it?" I asked him.

"I know what it says."

"Good." I then took a matchbook from my pocket, struck one of the matches, and set it ablaze.

"*What are you doing!*" he exclaimed.

"You're destroying a letter of promise. A contract."

"*You* met Hickcock and know that his word is solid. He told me after you read it to destroy it, to assure it didn't accidentally fall into anybody else's hands." The letter's red and black ashes rose into the air and then floated gently down into the sand. ';

Steed then sat back in his chair and stared at his bar for several moments, reflectively.

"It wasn't exactly my dream, the bar. It's just something I always wanted to try. I then told myself it wouldn't be any great loss if someone ever found me and carted me off to prison."

I ignored his meandering off the subject.

"What's your decision, Steed?"

"Say I agree to this...how do we do it?"

"Before I give you the particulars, tell me for sure that you're in."

Steed looked back down the beach in the direction of his bungalow, obviously thinking about the lady inside. He then nodded.

"Yeah, okay. What have I got to lose? You're here and now the U.S. Government knows where to find me. Anyway, I'm tired of playing hide-and-seek. If all this is on the up-and-up, I'm in. So, what's it all about and happens from here?"

I started from scratch, giving him a twenty-minute summary of everything that Johns and the agents had told me. "You pack up and go back with me. We then meet up with Hickcock and Larsen. They provide the latest Intel on this terrorist, who by the way is now considered the most dangerous of his kind in the world; and then we start to work. This target calls himself The Sand Viper and wants to be projected as the most venomous snake in the Middle East. His name is Asasif al-Massoud and he will soon arrive in the U.S. with the purpose of inciting an American jihadist group called Jamaat ul-Fuqra. He will give this organization his plan and orders to kill Americans and bring down our infrastructure in several major cities.

"The FBI believes this will begin to actively unfold in about three weeks. Al-Massoud is expected to enter one of the jihadist's thirty-five training camps, specifically one in Virginia, the first week of September and dispatch what will probably be several hundred suicide bombers and trucks to set out for the American cities. The government of the United States will then officially be under massive attack. You can redeem yourself, Mr. Steed, and at the same time do something good for your country...save a hell of a lot of people's lives."

"Why me, McGowan? I know you said Hickcock and Larsen considered this as payback for me saving their lives and helping them close a big-ass case, but a hell of a lot of shooters as good as me can take this target out."

"The agents have apparently convinced the National Security Advisor that you *are* the very best in the sniper business. I told them they were nuts engaging a nefarious hit man to do this job."

"Nefarious?"

"Criminal...evil."

"Criminal, yes. But I rather resent being called evil, McGowan. You might not think much of me, but you sure as hell don't know what I'm made of."

"Okay, so you're a real choir boy...I get it."

"What happens after I take that shot?"

"It depends. If you kill the guy, you're a free man. If you miss and he gets away, your ass had better disappear in a hurry, because you'll be fair game for every cop out there."

"I don't miss, McGowan."

"Another thing. You will be teamed with me and will follow my direction to the letter. In advance of putting, hhyou and a sniper rifle inside the compound, you and I will perform a recon and maybe pick out one or two of these jihadists, interrogate them using any measures necessary to obtain on-site Intel, and then cause them to disappear."

"What makes everything you've told me any different from what I did in my previous line of business?"

"The people you killed, Steed, were American citizens, innocent until proven guilty; these people are terrorists and enemies of the United States not subject to our laws. They get killed without us batting an eye."

Steed took a sip of the Margarita and then set his steely eyes on me.

"Just who the hell are you anyway, McGowan?"

"Let's just say I'm somebody who has served and *continues* to serve my country. Now, we call upon *you* to do the same. This is an opportunity to atone for your past and at the same time, wipe your slate clean."

Steed set his glass down on the arm of the chair and nodded reflectively.

"What do I do about Maria? I betrayed her once with my deceit. I can't do that again by walking away from her."

"Who says you have to walk away." I then did some thinking on my own and was silent for several moments.

"All right," I continued.

"You'll have to have a place to stay...some place where I can not only watch you, but work together with you on this plan, twenty-four seven, right up until we successfully take down the entire terrorist element. Here's the deal, and I had to get inside your head before I was comfortable in making this offer. You and Maria will stay at a country inn that my wife and I own and manage. It's in West Virginia, ironically about an hour's drive away from the jihad compound in Virginia. You and I will be away from our place probably more than we'll be there. My wife, Adriana, will be good with looking after Maria. I have a feeling they will enjoy each other's company."

"And my business here?"

"Do you have someone who can run it for a month or so?"

"Yes. The girls I hired mostly run it anyway."

"Then what other concerns do you have?" I asked.

"How will I convey this to Maria? She came here to be with me...to marry me. Now I'll uproot her again and tell her I'm going back into the killing game."

"*No you won't.* She can't know anything about this. I suggest you tell her that I'm from the government and that the American Justice Department wants you to work with me on a classified project so that you can clear your record. Tell her my meeting with you was no accident. Tell her also that what we are doing won't take long and I have invited you both to stay at our place while we're working on this government project. She can't know any more than that about it. If she loves you, she'll come with you. If you want me to sit down with her and explain it my way, I'll be glad to do it."

"I think it would sound better coming out of your mouth." He then took a deep breath and let it out slowly. "All right, McGowan. But this had better not be just a tricky way to get me on American soil without incident. I have never terminated anyone out of anger or revenge, and I don't want to start now."

I then shoved my index finger into his chest.

"And I have never handled threats very well, Mr. Steed. You sure as hell don't know what *I'm* capable of."

Seems that we were facing off again. But after a moment he said, "Okay. I suppose you've convinced me this is the real deal. You're right; I don't know you, but I did have a trusting experience with Hickcock. Like I said, I'm in. How about you coming by my house for breakfast tomorrow morning, and we'll talk this out with Maria? I make a great omelet."

"I'll be there," I said. "What time?"

"How about eight?"

"Eight is fine. After we talk, prepare to pack a month's worth of bags and then both of you be prepared to leave first thing Thursday morning. I'll make sure the Bureau's jet is at the St. John's terminal ready to take the three of us back to the states. We'll talk it over tomorrow."

"You're wanting to leave that soon?"

"We have less than three weeks until this all tentatively goes down. As Hickcock said, 'tick tock.'"

*****

 Later that evening, I bought a colorful arrangement of roses, carnations and lilies at the Jalousie gift shop before it closed, then set them in a jar of water so they would retain their freshness until I gave them to Maria at Wednesday morning's breakfast. It was important that this lady not only get to know me, but *trust* me after I laid out the reasons why Steed would have to return to the States with me. If she *wasn't* good with it and didn't agree to accompany him, there was a chance that he wouldn't go. And that would be a huge mistake on his part.

After showering on Wednesday morning in the six o'clock hour, I checked out the news and drank a cup of room coffee. It was nasty. I chided myself for not going down to the breakfast bar. As Steed appeared to be accepting Hickcock's proposal, I hoped that after sleeping on it, he had not gone in the other direction. Or that he had flown the coop with Maria during the night.

It was a pleasant walk that half mile down the beach, even though it was already 80 degrees. After entering the clumsy gate leading to the bungalow, I kicked the sand off my shoes on the step and then tapped the door knocker. Seconds later, Maria opened the door to greet me. I saw immediately that mornings agreed with her. Her thick black hair was pinned back with a tortoise shell comb and her deep, beautiful eyes danced like dragonflies on a pond. And then the silk white blouse she was wearing clung to every luscious curve of her body. Otherwise, I didn't notice much about her. When she saw the flowers, she smiled and said,

"They're beautiful. For me, I suppose."

I smiled back.

"Not for Atticus, that's for sure."

"Please come in. We have breakfast ready."

With the litheness of a butterfly she walked ahead of me down the hallway and into the kitchen where Steed stood with a Bloody Mary in his hand. He held it up and said, "One for you?"

"No, thanks. Maybe some O.J., though."

He then took the pitcher of orange juice from the counter top and filled the small glass at a place setting where I figured I had been designated to sit. Maria in turn placed a platter of bacon and stuffed omelets on the table alongside a plate of English muffins.

"Looks delicious," I remarked. I wasn't used to having a heavy breakfast like this, but as I only had a plate of nachos the night before with a couple of beers, I *was* fairly hungry.

We all sat down and Maria bowed her head for a short, silent prayer, after which she crossed herself. I dropped my head as well, realizing I needed to do this more often, considering not only my many blessings but my many moral impairments as well.

"Thanks for having me here for breakfast," I said, opening a conversation.

"It's good to have a fellow American in our house. And I'm happy you and Atticus had that chance meeting on the beach yesterday."

Steed and I shot glances at each other.

"Where are you from, Maria?"

"Dallas. That's where my parents live. But Atticus and I had an apartment in Atlanta where we stayed when we were not flitting around the country." She then gave him a sober look which I surmised reminded her that she was unwittingly traipsing around with a man who she found out was killing people.

"I like Dallas," I said.

"I was assigned there for a couple of years when I worked for the government."

"Are you still working?"

"No, I'm retired. But occasionally I do some contract work."

"What did you do with the government?"

"For just over twenty years, I was a special agent for the FBI. After that, however, I worked for the Department of State profiling people. Mostly terrorists." I wasn't about to divulge any more...such as my propensity to make them dead.

She laid down her fork, looked at Steed and then back to me. A former G man at her breakfast table. Somebody who actually may have been dispatched to bring him in.

"It sounds like you've lived an exciting life, Bruce."

I nodded and then cut into my omelet.

"Atticus said you've only been here a couple of days, but do you ever plan on going back to the States?"

"Well, I think I'll like it here just fine, but I know I'll soon be missing the states. Especially my parents and my older sister, Sophia, who is going through some medical difficulties. And I find that Antigua doesn't have all of the conveniences that we have back in America...the nice restaurants and movie theaters...Macy's. But back to my sister; she is in the third stage of cancer and I feel that I need to be at home with her as much as I can. We have always been close. And because of her condition, my parents gave me the devil for leaving home this time."

"Sorry about your sister, Maria. I hope whatever treatment she's receiving; she will fully recover." After a comfortable pause, I then looked at Steed. He nodded. It was time to begin that conversation we talked about.

I continued.

"Maria, I have a little confession to make. Atticus and I didn't just happen to meet by chance down on the beach yesterday."

A frown suddenly fell across her brow.

"You *didn't?*"

"I was sent here by the government to talk with him."

Maria then touched her napkin to her lips and laid it beside her plate. "I know about his past," she said.

Steed then broke in.

"I had told her about my trouble with the authorities, Bruce. That's the main reason she left me a few months ago. Then yesterday, I told her the rest of the story." He placed his hand over hers and gave her a rather doleful smile. "But as you can see, she's still here."

Maria didn't smile back at him, which told me that she was still adjusting to her startling discovery about the man she loved. Her face fully reflected her perplexity about it all. "Then you came here to arrest him."

"No. But let me ask you a question, Maria. If things could be different for Atticus, what would you like it to be?"

"That's easy, I'd want there to be no fear of him ever having to go to prison...no fear that some day a policeman will show up and take him away."

"And that maybe you two could travel freely to the U.S. and he no longer be considered a fugitive?"

Slowly she nodded her head, and her eyes began to glisten with tears.

"It's been very hard for me. I love him and I know I'm breaking the law myself by even being with him."

Steed reached around the table and took hold of her hand again.

"Mr. McGowan is not here to take me in, sweetheart. He came here to offer me a proposal."

Her eyes widened in surprise.

"Maria," I began.

"I spoke with Atticus yesterday evening. There are some people in Washington, DC who can have him removed from the fugitive list and make the cases against him go away for good. In exchange, he will go back with me and perform some work for the government."

"I...I don't understand," she said.

"How could that be possible? And why?"

"I am still working on an occasional basis for the government. There's a very important case that has been dropped in my lap...important to the security of the United States. Atticus has a very skilled background and the FBI wants him to collaborate with me on a mission that needs to be accomplished in just a few weeks. It will require his returning with me tomorrow."

"This is for real?"

"For real."

She then turned to Steed.

"And you believe it? You don't think this could be some kind of a trick?"

He squeezed her hand.

"I believe him, Maria. What he's told me is too specific and he handed me a letter from the FBI that spells everything out. It will give me an opportunity to do a kind of penance for my crimes. But, even if it *were* some kind of trickery, it's inevitable that someone someday will come and get me. And I don't want to take a chance on you getting hurt."

I said,

"Maria, this is a good thing for you *and* him. There's no trick here. He works with me on the case and he's a free man."

"And while you're away, Atticus, what will I do. I don't know anyone here."

"Bruce has an answer. I'll let him tell you."

"My wife is the proprietress of a very nice bed and breakfast inn in a rural area of West Virginia. You and Atticus will be staying there while he and I are working. There'll be a few days we'll be away...in Washington, DC and other places. You and my wife will become friends. You'll like her."

"Let me get this straight. It's like we've won the lottery. Atticus now works for the government; he'll no longer be a fugitive and I get to be on vacation while this is going on."

"That's about the size of it."

"If that's the case, I think I should go back home where my family needs me."

"That's up to you, sweetheart," Steed replied.

"You do what you need to do. But, we have been apart for weeks...months. I would like you to consider going with me. What I will be doing for the government should not take long. Do you agree, Bruce?"

I nodded. But Maria's face was stoic.

"What exactly *will* you be doing that will take you off the fugitive list?"

I stepped in.

"It's considered a Top Secret matter, Maria; something I really can't divulge." She didn't reply to that. But I could see both doubt *and* concern in her eyes.

Steed and Maria sat for a few moments, both in deep contemplation, not saying a word. I could almost hear the wheels grinding. We had all scarcely touched our food. Finally, Steed looked into Maria's eyes. His were not the same fierce, killer eyes I saw looking into mine yesterday afternoon when we faced off. And hers were soft, apprehensive eyes, waiting for his answer.

"All right, Bruce," he said.

"We'll go back with you."

She looked down at her plate and slowly nodded in agreement. Her reluctance was apparent.

"Good. I will arrange for tomorrow's flight. You both need to gather whatever you can carry that will last you a month or so. We'll leave here about 8:30 in the morning. I'll arrange for the plane to be at the airport at 10:00. Just meet me in the lobby at the Jalousie. We'll travel in my rental." Then I picked my fork back up and said. "It appears our breakfast is getting cold."

Maria finally lifted her eyes and then lit up the room with a smile.

"I'll warm everything up again in the microwave."

Just after 9:30 I thanked them for the good breakfast and left their front door. They had a lot to talk over and some packing to do. Steed walked outside with me and asked about his weapons.

"You won't be able to get them through security at St. John's. As a federal employee, I was given authorization for my .380 because of my government permit; however, I still had to place the gun and ammo in separate locked boxes, even though I was flying on a Department of Justice jet. Don't worry about it. I have the very weapon at home you will be using to make that shot. You don't need anything else."

He shook his head.

"I don't know, McGowan. My head tells me this is all okay, but my gut tells me to tell you to go to hell."

"Don't worry about it, Steed. By the way, you'll also get paid for the job."

"How much?"

"I'll let Hickcock tell you. But it's a nice little sum. We're meeting him and Larsen when we get back."

He smiled.

"I'm looking forward to seeing John and Maggie again. And I *know* they can't wait to see me."

While on my stroll back to the room, I called Hickcock.

"He's in, John. Have the Lear ready for us at St. John's tomorrow at 1000 hours. Three passengers."

"Three?"

Put the name Maria Cortez on the manifest. That's Steed's fiancée. She will also be staying at my place while Steed and I are out executing the plan."

"Was that necessary...to bring her along?"

"Yes. It was kind of a contingency to convince him to come back with me."

"What does she know?"

"Nothing. She knows only that he'll be working with me and that I work for the government."

"But she knows he is a fugitive from justice. She's bound to have had some questions about that."

"She did. And I did explain it to her that the government will be looking into dropping any charges. That's as far as I went with it."

"Did you destroy the letter?"

"It's in ashes."

"Good. By the way, I will have Steed's name removed from not only the no-fly list, but arrest list. He will now be able to go through security unchecked. On another note, we received new Intel from DHS. A message to ul-Fuqra's number two man in Saylorsburg, Pennsylvania, was intercepted yesterday. The Viper is slated to meet Maslama, the Goshen chief, in his compound on the 7th. No month mentioned. Again, we believe it is September 7th. You and Steed need to recon that camp sometime before then and then set up in wait the night of the 6th. I have some satellite images of the compound for you and will turn them over when we meet up."

"And when do you want that to be?"

"Your Learjet should arrive not later than 1500 at the Greenbrier Valley Airport. Larsen and I are driving down tomorrow afternoon and will be staying at the Brier Inn. We'd like to meet you two in the lobby there at 1830."

"Why don't you stay at our B&B? We have a couple of extra rooms." I knew they'd only need one.

"It'll be one big happy family...Steed and Maria, you and Maggie, and Adriana and me. We'll have some pretzels and beer, sit around in our P.J.s and watch the Bourne trilogy."

"Get real, Bruce. Thanks for the offer, but Maggie and I will be comfortable at the motel."

"I'll bet you will."

"All business tomorrow night, Bruce. We don't intend to get all slap-happy with the likes of Atticus Steed."

"I thought he was your hero, John. Seemed like a pretty nice guy to me."

"We don't form friendships with killers. His charm and charisma aside, you will find him as deadly as an Australian Taipan. Just be careful with this guy, Bruce."

"Remember who you're talking with, John."

"Yeah."

"We'll be at St. John's Airport at 10:00 tomorrow. Tell the sky boys don't be late. See you at 6:30. Kiss Maggie for me."

"Goodbye, Bruce."

# CHAPTER 14

We had no trouble clearing security and customs at the airport. I thought maybe Chief Reynolds might have had several of his officers watching to see if Steed would try leaving the country after my visit with him. However, we had a clean exit. I was actually surprised he hadn't already taken Steed into custody. Maybe Steed's 'friend in high places' was someone important in the Antiguan government.

I sat opposite Steed and his fiancée on the Learjet, even though there were plenty of seats around us. It was the sociable thing to do. He was wearing Navy blazer and khaki slacks, no socks and weejuns. She was also wearing a blazer over a pink, nylon blouse as well as a form-fitting skirt. I thought I looked pretty GQ as well in my tight, black Greg Norman golf shirt that showcased my massive biceps, my Popeye forearms and pronounced veins that demonstrated my immense strength.

For some reason, it was a seemingly long flight going back, so I thought it better served that we all got more so acquainted, considering we would be living together for the next few weeks. Steed and I, of course, did not talk *mission* at any point. We did, however, learn a little more about each other's history and even had a couple of laughs. A couple of times, I almost felt as though I was betraying my sense of legal ethics by becoming chummy with Steed, considering *his* history of having been on the other side of the law. But because of that, he didn't have much to offer about himself except his time in the Marines and with the CIA. His youth and early adult years neither Maria nor I wanted to hear about. And he definitely wasn't going to tell us about all of his hits. But, he and Maria had certainly otherwise enjoyed their travels together, about which they freely spoke.

I had told Adriana on the phone the night before that we would have house guests for a month or so and was sure the government would be footing the bill. What I didn't tell her was anything about Steed that would compel her to barricade the door. Neither did I tell her about anything the government and I had planned for him. But I knew she would like Maria, and Maria's presence might just take the focus off Steed and me and the upcoming mission. Of course, I always liked it when pretty faces stayed at our inn. But as much as I loved looking at beautiful women, I was tied down and on a short leash with only one woman. From here on, all I could do was run to the end of the chain and bark.

When we finally touched down at the Greenbrier Valley Airport, I thanked my Bureau aviators who had made two trips down to Antigua and back in three days...although what they did was not exactly tough duty. However, if we had flown into the jungles of Colombia and experienced a hail of gunfire from drug lords...

Adriana picked us up at the airport in my Suburban. She didn't like driving ol' Diablo very much, but it seemed her van's water pump had decided to quit. Steed immediately took account of the bullet holes that remained in my door from where Chuck and his fellow assassins ambushed me outside of Zulu team headquarters just after they had massacred my friends. He then merely smiled and began loading up his and Maria's bags. He might ask, but he would never learn how Diablo got its wounds. And neither would anyone else. As long as it was still running, I'd be keeping it and would never patch those holes.

As we had landed just before three and had nothing to eat except one of the Bureau's gourmet sandwiches, somewhere over the Bermuda Triangle, I'm sure we were all hungry. It was after we had driven out 219 to one of the more popular restaurants downtown for an early dinner, Maria commented about the village's quaintness and alluring ambiance. She said she loved little towns like this and wouldn't mind if she and Atticus ultimately settled down in such a place.

'No, Maria,' I thought to myself.

'Maybe you, but *my* town doesn't need a killer as one of its residents.'

I called Hickcock at five-thirty. He told me that he and Larsen had already checked in and were relaxing for a bit. I suspected since he was dipping his pen in the company ink...meaning Maggie...they were probably taking a little 'nap' together after their trip down from Washington, DC. We'd be sure not to be early.

I could tell that Adriana liked Maria right off the bat as they were enjoying sparkling conversation and smiling constantly over the dinner table. Steed and I mostly just listened and nodded. Adriana did comment to me, while the couple went to the restroom, that Atticus was nice and a good bit handsome as well. What she would think if she knew his past?

Maria thought the old B&B was lovely...even charming, she added. She knew she would love staying there, and since she had not had more than a couple of days with Atticus down in Antigua, she was anxious to spend "some sweet days there with him.

" What she did not realize was that she wouldn't see much of him, considering Steed and I would likely be in Washington DC a couple of days for the latest informational briefings, a day or two reconning the Goshen camp, and then finally who knows how long back inside that compound for D-Day execution.

*****

They were waiting for us in the Brier lobby. Both Hickcock *and* Larsen appeared almost frozen with that deer-in-the-headlight look when they saw Steed walking toward them. He had told me that the last time he saw them was when they all met on a D.C. street to discuss the people who were trying to kill them.

"Hello, Mr. Steed," greeted Hickcock. "We meet again. I see you're now sporting a goatee. Another disguise?"

"I've changed a lot of things about me, John. I rather like the look. You don't think it makes me look too sinister do you, Maggie?"

She merely glared at him and didn't respond.

Steed continued, "So, I guess this is where I find out if the offer you made is legit or whether I'll be going to jail."

"I had hoped after our recent history you would not question our word," Hickcock replied. "I will especially not put anything in writing that is not true."

Larsen then finally piped in, "If it was up to me, this arrangement would never happen."

Steed formed a wry smile. "And I thought you liked me, Maggie."

"I neither like nor dislike you, Mr. Steed. I just make it a point to never warm up to hired killers.

"Since you're hiring me for this deal, obviously you didn't have *that* much heartburn about me. I take it you're still wanting me to put a bullet in someone."

The lobby had been empty to this point, but then a guest approached.

"This is not a place we should be carrying on this conversation, folks," I said. "Do you have that conference room set up?"

"Yeah. Follow us down the hallway," Maggie said.

Steed and I allowed Hickcock and Larsen to lead the way to the third room on their right. It was small enough, to be sure. It appeared to be nothing but a reconverted guest room. The table was something like 3 X 7 with six chairs around it. Two more people and we would be jammed in like sardines. The agents took the chairs on the opposite side by the window and Steed and I sat across from them. Hickcock wasted no time working the combination lock on his briefcase and then popped open the lid.

"So, this *is* a real deal. I'm not in handcuffs," Steed remarked.

"Interesting, huh Steed?" Larsen said. "We brought in a criminal to take down a terrorist. Go figure."

"It goes like this, Mr. Steed," said Hickcock. "You take out the Queen and the colony of fire ants gets disrupted. Mr. McGowan here directs your activities all the way and then leads an FBI task force into the compound to destroy it and any resisters. It's your one and only chance to free yourself from prosecution."

Steed shuffled in his chair. "I'm good with *your* word, John, but what if you and Maggie just happen to fall off the edge of the earth? Does anyone else know about this deal? And what if some trigger-happy cop spots me and hasn't gotten the word that I'm no longer a fugitive? What then?"

"The answer to your first question. A very big and powerful player right under the President knows all about it. We'll get the word down to every federal, state, and local jurisdiction as quickly as we can...but not until you come through for the government. We've already taken your name off the domestic and international criminal list. That's why you were able to get through Antiguan security today and board a plane. But if you choose to flee, your name quickly goes back on. And to answer your second question...if some local yokel hasn't gotten the word that you are ultimately pardoned ...sorry about that. We can't control every scenario."

"That doesn't sound very promising for *me*."

"All I can say is that this is a chance for you to do something for the American people...and for a change, not *against* them."

"Ironic, isn't it, John," Steed said.

"You hunted me for weeks for killing people, and now you engage me to kill again."

Larsen responded.

"Only this time it's not civilian suspects...and I emphasize the word *suspects*. This time it's the enemy. Important difference."

I kind of had to agree with Larsen. She did not like the fact that Steed was getting a pass for the number of hits he had made. He needed to atone for his sins by going to prison like every other criminal, not get rewarded with a pardon and a million dollars. And I'd say he'd better get right with the Almighty before he checks out as well.

"All right let's get down to it," Hickcock said. He then pulled from his briefcase two pieces of paper...a 1 to 25,000 terrain map and a satellite close-up view of the Goshen compound.

"You will see several buildings here. This larger one, a cement block-looking building, we believe is some type of assembly hall that probably doubles as a mosque. Looks like it will hold about a hundred people. There are three other buildings in the camp...two that appear to be about 800 to 1000 square feet and this one that resembles a military World War Two style barracks that would sleep around seventy-five to a hundred people. The image also shows about two dozen people spread out in a line with weapons pointed toward a berm. We believe this is a makeshift firing range, although we can't make out targets. As you can see there are probably another dozen people scattered in different parts of the compound.

"About half of the jihadists live in the compound and the rest live in homes and trailers on the outskirts of Goshen. Some we think live in the mountains between Goshen and Lexington. Two-thirds are Middle Eastern. The others are a mixture of Blacks and Whites who as we told you, Bruce, are former convicts who had converted to Islam, receiving also a good dose of terrorist doctrine and a course in American Hatred 101.

"We have information that several meetings involving the jihadist hierarchy have already taken place in several of the ul-Fuqra camps in advance of al-Massoud's arrival. As we discussed, Bruce, the communique provides that he will definitely meet the Big Man on Campus,

Maslama, in the Goshen compound.  Again, we guess that will be on September 7th. Before then, he will meet with clerics at a mosque in Detroit and then travel to Islamberg in New York for another meeting. He's either already here on American soil or will arrive at the latest the first week of September."

"If he is spotted at an airport, would you then detain him and can the kill?" I asked.

Hickcock and Larsen very coyly exchanged looks. "No," Hickcock said.

"The National Security Advisor wants him dead. If he were captured, we'd get nothing out of him anyway. Killing him sends a message to all of his followers, both on the international terrorist scene and in these American training camps. Sending him to Gitmo will only allow him to hone up on his soccer skills like all the others down there."

"But killing him also makes him a martyr and inspires others to commit more acts of terrorism out of revenge. One of these fascist pigs like him goes down and another one pops right back up to take his place."

Hickcock's eyes were rigid. "There will be no other option, Bruce. He dies."

Steed seemed a little uneasy. "Here's *my* concern. Although I feel a little uncomfortable telling you people about my methods, I must say there are a lot of uncertainties associated with the hit on this al-Massoud character. I am used to taking my time on a hit, analyzing every minute detail, performing surveillance, conducting reconnaissance, rehearsing, and having absolute knowledge of a person's movements, routines, and plans. And I need to carry out these procedures myself."

"I will put you there, Steed," I said. "You'll have an opportunity to perform *all* of your pre-kill checks." I thought that was said rather cleverly, but Steed merely scowled.

"We'll supply the latest and best Intel on al-Massoud's activities and movements," Hickcock said.

"The Bureau can do this on a *strategic* perspective, but you two will need to get into that compound ASAP and use *your* best methods to gain *on-site* Intel. And Bruce, we had also talked about you snagging one of the Fuqua members outside of the camp to interrogate him as to what's going on *inside* the camp, specifically where that bunker of munitions is located and to verify the date of al-Massoud's arrival. As you can see from this image from outer space, there is no way we can tell where it is."

"Okay," I said. "We pluck out somebody in the element for interrogation. What do we do with him afterward?"

"He disappears."

"We kill him?"

"No. You either stow him away somewhere or we'll call in a chopper and send him down to Guantanamo Bay. We also need somebody in that camp to verify the

Intel that's coming our way. Will al-Massoud actually make the scene on the 7th or was that communication to the Fuqra leader in Pennsylvania just a ruse?"

"If we pick out a *nobody* to interrogate, privates don't know shit," I remarked.

"Nobody but Maslama, the Goshen ul-Fuqra leader, is likely going to know anything about whether al-Massoud is actually going to be there on the 7th of September...or at all. It may be he'll go to another camp. We then can't rule out the possibility that the explosives and the jihadists that drive the vehicles to the target sites will be located in a compound closest to their objective, like Reston and Hancock."

"We thought about that, Bruce. But again, we're acting on our best intelligence. It will be even more imperative that you verify our Intel through any means you can."

I leaned back in my chair and folded my arms.

"Is there a reliable human resource you have in the Intel community that can pinpoint al-Massoud's movement at this time?"

"We have a Middle Eastern contact who has regularly fed us information, but we haven't heard from him in weeks. Either al-Massoud's people found out about him and killed him or he just disappeared on us for another reason. Maybe the CIA wasn't paying him enough. It's been hit and miss lately. Sometimes we get lucky and receive something credible. Other times, because the Viper is so slick and cautious, we get nothing but false leads. We pretty much have to depend on the intercepted messages between him and his American jihad leadership. There have been several times we had knowledge he was in the U.S., but then he was already back in Mali or Pakistan before we even received the Intel. The radical community here in the U.S. takes care of this guy."

Steed then asked, "Why isn't a team of your covert agents and snipers taking out al-Massoud and this compound? Don't get me wrong; I'm grateful for the chance to do it. But you've got *how many* counterterrorist teams operating within your system?"

"Unfortunately, the Justice Department, CIA or *any* of our people can't take an active role in invading these compounds. Not only don't we have all of the proof that these training compounds are terrorist cells, these 3000 or so jihadists in the camps are protected under the constitution as well as under state law. We go in there and kill a foreign visitor and then we find *nothing* that verifies the camp was little more than a Muslim country club, our director and the man above him driving this mission will face a grilling by a congressional panel, not to mention having to answer a battery of lawsuits. But, *you* will be the groundhogs that get in there and get us that information."

"I see what's happening here now," said Steed.

"I kill this al-Massoud and we don't find anything significant about this camp, I, being a non-government operative, then become the scapegoat. You'll disavow any knowledge and McGowan and I will be classified as mercenaries. And by the way, I never got a copy of that little insurance policy you wrote out."

Steed had a point. Who knows what the Justice Department would then allege if this whole deal didn't work out as planned? And being a civilian former action guy, I would go down right along with him.

"That's not going to happen, Mr. Steed," Hickcock said. "You and Mr. McGowan will have to make the call and decision on the ground and then use your best judgment to act on what you find. You will have our ear and we will have your back. You just have to trust us on that. And, whatever happens, good or bad, and we know you did your job, your freedom comes back to you. Plus, you get a nice piece of bread for your three or four weeks of work."

"How much?"

"You didn't tell him, Bruce?"

"I thought I'd leave that up to you."

"A million dollars, Mr. Steed."

I thought Steed would come out of his chair as I saw him squirm a little. However, his expression never changed.

"That's about right, I'd say. The pardon, of course, would be the icing on the cake."

"And both arrangements will be made when the mission is complete," Hickcock said.

Hickcock continued his briefing well beyond eight o'clock, and then he said, "I think you have the crux of the mission, Mr. Steed. Do you have any questions?"

"Not at this time."

"The rule here is that everybody keeps everybody informed. Bruce, I'll give you our daily Intel as it comes across my desk and you let *me* know your specific plans and movements before you set them into action. Agent Larsen, do you have anything to add?"

"All I'm doing is listening. It's primarily *your* ball game and you're driving the train, John. I'll let you know if I disagree with anything."

I thought to myself "yeah, princess, and I'm pretty damn sure *you're* the one who drives the train in those strategic moments of intimacy. I've seen the fire coming out of you more than once."

"All right," I said.

"Tomorrow, we go to work and plan the recon. I'll let you know when we'll be going in, John. Maybe as early as tomorrow night...but again, I'll let you know."

He nodded and then handed me the map and aerial photo of the Goshen camp. "Good luck, gentlemen. And Bruce, do you have the kind of long-distance weapon that Mr. Steed will need in order to take Massoud out? If not, we can supply you one."

"I have something that even your ATTF marksmen would salivate over. The answer is yes."

"Good. Any further questions?"

We both shook our heads.

"You and Maggie sleep well," I said, smiling.

His glare told me he knew how I meant that.

# CHAPTER 15

It was well after dark when we returned to Wolf Laurel. Apparently, the women had become very well acquainted while we were gone as we heard laughter when we stepped onto the veranda.

"Let's sit out here a while and let them talk," I said in a low voice. "It'll be an opportunity for us to talk out things as well."

We each took a chair, and after we had sat a moment, the tree frogs started up their chorus again.

"Tomorrow morning we'll put our gear together. Tomorrow evening we recon that camp. I have a couple of night vision devices, binoculars and scopes, and everything we'll need to set up over there. I'm planning for us to find a spot on higher ground where we can scout out and observe activities within the compound. You wanted time to work out all of your minute details, so you'll get it. Prepare to spend the night and much of the next day in the woods. Sometime before we leave tomorrow, we need to study the area map...routes, such as roads and trails that might lead into the compound, the topography and lay of the land, et cetera. I think I have everything you and I both need to execute this mission.

"Goshen is a very small village of about 500 people. Like a lot of Virginia towns, it will be a picturesque little burg. According to the map, the Maury and Calfpasture Rivers run through it. The townspeople will be honest, hard-working, patriotic Americans doing a little farming and living the good life. The primary thing the town is known for, the annual Boy Scout Jamboree, is held close by. I seriously doubt that the ul-Fuqra members who have moved in, have integrated into the populace. They have purchased houses or are renting units outside of the town proper, and as Hickcock said, set up trailers and cabins in the mountains well off the beaten path."

"Sounds to me you've done a lot of homework already. I don't mind telling you, Bruce, not knowing anything about you to this point, I was a little apprehensive about working with you. I don't work with *anybody*. But now that I've been watching and listening to you, I think that methods-wise we are pretty much alike."

I wanted to tell him that *legal-wise*, we were *nothing* alike. But I let that one go.

"So, tomorrow we crank this up. You and I will be in each other's shadows from here on."

"Like I said, I'm used to operating on my own. I hope you don't slow me down," he said.

"And I hope you don't get in my way, Mr. Steed."

I saw a slight smile in the corners of his mouth.

"Sounds like *both* of us are used to doing our own thing. Two egos, one mission. Although you might have a problem with me and what I've done with my life, you're going to have to get past it. And since we're going to have to get along and trust one another, call me Atticus, Bruce." He then thrust out his hand.

I stared laser-like into his eyes for a short moment and then shook his hand. "Okay...Atticus."

We both then stood and I asked him, "What's your pleasure...bourbon, Scotch or a beer?"

"I'm partial to red wine, maybe a Moscato or Beaujolais, if you have some. Here's the thing, Bruce; I might be a despicable bastard with an atrocious past, but I do have a degree of refinement and culture about myself."

I had to smile at that.

"I think we have some Merlot. But from the sound of the laughter in there, I'd be surprised if there's any left."

Adriana gave the couple the larger of our rooms since they would be staying a good bit longer than any of our other guests had. It actually had a couch in it as well as a compact fridge. They were tired from their long day and so was I. Anyway, I had some honey-pie to catch up on before allowing my brain to sign off for the night.

*****

I am not without my inner haunts. For about a month after losing my team to mass murder, the same nightmare which had been invading my sleep off and on for years began to recur. It was the one where my guilty brain caused me to revisit the horrible mistake, I made in the Vietnamese village more than forty years before during a combat assault. The one where I sent a 40 mm M79 projectile into a bamboo hooch, killing an innocent mother and her young child.

Time and time again I had tried talking myself into believing that the woman was Viet Cong and that the glint I saw through the open window of the hut was the barrel of an AK-47. But in reality, it was only a cooking pot that had caught a ray of sunlight. I have many times tried to reason with myself that the mother and child were merely collateral damage, which unfortunately is one of the spoils of war. But even though that rationale rattles around in my head like a steely in a pinball machine, the recurring image of the woman's accusatory eyes staring at me in death continues to besiege my sleep.

The nightmares did subside for a couple of months until only recently when this Viper mission was dropped in my lap. Maybe all I have to do is *set* a killing mission into action and that alone will compel my unconscious brain to conjure up this ancient haunt. But now on this night, there it was again, as vivid and in living color as it had ever been.

I awoke in the dark that morning in a cold sweat which in turn caused Adriana to stir. She sat up and leaned on her left elbow.

"The dream again?"

"Yeah," I replied in almost a whisper.

She then stroked my hair and took a portion of our sheet to dab my moist forehead. "It seems they come back when you're involved in something you're doing for the government. Does that tell you anything?"

I looked at the clock on the nightstand. Three forty-two. Another night of interrupted sleep. My only response to her was "I'm going to get a bottle of water. You want anything?"

"I'm fine. Hopefully you'll be able to get back to sleep."

But I didn't. For the remainder of the early morning hours, I sat in our living room flipping through the channels...BBC News, ME TV, The Weather Channel, a half-over Butch Cassidy and the Sundance Kid. Not landing for any length of time on anything. Then finally at six-thirty, I saw through our window that the sky began to lighten.

Around seven, I brewed some coffee, made some toast and settled back down in my Big Easy. In a matter of minutes, I was back in la-la land. It was just after nine-thirty when Adriana's presence finally woke me. I sensed her nearby retrieving my empty coffee cup from the carpet which I had allowed to slip from my hand onto the carpet.

"Go take your shower, Skippy," she said.

"I'll make you some eggs and bacon if you want."

"I'm good, sweetheart, but you go ahead."

"I'm just going to get a Danish. Maria and I are having lunch over at the Magnolia in White Sulphur Springs."

"I'm really glad you two hit it off. It was one of my concerns before deciding on bringing her here."

"She's very sweet and I like her."

And so did I. I still wasn't sure whether I was going to like or accept her fiancée, however.


While I was asleep in the chair, a Cooter-looking fellow from the local garage had brought back Adriana's van complete with its brand-new water pump. So, all was well on the vehicle front. Just before noon, when the two ladies left for their early afternoon lunch, Steed and I were given that perfect opportunity to drag out of mothballs all my combat gear we needed to take with us. The ladies would be back in a couple of hours from their lunch, just in time to see us leave.

When the dust from her vehicle's wheels had dissipated, I went to my gun case and pulled out the weapons we would need. Steed's eyes quickly lit up.

"I have gone back and forth between these two sniper rifles...my Winchester 700, .308 with cryogenic-processed barrel, and my Walther WA 2000. But here...this is the latest. I don't know why I bought it. Maybe just to own it. It's the British-made L115A3 with an effective range of 1400 meters and uses the same .300 Winchester magnum round. The big difference is it has a Teludyne Straitjacket, a titanium composite barrel. Its recoil brake improves your accuracy by removing the harmonic waves that are always a troubling residual of the shot."

I thought Steed's eyes would pop straight out of his head. But then he surprised me by this disparaging, colloquial remark about my wonder gun,          "Beautiful, but I don't go in for anything as unnecessary and gee-whiz as this. I've gotten along very well with my own Winchester 700."

"Suit yourself, Atticus. But I guarantee after you compare the two..."

"You don't understand, Bruce. I don't miss. A lot of it is certainly the rifle, but most of it is the skill of the shooter. That wasn't meant to sound boastful; it's just that nobody can out-shoot me."

I *do* like a challenge...and that's what it sounded like.

"I'll tell you what. Before you take that shot, in the next couple of days, you and I will go to a local range just down the road and test both weapons."

"Fine," he replied.

"I need to zero whatever weapon I end up with anyway."

"All right, I'll also give you your choice of handguns. When I travel, for convenience I carry the .380, which you found aimed at your forehead a few days ago. But for business, I either carry this Glock 39 .45 caliber or my SIG Sauer P238 here."

"I see you also have a Springfield XD. I'd prefer it if you don't mind."

"Good choice. Now let's go to my storage shed."

From the locked metal bin, I pulled out our scopes, one each set of field glasses, my Night Owl optics night vision goggles, and a couple of ponchos, flashlights and protective vests. I also pulled down from a hook two large OD field packs, Vietnam War vintage. And then from an adjacent metal cabinet, I took down the all-important boxes of ammo.

From inside the house, I grabbed several protein bars and some bottled water to shove into the field packs along with the ammo. After all was loaded up in the cargo area of my Suburban, we took to the veranda for some cheese, crackers and a bottle of Shiraz.

We didn't say much to one another as we waited out the ladies. I was hoping Adriana would not become suspicious that we were heading out on an overnighter like this since we were very covert-looking in our black SWAT clothing. I made sure our shoulder holsters that contained our tools of business and K bars were tucked away in the back of the Suburban as well. It would be a real giveaway for the women to see us wearing them and they didn't need any more angst about what we were doing than I'm sure they already had. They certainly didn't have to know that we would have people under surveillance who we might just have to end up killing.

I had no idea what we'd find over in that compound or how long we'd be in recon mode. I was hoping Steed was the outdoors type, although I knew from his time in the Marines as a sniper he had lain for hours, even days in impossible conditions waiting for just that one shot. But perhaps he had also had similar experiences in the CIA and most recently in his more *disreputable* profession. As I watched him intently, sipping his wine in the style of a man of culture, I thought we might indeed be similar, although on different sides of the law, much alike in skill, patience and thoroughness. But I also perceived him as dark and brooding, something I am not. Nonetheless, I very much looked forward to seeing him in action to determine if he was a man with whom I was comfortable to have as a battle partner. We kissed the lady's goodbye just after 4:00 and I told them we'd be staying the night 'somewhere' near Lexington.

"And what is it you will be doing there?" Adriana asked just one more time. "You told me that you would be working on some research project. What kind of project?"

"All I can tell you is that we will be watching some people the FBI believes may have terrorist ties. Atticus and I both have the skills and experience that have been recognized by the government. Remember that Atticus was at one time with the CIA and heavily involved in such matters."

"And you'll be watching them where?"

She was doing her damnedest to put me in a position where I had to lie. And as I hadn't ever lied, *per se*, to her, I wasn't going to start now."

"Well, the location is classified, and you know there are things that in the past I wasn't able to tell you."

"And on those kinds of missions you came back with bullet holes in you," she reminded me.

"This is not like that."

"I'll be holding you to it."

I thought to myself, if I get shot up *this* time, I'd better *hope* it was fatal because I'd never hear the last of it. I laid another kiss on her lips.

"Goodbye, sweetheart. See you tomorrow sometime."

Steed and I made the Virginia border in fifteen minutes. It then took us another thirty to make it to the point where we left I-64 and turned off onto State Road 42. From there we drove another fifteen minutes to Millboro Springs, taking a right onto Highway 39. After crossing the Calfpasture River, we followed 42 again north just a bit until we reached the grid coordinate block 0634 on Hickcock's map where he had marked an X. The ul-Fuqra camp was supposed to be sitting in that grid square on 80 acres of hilly land in the Allegheny chain.

Just five hundred feet inside the grid, traveling very slowly, we spotted a dirt side road off to the right leading up a gradual slope into some triple canopy terrain. Not twenty feet into the road were two metal poles supporting a chain that held a sign. In bold red letters, it simply read, *No Trespassing. Violators Will Be Prosecuted.* It wasn't like *some* of the good ol' boy signs I had seen elsewhere, such as *Violators Will Be Shot and Left for the Crows* or *Is There Life After Death? Trespass Here and Find Out.*

But then I spotted something one doesn't usually see hanging on a tree out in the boonies...a surveillance camera. Steed saw it as well and nodded.

I continued driving slowly for another three hundred feet further north, when I saw a firebreak on the right. That's when I made the old 4-wheel drive Suburban jump the ditch and enter the trail. I drove about fifty feet in until I reached a small clearing where I brought it to a stop. From there, we would maneuver to the right until we reached a point where we could manage to get a concealed view of the compound.

From the rear compartment, we grabbed our field packs and rifles with their suppressors, donned the shoulder holsters containing our semi-automatics, and then I closed the hatch quietly. Before we moved out, I scanned the area for any roving guards who might be set up. There were *No Trespassing* signs all over the woods. I was set to wonder what would happen if kids on an exploring venture just happened to come across any guards...if in fact there were any. Considering the munitions bunker which was somewhere on the vast acreage and the training that was supposed to be going on deep in the compound, the place *had* to be heavily guarded.

I figured we were already on ul-Fuqra land; therefore, we had to move in gradually and with an immense degree of stealth, using the dense forest to our advantage. We stayed low, stopped every few feet to listen and used our field glasses to search behind every tree and bush before moving on. If there *were* roaming sentries and they spotted us, they would alert the camp by radio and fifty people would be down on us.

We didn't look like hunters, and it wasn't hunting season anyway. The way we were dressed, we would only be seen as a threat. I doubted there was anyone in a tree preparing to snipe us, but if there were enough guards out there, chances are *somebody* would spot us. Would they shoot and ask questions later or would they just order us off their land?

Again, my objective was for us to get ourselves into position on high ground to where we had good visibility of the buildings and activity in the camp. It would have been a bonus if al-Massoud would already be in the compound, but that would definitely upset the mission plan. First, I wouldn't be sure how to recognize him, and it would be a guess as to whose head Steed would be splitting open. But then, the task force which would be doing clean-up work wasn't on site...and *wouldn't* be until the morning of the 7th.

I was nearly a 100% sure al-Massoud *wasn't* there. He would not allow himself to remain in one place for two or three weeks before it was time to leave out and start blowing up America. I doubted he would even be setting foot on American soil until the first week of September, if the Intel was accurate.

Steed and I, still in crouch position, went perhaps another fifty yards, when we heard the motor of a jeep type vehicle approaching off to our two o'clock. Dropping behind a clump of brush, I brought my binoculars up and watched as a Toyota Land Rover came into view. It was moving along another firebreak adjacent to the one we were just on.

"What do you see," Steed asked me.

"Two heads inside, both wearing turbans. I suspect they're mobile guards...wait, they're stopping. The passenger is now signaling to someone in our direction. Get down."

I then looked to our left and spotted him. He was on our flank on foot moving toward us only twenty yards away...with an AK-47 in his hands.

# CHAPTER 16

"Bogey at nine o'clock. See him?" I whispered.

"Yes."

"Just stay put. If he advances onto us, I'll take him down." My K bar was in a ready thrust position.

Although we were lying flat on the ground, if the guard had continued in the same direction, he would likely have stepped on us. But because the vehicle's passenger yelled something out the window, the lone rover was more interested in what he had to say instead of continuing with sweeping his area. Instead, his head was up, and eyes focused on the Land Rover. The passenger seemed to be waving the guard in a direction that turned him away from us, more toward the south. A couple more words were exchanged and then the vehicle continued down the fire break. I was hoping the driver would not detour through the woods further to the east to the next fire break or he would surely encounter my Suburban. In hindsight, I should have parked it well out of the compound area.

Once the guard was out of sight and moving away from the direction of the camp, I reholstered my knife and signaled to Steed that we would pick up the pace. From my belt I then pulled out my compass and reshot the azimuth which according to my calculations would keep us on the bearing that would take us to the higher ground above the camp.

As we continued moving forward, I saw that the terrain *was* getting a little steeper...exactly what I wanted to happen. Stopping a moment to check the map, I saw that the contour lines were definitely getting closer, which meant we would hopefully be placing ourselves in a position where we could look down on the compound, provided our field of observation was not cut off by trees. After finding ourselves on what appeared to be the steepest part of the ridge, I saw that the real estate below us began opening. Suddenly, the woods disappeared, and we found ourselves on open terrain climbing toward an area that contained a series of large rocks. If my map coordinates were correct, we would ultimately be perched on the huge boulder that loomed ahead of us and looking down on the compound. Practically low crawling the last fifty yards, I looked behind me to assure there were no guards situated along the tree line we had just left. Steed was right on my heels.

"You having fun back there?" I asked.

"Having the time of my life."

I noticed that Mr. Steed wasn't huffing and puffing like I was. Of course, I had more than twenty years on him and tasking muscles I didn't normally use.

Once we reached the largest of the rocks that I found offered us concealment on both the military and reverse crests, I crawled closer to the edge, discovering exactly what I hoped I would. Perhaps 450 yards down below us was the beginning of the compound. We could see every building and the entire training area. Taking out the aerial map Hickcock had passed to me, I pointed out to Steed the large mosque-looking building, the barracks, and the other smaller constructions, all of which were situated between 500 and 900 yards from our position. And then I pointed to the open ground just beyond the assembly hall. There must have been a hundred fifty of the Muslims on their knees kissing the earth with hands spread out before them in prayer. Three platoons of men wearing kufis and either pants and shirts or the more traditional jubbas. In case I ever wanted to know, I now knew what direction Mecca was.

"Al-Massoud or not," I said to them, "I could easily call in an airstrike and vaporize the lot of you. But, by the grace of Allah, you get to live yet another day."

As I didn't know when the call to prayer had begun, I couldn't gauge how long it would go on. But as it was just after six, I figured it had started on the hour. However, right at six-thirty, when the evening shadows had slid over the compound, without command they all sprang to their feet in unison. It was then that they began to scatter. About half walked to the northwest area of the camp to a parking lot and within minutes began moving their vehicles out along the dirt road we had seen on the way in. As they staggered their departure, I figured they did so because they didn't want to attract the attention of the civilian populace in Rockbridge County by leaving in mass. Through the lens of my field glasses, I could see that most vehicles contained both a driver and at least one passenger.

Being the civic-minded citizens they were faithful to the government's conservation policies, many chose to carpool.

The people that remained in the camp then retired into one of two buildings...either the mosque, which likely doubled as the assembly hall or chow hall, and the barracks. The scenario we had just witnessed told me that clearly half of the little army lived at the compound while the others lived in houses or trailers off campus.

Dark fell on us around eight and the temperature cooled considerably. It then took me a full fifteen minutes to gain my purple vision. Still, there were two lights below us on poles, one at either end of the cantonment area, that played havoc with my night vision when I looked directly at them. We also saw lights radiating from several of the windows. By nine, only occasionally did we see anyone moving about in the came. Two men on a continuous path. Roving guards.

As we sat watching the diminishing activity down below, I said to Steed,

"Bring back memories of Iraq and Afghanistan?"

"As a Marine, yeah. Other than that, my experience with the CIA didn't involve me much with Middle Easterners or I guess I should say Muslims. Most of my assignments were in Central and South America helping our government topple dictators, drug lords, or rebel leaders who were threats to a country's democratic survival."

"And I'm sure you by yourself toppled a few heads with that sniper rifle of yours."

"I can't say that any kills I made for the Company were anything less than righteous, though. Maybe you and I were even doing much the same thing at any given time in the name of national interest...if I understand what you were about. But I have to wonder about these people's religion...a religion that would sanction the killing of innocent Americans, people who are peace-loving. Isn't the Muslim faith supposed to be about peace?"

I shook my head. "Those who adhere tightly to Sharia Law and take literally the commandments within the Quran, tend to be more fundamentally radical...intolerant, if you will. You might lose a hand if you steal; if you say something nasty about Muhammad, you'll even lose your head; and then a Muslim man marrying a non-Muslim woman will be executed. There are other alarming practices as well, such as, mutilating a young girl's clitoris so that she can't experience sexual pleasure with a male; a man can beat his wife just for insubordination; and if someone from another religion tries to disciple a Muslim away from Islam, he dies."

Steed remarked,

"Yet they claim they are all about love and peace."

I nodded. "Here's the thing...I don't doubt there *are* many peace-loving Muslims who don't buy into many of the laws that Muhammad established. We're told we need to better understand and respect the religion and ideology of

Islam. I get it. But as long as there are jihadist Islamic assholes spawning out of this religion intending to kill Americans just because we enjoy the blessings of freedom, that is something I refuse to understand. I will destroy any terrorist element, whatever its cause, that finds its way into my sights. And to hell with capture and interrogation. To hell with putting the bastards before a judge. Why should they spend years in a cell, costing American taxpayers millions each year; and then maybe in the end they'll be exchanged for some poor slob American tourist who is mere hours from having his head separated from his shoulders by hooded thugs wielding jambiyas? My old Special Forces motto has never rung truer...*Kill 'em all. Let God sort 'em out.*

"Hmm," replied Steed.

"Can you be just a little more passionate about that, Bruce.? I'd like to know how you *really* feel."

"Here's the thing. I've been to a good many of the Middle Eastern countries...even those that either harbor or spawn terrorists. I've been to their run-down airports and streets stinking with rotting garbage. Their marketplaces are covered with flies. Their arid deserts reach 125 degrees and kick up blinding sandstorms. You can't tell me their terrorist acts are all about religion and punishing American infidels who live evil, wicked lives. These assholes with *their* miserable lives are just downright fricking jealous...jealous of our way of life, our freedoms, and, oh yes, our beautiful women. No wonder their women hide their faces."

Steed smiled and shook his head. "You're brutal, McGowan."

My Seiko read two minutes past ten when we heard someone singing, sounding more like chanting.

"Their version of Taps, I guess," I commented. Moments later, all the building lights went off.

Steed then said,         "Appears it will be a long, boring eight hours until reveille."

"Not with what *I* have planned."

"Which is what?"

"When all the children are tucked safely in their beds, a little on-site recon," I replied. "I'm giving it a couple of hours and then we move out."

*****

Twelve-twenty. The cooling breeze had died down. The noises in the compound had dissipated into the night air like woodsmoke. Somewhere off in the distance, maybe a mile away, a dog was barking. It was pitch black out on those rocks. The moon was new and the stars were sharp and vivid against the night sky.

"Okay, Mr. Steed, grab your pack and weapon...we're going."

I donned my night vision goggles, but Steed chose not to wear his. He would just stick close to me. From the rocks, I could see where a makeshift trail began. It was a bit slippery, but the goggles helped me negotiate the difficult terrain. It took us about ten minutes to get to the bottom and as there was a set of trees off to the right before entering the cantonment area, I set us up there for a few moments to watch and listen for guards. No sounds of footsteps and no movement were detected. Still quiet. Slowly in a crouch, I led Steed into the nearest building, a shack, which was either a guardhouse or office. There were no lights on inside and I found the door unlocked. As quietly as I could, I slowly pushed the door open, allowing my Winchester to lead me in, just in case we encountered some sleepers. None apparent, however.

Considering our low-intensity mini-lights would still be noticeable from the window, I kept checking to see if there were any roving guards who might be in proximity. There was still enough light radiating into the room from the streetlight on a nearby pole for me to see jihadist posters on the walls of the center room. I then pulled off my goggles. One poster showed a Muslim dressed in traditional garb holding an AK-47 high above his head with something written in Arabic across the top. Symbolic blood dripped from the hieroglyphics. Another poster was a photo of the smoking WTC towers with a picture of bin-Laden in the background.

It was a small building, perhaps 800 square feet, with a central room and two doors leading to rooms on either side. In that middle room, I saw a desk, chair, and wooden filing cabinet. I then spotted a four-foot-high refrigerator on top of which sat a small microwave.

I quickly checked the room on the left, finding only an unoccupied folding cot. Steed canvassed the room on the right and found nothing but another door, which appeared to belong to a closet.

"All right, Atticus, while I watch the front door, see what's in the desk drawers and cabinet."

He nodded, and with his mini flashlight, he rifled the desk.

"Nothing but a couple of pens, a copy of the Koran, a few matchboxes, some crackers and what's this...hmmm, mouse turds," he whispered. He then went to the cabinet.

"Anything with a date on it and any papers containing the name al-Massoud?" I asked.

Steed found a handful of stand-up files which he pulled out and laid on the desk.

"Here's something interesting. I can't read it as it's in Arabic, but stapled to it are photos of buildings. For sure, one is of the Empire State Building. Others are of the Statue of Liberty and what looks like a subway train. Here are some more of the Nation's Capital and the White House." He paused a moment.

"Uh oh, Hickcock and Larsen are not going to like this. The Hoover Building."

"The obvious targets, just as everybody suspected. Go ahead and pull them out." He did so, then handed everything to me. I shoved them into a large pocket in my cargo pants.

"You say there's nothing in the room on the right?" I asked.

"Just a door."

"Let's take a look. No, wait a minute. I heard something." I then peeked out the window and saw him. A guard stepping up onto the steps leading into the shack. Quickly, I shoved Steed behind the door and then moved in beside him. Within a couple of seconds, the door opened, and the guard shined the beam of his flashlight around the room. Had he continued inside and checked behind the door, his gut would have been a mushy receptacle for the Ranger knife I had in my hand ready to thrust. But he didn't. Satisfied, he closed the door and continued on his round. Once he was out of sight, we entered the room on the right and Steed went to the closet door.

"It's locked."

I then went to the door myself, inspected the knob, and then brought the knife out again. The lock was simple enough. Placing the blade in between the jamb and the latch, I popped the door open in less than five seconds. I then pulled out my flashlight and shined the beam inside.

"Not a closet, Atticus. There's a set of stairs here. This shack has a basement."

I allowed the beam of light to lead me down two sets of wooden stairs until the area opened into a large room. A *hell* of a large room about the size of a warehouse. I was stunned at what my light picked up.

"My mistake. Not a basement. *This is the munitions bunker.*"

The lights were off in the bunker and unless someone was sleeping in there, which I doubted, the rat that scampered across in front of me was the only other living being in the room. Looking around with my flashlight, I found a light switch on the wall and flipped it. Just in case there *was* someone in there, I still led my way through it with the suppressed muzzle of the Winchester.

"Holy shit," I exclaimed. The bunker, which appeared to be about 75 feet wide and deep, had a concrete floor and a 12-foot-high ceiling. Immediately attracting my attention were crates stacked 40-50 feet wide that were labeled *explosives*. TNT and RDX. And then there was the ANFO. Four 55-gallon drums had stickers on them that read ammonium nitrate. That compelled me to look and find in a separate location bags and bags of fertilizer, which also served to give the bunker that nice, outdoors earthy aroma. Against a 55-gallon drum, the walls were stacked crates containing AK-47s, Mauser sniper rifles, and Kord and RPK Russian machine guns. Another very large crate contained four RPG-29s, also Russian. Shelves in the central part of the bunker had sitting on them boxes of small arms ammunition for both the AKs and M77 Chinese pistols...and blocks of C4.

"So much for ul-Fuqra's claim that they are a peaceful, benevolent organization living in poverty that exists only to pray and help their fellow neighbors," Steed commented.

"Yep, exactly." I continued looking.

"There has to be something like a garage door at the other end of the bunker that empties out into a concealed location near a road. There's no way all this crap would go up and down those stairs. Ah, there's a forklift over there."

We then walked around the shelving area to the very back of the room and saw it. Beside the large door was a metal pedestrian door.

All in all, it was a treasure trove of explosives, munitions, and firearms. I wondered if we kept looking if we would find any chemical or nuclear explosives. But I saw no red or blue drums with skulls and crossbones or a radiological symbol on them indicating Uranium 235 or Plutonium. Nor were there any boxes of initiators, tampers or pusher devices. There were, however, a couple of e boxes of wires and detonator switches that could be used for either a dirty or nuclear device or to blow a conventional IED.

Out of my pack I pulled my Nikon and took perhaps three dozen pictures. I also took a few with my cellphone so that I could send them to Hickcock via text message.

After the photo session, we walked back to the metal door that led to the outside. As quietly as I could, I turned both the top and bottom deadbolt locks to *open* and then rotated the doorknob. Pushing the door open just a crack, I looked for any guards that may have been posted outside the bunker. Cautiously, I stuck the upper part of my head through the crack, looking right and then left. At first, all I noticed in the glow that was cast from the pole light to my front were three cargo trucks sitting off the dirt road. I imagined come D-Day, there might be a dozen of these trucks coming in and going out, destined for New York and Washington, DC. They would likely leave at different times and travel different routes so they would not attract attention.

Because the bunker was such an important venue, I also knew there had to be at least one sentry in the vicinity. In turning my head to the left a little further, I spotted him about 25 feet from the bunker facing away from me, smoking a cigarette. An AK was slung over his shoulder. *Me* in the bunker full of explosives and *him* so close by smoking...well, I was just a bit unnerved. I hoped an errant red ash carried by the breeze didn't find its way through the crack in the door. I would remind myself later to tell Maslama, or whoever was immediately in charge, to be sure heretofore to post *No Smoking* signs. Slowly, I pulled the door closed and twisted the locks as gently as I could, praying there would be no sound of a click. I didn't hear anything, as close as I was standing near the door, so I figured he didn't either.

"You seen enough?" I whispered to Steed.

"Yeah. I don't mind telling you this place makes me a little nervous. I hope there's no spontaneous combustion in the air."

After retracing our steps back up to the building above us, I looked out the windows again to locate the whereabouts of the roving guard. Out the south window, I just caught a glimpse of the rover in his long white Cossack and skull cap walking in a direction away from us. Waiting until he was fully out of sight, we crept stealthily out the door and moved quickly at a crouch into the woods and up the steep hill to our observation point.

We then laid on the large flat rock until our breath returned, after which Steed commented,

"I'm impressed, Bruce. You're good. You know your stuff. I think that come action time; you will be a force to be reckoned with."

"Is that a compliment?"

"Just an observation."

I formed a smile he wasn't able to see.

"Well, in the immortal words of Popeye the Sailor, I yam what I yam." I then settled in comfortably, folded my arms and laid my head on my field pack. "I don't guess anything will be going on down there tonight. I'll reopen my eyes at dawn."

Steed replied, "I probably won't get any shuteye tonight, so I'll keep a look-out just in case somebody nosy comes along."

I then yawned and closed my eyes. "If he does, you have my permission to kill him, Mr. Steed. Now, good night."

I do sleep very lightly and have done so for years. When you've been in the danger business all your life, you wake up at the drop of a pin. My good intentions of catching a night full of Z's didn't quite work out...partly because I was sleeping bone to rock and partly because a damned owl in a nearby tree kept asking us *who* all night long. Every time I turned over on my granite mattress and looked at Steed, his eyes were glued to the camp below.

It was 0405 on my watch when I finally said, "What are you watching down there?"

"Nothing really. Just the roving guards as they make their rounds. But like I told you before, I have to spend time getting acquainted with my target area...specifically visualize the target *in* the area. Study my venue. I have sometimes sat for days watching, waiting, surveying, calculating. Through your starlight scope, I have spotted every part of this camp, measuring distance, dry firing on the heads of the guards and finally seeing in my mind the end result. I haven't wasted any part of the night. This is *my* way to recon, Bruce. And because this *is* my routine, I do not miss."

"Impressive," I said. "It's too bad you spent most of your life on the wrong side of the law. But, I will be most anxious to see your end result." I then dug into my field pack and retrieved a couple of protein bars and bottled water.

"Here. Something between last night's missed supper and today's breakfast."

"Thanks," he said. "I *am* a bit hungry."

"Look forward to the steak and baked potato we'll have this evening."

"And the shower," he added.

Just before seven, we heard vehicles entering the compound through the gate and onto the dirt road leading further into the compound. The sporadic traffic continued until it appeared the last one had been parked in the lot at the opposite end of the camp. A few of the hostiles had already come out of the barracks and chow hall and were milling around in the open area where we had seen them praying the evening before. A few moments after they had formed up, they fell to their knees and assumed the prayer position. Even at better than eight hundred yards, we heard their wailing, chanting, and singing in monotone. I thought for a minute I had been thrown back in time to the Freewill Baptist tent revival that my father took me to. The only difference was that these people weren't handling snakes.

After the morning prayers, they split up into two groups to engage in some imbecilic-looking training. Half of them were at an obstacle course, running, dodging, and jumping over and around some Virginia State road gates it appeared they had stolen. The remainder were going through the motions of martial arts, taking one another down, feigning the cutting of each other's throats and the like.

Their combative training was pitiful. Laurel and Hardy actually came to mind. After a while, as Steed and I were watching them through our field glasses, we found each other laughing, what with all of the stumbling and bumbling going on. And then there were their techniques. What techniques?

Following the Ringling Brothers act, there was another fall-down-on-the-ground prayer session around 10:00 that lasted nearly forty-five minutes. This prayer meeting, however, was more reverent and reflective without all of the moaning and chanting we heard earlier.

They apparently broke for chow around one o'clock as they, to the man, streamed into the larger building. Since we both were a bit weary and bored, not to mention the fact that our asses were sore from sitting on stone, I asked Steed, "Have you seen enough?"

He nodded. "Yeah. What an inept-looking bunch of idiots. Maybe that's why the government is not taking these jihadist camps seriously. I'd say we're not the *first* to spy on them."

"Don't sell them too short, though," I said.

"What they might lack in training, combative, and military protocol, they make up for in will, purpose, and motivation. Any one of them might be willing to park a truck on a street next to a public building and blow himself up, thinking himself a martyr and hoping to earn the opportunity to bed down those 72 virgins in Heaven. It doesn't take a highly skilled expert to do that...just some moronic fascist with motivation. These people are more dangerous than they look out there. And when some of them are done here, they will receive more intensified training in Pakistan and will come back here and to other camps ready to set the world on fire...literally."

"Yeah, I guess you're right," he said. "What we saw in that bunker does say a lot about their resolve."

"They've also given up their lives to be out here training and planning to make America bleed. They're not going away. A lot of them came out of our prison system with no job, money, family or purpose in life. Islam has opened up its gates to them and given them the promise of a new life, living within a caring, religious environment. And as this ul-Fuqra group hates America, the Brotherhood of Muslims, AKA Dar al-Islam, offers them not only a place in their organization, but a place in history."

Steed again brought up the Winchester and allowed the scope to zero in on various parts of the compound. I watched him for a while and then asked him,

"As parts of that camp are close to a full klick away, what's your maximum distance to target?"

"You're asking me what's the greatest distance I can make the kill? Depending on wind, humidity, and the accuracy of this sniper rifle you put in my hands...I'd say something beyond twelve hundred yards."

I grinned and shook my head. "No way. I'll give you seven, maybe eight hundred, but nobody's that good."

Steed held his focus on something down below us he had settled on and replied, "I might just have to prove it to you before this is over, old timer." He then made a couple of adjustments on the weapon and laid it aside.

"We'll see, Mr. Steed. I would hope your shot will be closer in than that. And watch the *old-timer* crap."

We had seen enough. The good thing was, we had gotten an unexpected look inside the munitions bunker. The ordnance was there for a purpose...to kill Americans, bring down our buildings and infrastructure and demoralize our citizens. But we were going to stop them. *And* their celebrated leadership

At just after one-thirty, we picked up our rifles and gear and moved back down the southern slope toward where I had parked the Suburban. I didn't think there were any guards out there at this point. Perhaps they all were mandated to go through the training. However, when we were within fifty feet of the SUV, I found out I was wrong. We spotted two of the perimeter guards trying to get into old Diablo. As the doors were locked, I saw that one of them had what appeared to be a screwdriver and working on the left side door lock, while the other stood beside him watching.

For a few moments, we remained in a crouch position watching and whispering to one another how to address the issue. They were either breaking in to see what they could steal, or they were intending to get to my registration to see who owned the vehicle. Maybe both.

"All right, Atticus," I whispered.

"We have to take them out. Follow my lead."

With all of the quickness and stealth of two copperhead snakes, careful not to snap a twig beneath our boots, we moved through the trees to a point where, given my signal, we would spring onto them. Just a second after each of them realized someone was behind them, they began turning their heads toward us. However, before they could see who we were, I first caught the observer with a horizontal butt stroke from the stock of my rifle, shattering his jawbone, while Steed, a mere second later, brought the butt of *his* rifle down on the skull of the man with the screwdriver. At such time they were found or whenever they woke up from their nap and stumbled back into camp, they would likely not be able to tell anyone what happened to them. Even if they *didn't* have amnesia from the assault, they would not be able to describe the Mack truck that hit them. The only concern I had was that the camp's leadership might surmise that not only had somebody come onto their property and assaulted two of their guards, but whoever did it might have been spying on their operation. Of course, they may also think that it could have been a couple of redneck good old boys who just hated Muslims and wanted to have a little fun.

But there was still something else Hickcock wanted to happen before that day the number one terrorist in the world would bite the dust. We also needed to pluck out somebody in the camp who could tell us for sure that The Viper *was* expected....and whether he would in fact be arriving on the 7th of September. I doubted very seriously that the two yahoos lying at our feet knew squat about al-Massoud's plan. They were merely guards. Peons. That's why I didn't toss their carcasses in the back of the

Suburban and take them down the road to interrogate them. And as they were Arab-looking, they likely did not speak English. That was going to be my concern *whoever* we plucked out to interrogate. It would be a waste of our time and resources to basically end up with nothing...not to mention bringing in the chopper that would cart them off to Gitmo.

After checking the guards for pulses, finding that they had not died from the blows to their heads, we moved them into the woods out of the clearing and threw our gear into the Suburban. Steed gave me a wry smile after we stepped into the truck. I think he rather enjoyed cracking the guard's head.

# CHAPTER 17

It was drawing on three when we arrived back at Wolf Laurel, but I didn't see Adriana's van. Maria, who we found in their room having a dialogue in Spanish with our maid, Juanita, said Adriana was out running errands. While they conversed, I then went up to my suite to take a shower. Steed waited until Juanita was finished making up the room and then did the same in his quarters. After donning a white golf shirt and a pair of jeans, I came back downstairs and found Steed already in the guest sitting room reading a copy of *Garden and Gun* magazine. I took it he *wasn't* reading about cultivating azaleas, however.

"Sandwich?" I asked.

"That would be great. I'll see if Maria wants something."

As he found that Maria and Adriana had eaten a late lunch about one thirty, we fixed ourselves each a ham and cheese on sourdough. By the time we were finished and had cleaned up, Adriana was back. Maria then came out of her room and down the hallway to join us.

"Well," Adriana said.

"Did you two boys have a good night?"

"Yep," I replied.

"The bed was a little harder than I'm used to and they didn't serve breakfast, but otherwise we were treated well."

"Where did you stay?"

"At a kind of rustic place over in the Goshen area where we had business." And I wasn't lying about that...just painting her a different picture.

"I was worried you might be somewhere in a danger zone like you generally are when you run off like this. What do you have planned the *rest* of the day?"

"I need to spend time on the phone with the FBI about some things we learned."

"Okay. I was thinking maybe we could have a little social...maybe order in some pizza around seven, and get better acquainted with one another. I haven't had an opportunity to talk much with Atticus."

"And then we can all sit around, hold hands and sing a chorus or two of kumbaya," I quipped.

I think I detected a partial smile on Steed's face, but Adriana didn't think that was funny. It was one of those "I'll deal with you later" looks.

"I'd like that," said Maria.

"Well good. Just let me know what you like on your pizza and I'll order it." I was sure mine would be coming loaded up with anchovies and mountain oysters.

"If you'll excuse me, I'm going upstairs to make my call," I told them.

From our fridge in the upstairs kitchen, I grabbed a beer, plopped into my Big Easy and got Hickcock on the phone. This time, I rang his cell so that I wouldn't have to endure the freaking telephone menu.

"I wondered when you'd call. What did you learn out there, Bruce?"

"We did manage to get inside the camp and just after midnight we found their munitions bunker, which was concealed rather cleverly under what appeared to be a shack. There were enough firearms and rocket launchers to equip a small army and enough explosives to blow up all of Manhattan."

"Any evidence of chemical material or devices?"

"No. We checked every crate and box. As far as I know, just conventional crap. There were a couple of boxes filled with what appears to be pressure cooker IED material...timers, wires, nails, ball bearings and the like."

"Where is the access to this bunker? How did you find it?" Hickcock asked.

"We actually found it by accident. As I said, it's located beneath the small shack we broke into. We found a door that led to a set of stairs to what we thought was merely a basement. They obviously dug out the bunker and then built the shack on top of it."

"So how were they able to get all of the munitions and explosives down there?"

"A large garage door on the back side of the bunker dumps into a road where a few box-type cargo trucks sit. What's amazing is there is only one relatively inattentive guard back there and a simple set of locks on a side entry door."

"And how many hostiles were you able to observe within the camp?"

"I'd say there may be a hundred to a hundred-fifty people milling around or playing games at any given time. During the day, they've either got their noses on the ground in salat (prayer) or running an improvised obstacle course. We saw some combative training...if you can call it that...and a makeshift rifle range with stationary targets. However, there was no firing going on today. The larger building you pointed out on the map is likely a mosque of sort that also doubles as both a chow hall and a place for lectures and X rated movies."

"You did well, Bruce. Can you give me a list of everything you found in that bunker?"

"Yes. I'll overnight some 35-millimeter pix I took. I also took a few with my cell. I'll forward those via text as soon as I get off the phone with you."

"Did you encounter anyone? I was hoping you might be able to snag someone for interrogation."

"A couple of sentries found my SUV a little further out in the woods and acted interested in buying it. After I caught them breaking into it, they suddenly fell into a deep sleep. Nobody messes with Diablo."

"Who?"

"My Suburban. Anyway, they were just privates and wouldn't have known shit. I doubt they even know who al-Massoud is. Anyway, they never saw us coming."

"Somehow, Bruce, we've got to get some information from somebody important in that compound to not only verify that Massoud will be in camp on or about the 7th to give them their rah-rah speech, but also that September 11th is the actual target date for their big show. If the date pans out, we will have the task force in position early on the 6th along with a couple of gunships in support. If our current Intel is not accurate, I'll be wasting a lot of manpower and resources. However, if the attacks *are* going down on the 11th, I would imagine those trucks along with others will be moving out with the explosives between the 8th and the 10th. We still need more tangible information on al-Massoud, Bruce, and whether he *will* arrive there on the 7th. Go pluck somebody out who knows something and shake him down."

I replied, "Like I said, the majority of the compound will probably not know the master plan. We'd have to snatch up the right person. Maybe one of Maslama's lieutenants. But then how could we determine who that would be? However, Steed and I will make another trip over there in the next day or so and see what we can do. We'll set up across the road somewhere *outside* of the compound, this time watching to see who's going in and out. If somebody's driving a higher-dollar car, we might expect that person is high enough up in the organization to have knowledge about al-Massoud and the overall plan. And hopefully, he will speak English. Of course, once we nab him, he's going to have to disappear. Cleanly. I don't mean we'll *off* him unless he wants to do battle; we'll just have to stow him away until you send down that chopper for his transport to Gitmo. And then we'd be banking on the fact that the disappearance of one of the members will not necessarily alarm Maslama that their plan has been compromised. People come up missing all the time."

"Sounds like a plan. But it's now the 18th of August. If you can get in there the next couple of days and pull this off, all the better."

"By the way, John, besides the pictures I'm sending you in overnight mail, I'm also enclosing a bunch that we pulled out of a filing cabinet in that shack we searched. They're photos taken of several of the buildings, key landmarks and national monuments in both Washington and New York. No doubt now that at least these two cities are the targets. And one other thing, John."

"What's that?"

"You and Maggie need to put on your asbestos underwear. One of the targets is the Hoover Building."

I didn't readily hear a response. I continued. "Makes the hairs stand up on the back of your neck, eh John?" "I'll look for the photos tomorrow, Bruce."

"What happens if there are other ul-Fuqra compounds involved in a more coordinated attack? We're here stopping *this* bunch, but trucks from other locations could be the ones to hit New York and Washington?

"I intend to have every federal, state, and local police jurisdiction in a state of readiness and security. But I won't put out the directive until the day before the raid. Most of America believes it's possible that al-Qaeda will strike somewhere every 9-11 anniversary date to celebrate what happened in 2001. So, a high state of vigilance would be expected anyway...even though we would not divulge the particulars of al-Massoud's plan. That's why the onus is on you, Bruce, to get somebody from that camp to talk."

"And that may be a chore. In my experience, most of these Islamofascist wouldn't spill their guts even if their mothers' lives depended on it. They are ready to die for Allah, if that's what it takes. But I can arrange that if necessary."

"I'm sure. My gut tells me you do have your methods. Use them at will."

When our conversation had ended, I immediately sent him the cellphone photos by text, and then after telling Adriana I needed to go out for a while to run errands, I took the memory disc from my camera to our Walgreens to have it developed. I asked them to put a rush on it so that I could take the prints to the Mail Box store before it closed. At nine minutes till six I was standing at the UPS counter overnighting my package to Hickcock.

When I returned to the inn, I was beat. At twenty after six, I stretched out on our bed and closed my eyes. However, Adriana, who was preparing to order the pizza, said to me,

"None of that, Skippy. We're getting ready to have supper."

I then grabbed her by the hand and pulled her down on top of me.

"How about..."

"No. None of *that*, either."

"Just a quicky?"

She gave me that teasing grin.

"I said *no*. Anyway, I'm not that kind of girl." She then wrestled herself free and slid off the bed.

"Go take a cold shower or something."

"I had a shower earlier."

"Well, take another one. The pizza will be here in a half hour."

"All I can say, Mizz McGowan, is you missed your chance."

She ignored my impudence by waving me off and then picked up her cellphone to make her call.

I piddled around a while, but when I finally went downstairs, I found that Pizza Boy had already been by and Adriana had brought out several bottles of Sam Adams in a bucket of ice. Steed and Maria were seated on the couch and already conversing with my social butterfly. And I was missing the Braves and Reds on TV.

I sat down about the time everyone was pulling slices of the pizza out of the two boxes and slapping them onto plates. Adriana did take care of me by making sure one of the pizzas was pepperoni. I could tell that Steed, the hard-case stiff that he was, was just a bit uncomfortable in such urbane, social settings, but as he obviously would do anything to please the woman beside him, he would give it his best.

It was when Adriana asked what his line of work was that I saw him choke on a piece of the pizza. He also might have noticed the slight smile on my face. It was while he was taking a swig of his beer to push down the stuck morsel that I noticed that the little gerbil in his brain was running as fast as it could to keep from falling off the wheel.

"More recently, I worked as an independent contractor," he finally said.

"Were you in construction?"

"I did some work for the government."

It was *my* turn to choke. It just so happened that the government people who engaged him were now doing time.

He then added. "I was in the CIA for a while and before that, the Marines."

'Good answer,' I thought to myself. Well, that part was certainly true. I then looked at Maria whose eyes were looking down at her plate. I wasn't sure how much she knew about Steed, but the fact that she had left him a few months before over what she *did* find out, the conversation seemed to be affecting her. It was time to bail him out.

"Let's talk about you, Maria," I interjected, taking the focus off him.

"You said you're from Dallas and your folks still live there."

Steed's eyes showed his appreciation. He knew he owed me one.

"I worked for a pharmaceutical company for a while and then I met Atticus one day when I was working out at a gym. His...uh job...required him to move around a lot and after we began dating heavily, he asked me to travel with him. I was reluctant at first, but then as I knew I had fallen in love, I just couldn't stay separated from him. So, we got an apartment in Atlanta for a kind of home base and then I went on the road with him for almost two years."

Obviously, she left out the part about him killing people all over the United States.

Adriana, the inquisitive person that she is, wanted a little clarification.

"The CIA sent you all over, Atticus?"

"Hey, sweetheart," I broke in.

"You gotta understand most of these CIA types can't talk about what their jobs entail. I think it's your turn to talk a little about *your* history and how you came to be known as the Mistress of Wolf Laurel."

*You now owe me twice, Steed.*

Adriana then began telling them she grew up in the county, never really leaving, except for college, and then married her first husband whose parents owned the B&B that bore the family name. His parents passed away shortly after they were married and then he developed cancer a few years later, subsequently dying as well. But, Adriana chose not to open another old wound by telling them about her little boy who also died...of leukemia. She obviously didn't want to put a damper on our pizza party. She did convey that when she was a little girl and I was a high school senior leaving for college, she got me off to the side and told me that she had been in love with me all of her young life...and that one day she would marry me. Then thirty some years later, here we were. The most important dream of her childhood had come true.

"What a sweet story," Maria remarked.

"Like a fairy tale where Cinderella lives happily ever after with her Prince Charming."

I thought Steed was about to choke again while stifling a grin.

"But, Bruce, you haven't told us anything about you," he said.

"Like what *your* last job with the government was."

I felt my eyes searing into his like lasers. *I saved your ass and you pay me back this way?*

"Well, I too was kind of a government contractor after the FBI. Basically, I was with a group that profiled subversives, especially Middle Eastern terrorists whose mission it was to harm Americans."

"In other words, you hunted down terrorists," he remarked, displaying a mild smirk. "What did you do with the bodies?"

"*Atticus*!" Maria chided.

I glared at him again for trying to throw me under the bus and then turned softer eyes back to Maria.

"Most of my responsibilities were to locate the suspects and interrogate them, then turn them over to the Justice Department where they would potentially face prosecution." And sometimes it did actually go that way. I of course *didn't* tell them that I had sent an equal number of terrorists to the Great Beyond to meet Allah.

"Well, it all sounds very exciting what you did for your country...and patriotic."

"It had its moments," I said.

"Tell me about Greenbrier County," Maria continued. "The countryside is beautiful...the surrounding mountains and rich green farmland."

Adriana said, It's a historic place where an important Civil War battle was fought. And then there's the hotel they call America's Resort, The Greenbrier Hotel, only a few miles from here. Nearby is also some rich and wonderful farm country. Some of the best beef in the world comes from here...Herefords and Black Angus breeds. Actually, you can see them at the State Fair just south of town. The fair is always in August and actually going on now."

"Hey, I have a little story about the fair," I added. "My dad used to take me there every year. I remember the year I was eleven or twelve. He left me to walk around by myself for the first time. I saw this tent that had a sign on it that read, *Girls, Girls, Girls.* Well, that was the age I was starting to like girls, so I thought I'd go in. But the guy out front said I'd have to be eighteen to get in and turned me away. So, I went around to the side and crawled under the tent flap to stick my head in. Suddenly, I felt somebody pulling on my legs and found it was my dad who yanked me out and chewed my ass. He said,

"Boy, you be peaking at stuff like that, and you'll turn to stone. You remember what happened to Lot's wife when she turned into a pillar of salt." Well, that scared me a bit, but as soon as he left to go check out the livestock, my curiosity got the best of me. I ducked back under the flap. And then when I saw all the women in there taking off their clothes, I'll be damned if I didn't feel myself turning to stone. After that, I definitely avoided peeking into girls' locker rooms."

And that's when I saw the stone-faced Atticus Steed lose it. When he laughed, I thought his face would crack open like a glazed donut.

Adriana then narrowed her eyes. "Bruce McGowan, shame on you." She then turned her face to our guests and said, "Would anyone like another beer or a glass of wine?"

I guess it was me who finally broke up the party since Maria reported she was a little tired and it was going on ten. What was left of the pizza was cold and rubbery anyway. And as I was bushed, I *knew* Steed was. After they left the room and I had finished helping Adriana with the cleanup, she said something so out of character for her it blew my mind.

"All right, come on, lover boy. Let's go see about turning that little brain of yours to stone." It appeared my State Fair story that she found so off color, must have in fact turned her on.

# CHAPTER 18

My cell phone went off at 9:23 the next morning. It was Hickcock.

"I got the photos you sent by text, Bruce. Enough combined yield to equal a couple of nukes."

"Yep."

"That bunker has to be taken down before those trucks hit the road. By the way, Interpol provided me with new photos of the man they say is al-Massoud, The Viper. I'm sending them to you by e-mail attachment. You'll see that he's aged some from the photos we have in our database. But he is forty-six and his full, black beard now has some salt in it. The beard is also a little shorter than in other pix we have."

"But," I said. "As he's changed his looks frequently, alternating from clean-shaven to a beard, mustache only, added glasses occasionally, this may just be another attempt to disguise himself. If and when we capture his image in our scope, he might even have a *different* look. Who knows; we might see a man with white hair and a beard made up to look twenty years older."

"Perhaps. There are a series of photos taken of him by an MI6 operative in a Mali marketplace last week.

Whether he shaves off that beard in another two or three weeks before he lands here in the U.S., remains to be determined. We have provided the TSA and customs in every major airport with copies of photos showing him with several different looks. The problem is, he will likely have even another alias on his passport and possibly a new look. One of our informants in Detroit has what we believe to be accurate information that The Viper plans to meet with a contingency of Imams there. We have especially alerted DTW, Wayne County, to make sure they take a good look at every Middle Easterner coming through."

"That's a bit politically incorrect, isn't it, John? The FBI...profiling?"

"Ask me if I care, Bruce."

"Since Johns wants him dead, what if some TSA agent or airport cop detains him?"

"We have put out instructions that they will *not* detain him, but notify the FBI ASAP. Agents will be on-site at DTW. If he's spotted, then we'll have an opportunity to track him to be sure he's on that expected timeline to enter the Goshen camp on the 7th. Again, we expect he might step on American soil on or about the 1st, meet with his Islamic brotherhood, visit the Hancock ul-Fuqra headquarters, and then motor down to the Goshen camp or take a small plane to a Podunk airport in your area. We still need to snap up somebody from that camp to solidify that timeline, however."

"All right, John, tomorrow, sometime around EENT, Steed and I will be positioned outside the entrance to the compound to determine who that lucky terrorist is going to be. We'll follow the vehicle and at an opportune time, take him down. Whether or not he knows anything will be *his* bad luck."

"What's EENT?"

"Come on, John. Didn't you study your government and NOAA abbreviations at the academy? Ending Evening Nautical Twilight...when night starts to happen."

"Okay, I knew that," he said.

"Then why did you ask me?"

"Just keep me informed, Bruce."

"Goodbye, John."

I printed off Hickcock's photos and then rapped on Steed's door, hoping I wasn't committing *coitus interruptus*. He opened their door and I could readily see both were fully dressed and watching the nice, new flat-screen TV we had put in the room a couple of weeks before.

"Let's go out on the veranda. Something to show you."

Without a word, he followed me out to where we each took a rocker.

"New photos of al-Massoud from Hickcock. I enlarged them on my printer so that you can make out his facial structure, eyes and other features. You can compare these with what we already have. Although we may not be absolutely sure which of these images you'll see in the scope, this could be the one. It was supposedly taken only recently."

"If someone got close enough to take these pictures, why hasn't someone gotten close enough to kill him?"

"You're asking the wrong guy," I replied.

"These were taken by British Intelligence and maybe he's not on their target list."

"If not, then why take photos?"

I shrugged and shook my head.

"As everything still points toward the 7th, we'll be situated on that observation point the night of the 6th. I also need to recon a site for the SWAT element to use as a staging area well before we marry up with the force commander. The attack will need to be coordinated with our time-on-target in the compound. You take the Viper down and I radio the task force commander to sweep in. I think the enemy will be moving the trucks out on the 9th, not later than the 10th. A lot of collaboration will need to take place between us, Hickcock and SWAT."

Steed shuffled his weight in his chair.

"Seems like you've been doing all the work so far, Bruce. I feel like I'm just along for the ride and really haven't been involved in much so far."

"I was hired to plan this mission, Mr. Steed; you were hired to make that one shot that kills the leading terrorist in the world. You'll be doing a hell of a service for the citizens of the United States. The thing is, though, no one will ever know just who fired the shot, so forget about becoming a national hero and getting the Nobel Peace Prize."

"I'll just be happy to earn that pardon."

"And your million," I added wryly.

"A million bucks for one bullet."

And then like a cloud had formed over the sun, he was rather quiet for a long moment and began darting his eyes around as though he was chewing on some words to spit out. Finally, they did come out. "Don't get me wrong, Bruce; I feel I can respect you as a true professional. But since I've been around you these days I get the impression you're just *condoning* me on this mission. Like I'm a means to an end. I also get the impression you think of me as nothing but a killer. And if that's the case, then you and I might ultimately have a problem here."

Now it was time to chew on *my* words. "Look, Steed. I like you. I like what I've seen. I like what comes out of your mouth. I believe if things had worked out differently for you and then somehow we met up, we might have even been friends. It's just that I can't get past what I read about you in the CJIC file...about the numbers of potentially innocent people you may have killed."

To this point, I had not seen the icy blue eyes glare that I was getting from him now. But along with it came the fiery words.

"I wondered when you would get in my face about that, McGowan. I took both time and great pains studying each and every target before performing the hit. I will assure you, sir, that every goddamned parasite I killed was guilty of murder. I might have been killing *for* the *wrong* people, but I damn sure killed the *right* people. And now that I do know something about you, how many people have *you* killed?"

I knew I needed to de-escalate the situation...and quickly...or he would disappear on me overnight. "Only the ones who *needed* killing, Mr. Steed."

"And *you* decided that." His tone was now more abated.

Steed had held a mirror to my face and I'm not entirely sure I passed the litmus test. My victims were generally opportune...and most were terrorists. Or people who were out to end *my* life. And that would be called self-defense. But I did not want to get into an apples and oranges argument over righteous kills. The only killing that I might not be able to sanction as valid was the murder I committed on Congressman Jack Randall, whose own killing streak spanned over forty years. Each notch on his gun put him a step closer to the White House and fame. He *had* to die.

But, in taking his life, I also took away his right to a fair trial. Maybe in that split second, it took me to pull the trigger, I saw an image in my brain of him walking out of the courthouse a free man.

I then held out my hand.

"Can we end this by saying that perhaps both of us made some decisions that we were not proud of? Maybe you're right, Mr. Steed. My life is a glass house and I should think first before picking up a stone to toss. Now are we good here?"

He nodded, but his expression was one of flat affect. "Maybe we needed to get all this out," he said. "Sometimes it's what is *not* said that causes people not to trust one another." He then shook my hand.

From there I quickly changed the course of our discussion. "By the way. Enjoy the next twenty-four hours. Get ready to spend another night in Rockbridge County."

"Back to the rock mattress?"

"No. We're going to try grabbing one of the more high-ranking ul-Fuqra members and do a little interrogation. We'll have to find a place to park the Suburban in proximity to the camp gate so that it will not be detected."

"When do we leave?"

"Tomorrow about three...just in case there are any early departures after their day of fun and games."

"Good. Uh, I was wondering about something."

"What's that?"

"If I could take you up on the use of Adriana's van...that is if she's not using it this afternoon. Maria and I would like to drive around the county a bit and see some of the sights...maybe have some dinner downtown."

"I'll ask her. I don't know if she's going anywhere. There's a family coming in from Tennessee a little later...a young couple and their kids. She'll want to be here."

"Kids, huh?"

"You have a problem with kids?" I asked.

"You mean besides the fact they're loud, snotty and get into everything? Not really."

"I assume you and Maria don't plan to have any."

"We actually haven't discussed it. I think she wants to be sure about *me* before we invite any rug rats into our lives. Anyway, I'm getting a little too long in the tooth to start having any."

"And then there'll be that question one day that you're sitting with them watching a Bruce Willis movie...have you ever killed anyone, Daddy?" I don't think Steed liked the comment. He merely turned his head away and scowled. "Sorry about that," I said. "It wasn't my intent to revisit your past and start this all up again."

"No. You're probably right, though. Something to think about. I wouldn't want to lie to my son; but I wouldn't show him all of the notches on my gun, either."

"You'll have a clean slate after this mission, Atticus. I hope you'll make the best of it."

"I intend to. I've got a wonderful woman in my life, and I want to keep her. A lesser person would have already walked away for good."

I then stood and placed a hand on his shoulder.

"Yeah, it's women like ours that keep us from tumbling off the end of the world, brother. Let me go check about that van."

*****

Steed and I left a little earlier than I said we would so that in advance of our surveillance, I could pinpoint a clearing where a chopper would land in case we had to evacuate our detainee. And getting him out of the area was our only real choice, other than killing him and dumping his body in the nearby Maury or Calfpasture Rivers. There was no way we could allow him to return to his brotherhood to spill the beans about his being taken prisoner. I envisioned that the clearing might also serve as a staging area for the task force on D Day, so it had to be located no more than a kilometer from the compound. On the way to our target area, I pulled off at a mom-and-pop store on Highway 42 for a cup of coffee and to study the topography on the map Hickcock had provided.

Beginning with the grid square that contained the compound, I reviewed the contour lines and vegetation a full kilometer in all directions to locate a flat, open piece of terrain, making sure there were no houses, businesses, or power lines in the immediate vicinity. In checking the legend, I saw that the map was two years old and buildings can spring up in a matter of months. I also didn't want the landing zone to be anywhere next to the highway. Still, the Landing Zones had to be in close enough proximity as possible to the compound so that the strike team could move in quickly. It was a tall order to get all of these requirements into the equation, but it had to be done.

There were two possibilities and I drove to each one of them. The first was just over a klick (kilometer) away from the camp toward the eastern mountains and would have been fitting had there not been two log cabins sitting in the middle of the clearing. But then I found one very solid candidate for the LZ just off a firebreak across Route 42 and 800 meters west of the compound. On its south edge, the tree line was low and provided an excellent approach route where a chopper could fly nap-of-earth for a half kilometer before setting down.

I canvassed the site thoroughly, first with my field glasses, and then Steed and I performed a walking recon around its perimeter to determine if there might be houses and human activity nearby. The noise of a chopper or sounds of tactical vehicles come mission day could certainly bring people out of their homes and into the clearing to find out what all the commotion was about.

# CHAPTER 19

Having stepped out of the tree line into the open field and bright sunshine, we found the temperature to be nothing less than stinking hot. No breeze. Gnats swirling. The air heavy. Ankle deep in pungent musk thistle and Johnson grass. As we were wearing protective vests and light field jackets that partially concealed our weapons, I felt like I was boiling inside. And as it took us a full fifteen minutes to circle the clearing, stopping occasionally to zoom into the trees with the field glasses and check for life, I was just plain damn miserable. Flashback to Vietnam. It's hell to get old like this. Then I looked at Steed, and except for a few small beads of perspiration on his forehead, the heat didn't seem to faze him, the cool kid that he was. Bastard.

We had covered the turf counter-clockwise from about six on the clearing's clock face until we reached nine, mainly looking for deep-woods residences. That's when I caught a glint off something metallic approximately fifty yards in. Positioning myself steadily against a tree just off the perimeter, I brought the glasses to a point where the lens zoomed in on a tin roof that reflected a shard of sunlight streaming through the tops of the trees. Obviously, the house belonged to someone who preferred solace far away from the madding crowd's ignoble strife. But, it appeared to be the only house around.

"Shall we?" I said to Steed.

"Are you going in to take a closer look?"

"Just to see if it's inhabited. Looks pretty run down from here."

With Steed on my heels, I closed in on the place. The house was little more than a shack, largely dilapidated, constructed of shabby, unpainted wood, kind of grey-brown in color. A cord and a half of cut, well-seasoned poplar lay ahead in our path and off to our right front sat a rusted-out late fifties Chevy pickup covered up to the tops of its wheel-less brake drums with shin-high weeds.

The house looked to be inhabited by a family with younger children considering the trike that was absent a front wheel and a couple of rusted-out Tonka toys that lay near the front steps. But then I considered because of the condition of the toys, perhaps the children were currently in their teens or early adulthood and the relics were now nothing but yard ornaments. Also, the Tonkas were made of metal as few were these days. One thing for sure, the house would never be featured in Southern Living or Better Homes and Gardens.

"I've seen hundreds, maybe thousands of shacks like this scattered all over West Virginia," I commented.

"Don't be surprised if we stumble over a still."

On the opposite side of the house I spied a dirt road that led from somewhere out yonder up to the house. Then as we moved farther in at our seven o'clock, the rear end of a white, late-model Ford pickup came into view. And lying in the cool grass, what there *was* of it near the porch, was a hound. Looked to be fifteen to seventeen and obviously on his last leg. Apparently, he had heard our approach, but as he was too old to do anything about it or even care, he merely lifted his head and uttered a feeble *woof*.

When we had advanced to within fifty feet of the front porch, the door suddenly sprang open and the double barrel of a twelve-gauge swung in our direction. Although I knew Steed saw it, my instincts caused me to yell

"Gun!" I then placed my hand inside my jacket and went down on one knee. Steed dropped down as well.

"*Whadda ya want!*" bellowed the man's voice from inside. All that was still visible was the shotgun.

"*To talk!*" I yelled back. I didn't add that we were from the government. If he *was* a moonshiner or was running a meth lab, we would for sure catch a load of buckshot.

Then the man's large form appeared in the doorway. The gun was still trained at our heads. When I say *large*, his Caterpillar hat nearly touched the top of the doorway. Maybe three hundred pounds he was. I still couldn't make out his features, however.

"About what?!" he yelled back.

"Can we approach?" I raised both hands to show him they were empty. Steed followed suit, but muttered something like, "What the hell you got us into, McGowan?"

The man stalled for a moment, continuing to check us out, then said, "All right. Come on up. But don't try nothin.' I hain't killed nobody today, but the day ain't over."

Slowly we moved forward, hands well above our shoulders.

"We come in peace," I said. And then I almost laughed at myself. I don't know *why* I said that. We weren't the cavalry entering an Indian village or aliens that had just landed on the planet.

When we had negotiated a couple dozen beer cans scattered at our feet on the path that led to the porch steps, the man said, "That's far enough." A few seconds later, he asked,

"You the law?"

"Not exactly," I replied.

"We just saw your place and were curious to see if anybody lived here."

"Now you done found out. So you can git off my prop'ity."

"Can we talk anyway?"

"Got nothin' to talk *about*. You boys is truspassin,' Now *git*!"

"Just hear us out," I said. "You might be interested."

"If yer here sellin' somethin,' yer wastin' yer time. And unless yer here to tell me I done won the sweepstakes, we got no business at all." He paused a moment and cocked his head.

"Just what does 'not exackly' mean?"

It occurred to me that his IQ may in fact not have exceeded his waist size. Standing over six-six, the man's stomach looked as though he might have swallowed a watermelon. If I had stuck a pin in him, the entire place might have gone up. Dressed in a checkered shirt and bib overalls, he was as *Junior Samples* as they came. From both corners of his mouth, tobacco juice had run, dried and caked before reaching his neck.

"My name's McGowan and this is Mr. Steed. We just want to talk with you about something that's fixing to happen around here in the next couple of days."

Fixing? It was obvious that I had been unwittingly lulled into his manner of speech.

"Like whut?"

"Can we come up and sit on the porch to talk?"

He motioned us toward two broken down porch chairs with the barrel of the shotgun.

"Suit yersef."

Steed and I passed Old Blue, who still paid us little mind, then walked up the steps and across the rotted and broken slats of the porch. With each of our steps the porch creaked and groaned. It was a wonder that elephant man hadn't fallen through the boards by now; but since he hadn't, I figured we'd be safe. We eased ourselves carefully into the chairs which appeared even more fragile than the porch.

"All right then...*talk*," he barked.

I opened up the dialogue.

"First, can we ask a couple of questions?"

"Shoot."

"You live here alone?"

"If it's any of yer business...yeah."

"I just thought with the toys in the yard, you had kids."

"I'm sixty-two years old, feller. Do I look like I got little kids? They done grow'd up and got families of their own."

"Your wife?"

"Daid. Died of cancer years ago. Like I said...I'm by myself. Now talk about why yer here or git."

"We're with the government and..."

He then raised the shotgun even with my chest.

"Let's see them badges."

"We're not law officers, I told you. We just *work* for the government."

"Doin' whut?"

Steed handled that question.

"Investigations, sir."

"You investigatin' *me*? Fer what? I don't make bootleg wine or shine. I ain't cheated the gov'ment and don't make enough to pay you bastuds any taxes."

"It's not about you, sir," Steed continued.

"We're investigating another matter."

"If that's the case then why you on my prop'ity?"

"Good question, Mister...uh..." I replied, soliciting his name.

"Huggins...Cletus Huggins."

Of course he was. The name rightly suited the man.

"Right, Mister Huggins. Here's the thing. In the next day or so and maybe again in a couple of weeks, you're likely to hear some things going on around here fairly close to your house. It'll be a kind of government activity, so we were just trying to see who might be living close by. That's why we're here. We just didn't want people to become alarmed when they heard some things."

Actually, I hadn't intended to make *any* contact with homeowners in the area. And here we were...on Cletus' porch chatting away. But it was good that we were talking. When that chopper came in and when the ATTF war party converged on the scene at some point in the future, we had to be sure that all the Cletuses out there wouldn't come out of the woods, set up lawn chairs and start picnicking with fried chicken and Jack Daniel's, watchin' what wuz goin' on.

"Got anything to do with that bunch down the road and across the way?"

"And who would that be?" I asked, playing ignorant.

"Them A-rab lookin' people that come in and out most days. I hear'm over thar firin' guns sometimes. You here about them?"

Rather than answer the question directly, I retooled the conversation by asking one myself.

"What do you know about them?"

"I think they's terrorists, if ya wanna know the truth. Most people around here don't pay 'em no mind. But the neighbors ain't got no sense. They's a bunch of chuckleheads. They wouldn't reckon-ize danger if it come up and bit 'em on the butt. I *will* say the A-rabs don't bother me none...or nobody else. But I know they's terrorists, and the cops don't pay 'em no mind neither. That sticks in my craw, bein' a law-bidin' American. Me and a couple my friends, we reported our suspicions a bunch of times, but nobody's made no attempt to move 'em out."

Steed jumped in.

"Speaking of your friends, do any of them live nearby...specifically in proximity to that field over there?"

"I'm the only person whut lives out here. I don't like havin' my neighbors breathin' down my neck. Next family lives over a half mile from here. I own all the prop'ity far as you can see. Fifteen acres includin' that field. Up until three years ago, in the spring I always put in a two acre garden there. Ain't able to no more."

That answered my question about any other houses being in the area. And as ex-farmer Huggins obviously didn't use his bathtub or slap on Right Guard on a regular basis, I doubted anyone *wanted* to live around him. So, ol' Cletus was all we had to be concerned about when it came to somebody witnessing our operation or interfering in any way with mission conduct.

"You can lower your gun now, Mister Huggins. I hope you've discovered we're no threat to you...and we're not a part of the government that's looking to cause you any trouble."

"But under your jackets I see guns, Mister. If you're not lawmen, who are ya?"

Maybe I misjudged the man *and* his IQ. He was more perceptive than I figured.

"Just a couple of guys who will be laying the ground work for that activity you are likely to see and hear nearby."

"Then I gather you boys *do* intend ta take out them A-rabs, eh."

Again, perceptive. Eventually, he'd find out that's exactly what we were up to. But until the aftermath, I had to either get him out of the way or think of a way to engage him to make him feel like a hero. After all, it *was* his land.

"Can we trust you, Mr. Huggins?"

"*Everybody* trusts me."

"I'm sure. But can we trust you to not divulge to anyone that we were even here?"

"Are you gov'ment spies?"

I chuckled.

"No. We're not spies, sir."

"Well, anyway, I don't tell nobody nothin'."

"Good," I said.

"And we can hold you to that."

"Yeah. But you gotta tell me whut you people got planned. Yer not gonna do somethin' that'll blow up my house, are ya?"

Like that would be any great loss.

"The activity we have planned won't be anywhere close to your house, Mr. Huggins."

"So whut you boys *got* planned?"

I looked at Steed and his response was raised eyebrows. Finally, I said,

"Well, Mr. Huggins, here's the thing. Generally, the kind of government maneuvers I'm talking about are confidential. Normally, I'd be telling you I can't divulge the nature of what we will be doing. But since you appear to be a straight-up, trustworthy gentleman and a true patriot, we want to let you be a part of this exercise."

Huggins' widened his eyes and then set the shotgun down against the door frame.

"I'm all ears. Always wanna hep the gov'ment when I can."

I looked at Steed and he then shrugged.

"All right, Cletus. Can I call you by your first name?"

"Yessar."

"In the next day or so, you're likely to hear a chopper over there in your field and then a few days later, men and vehicles coming in to set up what we call maneuvers. What we'd like you to do is act as a kind of security agent for us. When you hear anything like I described, I'd like you to quickly position yourself somewhere in your yard here. I see there's a dirt road over there that leads up to your house and it would be easy for anyone to come down that road, continue on the path and enter into that clearing where the action is. It appears to be the only way anyone can get into the field except the firebreak on the other side where we came in. And our men will take care of that. We can't be disrupted, Cletus. You have to keep out any intruders. Can you help us?"

"Yessar. Be glad to."

"And since you own that vacant field, can we use it?"

"Yep."

"Another thing...you can't tell *anyone* we had this conversation or leave your post during any activity."

Huggins stiffened up and assumed the position of attention. I wondered if at one time he had served in the military the way he placed the heels of his boots together, put his feet at a forty-five degree angle and cupped his pork chop hands along the seams of his overalls.

"You can count on me, Mr. McGowan."

I then stood and said, "Please stand beside Mr. Steed, sir, and raise your right hand." Huggins did as instructed. "Repeat after me. I, Cletus Huggins, United States citizen, do solemnly swear..."

He began repeating the oath.

"...to uphold the constitution of the United States..." He again echoed the pledge."...and to protect and defend my country when called upon to do so to the best of my ability..."

He had just a wee bit of trouble repeating that last part, and in retrospect, I should have broken the sentence up a little more. Speaking of breaking up, Steed was doing all he could to keep from laughing out loud. "...so help me God."

"So hep me Gawd."

"All we now ask you to do when the time comes, Cletus, is just shoo anyone away back in the direction they came. But please don't shoot them." I didn't think anyone would be venturing onto the place; I just wanted to keep him out of the way and make him think he was contributing.

He nodded patriotically. "Who am I s'posed to keep out?"

"Anyone who is not dressed like we are. And for safety purposes, don't venture over into that clearing. Again, you can't leave your post here at the house at all. Understood?"

"Yes...yessar."

"So," I continued, "what are your two responsibilities?"

"To make sure nobody gets near that garden field and to not kill nobody."

"And?"

"And..."

"Don't speak with anyone about us being here or that the government might be using that clearing. Mum's the word."

"That's more than two," he said.

"What?"

"You said they was two responsibilities."

I stifled a smile. He could count to three.

"You're correct, Cletus. Thanks for catching that. You'll be doing your country a great service, you know." I shook his hand that totally engulfed mine, but then I found out he had no grip. It was like he had merely laid a big clammy fish in my hand. I hate that.I then turned and descended the steps. Steed shook Huggins' hand as well and turned to follow me.

We both turned again after stepping through the maze of beer cans and saw that he was back at attention saluting us. We returned his salute and then began making our way back through the woods and into the clearing. We waited until we were within just a couple of yards of the Suburban in the firebreak before looking at one another and grinning.

Steed then said, "You should be on stage somewhere, Bruce. What a load of bovine scat."

"A load of what?"

"Bullshit, McGowan. Bullshit."

# CHAPTER 20

After marking the spot and recording the coordinates on the map with my thin-pointed grease pencil, I turned the Suburban around and drove back toward the camp's entrance. What we didn't see the last time we passed by the entranceway were the two sentries back in the woods about fifteen meters from the posts and chain. I assumed besides guarding the gate, their purpose was to lift the chain for any member vehicles coming in or going out. One of the guards was a little difficult to make out, but the AK in the other sentry's hands made him clearly visible.

I then picked up speed and continued on past the entrance, looking for some place nearby but on the opposite side of the road to enter the woods and set up an observation point. I had to go about a hundred yards further west before I found a wide spot between the trees to pull into. Once I went in, I found the the terrain fairly level with sparse vegetation between the hardwoods. But then I turned back through the forest in the direction of the compound, maneuvering as best I could about twenty feet off the highway in four-wheel drive until I was approximately fifty feet down and across the road from the camp's entrance. If I had gone any further, the guards would not only have seen my SUV, but heard its motor. I then turned the nose of the Suburban toward the road to a point where we could quickly pull out of the woods when we had to.

I set Steed up with a two-way radio and ear bud and put him behind the wheel. Then I began walking toward the east through the woods to where I could remain concealed about twenty feet back, but still see every vehicle exiting the compound. When I was finally in position and set up, I said in a soft voice, "Radio check."

"Loud and clear," was the response.

"Good. If I spot a possibility, I'll let you know and then hoof it back in your direction. Be ready for me to jump in and move out. We'll follow at a distance. Copy?"

"Copy."

I had two important items with me...my field glasses for daytime observation and my night vision scope on my Winchester. Both had power lens that would put me inside the passenger cabin of any vehicle coming out. My night vision scope would pick up just enough light from the instrument panel on the vehicle for me to see every feature on the driver's face. The only concern I had was that the vehicle's headlights coming out of the road might blind me and impede me from making out *anything* about the driver *or* car. I wouldn't be able to then see anything until the car turned left or right.

If *this* evening ended the same as a couple nights before, after the formation and prayers, the hostiles not living in the compound would be leaving at different intervals sometime after six. It was now only five twenty-five.

We had been in position for about forty minutes when one of the guards dropped the chain and allowed an early model pickup to exit. Through my lens, I could see that the driver was a Black man in a skull cap who did not fit the usual profile of a Middle Easterner. Most likely, he was one of the American inmates who been evangelized to Islam by fellow Muslims in some penal institution and recruited into the Jamaat ul-Fuqra organization upon his release. He was not a person I was looking for. He was probably someone living on a shoestring in the community with a family. What I was set to wonder was how any of the camp members, living in or out of the compound, were getting by financially unless they were working part-time night jobs. I assumed some were taking welfare money while others had working wives who were being treated by their husbands little better than slaves. The women were bringing home the bacon and the men were spending their days at the compound striking the gong for their cause, plotting to kill infidels.

A '90s model Dodge exited the camp after the pickup was well down the highway, so they were indeed coming out in piecemeal fashion. The driver was a fairly dumb-shit looking Arab and I was not interested in him either.

The skies gradually darkened and around seven-thirty a couple more cars exited, both with two to three people in them. Neither were high-dollar vehicles and I wasn't interested in multiple passengers anyway. *One* was my target; and he had to be driving something valued over $30,000. It would hopefully be *that* person who would tell us something we could use.

It was now eight-twenty-five and totally dark. The string of vehicles coming out at this point were few and far between.

I figured all of the peons had left anyway. Each time a vehicle had pulled onto the highway, I radioed Steed. And each time, we agreed that we'd let the driver go. The more important people might stay around to conduct a meeting or lecture about those arrogant, greedy, morally challenged Americans.

But at eight thirty-three, I spotted a boxy-looking Mercedes G Class SUV coming out. A $130,000 vehicle at least. For a moment, the driver stopped at the intersection and had a dialogue of sorts with one of the guards. This guy *was* somebody. When the driver then made his left turn toward Goshen, through my scope I sized up the man we would nail.

"This is the one, Steed. A Mercedes SUV coming toward you. Keep your eye on him. I'm on my horse," I said, running at a good clip. "I'm almost at your location."

By the time I jumped into the passenger seat and Steed had begun moving out of the woods toward the highway, the Mercedes was already out of sight. I knew it would be, but unless the driver was standing on his accelerator, the way Steed was driving, we were going to be on his bumper in a matter of minutes.

And Steed *was* mastering the Suburban on the curves and hills with remarkable ease. I had no concern that we might find ourselves upside down at any point. After we had traveled about a mile, we spotted the Mercedes' taillights just in time to see it slow and make a right turn onto a secondary road. Steed kept his distance so as not to make the driver suspicious he was being tailed. We followed him about three miles further and he then turned left down a narrow lane that proved to be very dark without any street lights. Being the smart guy that he was, Steed went on past the road and then whipped around like a stunt driver, shutting the lights off and making the turn behind the Mercedes.

"You can see the road?" I asked him.

"My eyes haven't started to fail me like yours, old timer," he quipped. "My purple vision is 20-20."

And I was sure glad of that. I couldn't see a *damn* thing.

Finally, after a country mile, the Mercedes turned into a driveway that led up to a sprawling 5000 square foot stucco house which looked just a little out of place among the sparsely scattered shabby shacks along the road. The lights were off inside the house, which gave the impression that either the driver lived alone or his family was not at home.

As we were still situated on the road, I said to Steed, "Okay, zoom in on him."

With the headlights still off, he accelerated down the driveway and came to a stop within inches of the Mercedes' rear bumper. Like a flash, I jumped out and converged on the driver's side door. I then placed the muzzle of my Glock on the door glass and yelled, "Out of the car, now!"

The man stalled on me as though he were in shock. The whites of his eyes were as big as mothballs. I yanked on the door handle, but the door was locked. "Get the hell out of the car, I said!"

As the engine was still running, he then threw the gearshift into reverse and gunned it. Unfortunately for him, my Suburban was behind him. Unfortunately for me, my front bumper was now damaged. Unfortunately for Steed, he probably had a sore neck. The driver could have hit the garage door button, but unless he drove the Mercedes through the wall and out the back of the house, he was going nowhere.

"What do you want?" the man yelled back at me in a slight Middle Eastern brogue.

And that's when I slammed the butt of my Glock into the door glass, shattering it into a thousand pieces all over him. I then placed the muzzle into his left ear. "Don't make me blow your head off. Now get out."

Without further hesitation, he popped open his seatbelt and swung his legs out of the car. "Are you here to rob me?"

"Is anyone in the house?" I shot back.

He shook his head.

"I live alone."

"Then open the front door. We're going inside."

But he didn't move. "What is it you want with me?"

I shoved him ahead of me and drove him up the front steps with the muzzle of my Glock. "Go! Inside!"

As his keys were still in his hand, he found the one to the door and unlocked it. We then entered the foyer and Steed came in behind us.

I flipped on the hall light and pushed the man again, this time toward the massive living room on the right. Finding the switch to that room, I flipped it and a half dozen table lamps came on. I then sat the man down hard onto a white sofa chair and looked around. This guy may have belonged to Jamaat ul-Fuqra, but he was not one of the 'impoverished.' The furniture and decor alone in the room had to be valued more than our entire Wolf Laurel estate. A huge ornate tapestry graced one wall while other walls contained several original paintings undoubtedly created by world famous artists. What seemed to be a dozen white sofas and chairs sat on a room-size six-inch-thick Persian rug.

"Now stand back up," I barked.

Slowly, the man stood in front of the chair, hands noticeably shaking.

"Keep your gun on him, Mr. Steed." I then shoved my Glock back into its holster and began searching our prisoner. He was not exactly dressed as others we had seen in the compound. His clothing was more westernized...a blazer type jacket, silk shirt and a pair of black sports slacks. None too kindly, I then ripped his jacket off and began patting him down. To no surprise, inside his waistband I found a T-55 pistol. And strapped to his calf was a K bar. After removing them both, I also pulled his wallet from his back pocket and then shoved him back down into the chair.

When I opened the wallet to check out his driver's license, did I ever find the surprise that might have just blown our entire mission. The man was Tahir Maslama, himself...the Goshen ul-Fuqra's big man on campus. I then glanced at Steed who saw the alarm on my face. When I tossed him Maslama's wallet and he read the name on the license, he tightened his lips and shook his head, also realizing our dilemma. If al-Massoud tried to contact Maslama and found that he had disappeared, he might avoid the Goshen camp altogether.

Maslama was thirty-one, about five-eight with a short-cropped beard and light bronze skin. He was a distinguished-looking man who in my mind epitomized the features of the new young lions of Islam.

With venom spitting from his eyes, he then asked the same question as before. "Why are you here?" The man appeared to speak nearly perfect English...maybe even 'gooder' than me.

I pulled up an arm chair and placed the muzzle of my Glock against his left knee.

"We know you are the Jamaat ul-Fuqra leader in that jihadist compound back there. Do you want to walk without a cane for the rest of your life? I'm going to ask you some questions and you *will* provide me the right answers."

He merely glared at me. I continued. "Where are you from?"

"I am from Libya."

"Of course you are. What are you doing here in the United States?"

"I am here on a Visa."

"Doing what?"

"I am in what you call the imports and exports."

"Good. Then you won't be too upset when you find *yourself* exported."

"That will not happen. I am protected as a legal alien under your laws. I have rights."

"Gee, what a coincidence. So do we. We have rights as American citizens to not being blown up by assholes like you."

He then sported one of those Elvis-like turned up lips that ended in a snarl.

"What gives you the right to harass someone like me who has the proper papers?"

I placed the muzzle of my Glock against his left temple.

"I believe *this* does. If you're here as you say doing business in our country, why did we find you back there in that jihadist compound?"

He didn't answer. I guess I had him there." Let me answer for you, Maslama. We know you are the camp commander. We've got all the Intel on you...and on al-Massoud."

His eyes widened which told me he was surprised to learn that we knew about The Viper. ""That's right. We know all about him...and your planned rendezvous. We know al-Massoud will soon come to your camp. So, tell me, Maslama, how will he be arriving and exactly what day and time will it be?"

"I do not know this al-Massoud you mention."

I know it might be hard to believe, but I actually wanted to try an open dialogue with him as I don't favor beating the hell out of people for information. But Maslama was a terrorist. An arrogant and defiant one at that. I knew his type, and he wasn't going to readily volunteer any information to save himself from pain...which was definitely coming. So, I then shoved my Glock into my left hand and gave him a quick shot in the Adam's apple with the knuckles of my right. He grabbed his throat and began gagging.

"Wrong answer, Maslama. Save yourself some pain. I might not kill you, but I *will* break every bone in your body to where you'll be on a feeding tube for the rest of your miserable life. Now, what day is al-Massoud planning to go to your camp?"

Maslama coughed and wheezed to get some of his breath back, but still glared at me with a snide, sardonic smile on his face. "Why don't you ask *him*?"

I looked at him with narrowed eyes for a moment and then cracked him across the nose with the butt of the Glock. Blood gushed immediately and splattered onto the seat of his white chair. As blood was also pouring into his mouth through his sinus cavities, he began to gurgle and choke.

"When the nose bones are shattered like this, there's no way they can be repaired. And that looks nasty, Maslama. Michael Jackson might have had better looking noses than you will end up with."

"You ...can beat on me all night and I will tell you nothing. I am not afraid to die."

"And I am not afraid to kill you."

He then coughed and spat out blood that had pooled in his oral cavity...into my face. I wiped away the blood with my handkerchief, then stood and walked around behind him, quickly placing a choke hold on his neck.

"And then there are the bones in the neck. Remember the unfortunate injury to Superman, Christopher Reeve? Now that was a real tragedy. It's been a long time since I snapped anyone's neck. It's an art, you know. Being able to break a man's neck without actually killing him. But I think I remember how. Your choice. Tell us what you know about al-Massoud or spend the rest of your life in a wheelchair sucking on a straw."

Suddenly, out of the corner of my eye I saw Steed raise his pistol in my direction.

"What the hell, Steed!" I exclaimed. The two quick shots he fired were muffled by the suppressor. For a split second, I thought my life had ended. But as I stared at him, frozen in disbelief, wondering why he had fired the rounds within inches of my head, I saw him point behind me. I then turned my head to find the body of a smallish woman lying in a pool of blood on the tiled floor in the hallway. Two holes were in her forehead just above the brow. Her gun was still in her hand. Her body first went through some involuntary death throes and then, momentarily, she was still.

Once my heart restarted, I looked back at Steed and nodded my thanks. Now, I owed *him* one. A *big* one.

I then sat back down and glared at Maslama.

"Who was she?"

The tears then came streaming along with the blood. Still sputtering, he stammered,

"My woman, you b...bastard. You killed her. When you let me go, I...I will kill you both." His cold, deadly eyes bore into me like lasers, unlike his woman's cold, *dead* eyes, which remained fixed on the ceiling.

"B...but we will *not* let you go, Maslama. After we're through with you here, you will never see this house or that compound again."

Eyes still bearing down on mine, he then demanded,

"Get me a towel or...something to stop my bleeding." His voice was garbled and nearly unintelligible.

I looked at Atticus.

"If you would be so kind, Mr. Steed."

Steed by-stepped the woman's body and went to the kitchen. A minute later, he returned with a wet towel and a frozen bag of peas. Maslama applied both to his face and laid his head back against the chair.

"Why?" he said.

"Why what? Why did we shoot your woman? I guess because she was going to shoot *me*."

He then took a deep breath.

"Why do you want to know about al-Massoud?"

The question surprised me. "Mr. al-Massoud seems to be an important figure in the terrorist world," I replied. "And Mr. Steed would like to meet him."

"I do not understand." He choked again just a bit.

"There's nothing that you need to understand. But, because you asked me that question, you just admitted you do know about him. Now I'll ask you one more time...what day is he to arrive at your compound?"

He shook his head, then closed his eyes without responding. For a moment I thought he might have passed out. But then I saw that he was just not going to volunteer anything else.

As Steed was quickly learning, I am not a gentle interrogator when it comes to terrorists. I can be *particularly* vicious, even sadistic as the process wears on. It's one of my shortfalls, I admit. But generally, my methods are successful.

I re-holstered my Glock and walked into the kitchen. After checking behind several of the cabinet doors, I then pulled from a lower shelf a saucepan. When I returned to the living room, I grabbed Maslama by his jacket and flung him to the floor. Then I propped him up against the sofa chair and took from a pouch on my pistol belt a small vial and a syringe. After placing the needle into the vial, I drew in ten CCs of the liquid and jammed it into the left side of his neck. Maslama grimaced and cried out. When he again opened his eyes, he said calmly,

"Truth serum will not work on me. You will see."

Steed continued watching intently but said nothing. I got the impression that hit man or not, he was just a wee bit uncomfortable with what I did.

I let our prisoner lie there against the chair for about fifteen seconds and then said,

"As you're by now coming to realize, this is *not* truth serum. In just a few seconds, Maslama, you won't be able to move. I injected you with Quelicin...suxamethonium chloride to be exact. It induces muscle relaxation and paralysis. In about ten more seconds, you won't be able to move at all. You might be able to blink or utter a word or two, but that's all."

He tried for a moment to get up, but then was alarmed to find out I was telling him the truth. His eyes widened and for the first real time they showed fear.

I then placed his right hand into the saucepan, pulled out my Ranger knife and allowed the blade to sever the veins in his wrist. Blood poured immediately into the pan.

"Uh, partner." *Steed's* eyes showed alarm as well.

"Concern from a man who's done his *own* share of carving? Don't worry, Atticus. Here's the thing. I only gave him a few CCs...not enough to cause either respiratory failure or to kill him, but just enough to temporarily immobilize him. The problem is, will the blood fully drain from his body before the paralysis wears off?" I then turned my head back to Maslama. "And that would be up to you. Can you speak, Maslama?"

At first, the words would not come forth. He then formed as best he could a

"Y...yes."

"Good. Alright, now let's talk about al-Massoud. What day is he to arrive?"

I thought I saw his lips quiver and wasn't sure if he was trying to form words or if hypothermia was already setting in. I looked at the saucepan and then said, That's about a pint, Maslama. In thirty seconds, it'll be a quart. Roll the dice if you want, pal. I'd say you have three minutes. The paralysis will continue for just about ten." I then realized, he *was* trying to say something. I asked him,

"Will you now tell us what we need to know? Blink once for yes."

Slowly he closed his eyes and then reopened them. I guessed that was his best attempt at blinking.

Quickly I pulled my belt from my pants and formed a tourniquet on his bicep, twisting it tightly and holding it until the blood stopped dripping into the pan.

"Mr. Steed, would you be so kind as to retrieve my first aid kit from the back of the Suburban?"

In looking at my compadre, Steed, I thought maybe *his* complexion was nearly as pale as Maslama's. However, he nodded without word and went outside. In a short minute he returned.

"While I continue to hold the tourniquet, take out some gauze and apply pressure to his wrist. Once the bleeding has fully stopped, apply one of those alcohol pads and wrap him up tightly with the gauze bandage."

Steed then pulled Maslama's bloodied hand from the saucepan and did as instructed. I saw that Maslama had already passed out. It would be a while before he came around.

While Steed watched our prisoner, I poured the saucepan of blood down the sink drain and flushed the stainless-steel bowl out with water. On the way back to the living room, I checked on the woman. She was still dead and her body temperature had now begun to cool.

About half past nine Maslama came around. He was still wanly but was now able to move around. Gratified he was neither dead nor paralyzed, he then fixed his venomous eyes back on mine.

"Did you have a nice nap?" I asked him. "And are you ready to talk or would you like another dose of Quelicin?"

"What is it you want to know?" he replied in a raspy voice.

"We'll start over. When is al-Massoud going to be in your camp and how is he getting there?"

For a moment, he turned his head away and I thought I was going to have to get ugly again. He then glared at me and said, "I do not know how he plans to come here."

"Then what day?"

He shook his head.

"I don't know."

"You *do* know, Maslama. There's a reason he's coming and I want to hear the words spitting out of your mouth."

He turned his head away again and clammed up. Now he was *really* testing me.

Once again, I pulled my knife. He saw that his blood was still lining the edge of the blade. His eyes enlarged and I could see his pulse pounding away in the vicinity of his carotid. And that's where I laid the blade. He knew this time there would be no stopping his death.

"*All right*. Al-Massoud is to be here on the 7th of next month." But then to save face he threw in,

"He will watch with much pleasure as our people attack New York and Washington, DC. Many of you infidels will die and many buildings will fall. You will not be able to stop the jihad. It will be unlike anything that has happened to America before."

"What other ul-Fuqra elements are involved?"

"I do not know."

"But there *are* others."

"Yes."

"Do they have bunkers of explosives as well?"

"I do not know," he said again.

I then lightly tapped the knife's blade on his chin and ran it down his neck.

"*I do not know and that is the truth.*"

Satisfied that he probably *was* telling me the truth, I asked,

"How many trucks will leave your bunker."

"Ten, maybe twelve."

"Which means at least twelve targets. Specifically, what *are* the targets?"

He shook his head as he probably thought he had told me enough already. Just enough to save himself from further pain. He was wrong. I then placed my knife back into its sheath, grabbed his left pinky and snapped it. The bone cracked loudly like a stick. I think *Steed* even felt that one. He winced again.

Maslama cried out again in pain.

"All right! All right! In New York, the Empire State Building and Time Square. Many...buildings in Washington, DC."

"What buildings?"

"The...the museums...Smithsonian, the FBI building, and we will place bombs in back packs in the Lincoln and Jefferson Memorials. We will also bring down the Washington Monument, all symbols of American arrogance and evil."

I looked at Steed and his eyes reflected what mine probably did. Fury and rage. I wanted to cut the guy again just to get the ire out of my system. But what he told me I took to be the truth and I needed to keep my end of the bargain.

"See? That wasn't so hard," I said as calmly as I could.

"Now you will let me go?"

"You know that can't happen, Maslama. It wouldn't take you any time to warn al-Massoud. I have plans for you, anyway. But for tonight, we become your guests. Got any good beer in the fridge?"

Maslama scowled and turned his head. Without looking at me, he said,

"What is it you plan to do with me?"

"Give you a nice, scenic helicopter ride tomorrow morning. You will have a new home, but not anything as plush as this. Think tropical."

Steed, who had been watching the show but not said anything to this point, asked, "What do we do with him tonight?"

"We give him a glass of orange juice and a piss break...unless he's already taken one in that chair...and then tie him up. But we'll have to watch him closely."

"You will tie me up? Please do not do that."

"We can't sit here and watch your ass all night long, Maslama. We'll need to get some sleep."

He formed a snide smile.

"You will get *no* sleep. If you do, I will find a way to escape and cut both of your throats."

"Sure you will. By the way, Maslama, we found that munitions bunker of yours. Quite impressive, I should say. Too bad nothing out of it will leave the compound bound for any of the target cities. And neither will any of your people. When our attack force swoops down on it, all the best laid plans of mice and serpents suddenly go awry. We'll finally have the proof we need for the government and the liberal media to see who you really are. Terrorist assholes bent on destroying America. And then *all* the compounds get shut down."

Maslama grinned, revealing his blood-stained teeth. "I will share this fact with you with much glee, infidel. My people are under orders that any infidels who try to capture us will be sent to the fires of Hell. As we are not afraid to die, we will also not be captured. As soon as your men enter our camp one of my people will blow up the bunker. And the shock wave will vaporize anybody within a kilometer in all directions. If you send in a hundred, they all die. If you send in a thousand...well, you get the picture."

"Thanks for the warning, Maslama. If that's supposed to scare us out of taking down your compound of incompetent boobs, think again."

But then I was immediately set to wonder *why* he volunteered that piece of information in the first place, unless he just wanted to convey he was still in control, captive or not. Whether what he told us was true would remain an issue for us to ponder. A kilometer? Perhaps. But doubtful. Since the bulk of the munitions was below ground, the majority of the blast would be propelled upward. However, it would be a hell of huge fireball to behold. But what he told me did register. We might just have to re-assess how and when the task force would go in.

"Mr. Steed, while I watch this piece of shit, see if you can find some rope out in the garage." I then went again to get a closer look at the woman's body in the hallway. She appeared to be about twenty-one or two and probably only weighed a hundred pounds. Although moderately attractive, she was as deadly as a snake. *Was* being the operative word. "And see if there's a blanket or tarp to wrap her body in. We'll put her out in the garage for the night and dispose of her tomorrow morning."

At the very mention of his dead woman, Maslama then again showed his anger and jumped to his feet. "You are murderous bastards and you will pay for her death."

I pushed him back down in the chair.

"Now you sit there until Mr. Steed returns. If you give me any trouble or try to escape, I will shove the barrel of my Glock in your mouth and pull the trigger. And don't think for a moment I *won't*."

Steed left the room and found the door that entered the garage. As soon as he was out of sight, Maslama pushed himself back up to his feet once more.

"I want to go to the bathroom and wash the blood from my face and hand."

"*Sit the hell back down. You're not going anywhere,*" I barked.

He formed a sarcastic smile. "You will not shoot me or you would have done it already." He then weakly balled up his nine good fingers into fists and took a step toward me. And that's when I threw *my* left fist into his right temple, knocking him to the floor. He didn't move after that. I didn't want to keep pounding on him, but until we had him bound and secured, I couldn't risk him getting away. Honest, I really am not a sadist. Just a little rough in my interrogation techniques is all.

Steed returned in less than five minutes with some hemp rope and a huge piece of blue nylon.

"This was covering a vintage Jag XKE sitting out there in the garage." He then saw Maslama taking a nap on the high-dollar afghan rug.

"What happened to *him*?"

"He made a lunge at me and hit my fist with his face. Help me get him up. We'll sit him in the kitchen in a chair and tie him to the bar."

When we had secured him and had wrapped the woman's body in the Jaguar's car cover, I said,

"I need to call Hickcock and tell him what we have so far. I'm hoping he can have his chopper in that clearing by 0900 tomorrow. You will drive Maslama's vehicle when we leave out of here and then dispose of it and the woman in a ravine somewhere. If someone would happen to come *here* looking for him in the next day or so and finds the Mercedes and the body, they'll know for sure somebody got to him. This way, no one will have a clue as to whether he just took off or what."

Steed nodded. "We also need to get rid of that bloody chair and clean up the mess in the hallway."

"You're right. But as the chair won't clean up, we'll just take it with us."

"We can't keep the Jag?" Steed asked.

"Maria would look like a Latina princess sitting up in that gem."

I smiled. "Come payday, you can buy her a *Maserati*."

# CHAPTER 21

Before I called Hickcock, Steed and I split up to search the house and the Mercedes for any documents that might pertain to the tentative attacks on Washington and New York, and that might also contain the name, Asahif al-Massoud, The Viper. From an oak secretary, I did pull out a notebook and some loose material, all written in Arabic hieroglyphics, which I do not read. I would have to zip them off to Hickcock to have them translated.

Steed returned from the car with Maslama's valise that also contained some papers which again were penned in hieroglyphics. However, stapled to several sheets was a photo of a 40-ish medium, brown-skinned man with a salt and pepper beard who looked much like a couple of the photos we had of al-Massoud. I could not, however, find his name on the attached papers. I surmised that Maslama had never met al-Massoud and so the photo was all about recognizing the man when he arrived in the compound on or about the 7th of September.

While we both were rifling through the remainder of the house, Steed and I shook our heads at Maslama's wealth. Not only did we take note of the dozen or so finely-made Armani suits valued at anywhere from $600 to maybe $2000, we whistled at finding more than thirty silk ties and scores of solid gold cufflinks that would adorn at least that many high-dollar monogrammed shirts. In a separate bedroom closet we found the woman's jihab and a couple of burkas, but on the same rod were several expensive, very colorful dresses with hemlines cut about four inches above the knees. Back when I was a smart-ass adolescent, we guys called them jet skirts...four inches below the cockpit. On the floor neatly situated in a row of racks were dozens of westernized shoes, mostly open-toed, containing three inch heels and 'come do me' straps. In nearly every drawer of her door chest we found a treasure trove of frilly Victoria's Secret lingerie. Was there any of this that might in any way conflict with the teachings of the Quran or with Sharia Law? I wondered what the poor brotherhood would think if any of them knew about their leader's lavish, lewd and lascivious lifestyle. Pardon the alliteration.

When we returned to the kitchen and saw that Maslama was still in la-la land, I picked up my cell.

"Hello, John. Did I catch you in bed?"

"At ten thirty? I'm not as old as *some* people I know."

"I wasn't referring to age. While on the subject, how's Maggie?"

"What do you have for me, Bruce?"

"A bit of a snafu, I'm afraid."

"How so?"

"You want the good news first?"

"Shoot."

"We grabbed one of the ul-Fuqra people who is well in the know. With a little friendly persuasion, he confirmed that al-Massoud will be on site in the Goshen compound on the 7th after which a dozen or so trucks will be leaving there for New York and Washington, DC. Time Square, the Empire State Building, the Smithsonian, the Washington Monument and Lincoln Memorial are among the targets. They will lay satchel charges inside the monuments. Appears there will also be combined truck *and* pedestrian bombings. This will be a big deal, so it will be imperative that the bunker is taken before the trucks move the explosives out."

"Of course our task force will be in position to make that happen. As we had hoped, it sounds like your captive is well informed."

"He *should* be."

"How's that?"

"That's the *bad* news. By pure coincidence, we picked up Maslama, the BMOC himself."

"Hmmm. That *does* present a problem. That means if al-Massoud tries to contact him over the next couple of weeks and isn't able to, he might get suspicious and re-think the mission."

"I'm thinking he *won't* put it off. He's got a lot invested in this. These people plan such missions for years. They're very patient. My experience is that once the wheels start turning, they continue on unless there's some very evident threat to their plan. It could be perceived that Maslama made himself inaccessible for a *lot* of reasons. Maybe he just took off for a few days in his Mercedes for a little R&R in advance of the big show. He's high enough up on the food chain where he could get away with that and not have to answer to anyone."

"I don't know, Bruce. His people would certainly question the timing of him taking off...and without telling them in advance."

"Well, as a former boss of mine liked to say, *it is what it is*."

"So, he gave up his brotherhood and al-Massoud. That surprises me. Terrorists are not that easy to give up information."

"It surprised me as well," I said.

"But considering Maslama's lifestyle and how Americanized he had become living his life of luxury, I guess he felt he had a hell of a lot to lose. And he was terrified I was going to kill him, which would not happen with his more heroic and dauntless jihad brothers. Anyone else would have welcomed the opportunity to die for Allah."

"Where is he now?"

"Sleeping. We followed him to his house, where we are now."

"What do you mean *sleeping*?"

"He suddenly went out on me while I was interrogating him."

"What condition is he in?"

"Not bad," I said.

"A few broken bones, some nasty bruises and a little less blood in his arteries."

"I was afraid, considering your sense of humor, when you said *sleeping*, it might be a permanent condition. What's your plan from here?"

"We'll need that chopper first thing in the morning to cart him off. Maybe around 0900?" I told him.

"Tell me where."

"In a field, Rockbridge County. Got your map close by?"

"Yes."

"Coordinates 07123467. I'll pop smoke. I have a canister in my Suburban."

"You've got a *lot* of toys for a civilian."

"Just some stuff left over that I didn't turn back in. Like a..."

"I don't want to know," Hickcock said.

"So, do you have an extra bunk down in Gitmo for Maslama?"

"Always room."

"Who'll know he's there besides us and the people that stow him away?"

"Certainly not lawyers or the ACLU. Maslama just disappears. Nobody knows why. Nobody finds out how."

"What if the media gets wind he's being held without charges?"

"We'll do our damnedest to make sure that doesn't happen. Anyway, once we raid the compound, we hope to gather enough evidence to prosecute everyone involved. That will also open the door for us to close all the other camps without concern of taking heat from our own justice system."

"With the exception of al-Massoud, who escapes prosecution by digesting a well-placed bullet," I added.

"Right."

"One thing, though; I've got something different in mind about that bunker when we take Goshen down. I'd like to work it out in my head if you don't have any problem with it."

"You want to change our plan? In what way?"

"I'll let you know."

Hickcock was quiet for a moment. Then he said,

"All right, but just keep me informed. You're the ground commander and it's your deal. Your protocol."

"I just want to tweak the plan a bit, that's all."

"We'll talk."

"And I'll have your package wrapped and delivered to the Landing Zone (LZ) tomorrow at 0900. Ciao."

Maslama woke to find himself bound and unable to move. He looked pitiful. His eyes were swollen and blackened from the nose shot I gave him. He was now having to partially breathe through his mouth, considering his nasal passages were no longer wide-open breathing tubes. The lower half of his face was still partly covered with dried blood. Finally, his pinky finger was badly distorted and colored purple. Other than that, he looked fine. I checked the bandage on his wrist to see if he had sprung a leak. He hadn't. I expected he eventually would have to visit the toilet, but in doing so, he might think that was an opportunity to rabbit. His eyes, searing and penetrating, stayed fixed to mine.

I then said to Steed, "Tell you what. I'll catch a few winks on Maslama's couch and then you wake me around two. I'll take the latter morning shift."

"I have a better idea, infidel," Maslama interjected.

"*Neither* of you get to sleep." And then he broke into some kind of chant in his native tongue, whatever the hell that was, also apparently wailing proverbs and prayers to Allah. At least that was my guess. After he had carried on for over fifteen minutes, many times shouting. "Allah Akbar!", I then went to the garage and rifled through his metal toolbox drawers until I found what I was looking for.

"Here's an old *American* proverb, Maslama. Silence is golden, but duct tape is silver." I then tore off a large piece of the tape and stuck it on his mouth. "As-salaam alaikum," I added. *Peace be unto you.* He looked surprised that I actually knew a little Arabic. *Very* little.

Maslama then squirmed and fought to loosen himself from the ropes in vain. Now forcing himself to breathe through at least one of those nasal passages, he either began humming his chants without vocals or humming what appeared to be the chorus of Les Misérables. But it was faint enough that it wouldn't bother us. Still, I was surprised his strength had returned so quickly.

When we then moved back into the living room, Steed sat down opposite me and shook his head.

"Damn, Bruce, I don't know about you."

"What don't you know?" I replied.

"Your interrogation techniques. You are indeed one cold and ruthless bastard."

"And what was your first clue?"

He forced a smile.

"That deal with the injection and blood-letting made even *me* a bit queasy. Just remind me never to piss you off."

I then firmly fixed my eyes onto his.

"Don't like my methods, Atticus?  My tactics too callous and brutal for your taste? I guess it doesn't matter that Maslama verified everything we suspected. What you need to understand is...*I get results*. And because I *am* to a degree admittedly ruthless, thousands of innocent lives will be saved. Even so, I take it you don't find favor in how I do business."

He stared at me a while with a smirk on his face, perhaps thinking of an appropriate retort.

"I'm just wondering where the hell you got that vial of Quelicin? Left over from your cold war spy days?"

"One can get it from any hospital lab or veterinarian."

"Which of course is not intended to be utilized for interrogation."

"And where did you get the cyanide capsule that killed the woman in San Francisco? Left over from your CIA days? I read your file, remember?"

It was one of those *touché* moments.

"I've been wondering, McGowan, why weren't you just a one man show on this mission? I have no doubt you could nail this al-Massoud with that sniper rifle of yours just as easily as me. So why *me*?"

"We talked about this before. Hickcock and his sidekick know what a crack shot you are, first hand. And, I know they feel you did the Justice Department *and* them a huge service. You also didn't kill them when you were hired to do so, which says a lot about your integrity. I think they believe in a way that they owe you; and so, they're giving you this one opportunity...to make your past go away."

He sat for a moment, head down and looking at his hands.

"The word you mentioned...opportunity. Yeah, it *is* my opportunity and I'll be *taking* it. But then, after that, after I kill this Viper, I lay the gun down forever." He nodded in self-reassurance, looked up at me and smiled."I do make a pretty damn good bartender, you know."

There was a little small talk between us for a while. But then instead of sacking out, Steed took the time we had in waiting for the dawn to do a little self-disclosing. For some reason, he began telling me stories that he had told no one else...especially Maria. He freely talked about his days with the mob and the hits he was compelled to perform as a young man. He didn't actually get graphic on me or tell me how many kills he had made, but I could see how remorseful he was about them. He hated the handle the mob had put on him...Billy the Kid. However, it was apparent from what he was telling me that Billy Joe Cavanaugh had ceased to exist long ago.

Steed was also contrite about the hits he did illegally and under coercion for the Justice Department kingpins. Although he had little doubt as to the guilt of his victims, he still knew in his heart that killing them was the wrong way to address the problem, regardless of what he had told me on my front porch. But even though the justice system, as he experienced it, had become corrupt and depraved, he still wanted to believe in it. And it took his association with two of its finest, namely Hickcock and Larsen, for him to begin seeing things a little differently.

I got to know and appreciate Atticus Steed a little more that night, even though I still realized that I was collaborating with a cold-blooded killer. But sometimes, if we try hard enough, people like us can turn our heads the other way...especially when we hold the mirror up to our own faces. And especially when we are associating and combining our skills on a mission that will keep Americans from being harmed.

It was nearly two o'clock and Steed and I were still talking like a couple of thirteen year old girls at a pajama party. I did go back to check on Maslama one more time and found him asleep. I needed to determine if he was truly asleep and not dead, considering he could have suffocated from his badly swollen membranes; but his neck was warm and its carotid area was still throbbing.

Steed then reminded me I hadn't taken the opportunity to grab some sack time; but if I did now, *he* wouldn't get any sleep. But as obviously he wasn't *intending* to sleep, I supposed I wouldn't either. As he flipped through the channels with the remote while watching our host's big screen TV, the capitalist hypocrite that Maslama was, Steed settled on an old World War II movie, *The Sands of Iwo Jima*, the ultimate John Wayne Marine flick. As Steed was a Marine sniper, of course, and I was Special Forces, we bantered back and forth competitively about the better of the two groups. He *had* me when it came down to who generally goes into the combat zone first, but I think I scored the most points where it came to *my* group's special skills and abilities. But as we had reduced ourselves to a couple of childish braggarts, touting our branches of service, I figured that it was because it was now four in the morning and having had no sleep, we both were wasted, mentally and physically. And we still had four hours before we needed to gear up and leave for the LZ.

Steed was good with just watching more TV. I would not have thought it, but he was a Trekkie, a Star Trek fanatic of the first degree. And from four o'clock until mid-day, there was scheduled a series of syndicated episodes airing, one after the other. I could see there would be no more conversation well into the morning hours as we waited for dawn.

When I finally picked up my bones and dragged myself to the hall bath to empty my bladder at six forty-five, I noticed that Maslama was awake with eyes that said he still wanted to kill me. Fine. It was mutual. I still wanted to kill *him*. Seeing that he had not pissed himself during the night and knowing that his bladder had to be on the verge of exploding, I then asked him if he wanted to hit the toilet. He nodded.

That is when I inflicted just a little more pain on him by yanking the duct tape off his mouth that brought with it some hair from his beard. I then had Steed hold his gun on Maslama while I untied the ropes that were attached to the bar and helped him to his feet. I did, however, leave his hands and ankles tied together. Able to take small steps from the kitchen to the bathroom, it took him nearly a full minute to get there. I had already checked the medicine cabinet and beneath the sink for anything sharp that he could put his hands on. At that point the only thing he wanted to put his hands on was his manliness...and of course me. After he had completed his lengthy piss, he baby-stepped back out and stood in the hallway.

"Then you are still taking me away from my home," he said.

"Yes."

He turned his head away and scowled. "Will you keep me tied up here until we leave?"

"If you behave, I'll set you back in the living room. I'll untie your ankles, but not your wrists. Do you want a piece of toast or some water?"

"What I want is for you to release me. If my brothers do not see that I am with them this morning, they will come here looking for me."

"Somehow I don't think so, Maslama. You're the big cheese in that camp. I'm sure you pretty much go and do as you please. Maybe they'll look for you in a day or so. But maybe they'll think you've just tired of them and took off for the Bahamas."

I then escorted Maslama to the living room and sat him down in the same chair that was saturated with his blood. Steed took the chair opposite him, placed his gun in his lap and stared at him.

"Nice TV," he said.

"Do you invite your poor Muslim brothers over for parties so that they can enjoy all your American capitalist luxuries?"

He didn't answer.

I asked him, "What are you really about, Maslama? You don't dress like your brothers...like Bedouin tribesmen. And you don't appear to be the devout, praying kind of Muslim. When we searched your house, your Mercedes and the clothes you're wearing, we found no prayer beads. You know what I think? You're nothing but a capitalist opportunist...the same as any rich American. You're the same kind of person you terrorists claim to have disdain for. You're all about money and self-gain." I then placed my face within inches of his. "How much do you stand to make from this despicable plan to kill Americans? And who is it that will put the money in your pocket?"

He turned his face away from mine and for a while allowed his eyes to fall on several pieces of his terribly expensive artwork, all of which would go away in a matter of hours. He then returned his eyes to mine and said, "Just so that when I am able to break free from wherever you take me and I am able to come hunt you down, infidel, what is your name?"

"You're planning to escape?" I laughed. "That will never happen where you're going. But let me give you a name that will haunt you the many days that you're in that six-by-six cell. It's Chuck Norris."

Steed allowed a smile to break out and turned his head.

Maslama then replied, "I will then one day kill you, Chuck Norris...and you as well, Mr. Steed."

Steed then looked up at me. "Does that make you very afraid, Mr. Norris?"

"I'm shaking in my boots, Mr. Steed."

# CHAPTER 22

At 0750 I pulled out my Glock and stood by as Steed cut Maslama's ropes. He then snapped a set of my handcuffs onto our prisoner's wrists and set him into the front passenger seat of the Suburban. Finally, I placed a piece of rope around Maslama's neck and tied it to the headrest tight enough to keep him pinned against the seat just in case he had any ideas of wrecking me on the way to the Landing Zone (LZ). I made sure there were no weapons or anything sharp in the glove compartment that he could reach.

Once he was secured, I hit the garage door opener in the Mercedes and then both Steed and I went inside to remove the small body of my would-be assassin. After we carried her carcass out, we then placed it in the rear compartment of the Mercedes. Seeing us with our wrapped bodies brought tears to Maslama's eyes and he sobbed bitterly. In a way, I felt sorry for him. For maybe three seconds.

Lastly, I went inside and made sure there was no more of either Maslama's or his lady's blood on the floor, tossed the rope fragments in the trash, and then carted the white chair out the front door to the Mercedes. It joined the body of the woman in the cargo area. After locking the front door of the house and bringing down the garage door, we were ready to shove off.

"Just follow me to the clearing, and after we send Mr. Maslama up, up and away, we'll dispose of the Mercedes in a reservoir I think I have located." I then spread Agent Hickcock's map out on the hood of my SUV and pointed to a depression in a grid square southeast of the Town of Goshen.

"We'll check this one out, and if it doesn't suit our purpose, we'll look elsewhere."

"What if one of Maslama's followers recognizes his Mercedes on the road and sees that someone else is driving it?" Steed asked.

"It's a chance we'll have to take. Whoever follows or tries to stop you, joins the woman in the back of the Mercedes. Simple as that."

Within thirty minutes we were parked in the clearing about a half hour early. I assumed that no one spotted the Mercedes because we found no one on our tail. Steed parked the vehicle at the edge of a tree line and then slid into the back seat of my Suburban.

Maslama hadn't said a word to me all the way to the LZ. And then for more than five minutes after Steed had gotten in, neither of *us* conversed as well. Finally, it was Maslama who broke the silence.

"I can make you both very rich. More money than you have ever seen in your lives."

I glanced over at him and replied,

"How much are you talking about?"

"A million dollars...maybe two."

I then looked back at Steed.

"Two million. That's a hell of a lot more than we're getting paid on this job. What do you think, Mr. Steed?"

"Tempting," he said.

"I assume that we would let you go, Maslama, and you would send us a check for the money."

"I do not think you are fools, but neither am I a fool. I can take you from here to two million dollars in cash."

"Where?" I asked.

"To our camp."

I laughed.

"I thought you didn't think of us as fools, Maslama. Let's see now. We drive through the gate past your guards and then you take us to one of the buildings where there's probably a safe. You tell your people we're your new friends who are thinking about joining the Jamaat ul-Fuqra. You tell them to open the safe and give each of us two million...and then we let you all go out and blow up America."

"You make light of my offer, which is something I do not appreciate."

"I'll tell you what *we* don't appreciate, Maslama. All you terrorist sons-of-bitches coming into this country, recruiting America's riff-raff and planning jihads that will destroy our people, our properties and our way of life. If you bastards want to blow yourselves up, do it in your own dammed countries and leave the United States alone. Get this straight, asshole, no amount of money you could ever put out there would convince Mr. Steed or me to betray our country and help you kill our people." I then pulled out my Glock and placed it against his left temple.

"I should just go ahead and shoot your ass where you sit."

Maslama closed his eyes tightly. I believe he actually thought I'd pull the trigger. And maybe I *wanted* to. But then, off in the distance, I heard the wop-wop of the chopper's blades. It was 0900 on the money.

In no time at all, it swept on top of us after coming in nap-of-earth. The aviator then circled the landing zone once, likely to assure there were no obstacles, power lines or civilian observers and that we were friendlies, and then headed back out to the north over the trees. I then jumped out, ran to the four o'clock of the LZ and popped the canister of smoke.

The wind was with us as the smoke was drifting away from the ul-Fuqra compound which again was nearly a klick to the south. Since the camp was in a valley at the base of the mountain range, no one should be able to see the smoke *or* the chopper.

The UH-1N, an older tactical bird, then appeared again on the horizon and began banking where I could see that the side door was open and a SWAT agent was positioned inside with a very visible MPS/10 machine gun. As I did not have any way of establishing radio contact to this point, my cellphone began to vibrate. Plugging the ear bud in, I answered,

"This is McGowan."

"McGowan, this is Special Agent Collins. I see yellow smoke."

"Affirmative, Collins. You're good to come in."

"Excellent. Will you bring us in?"

"Wilco. I'm the signalman standing on the east perimeter."

"Roger. I see you. Out."

Standing with my arms spread in a Y, something I had done a hundred times in Vietnam as well as when I was with the Bureau, I guided the chopper in. Then when I dropped my arms to a spread eagle, the bird descended to about ten feet off the turf. Finally, I brought my arms further down into an inverted Y and the skids touched ground.

As the tornado-like wind generated by the blades kicked up dust, scattering the smoke, my eyes were suddenly stinging to a point where I could barely see. An agent in black then stepped off the chopper along with the door gunner and began running at a crouch toward me. I signaled to Steed to bring up Maslama. In the meantime, two more figures dismounted from the bird...one with a medium build and the other much smaller.

By the time the men in black got to me, Steed had our prisoner ready to hand over. The man with the machine gun then approached me.

"I'm Collins, McGowan." We shook hands. We had to yell so that we could hear one another over the chopper's deafening roar and whipping blades.

I shouted,

"This is Tahir Maslama, late of the Goshen ul-Fuqra camp! I understand you have a place for him!"

"Roger that! You interrogated him I see! Either that or he had a clumsy fall! We will be squeezing him for more!"

"Watch out for him! He offers big money to let him go!" I yelled.

Collins laughed.

"Big, huh? Maybe I'll listen! By the way, I'm leaving these two agents with you!"

"What?!"

"See you in a few days, McGowan! We'll talk!" He then grabbed Maslama by the arm and steered him toward the chopper.

Maslama looked back at me and started yelling. Unfortunately, since the noise drowned out his voice, all I could hear was the F word. Considering how nice I was to him by allowing him to live, my feelings were hurt. They then passed the two agents walking toward me and more words were exchanged. Once aboard, the chopper quickly became airborne.

After the dust had cleared, I was finally able to make out the agents' faces. Hickcock and Larsen had come to pay us a visit.

"Hello, Bruce...Mr. Steed," Hickcock greeted. "

You having a good day?"

"Well I'll be damned," I said.

"I didn't expect you two."

"We just thought we'd get a first-hand look of the area," said Larsen.

"I'm glad you did. First, though, we need to dump some things."

"Maslama's vehicle?" asked Hickcock.

"And the body inside it."

"What?"

"Maslama's girl friend, or maybe his wife, was waiting for us at his house. She wanted to give me lead poisoning, but Steed here put two holes in her head. By the way, Atticus, I forgot to thank you."

"Don't mention it. All in a night's work."

"What was her name," Larsen asked.

"Mrs. Maslama, I guess. She didn't have any ID on her, but I really don't give a rat's ass *who* she was."

We then reached the vehicles. "John, Maggie, you ride with me and Mr. Steed will follow in the Mercedes. I'll be looking for some place to drop a few thousand pounds."

I was just getting ready to pull out when I saw on the nine o'clock edge of the clearing a large human form standing just outside of the tree line. I then stuck my head out of the driver's side door to get a better look. Huggins. When he saw my eyes on him, he threw up his hand. I groaned.

"Who is that?" Larsen asked.

I shook my head slowly.

"Never mind," I replied.

After we drove down the firebreak that intercepted with Highway 42, we turned right on the road and I proceeded slowly toward the entrance to the compound. When we were within 500 feet, I alerted them to watch for the road that led into the camp.

"There...on the left. See the chain? Now look further back and onto each side of the dirt road."

"I see them," said Hickcock. "And their AK's."

"The compound sits just over that rise and in a valley at the base of one of the Allegheny humps. We have a good point of observation that looks down on the central part of the camp from six to eight hundred yards away. That's where Mr. Steed will make his shot."

"From 800 yards away? Are you kidding me?" said Hickcock.

"He says his range is actually farther away than that, John," I said.

"I thought you knew that. You supposedly know *everything* about him."

"I know he made the shots that saved our necks from 250 yards. But 800?"

"Parts of that compound are even up to 1000 yards from the Observation Point. The distance depends on where the Viper exits his mode of transportation. We'll see come time for the big show."

We then came to the intersection I had plotted on the map. I turned left on Route 15 and traveled approximately three-quarters of a mile until I saw a well-weathered sign that read 'Quarry." Ergo, the depression on the map. After turning left onto the rugged gravel and dirt road, we traveled another mile until the cavernous pit came into view. It was a good find. The quarry appeared not to have been worked in years. It had to be a mile long and just as wide. To our right, a road began that snaked a half-mile down into the abyss. A part of it was filled with water about the size of a small pond. Kids sometimes went swimming in these abandoned quarries, but not this one. The water, green and slimy, was good for only one thing...the final resting place for one G Class Mercedes and one dead female hostile.

Steed drove the SUV to within two feet of the edge, placed it in neutral and then exited the vehicle to join Hickcock and me at the rear bumper. Without much effort, we pushed and set the Mercedes in motion.

It was like watching something out of the movies. At first, the vehicle flew off the cliff, gracefully through the air, seemingly in slow motion, until it struck the side of the quarry, tumbled and bounced and then did a bellyflop into the gunk. It took some time to sink, but after a couple of minutes, it finally succumbed to the deep water and drowned. It was a beautiful thing to see.

"A hundred forty thousand dollars...down the drain," Steed lamented.

I slapped him on the shoulder and said,

"Don't worry about it, Steed. You can have one of your own soon." I then turned to Hickcock and winked. "Right, John?"

"Whatever," the agent replied.

Tooling back to my place, Maggie rode shotgun with me while Steed and Hickcock took the back seat. They just climbed in that way. I wondered if John and Maggie were fighting for some reason. Maybe it was because I had been giving Hickcock so much grief about their sleeping together, they wanted to henceforth display a bit more discretion. Too late, kids.

"Have you and Maggie come to stay with us, John?"

"We're not staying over, Bruce. Maybe some other time. I arranged for the chopper to retrieve us at Greenbrier Valley at 1700 this afternoon. Anything more for us since we talked last night?"

"No. I think we got what we needed out of Maslama."

"From the looks of him, he wasn't all that cooperative," Larsen commented.

"A little blood was lost in interrogation. But, in retrospect, I should have saved a pint or two for the American Red Cross."

In my rear view mirror I caught Steed rolling his eyes and shaking his head.

I continued.

"I guess in ten days or so we can expect al-Massoud to enter the country to go on tour," I remarked.

"I'm still concerned about the TSA identifying him at one of the airports and allowing him to go through. If for some reason he doesn't come here, then we've let an international terrorist slip through our clutches. You're turning a killer out into the streets, who if he is successful, will cause the death of thousands."

Hickcock shook his head.

"You know what Johns wants to happen. Again, the Viper is not on the capture list; he's on the *kill* list. Killing him where we find all of the munitions and explosives makes a statement and solidifies our position that ul-Fuqra is tied to al-Qaeda and terrorism. Goshen is obviously the storehouse of the instruments of destruction that will cripple this country. When al-Massoud's dead body is confirmed in that camp, there's no court, no batch of lawyers and no panel that will be able to dispute our reason for going in there...and ultimately into other compounds."

"What keeps them from speculating you just didn't fabricate all that and plant evidence...even plant his body there?" I asked.

"I guess we can tell you this, gentlemen. Collins, the task force commander, is bringing with him a freelance combat photographer. As this is a classified mission, the journalist will not know about the mission until the day before the takedown; so there should be no way anything will leak out in advance. By the way, this photographer is ex-CIA , but because he's been involved in other missions, military and Bureau, he enjoys a top secret clearance. He will *not* photograph either one of you."

"I'm good with that and I'm pretty sure the man sitting next to you is as well."

I saw Steed nod 'yes.'

Hickcock then continued.

"Johns wants this to be a metaphorical double tap...kill the Viper and take down the conspirators before they leave the compound. Then we'll have the green light to invade the 35 other camps."

"All right," I said.

"You folks are running the show".  I then turned to Larsen.

"We haven't heard much from you, Maggie. Seems like these times we've met, you've been fairly quiet."

"Just a woman along for the ride in a vehicle filled with patriarchy and testosterone," she replied.

In my rearview mirror, I spied Hickcock with a snide look on his face. Maybe the lovers *were* fighting.

"Do you feel all of us guys are hogging the game?" I asked.

"I've seen Maggie in action, Bruce," Steed remarked.

"She can hold her own."

"Don't try to patronize me, Mr. Steed," she snapped.

Sounded like from where I was sitting Maggie wasn't good with *either* of the back seat passengers. I hope she still loved *me*.

"Let's not get into a tete-a-tete, people," Hickcock said. "We don't need any egos and attitudes to sabotage what we're doing here."

I then thought it best to change the atmosphere in the Suburban by changing the subject.

"Anyway, since you're spending much of the day with us, I'll call ahead and ask my wife to whip up a nice lunch at our place."

"We can get something on the way in, Bruce," Hickcock said. "No need to bother her."

"I think that sounds nice, Bruce," Maggie overruled. "We'll take you up on it. I only saw Wolf Laurel from the outside, anyway. Are you sure she won't mind?"

"She'll enjoy doing it, if she doesn't have other plans. If she does, then you feds can treat us to lunch at the Greenbrier."

"And how would I be able to explain a $300 lunch on my expense account?" Hickcock said. "No thanks. I guess it's your place or McDonald's."

*****

Day after day, when we had guests, sometimes even seven days any particular week, Adriana prepared nothing but breakfast. Usually, it was sweet rolls or blueberry muffins with fruit, or maybe poached eggs on English muffins, or perhaps her special oatmeal with brown sugar, raisins and nuts. Lunch was always a nice change for her. So, when I called her to ask about lunch, she said she was absolutely excited about preparing us something good. Or words to that effect.

I actually expected that she would just make up a Cobb salad with some ham or turkey, but instead, she sautéed some shrimp and placed it over some pasta with a special sauce containing garlic butter. But, she still couldn't pass up making a side salad to complement the dish.

Adriana liked the agents, especially John Hickcock, who she thought was rather handsome in a roguish sort of way...like yours truly, she added...twenty years ago. She and Maria both also thought Maggie came across as sweet and shy, much to my surprise. As Maggie was of course on her best behavior, she obviously had my usually perceptive bride well-fooled. But, I'm sure Maggie could be sweet whenever it suited her.

During lunch, almost everybody had something to say about their families, places they'd been and even favorite foods and wine...mostly meaningless small talk. Then, just after two when lunch was over, there were compliments all around to Adriana for her splendid meal. And it damn sure beat the Big Mac that Hickcock was prepared to buy, the cheapskate.

As it was still a couple of hours before the agents' flight out, they wanted to capitalize on the time left to carve out final details of what Hickcock continued to refer to as Operation Firestorm. So, I set them and Steed up down the hall in an unoccupied guest room with four chairs and a pot of coffee.

Hickcock then kicked the conversation off.

"Okay, Bruce, you said you might have a little different idea of how you envision the mission going down. What do you have in mind?"

"All right. We got some information out of Maslama that when our task force stormed the compound, one of the hostiles would wait until they were fully inside and then blow that munitions bunker."

"*That's* not good," Hickcock commented.

I continued. "But, let's start at the beginning. We will anticipate al-Massoud enters the camp sometime during the morning as expected. We have a good vantage point where we can see all vehicles after they have gone about a third of the way in. The road then splits. The left fork runs down between several buildings and the right goes behind the buildings under a canopy of trees that leads to the large door at the rear of the bunker. The larger building off the left road which sits up on higher ground apparently does double duty as a mosque and meeting place where you believe al-Massoud will hold some kind of summit the day he arrives with two or three other ul-Fuqra leaders. He will of course be surprised when Tahir Maslama is not there. He *could* find that out days before he gets there. But, I digress. The vehicle rolls in and likely will come to a stop somewhere near the meeting hall. That would make it between 600 and 800 yards from our position. As soon as the Viper exits the vehicle that brings him in, he goes down."

Steed added, "I have zeroed in on every part of that compound and with the exception of the back end of that bunker, I can hit him anywhere. Bruce is right. It's best to hit him as soon as he shows himself versus allowing him to mingle in with several people or move quickly into one of the buildings. Of course, if I'm not able to nail him right away, sometime during the day it's probable that the camp might put on a show of their combative skills and training for him. He'll be standing somewhere and watching. We might just have to be patient in taking that shot."

"Okay, McGowan, fine" Larsen began. "We've gone over this before, but what is it that's different you're bringing to the equation?"

"Initially, we had Mr. Steed perched up there on the high ground by himself, ready to take out the Viper. I would be in the staging area with the attack element. Once the shot is made, I am supposed to bring Collins and his Red Team in. They raid the camp and likely engage in some semblance of a firefight. Collins could lose a few of his men. But what is *more* concerning to me is that one of the hostiles would, in fact, blow that bunker when the action begins. And because Collins' men and I will be sweeping the compound, quite a few of us could be blown sky high. Maybe everyone."

"We expected there might be casualties," Hickcock said.

"But there needn't be. I got into that bunker before and can do it again. The night of the 6th, I go in and line it with charges. Of course it all depends on whether you *want* the bunker blown. If you want to show the world on film what kinds of storehouses these camps will have, that's up to you. Is that what you want?"

Hickcock and Larsen looked at one another and shrugged. He said,

"When we talked with Johns about this, I think he anticipated that the bunker would be salvaged. The liberal organizations that have been pounding the Bureau on its supposed harassment of these ul-Fuqra camps *do* need to see official film of all the munitions stored in that bunker. Maybe Maslama was lying to puff himself up. There's no guarantee one of his people *has* been slated to blow that bunker when our team comes in."

"There's no guarantee as to the contrary either. I'd rather we not take the chance of getting the good guys hurt. If that bunker does go up, it'll make a hole in the ground the size of that quarry we dumped the Mercedes in. I'll blow that bunker *before* the troops move in and any casualties will then be the bad guys. And I already took a copious amount of pictures that you can show the world."

"So, what you're saying is, you'll remain in the camp with Steed and not enter in with Collins."

"As soon as Steed makes the kill, I'll blow the hell out of that compound by remote detonation. Then while it's still raining eyeballs and gonads, Collins and team sweeps in and polishes off or captures any survivors."

"But blowing that bunker could kill 75 or 100 ul-Fuqra members," Larsen remarked.

"And your point?" I replied.

"I'd think we would want as many people left alive as possible that we could crack under interrogation," she added.

"They'll likely be scattering after Steed makes the shot. Not everybody dies when that camp goes up. And anyway, once al-Massoud is dead and the camp is compromised, what else would we get out of them that would be worthwhile?"

She shrugged. I think both of the agents were getting my point.

"What if there are chemical weapons among the munitions?" Maggie asked.

"Again, I didn't see any, but just in case, I'd be sure that Collins' Red Team is equipped with protective masks. Steed and I will need them as well. The camp will also need to be cordoned off so that civilians aren't in proximity. Suggest the local police, fire department and paramedics are notified around 0800 on the 7th to stand by. But make sure they do not set up anywhere in sight within five miles of the compound or al-Massoud will just drive on by."

"All right," Hickcock said. "We'll chew on all of this. I think Johns will actually agree with your plan. I didn't anticipate that the hostiles might blow their bunker when the attack ensues. Johns would rather explain the deaths of people who want to kill Americans than the unnecessary deaths of our agents. I guess that's why he picked you for the job, Bruce. You've got a good, strategic nose for these things."

Larsen leaned back in her chair and folded her arms. "Okay, I admit it might make sense, Bruce, but what if you get caught this time when you go in. Somebody sees you, yells out and the whole camp is down on you and Steed."

"I won't get caught, Maggie. I appreciate what you're thinking. I'm not saying it's impossible, but I believe that Steed and I are a good bit more skilled in what we do than any one of the sentries. We'll get in and do this thing without any glitches."

No one said anything for a few moments. The agents were either darting their eyes around the room or had them closed in contemplation, replaying the scenario in their minds over and over.

Hickcock then reached over and shook my hand. "Like I said before, Bruce, it's your deal...your protocol. We have complete confidence in the both of you. What do you need from the Bureau if you do it this way?"

"I'm going to need either some Semtex or C4...I'm thinking six blocks. Also, a dozen or so blasting caps and a remote detonation pack."

"I'll make sure Collins has what you need, including any additional ammo."

"I have all the ammo we need," I said.

"I'll bet you *do*. You probably have enough guns and ammo to supply a small army." Hickcock then held up his hand like a traffic cop.

"*But*...I don't want to know. By the way, Mike Collins is ex-Special Forces like you. You two ought to hit it off very well."

"Hooah," I grunted.

We continued to iron out some of the more intricate details for the better part of the afternoon and then rejoined Adriana and Maria for another half hour or so out on the veranda. At four-fifteen Hickcock received a call from the aviator that had just landed at Greenbrier Valley Airport. At four-thirty, I drove the agents to the airport, watched their Blackhawk take off into the wild blue yonder bound for Andrews, and then returned to Wolf Laurel for a much-needed shower.

Barring any unforeseen complications, we were good to go. In two weeks, the Sand Viper would die...and it would be the beginning of the end for Jamaat ul-Fuqra in America.

# CHAPTER 23

On the 26th, sometime around eight in the evening as I sat in my over-stuffed leather recliner, The Big Easy, there was a rap on our door. I opened it to find Steed standing there with a solemn look on his face.

"Bad news, Bruce. Maria's brother called. Their sister passed away this afternoon. The breast cancer was too far advanced and her body gave up on her. Maria...er, *we* will be flying out to Dallas first thing tomorrow morning."

"We?"

"Yes."

"I'm very sorry for Maria, Atticus, but, *you* leaving is not an option."

"Staying here while she faces this crisis by herself is not an option for *me*, Bruce. This is the woman I'm going to marry and she needs me with her."

"Don't get me wrong; I'm sympathetic here, Atticus, but we have only a week until our Intel says al-Massoud is landing here in the U.S. And we might just find that his timeline is actually different. He could go directly to the Goshen compound. We both have to be ready for any change of plans from here on."

"I hear you, but I'm going with her, Bruce. Look, I'll be there only a few days and I can't imagine not being back by the 1st of September."

I leaned against the doorway, looked away for a few moments and then blew out a puff of air. "I guess I can't stop you. If the shoe were on *my* foot, I'd have a hell of a decision to make. All right...go. But you have to be in touch with me every day."

He nodded.

"Our flight leaves the Greenbrier Airport for Charleston at 10:50 and then we fly to Cincinnati. From there to Dallas tomorrow evening." He sighed.

"It'll be a long day in the air with a very sad woman."

"I'll take you all to the airport in the morning. Tell Maria that Adriana will be down to talk with her."

"Thanks for understanding," he said.

"Yeah." I shook his hand and he walked back downstairs.

Shortly after I told Adriana about Maria's sister, she went down to the their room and spent a few moments consoling her. While she was gone, I got Hickcock on his cell and told him that Steed was leaving for a few days.

"What? Bruce, I hate it about Maria's sister, but you cannot let him go."

"Has anything changed since yesterday?"

"No."

"Would his presence here have made any difference over the next week?"

"Probably not."

"Then what's your concern, John?"

"That he'll not return on his own."

"He'll be back, I assure you, and well in time to carry out his part of the bargain. He's not going to miss the opportunity for that pardon."

"I hope you're right, Bruce. Maggie and I learned a few things about him last year, you know. He's a hard case and used to calling his own shots. Excuse the unintentional pun. So, the question is, can we depend on him to be dependable?"

"At first, I wasn't sure, John. But in the past few days, I've seen a growing commitment in his eyes. This deal has given him another chance at life, even though he's planning to do the same thing he's done for years. But this kill rids the world of a dangerous icon in the the terrorist arena and Steed is once again contributing to a mission that will save a lot of people's lives...like he did as a Marine sniper. No, he *will* be back."

"Okay, Bruce. I have complete confidence in what you tell me. Like always. We'll talk in the next couple of days."

On the way to our small airport, Maria was still experiencing such grief that she was barely able to communicate with Adriana and me. I think what fueled her grief even more was the guilt she was hanging on herself about not spending time with her ailing sister. Her father had also begged her to be there while her sister was apparently spiraling. Instead, Maria had chosen to follow Atticus and try to mend their broken relationship. And then her mother had been all over her about the lifestyle she had chosen the past couple of years in traveling with a man to whom she was not married. Now, emotionally crippled with all the guilt, regrets, self-blame and immense sorrow, she did need the man she loved to be with her.

*****

For five days in a row, Steed called religiously on or about nine in the evening, EDT. He reported that Maria was fairing well, but her father and mother were not. They were distant with her, especially after the funeral, which added to Maria's anguish. Steed said he was glad that he had gone with her for support.

On the 31st, he called and asked,

"Is anything happening I need to know about?"

"Nothing much from Hickcock. Al-Massoud has not been spotted on the move anywhere. No recent Intel from Interpol or other resources. The informant knows nothing as well. Speculation is that the Viper may already *be* in the U.S.; however, nothing but negative reports from airport security throughout the country."

"Okay, I'll be wrapping things up here tonight and leaving out on the first Delta flight tomorrow for Cincinnati. My flight from Charleston is supposed to land in Greenbrier Valley at 8:25 tomorrow night. Maria won't be with me. She felt she needed to stay with her parents and help them with her sister's affairs. Sad deal here, Bruce."

"Sorry about that. Hopefully, time will help Maria and her parents reconcile their differences. Anyway, I'll be at the airport to pick you up. See you tomorrow."

Flight 1542 from Charleston arrived on time and I saw eighteen people come through the door. Steed was not among them. I then checked with the agent on duty at the counter to see if Steed was listed as a passenger. He was not on the manifest. I called his cell, but only got his voice mail.

"Steed, I'm at the airport and you're not. Where are you?"

I fully expected him to return my call right away to explain why he hadn't materialized; but even after an hour, nothing. I called again and had to leave another message. "Steed, call me ASAP."

Back at home, I continued to wait for his call. At ten after eleven, I broke down and called Hickcock's cell. It was

Larsen who answered, however. It was not the time for me to make jokes about their little arrangement.

"Maggie. Got a problem."

"Is the problem *Steed*?"

"Yes. I went to the airport to get him and he wasn't on the flight. Now I can't raise him on his cell."

"Exactly what we were afraid of, Bruce. We let him out of our sight and he disappears."

"There has to be an explanation, Maggie. He has a lot at stake in this game...mainly his freedom."

"It appears he got himself free on his own."

"It doesn't make sense. Why would he take off when he would have been given a full pardon?" I asked.

"*You* tell *me*, Bruce. The bottom line is, he didn't make it back and he hasn't called you."

"Okay. If I don't hear from him in the next twelve hours, I'll call you or Hickcock and we'll reassess our situation."

"Fine. Talk tomorrow, then."

"By the way, where's Hickcock?

"He's...asleep."

"Was it you who made him that way?"

I couldn't resist, after all.

There was a brief pause.

"If you're trying to embarrass me..."

"Just having a little fun with you, Maggie, that's all. Sorry."

"Tomorrow, McGowan."

It was ten in the morning on the 1st. Still nothing from Steed. I made yet another attempt to reach him to no avail. I was now feeling pretty damn sheepish about letting him go. However, he was going to leave with Maria anyway and if I had tried to stop him, I'd have had to hog-tie him and then we would've lost him on the mission. Either that or he would've turned on me and there might have been a face-off. We definitely didn't need that.

I called Hickcock's number again. This time *he* answered. When I conveyed that I hadn't heard anything, he was livid.

"I'll give it another day, Bruce, and if we don't hear from him, you, Maggie and I are going to talk about a *new* plan. Johns won't be happy to say the least."

"Does he know about Steed?"

"Not yet, but I'll call him tomorrow about the situation. We will then be five days out. *Four* days until you and the Red Team will set up. That cuts it close."

It was now midday on the 2nd. By then I had already had two more conversations with Hickcock...and none with Steed. In my third conversation that day, I could tell John Hickcock was out of patience.

"I can still work this out, John."

"One man show?"

"I've been a one man show more than once."

"And some day I'd like to hear about it."

"You won't."

"I guess I need to dispatch a couple of Dallas agents to pick Steed up. Did you get Maria's last name? I don't think Maggie *or* I ever heard it."

"It's Cortez. You know there'll be hundreds of Cortez's in the Dallas area. But suggest you just check the obituary from a week ago. Steed told me Maria's sister's name was Sophia Cortez Benviende."

"Okay. Good idea about the obit. I'll get the ball rolling on that. Four days, Bruce. You'll need to meet Collins the afternoon of the 6th and be inside the compound before dark."

"I *can* make that shot, John."

"You said your O.P. was maybe 800 yards away. Have you ever knocked the center out of the bull at that distance?"

"The target will appear a little bigger than a bullseye in my crosshairs, John."

I heard him sigh.

"I don't know, Bruce."

"It'll be all right. I have never failed to deliver."

"I guess I've got no recourse but to trust you on that. Okay, I talked with Agent Collins this morning. You'll meet him on the 6th at the Ingalis Airfield in Rockbridge County, which is 5 to 6 miles from your target. It shouldn't take you long to brief one another on your portions of the mission. He'll have a radio for you as well as your protective mask, plastic explosives and remote detonator."

"Let's not write Steed off just yet. I gotta believe he'll be back. Something has to be wrong."

"I hope you're right, Bruce; but he'll have a hell of a lot of explaining to do."

*****

I had just slipped under the sheets after showering and splashing on a little Bvlgari with the intent of enticing the hot Mrs. McGowan into our bed after I saw through her see-through nightie the body of an eighteen year old goddess, when my cell phone went off. *"No!"* my libido shouted. But then I thought it might be Steed, so I snatched the phone off the nightstand. Hickcock.

"You very nearly interrupted something over which I would not soon forgive you, my friend."

"Our agents found Steed."

"Where?"

"In a Dallas hospital. He was in a taxi on his way to the airport when he was broadsided by a truck. *His* side."

"How bad?"

"He has a concussion. Was unconscious for over twenty-four hours."

"How is he now?"

"He's up and walking, but has double vision. His cellphone was smashed in the impact and as he had temporary amnesia, he had no idea he was supposed to call you. He still doesn't remember your number...but the good news is, he remembers *you*."

"I'm hard for *anyone* to forget."

"They want to keep him for observation another forty-eight hours, but he's putting up a ruckus."

"Well, whatever the case, even if he does make it back, with vision problems he won't be able to take that shot," I said.

"It's now up to me."

"I could assign the task to one of our best sharpshooters, but Johns is emphatic he doesn't want the kill shot made by any of our people."

"Just trained killers like Steed.

"Well, that won't happen now."

"I can still make the shot and then press the buttons on the detonator to blow the bunker."

"Apparently, that's our only recourse" he sighed.

"We'll just have to make it work. I gotta go. Will get back to you later."

On the afternoon of the 4th, I was standing at the rear of my Suburban rechecking my pack list. Most of my necessities were still in the cargo area from our last trip over the mountains, such as my field glasses, starlight scope and goggles, flak jacket and other ash and trash I go to battle with. On mission day, I would throw in either my new British L115A3 or Winchester 700...I hadn't yet decided. Of course, either my Glock or my .380 were *always* packed under my left arm in the shoulder holster.

I had just closed the rear door when a taxi pulled up in our gravel driveway. And then a man with a bandage on his head, carrying a travel bag, got out. Atticus Steed had returned. His head was swollen on the left side, his left cheek was lacerated, and his blackened left eye was nearly closed.

"What the hell are you doing back here?" I exclaimed.

"Living up to my part of the deal, McGowan."

"No, no. A cracked head and double vision? You're no value to me on this mission."

"We've got two days, Bruce. All I need is a little R&R and some of Adriana's good cooking and I'll be back in the game."

"Hickcock told me the hospital would hold you for 48 hours for observation. What did you do, escape?"

"I'd prefer the term, *eloped*. They wanted to talk to me about my bill before I left. Having no insurance, there wouldn't be much of a conversation."

I let out an audible sigh.

"Well, come on in the house and have a beer. You look like shit."

"I feel like it, too. But, I'm a hell of a lot better than I was a couple of days ago."

Adriana had the same reaction that I had. But *she* gave him a hug. I didn't.

"You poor guy," she said.

"You've *got* to be in a lot of pain. Now all you're going to do for the next week is relax. Are you hungry? I'll fix you something to eat."

I can remember a few times *I* came home looking worse than him...dirty, bleeding, nursing a bullet wound...and all she did was stand there with her hands on her hips, giving me a bad time. But, I guess the difference was, she only *pitied* him. She *loved* me.

*****

Steed and I sat on the veranda late that evening, swigging down a couple of Heinekens and filling one another in on the the past week's happenings. He told me a little more about Maria's situation there in Dallas. She and her parents were slowly coming to terms, thanks to the efforts of her brother. But she *was* staying at her folks' home until our mission was done. I told him that everything seemed quiet on the Western Virginia front as we had received no further information on al-Massoud's movements. It was probable that he had somehow made it into the United States without being spotted, the snake that he was. FBI agents had the mosque in Detroit under surveillance and had reported that hundreds of Arab faces had gone in and out of the building; however, their lenses could not ascertain that al-Massoud was among them.

"I appreciate Adriana's good intentions of playing nurse-maid while I'm recuperating for a week here at your home, but that's not going to happen, Bruce. In two days, you *and* I will be inside that compound ready to finish this mission. I might be a bit beat up, but I can still make that shot."

"With your brains still rattled and your left eye half closed? Who are you trying to kid, Steed?"

"Like most right-handed shooters, I close my left eye, anyway. And the double vision is almost gone."

"*Almost* won't get it, Atticus."

"All right, I'll tell you what. If you have a shooting range nearby, we'll take our weapons out there and I'll match you shot for shot. If I beat you, I make the shot that kills al-Massoud. If you beat me, I'll stay here and play Rook with your wife."

"I don't want you playing *anything* with my wife, Mr. Steed. She's already been hugging on you."

"Only because she feels sorry for me. So, are you game?"

I leaned back in my rocker and then took another swallow of the beer.

"I'm friends with a couple of State Police detectives and they let me use their range whenever I want. All right, I'll take that challenge. Tomorrow at first light, we go."

That night, I called Hickcock and told him Steed was back.

"From how you describe him, he won't be any value to the mission. You'll still have to go without him," Hickcock said.

"He says he can do it."

"I can't take that chance. You'll make the shot and then immediately detonate the explosives as we discussed."

"Not that it matters to me, but is the deal off as to his pardon and fee for services?"

"That will be up to Johns. I know this hiccup was not of Steed's own making, but the deal required his sniper services."

"All right. I won't mention anything to him until the decision is made. He and I are doing a little target practicing tomorrow. I'll then be able to assess both his medical *and* readiness states."

"Fine. Keep me apprised."

# CHAPTER 24

The State Police firing range was not far. After traveling north on 219 about four miles, I turned left onto a narrow state road where we came upon the sign that read *State Fire and Police Training Center*. At the gate stood my old Wackenhut friend, Dave Traynor, a retired county deputy, who waved me in. I then passed the main campus and drove about a half mile until I reached the KD (known distance) rifle range. No one else was on the range and I saw no one in the control tower, either. On the adjacent pistol range, three state officers were pop-popping rounds at 50 foot targets. As we could not do any firing until a safety officer was present, we had to wait until someone caught sight of us.

On the rifle range there were silhouette-type targets set at 100, 150, 250 and 350 meters. No sooner had we begun to set up in the prone, range safety officer Larry Simezko, who I had known since military school days, approached from our right.

*"Attention on the firing line,"* he yelled through his bullhorn. *"I need to clear everybody off the range. Bruce McGowan is here. I don't want anybody shot up."*

"Very funny, Lawrence," I said.

"I hain't seen you around for months. You still with the government doin' whatever it was you was doin'?"

"No. I'm fully retired now, with the exception of my part-time teaching job over at VMI. I just thought I'd come by with a friend to give him a clinic."

"And you can do it. I don't know how good this guy is, but..."

"The name's Atticus Steed." He then stood and shook Simezko's hand.

"Good ta meet ya. You'll have ta be pretty damn good to beat this guy. I'll tell ya what...give me a couple of minutes and I'll take my jeep down range and paste these here targets on a few of the silhouettes at the 350 mark. If you beat ol' Bruce here, I'll give ya a box of 7.62 ammo. By the way, what happened to yer head, man?"

"Auto accident a few days ago in Dallas."

"Yeah, I been to Texas. Them people drive like they're zippin' around Daytona. Well, I'll take care of them targets and be back in a jiff. Don't shoot at me."

When he had finished pasting the targets, Simezko bounced his jeep back down the dirt side trail and stopped it at our firing post. He then took out his bull horn and allowed his deep, bellowing voice to cut through the humid summer air.

*"Is there anyone down range? Is there anyone down range?"*

He paused the required ten seconds to listen and then announced,

*"The firing line is clear!"*

I said

"Okay, Atticus, you take the target on the left and I'll take the right one. Three shots each. The shooter closest to dead center of the bull wins the challenge."

Simezko said,

"I'll flip a coin. You call it Mr. Steed."

"I'll just let you go first, Bruce," Steed said.

"You're the home team."

"Fine." I then put on my ear covers. As I already had my Winchester zeroed from the last time I was on the range, I figured I would not have to make much adjustment. Mostly, all I needed to do was get my sight picture and sight alignment. I then relaxed my arms and hands, took a breath and let it out. Regaining my sight picture, I took another breath and let it out as well. B.R.A.S.S. Breathe, relax, aim squeeze, slack. Something I never forgot from my days with Uncle Sam. After squeezing off the first round, I took a little time before the second shot. Then working the bolt and shoving another round into the chamber, I fired again. Repeating the action a third time, I was done.

Simezko had been spotting my handiwork through his telescope. When I had placed my rounds in the target, he merely nodded and smiled. I checked the target myself through my scope and saw that the angels had to be singing.

But then after Steed established his sight picture, he wasted no time. He put all three rounds on target within ten seconds. I could see from my scope that Steed was in the bull as well, but couldn't see *well* enough to compare the two targets.

Simezko again handed me the telescope. I had placed two rounds dead center, but the third was partially in the bull but halfway into the white at two o'clock. I then swept the lens over to Steed's target.

"Holy shit," I said under my breath. He had knocked the center out of the bull with all three rounds. Each of the holes was touching the other two. Nothing in the white. And this was dealt by a man who was still nursing a concussion.

"Where'd you find this guy, Bruce?" Simezko asked. "I never seen nobody that good. I think you ain't top shot around here no more, old man."

I said nothing in return. What *was* there to say. All I could do was shake my head.

And Steed didn't say anything either. He didn't even look at his target. He didn't have to. He knew where the rounds would land as soon as he pulled the trigger.

"Larry, is there anything to shoot at out there at a distance of 500 meters or more?" I asked.

"Hmmm. I'd say that dead tree out yonder is 250 to 300 meters further down range." He then took from his pocket his range finder he mostly used on the golf course.

"Yep. 756 yards if this thing is accurate."

"Can you hit it, Atticus?"

"We'll see." He then made a few clicks on the scope reticule to adjust for windage and deviation.

"That should be about right." He held steady for a moment and then backed off a click.

"See the two limbs on the right side of the tree?"

I looked through the telescope and replied,

"Yes."

"Watch the top one."

He fired. Just under three seconds later the one inch thick limb separated from the tree. When he fired again, the second limb disappeared.

"Yes, sir," said Simezko. "We got a new Top Gun out here."

On the way back, I guess I was noticeably quiet. My pride had taken a major hit. But I wasn't pouting, mind you. It's just that I was beaten by a shooter with a broken head and by all laws of physics and medicine, he had no right to be that good. But one other thing impressed me about Atticus Steed. He neither gloated nor rubbed it in. It was his style, I guess. Cool and all business.

Finally I said, "Well, I'm pleased to tell you, you're back in. You proved yourself out there. Just don't relapse on me."

He looked at me and nodded. As we began passing the Van Meter farm, he then turned his head back to his right to take account of the dozen or so herefords as they grazed in the lush, green meadow just to the other side of the perfectly-erected white fence that continued on for a half mile.

*****

While she was in our upstairs kitchen making breakfast just for us, that morning of the 6th, Adriana asked me how many more of these 'overnight exploits' Steed and I would be doing.

"This will be the last one as far as I know. We will likely have to do a de-brief with the FBI sometime after that and then Mr. Steed will be rejoining his fiancée in Texas."

"I don't know what you all will be doing, since you haven't seen fit to give me all of the details of your...*mission*...as you call it; but is he improved enough to be doing it?"

"He says he is and I think he looks better. His eye is healing up and he tells me he no longer has the headaches."

"I've been fairly accepting about you going off again like this doing God knows whatever. But I have especially been concerned because you and your people in that black limo had to bring Atticus in on it. What skill does he have that somebody in the government *doesn't* have?"

"Adriana, we don't need to keep going back through this. Just know that this is the last time we'll be in a surveillance mode. It's a very important mission that affects the safety and security of this country."

"It's *your* safety and security I always worry about. And I don't have a very good feeling about you going off this time. Call it intuition, but I'm sure there's some kind of danger involved."

Throughout the short time we had been married and I was with Team Zulu, we had had similar conversations a dozen times. And I had discovered that her fears and worry had everything to do with losing her first husband and her nine year old son. Although their lives were lost to diseases that were uncontrollable, my brushes with danger *were* within my control. And many times, she asked me to please don't go. Sometimes I told her *where* I was going, but never have I shared with her the total *nature* of my missions. I should be dead five times over, considering what I have experienced. The fact is, if she had the slightest inkling *this* mission was anything more than merely spying on people and providing intelligence to the government, at noon today when I left out the front door, she might just lock it behind me for good. I agree it's not the way to maintain trust and honesty in a marriage, but there's no way a wife should ever know the kind of danger that I have experienced in order to protect America and its citizens.

As I sat in the kitchen chair watching her at the stove, I thought about how lucky I was at this stage of my life to have her...somebody sweet, caring, loving and did I mention, beautiful. I then stood up and placed my arms around her tiny waist. "I love you for worrying about me, Babe, especially the times I've answered my country's call. Just realize that I'm very good at what I do and I take every precaution to protect myself. I avoid danger like the plague."

"I thought all this clandestine stuff was long behind you when you gave them notice a few months back. But, something tells me this won't be the last time someone calls you, either. There has to be a cut-off point with all of this, that's all I'm saying."

"On *this* mission there is. Tomorrow afternoon."

"And is the government paying you for your time or is this just volunteer work for good ol' Uncle Sam?"

"They'll pay me nicely when it's all done. You'll see." I was hoping she wouldn't ask me how *much*. She'd never believe the government would pay me a million bucks for just a few days of collecting intelligence.

"Yeah, I'm sure," she said.

"Probably enough to put gas in your old bucket of bolts out there...and maybe an oil change."

"Actually, I'll be able to afford to put brakes on it as well."

"Funny man. Now go down and tell Atticus that breakfast is ready. I asked him last night if he'd like to join us."

"I thought it was just *you* and *me*. You're obviously well-taken with him, aren't you?"

"He's alone, his fiancée, who I'm sure is still grieving, is far away from him, and he's still smarting from that auto accident. He needs looked after."

"I guess you're right. But that's *my* job. I brought him here, so I'm responsible for him."

I went and got him, finding that his head actually looked a little better. I guessed that he'd had a good night's sleep...certainly well-needed. He spoke and smiled at my pretty wife, who was a pretty sight for any man, sore eyes or not.

It was probably going to be our last hearty meal for a good day or so. We would need something that would stick to our ribs. I hadn't noticed, but to my dismay, I saw that Adriana had made us oatmeal.

"Uh, sweetheart. I see oatmeal, but not much of a *meal.* Are we out of eggs and stuff to make flapjacks with?"

"How about if I add some wheat toast and blueberries," she replied.

"I'm not contributing to your heart attack. We've also had *this* conversation. Neither one of us needs to find ways to kill you off."

I looked at Steed, who I thought might also be expecting a big breakfast, but he merely shrugged. He didn't say a word. I guess he was wanting to score points with my wife.

After the meager breakfast, Steed helped Adriana clean up, which may have scored even more points with her...but *zero* with me. Now Adriana would henceforth be expecting the same from me. Hey, my job around the house is *outside* the house. Don't give my Mrs. anymore ideas, Steed.

At 1030 hours in a part of the parking lot where Adriana could not see us from the house, Steed and I took inventory of our gear, which included putting our spanking-clean rifles through their final checks, assuring that there were fresh batteries in our flashlights and starlight equipment, and that we had plenty of water. I didn't need to give Adriana the impression we were preparing for war. At such time we were at the small airport in Rockbridge where we would meet Collins and his CIRG (Critical Incident Response Group), we would don our protective vests, shoulder holsters containing my Glock and his XDM, equipment belts containing 7.62 and .45 caliber ammo, suppressors and K bars. Both of us were outfitted in SWAT team black with black field caps. I also had camo sticks to apply to our faces and hands. That would go on after we arrived at the airport as well. My field pack would stay empty, except for a few protein bars, as it would ultimately be containing the plastic explosive, remote triggering device and receivers.

Once we had double-checked everything and loaded up, we returned inside to kiss the wife. At least *I* did. Steed would stay the hell away from her.

"What time tomorrow do you think you'll be back?" she asked. "I can have dinner ready."

"Don't know, pet," I said. "It might be late. Don't go to any trouble. We can pick something up on the road. However, if we're back before six, I'll take you to dinner."

"Be careful, Skip. And you too, Atticus. You know you shouldn't be doing anything but resting."

"I'm doing okay now, Adriana. I appreciate your concern."

After we had slid onto our seats in the Suburban, Steed said, "I meant to ask you the other day, why does she call you *Skip*?"

I wasn't about to open up *that* dialogue at this time. "Maybe because I'm always skipping out on her, I don't know." It's just not something two tough guys talk about on the way to a killing zone.

*****

It was actually about a quarter till eleven when we left since we needed to make the Rockbridge County Airport by 1300. When we arrived, Collins was already waiting for us. Off to the side of the runway was the Blackhawk that he and three members of his Red Team came in on. Beside of it, I then spied an AH-6C attack helicopter. I couldn't help but notice the armament on the warbird...a 30 millimeter M230 chain gun, two .50 caliber GAU-19s and two LAU M260 rocket pods loaded with 70 millimeter rocket projectiles. Not only am I damn good at my aircraft recognition, but I get into all that firepower shit with a purple passion.

In sizing Collins up, I found him to be a wiry little fellow, around thirty-five,  about five-seven with the Body Mass Index of maybe *three,* and with dashing Audie Murphy looks. But his slung M4 made him appear a force to be reckoned with. I could only imagine that he was nothing but dynamite in a small package.

"Nice ride, Agent Collins," I said, still eyeing the attack helicopter. "Going to war somewhere?"

"Just out for a Sunday ride and thought I'd bring my boys down here for a little target practice."

"They didn't have anything like that in the inventory when *I* was with the Bureau," I said.

"I'm sure Mr. Hoover had *some* kind of aircraft in his repertoire. A couple of bi-planes maybe?"

"Funny, Collins.  Where *are* your boys? I'm sure that your CIRG isn't comprised of only you four."

"So as not to get people around here excited by flying them in on choppers, they're driving down as we speak. They'll meet us in the staging area at 1600. I assume it's the same clearing that we used when we took Maslama out of here."

"It is. By the way, did you have a good trip back to Andrews with him?"

"At first, he was scared shitless. I guess he was afraid I'd dump him out somewhere over the Atlantic. But, by the time we got to where we could see D.C. on the horizon, he began yelling about how the City of Miscreants, whatever the hell that means, would soon be nothing but rubble and our infidel President would be hiding in fear for his life."

"Yeah, I wondered if he might 'accidentally' stumble out of the chopper?"

"Don't think I didn't consider it with the hell he was raising, but I didn't want to take the chance of him falling *on* somebody."

"You people are barbaric, you know," Steed said, smiling.

"It's how we ex-Special Forces think, Mr. Steed," I replied. "You remember our slogan...kill 'em all; let God sort 'em out."

"Yeah, yeah. How many times do I need to hear *that*?"

I spread my map out on the hood of my SUV. Collins, who had the same map, did likewise.

"Alright, Mike, see that dot right on that wide contour line? That's the center of the compound." I then moved the tip of my grease pencil a klick to the northeast. "Here's the clearing where we set up the LZ. It sits near a firebreak that leads down to Highway 42. As you can see, once you cross 42, you are within 700 meters from the entrance to the compound. Your men can park their vehicles just off the clearing and set up their perimeter in the woods here by this stream. The location will not only be close for your rapid advance into the compound, but provide you concealment from the road. How many people on your team?"

"Seventy-six including me."

"What kind of vehicles are rolling in?"

"Two unmarked Lenco BearCats, an SRT van, three Pit Bull VX units and three nine passenger SUVs. All FAVs, (Full Armored Vehicles)."

"Unmarked or not, *that* convoy ought to raise some eyebrows on the road," I commented.

"Is the firebreak that leads into the clearing accessible for these vehicles?"

"Easily. They'll go in here." I pointed to a dotted line on the map.

"I'm suggesting they park here." I then pointed to a small open space without foliage.

"Good," he said.

"Here's the deal. Once our target arrives...I don't know the hour or mode of transportation...Steed here will take him down. This will cause panic within the compound and they'll be looking for the location of the shooter. Before they start fleeing, I will blow the bunker. The explosion, I promise you, will have a devastating effect and take a good many of them out. This will then cause mass panic among the rest and they will scurry like fire ants. It shouldn't take your men more than a few minutes to then sweep in and envelop the camp. As they'll be scattered everywhere in the camp and the woods, I suggest you deploy small patrols to hunt them down, with special emphasis on this area where they park their vehicles. Some of the vehicles will likely be wiped out by the explosion. Although there's only one road in and out of the compound, some might hit the woods and try getting away on this firebreak. You can intercept them there." I then placed the pencil on that area of the map.

"Seems simple enough," Collins said.

"You need to be on our freak, so here's a couple of ear buds and mikes. If for some reason you're not able to blow the bunker, just tell me and we'll move in. Of course, we'll also hear your shot when you take down your target."

"Actually you won't. We have suppressors on all our weapons. We don't want the bad guys to be able to pinpoint our position. When the charges are detonated, watch out for secondary explosions when you enter the compound."

"Where will you be perched?"

"Here." I pointed to the narrow contour lines that depicted the high ground and the number 589 (Hill 589).

"We'll be sure to look out for you," he said.

"Tell your men we'll be the guys dressed in black and not wearing turbans or skull caps."

"By the way, three of my men are actually women and tough as nails."

I smiled.

"I know a Bureau gal just like them."

"You're obviously talking about Maggie Larsen...Miss Congeniality. Remember, she rode down with me in the chopper when we came to pick up Maslama. And you're right."

"Okay, my highers want al-Massoud's body secured and photographed. You'll also be transporting it to Quantico."

"If there's anything left after the explosion. But, understood," Collins said. "However, answer me a question. I still don't know why you two are involved in this mission. This is an exercise for a CIRG like ours which is also fully capable of infiltration, surveillance and long-distance sniping. I'm also especially not sure who *you* are, Mr. Steed."

I placed my hand on Collins' shoulder.

"This is intended to be a covert, low-visibility mission. Liberal special-interest groups, media hounds and even congressional left-wingers have been all over the President and Justice Department about their *alleged* persecution of these peaceful, non-threatening Jamaat ul-Fuqra groups. This operation is being directed at the highest level of government and they want to be sure this Viper, considered the most dangerous terrorist in the world, gets a bullet put in his brain. And they called in the best marksman in the world to make that shot. And that's Mr. Steed. Once al-Massoud is taken down, we disappear. We were never involved. You and your team get the credit...or catch the flak, whichever. I know that a number of Special Ops guys or FBI marksmen could do the job. But there are reasons you don't know about that put Steed here behind that sniper rifle."

Collins shook his head.

"Still not understanding."

"Just accept it and go on."

"Okay." He then reached down into a large canvass bag and pulled out a box. "Here's your plastic explosives. Semtex, like you asked. Much more effective than C4. Here are your blasting caps and your remote detonator."

"Cool," I said.

"Are you familiar with the device?"

"Not really."

"Then let me give you a quick schooling. This is a new, state-of-the-art Quantum RK500 control mechanism with four possible circuits and receivers. You can have up to 10 igniters per circuit. And here is your hand-held transmitter. Once the receivers are laid in the bunker with the explosives and connected to the electrical firing circuit, you operate this transmitter. The signal from the transmitter and receiver must be set with a matching code. Basically, it prevents a premature explosion from occurring due to radio traffic, car alarms going off or electrical storms. I have matched the code for you already. These are your firing triggers for as many receivers as you set up. Now that you have all of this together and there are storm clouds rolling in, are you just a wee bit nervous?" He had a shit-eating grin on his face.

It was Steed who said, "Standing next to somebody with all explosive shit on his person, *I* sure as hell am."

Collins laughed.

"One problem with blowing the bunker. You said your observation point from where you will take out the bunker is over 550 meters away. You, Bruce, are going to have to set up closer than that with your transmitter. Its range to target is only 400 meters."

"That does present a problem since I'll be helping to spot for Steed. We'll just have to work that out, Atticus."

I then very gingerly placed the Semtex and detonator devices in my field pack.

I guess that's it, except for our protective masks."

Collins then pulled two of them from his magic bag,

"Here. Make sure you prepare them for use. Being an old warrior, I'm sure you remember how."

Steed and I then shoved them into our packs.

"And the commo?" I asked.

"Just getting to that. You have your ear buds and wrist mikes. I've set up a Mulit-band IntraTeam Radio system or MBITR. 300 MHz and a range of about four miles. We're on a freak that won't be compromised...that is unless they have the latest interception equipment called StriCom, which I doubt. By the way, my call sign is Yankee 6. I'll be the only one on my end on the net with the exception of that AH-6 aviator over there. He'll be at my beck and call when I need him tomorrow morning. What do you want to be called."

"By my usual...Scorpion."

"Scorpion?" Collins said.

"Who gave you *that* handle?"

I placed my index finger over my lips, which told him it was a clandestine part of my past that needed to stay that way. *In the past.* I then picked up my pack and swept it onto my shoulders.

"Will you send in the clear or do we use encrypted dialogue?" I asked.

"I doubt these people have any communications intercept ability or will be monitoring radio airways for any reason."

I nodded in agreement. "Alright then. If that's all, follow me. You and your men will ride with me to the staging area. I'll leave my Suburban in a location near the clearing where your team can see where to park when they arrive. I'll also walk you through what I think will be a good location for you to set up your perimeter, TOC and jump off point. From there, Steed and I will take off and began our infiltration to set up for the night."

"Lead on," he said.

# CHAPTER 25

Collins appeared satisfied with my selection of the staging area where I had placed his team. After spending a very thorough hour of walking the perimeter, compiling notes and placing marks on his laminated map with his color-coded grease pencils, he established his commo net and at a distance of about 250 meters performed a radio check with Steed and me.

"Loud and clear," each of us said.

"Then see you on the battlefield," he replied.

Operation Firestorm had officially kicked off.

Just as the Red Team was beginning to arrive, Steed and I pulled on our field packs, grabbed up our sniper rifles and then moved to the northeast about 300 meters before crossing over Highway 42 into enemy territory. We were careful to watch and listen for vehicles on the hardtop whose drivers might just get a little excited about two Swat-looking characters armed to the teeth crossing in their path.

Once we were well into the woods, just as we did the last time we ventured into Fuqra-land, we eased along a few yards at a time, stopping frequently to look for people wearing skull caps and turbans. I doubted any of the stationed or roving guards would be set up in tree stands or behind logs waiting in ambush; but, just in case, every few feet I stopped to canvass the trees and bushes with my field glasses. I also stopped a couple of times to check my map with the terrain to be sure we were moving in the right direction toward our O.P. on Hill 589. It was now drawing on 1600 hours.

In moving through heavily wooded areas, one needs to rely on the senses...not only watching for the shaking of bushes and the scurrying of small animals off in the distance, but listening for the sound of twigs snapping beneath feet or sudden rousing of birds and their flutter of wings. Whether it's an innate ability or a learned skill, I can almost smell and feel the presence of another human being in the woods. And I'm sure it was in the jungles of Vietnam years ago that I had honed these skills out of necessity, learning to heighten all of my senses, that when summoned, fell into perfect union. Cemented together, they became that sixth sense that on many occasions since has served as my radar.

Having entered the camp's acreage from a slightly different route than before, I was checking my map when my antenna went up. I then placed my hand on Steed's arm and motioned for him to drop down. I didn't see or hear the guard, but somehow felt his presence. Moving my head slightly to my left to where I could peer through a series of bushes to my front, I spotted him. Had we continued on another twenty yards, we would have walked directly into him. Crouched down in a squat position, he rotated his head continuously a hundred-eighty degrees, AK-47 at port arms and ready to engage. If we had been a couple of hikers or adventurous kids in the woods, the sentry would merely have shooed us away. The assault rifle alone would have sent the average civilian fleeing in terror. However, dressed for business and armed as we were, he might have just started shooting, then asked questions later.

I tapped Steed's arm once again, placed two fingers up to my eyes and then pointed in the direction of the guard. Steed nodded and put up his index finger, which I took to mean that he was going to try something. After he began searching the ground with his eyes, he then picked up a rock about the size of a baseball just off his right boot and pointed to a flock of crows that stopped to take a break in a large oak about forty yards away to our three o'clock. Still in a squat position, with the arm of Johnny Bench, he hurled the stone into the tree's branches and scattered the birds. The sentry then popped up quickly and began moving toward the oak, AK leading his way.

When he had almost reached the tree and had begun searching through the brush for a possible intruder, I motioned for Steed to follow me. After flanking the man, we moved quickly and quietly away from him for another fifty meters until we were back on our course. In less than five minutes, we were in sight of the rocks where we had set up two weeks before...our point of observation. The spot where Steed would be killing the Viper.

Suddenly, it was *Steed's* eyes that spotted another guard with a skull cap and AK moving parallel to us. "Over there," he whispered. "Do you see him?"

"Yeah," I said. "We need to stick here to see where he'll go. Get down."

It didn't take us long to find out. The man then began trudging to the top of the hill where he came to a halt at its crown. He was standing in the exact spot where we again intended to set up. Three of us together there on that series of rocks was just not going to work out. "He might move on, soon. If he doesn't, he has to go down," I said. "We'll wait him out, however."

And that we did...for nearly a half an hour. On one occasion, he was either signaling someone down below in the compound or waving at his friends enjoying their fun and games. Finally, he turned around, looked down over the terrain below and then slowly descended the reverse crest of the slope until he disappeared into the trees a hundred yards or so away from our position.

Once I was sure the guard was well into the woods and would not return, we ran at a crouch up the slope to the rocks and to a point where we wouldn't be spotted from either the compound or the reverse side of the hilltop. We then unslung our packs, laid our rifles aside and brought up our field glasses to view what was happening below. It appeared there was more of the same going on, the training and games, like we observed the last time we were spying on them. A squad of men was engaged in combative, practicing their lame take-down exercises, while others were concentrating on bayonet drills...modified perry and thrust techniques with their AKs. Through the telephoto lens on my Nikon, I snapped off several shots of a half dozen yahoos with huge, gleaming jambiyahs practicing throat-cutting and head separating techniques. The film would serve as evidence along with the photos of the underground ordnance that ul-Fuqra was a genuine threat and had to be taken out.

But then we watched something a little different. After thirty seconds or so of each exercise, a leader would stop them, provide verbal instruction or demonstration, and then let them resume. It didn't take us long to figure out they were choreographing all of their monkeyshines for show. They were likely practicing all that shit to impress al-Massoud when he showed up the next day to observe. Watching their little Barnum and Bailey act again put grins on both our faces.

It was now nearly 1700 and the sun was starting to hide behind some darkening clouds. And that was actually a blessing on this 91 degree afternoon where the 91% humidity had made the heavy air quite steamy. And then lying on the scorching rocks under the oppressing rays of the sun had all but sapped the both of us.

Suddenly, we heard not far behind us the sounds of footsteps and an occasional kicked up stone that might be sent toppling back down the slope. We were trapped. Although the person couldn't see us yet, since we were imbedded into the rocks, all we had to do is stand up and we would be seen. I looked at Steed, but he was looking back at me for suggestions. Slowly, I pulled my Glock and then unsnapped one of my pouches to retrieve the suppressor. I had just finished attaching it when the surprised man approaching from our rear began bringing up his AK. But within the split second that I saw him, I also caught sight of another head behind his. I had no choice. As the muzzles of two AK-47s were bearing down on us, I pulled the trigger in less than two seconds on both heads, sending the men's bodies several feet back down the rocky slope.

"Chee-huahua, Bruce. Great shooting," Steed exclaimed in a low voice.

Both of us then low-crawled out of our positions. When we were out of sight of the camp below, we stood up and scampered down the hill to check the bodies. One each hole was centered in the middle of both foreheads. One was obviously an Arab with a full beard, while the other appeared to be a Black American. I then grabbed the Arab by his collar and dragged him the forty yards or so back down the slope until we entered the woods. Steed was right behind me hauling the other man.

"We need to somehow cover these guys up so they won't be readily found," I said. We then pulled the corpses ten to fifteen feet inside of the tree line after which I took my K bar and sawed some branches off a couple of hardwoods to conceal the bodies the best I could. Checking again for any movement afoot from any other sentries and then finding the area clear, we ran back up the hill to settle in on our perches.

We laid in position for a while, both of us out of breath, and then Steed remarked, "They're going to be missed by somebody, you know. What happens if they are and that brings more up here to look for them?"

"We'll cross that bridge when we get to it. It'll be dark in a couple of hours and a storm has been brewing all afternoon. That might send everybody else down there for cover. Other guards will have their assigned areas to patrol is my guess. We'll just have to stay vigilant otherwise."

Steed then began smiling.

"Obviously, whoever and whatever you were before you retired, you can still bring it, old man. I gain an increasing respect for you every day."

All I said in response was,

"Watch the 'old man' talk, Steed."

The combatants below ceased their comedy routine around a quarter till six and instead of forming up for what we military types call *retreat*, they organized themselves into a company-sized element and spread out on their hands and knees to begin salat. They'd *better* pray, I thought. Tomorrow was going to be a hell of a day for them.

But I had to hand it to them. They were a devout bunch...praying in mass two or three times a day, humbling themselves, and spending more time talking to Allah in one session than I remember my old man spending in Wednesday night prayer meeting at the Baptist church.

After a good while, they all broke up and although some made a bee-line for their vehicles in yon parking lot, the majority began filing into the large assembly building, likely for either evening chow or a meeting. I doubted many of them would be coming out until after dark.

But at eight-thirty five, something happened that I had earlier prayed to God wouldn't. Flashes of lightning began to our west. And I'm talking about *serious* lightning and ensuing thunder. Getting closer by the minute. It wasn't long before the wind began to kick up and then the spotty rain began in big drops.

Steed kept eyeing my field pack that contained the Semtex and blasting caps.

"I don't know, Bruce. Maybe you ought to find yourself *another* O.P."

I had to laugh...but it was kind of a nervous laugh. I wasn't too keen about being that close to the stuff either. And lightning does have a tendency to seek out the highest places. Suddenly, the rain began to come down in sheets. A squall line was coming through. Although we had our ponchos with us, part of them had to cover our weapons and packs. It wasn't long until we felt the straight-line wind. The rain, now coming at us sideways, began to pelt and sting our faces. It made me think of the many days I stood out on rifle ranges with my troops when these things blew in. We couldn't seek shelter under trees or in the metal bleachers and we had to stay away from high places. So, in essence, where we were now situated on high ground with metal and explosives around us...we could be in deep ca-ca. I then remembered Collins asking me, "...you nervous?" I sure as hell...pardon me... *heck*...was now.

Actually, Collins did check in with me twice for a radio check. The first time was at 1856 or six fifty-six and then again while the storm was raging.

"You enjoying the monsoon, Scorpion?"

"Brings back memories, Yankee 6. I remember it raining once for four months up in Kontum. Hey, what am I saying? You have no idea where that is. Your war was Iraq. See what being vintage does to you?"

"I assume you're in no place dry," he said.

"I assume you're in one of your vehicles."

"And having a nice, hot cup of coffee."

"Bastard."

"Good luck. See you in the morning, Spiderman. Out."

Sometime within the next few hours, I was going to have to move down inside the compound with the plastic explosives and blasting caps on my back, dodging raindrops and lightning bolts. Even so, the fact that we were lying there on that high ground with that field pack at arm's length...well, it was sphincter-tightening time for sure. Should I wait it out or go ahead and get it done? I could still get the charges planted at three or four in the morning, but no later.

The longer we laid there, the more we both began drowning. Steed said nothing for the longest time and I thought for a moment I saw him shivering. The longer and harder it rained, the cooler the air became. After all, it was a cold front moving through. A few lightning bolts *did* hit around us, but thank God...and I did every couple of minutes...none came dangerously close. I was hoping that He wouldn't kill off the very people who were seeing to it that His innocent sheep didn't get harmed or killed by these Godless terrorists. I figured that all the guards had by now taken shelter indoors and we shouldn't have to worry about anyone else creeping up on us. The two dead guys in the woods I was sure weren't minding the weather, however.

Midnight. The storm was not letting up. I checked the Weather Channel radar on my cellphone and the mass of pretty red and green looked like there was a freight train of raging storms still coming, one after another. I doubted the crap would clear out before 0500. So, as much as I hated to admit it, there was no time like the present to make my move.

I tapped Steed on the shoulder.

"I'm going down now. If I'm not back here by zero two, something probably went wrong and you will have to make that shot on the Viper without me. As soon as you do, get Collins on the horn and tell him to go ahead and advance on the compound. Then he will need to sweep the camp, set a delayed charge and get the hell out of Dodge. You along with him."

He nodded.

Gingerly, I donned my field pack and poncho, then stood and began flanking my way down the front slope toward the cantonment area. I left my Winchester with Steed.

At the edge of the compound's eastern tree line, I stopped to assess where I was. With the steady hard rain and the fact that both of the lights on the poles in the camp had been knocked out, I had lost my bearing. And my night vision goggles would do me no good. I basically had to feel my way into the compound until I came upon the buildings. But, then I found the very road, muddy as it was, that would lead me around to the rear of the bunker.

Suddenly, a horrific bolt of lightning struck a large elm not ten feet from where I was moving. It was like deja vu all over again with the monsoon rain and what seemed like an artillery round practically knocking me off my feet. Good thing I was not a victim of PTSD or somebody would find me tomorrow morning lying in a mud puddle in a fetal position sucking my thumb. I actually smelled the sulphur and felt the shock enter my feet from where the lightning had fanned out. The good thing was that the Semtex hadn't been set off. The bad thing was that I had forgotten to bring toilet paper.

"I'm still here, God," I said under my breath. "And thank You for that."

Still, I continued on ever so slowly, stopping to listen and straining my eyes to pick up any object that would give me a clue as to where I was on the road. But then as suddenly as they had come, the rain, wind and lightning all but ceased. The next few flashes of the lightning were now further away and their flash-booms a greater distance apart. Finally, even the drizzle waned to nothing but a mist. I figured I was in fairly close proximity to the back entrance of that bunker because the road began to drop down several degrees and curve to the left behind the series of buildings in the compound. I also figured the bunker, which had been tunneled out of the high ground on which the guard shack was sitting, had to be coming up on my left.

When I was inside the bunker on my last visit to the camp and I had peered out the back side door, I was not able to get a good look at the area around the larger cargo door. As such, I wasn't sure how to recognize what it looked like from the outside. *And* I wasn't sure if I was even in *proximity* to the bunker. But, then just one more distant flash of lightning brightened my way, and I could at least see that I was definitely on the dirt, now muddy, road that led around to the rear of the compound.

And then I heard something up ahead of me that sounded like a vehicle door shutting. Momentarily, I ducked back off the road and into the woods. It was a good thing that I did. As I had found myself nearly opposite the bunker door, the light on the nearby pole decided that it would come back on to fully illuminate the area. It seems that one of the hostiles guarding the rear entrance to the bunker had decided to seek shelter from the storm in one of the cargo trucks sitting back off the road and had just gotten out. Maslama would not have liked that. But what did he care now? He had a few other things on his mind.

The man then took his position on the right side of the door. From what I could see from my vantage point, he was Middle Eastern. And then he decided to light up a cigarette. If he didn't get away from that door he was leaning on, he might just light up all of the pyrotechnics inside as well. Moron.

There was only one way I was going to get in there to plant my own explosives...and that was to take him out. I didn't want to kill him, but he was going to die anyway if he was still guarding the bunker when I made that very big hole in the ground.

One good thing about the rain...it made all of the brush, branches and twigs on the ground soggy and mushy. Very little beneath my feet was going to snap, crackle or pop. It took me a few minutes, however, to continue on through the woods parallel to the road to where I could envelop him and come around behind him. Using the three vehicles that were parked off the road to my advantage, I then circled in behind them and stopped at the rear bumper of the far truck to where I could get a good look at the entire area.

The ul-Fuqra element had done a good job concealing the rear of the bunker. I could readily see the point where the bunker had been dug out of the high ground, but a gigantic camouflage net was covering the large cargo door. Only the pedestrian door was visible. And that's what smoking man was leaning his right shoulder against, the lazy bastard that he was.

Quickly, I crossed the road from the truck to within six feet of his location behind him. No sooner had I done that, tromping lazily down the road from the opposite direction, came another sentry, likely the guard's relief. They then greeted one another in their native tongue. As I was tucked in behind smoking man, the second sentry probably didn't see me. But, it wouldn't be long until he would. I had to make my move. With my left hand, I grabbed smoking man's collar and pressed the suppressed end of my Glock against the back of his neck.

"Don't move," I whispered. My voice and the sudden cold steel against his flesh shocked and surprised him to a point that he dropped his AK...and his cigarette. The second sentry must not have readily seen me in the dim light. All he saw and heard was the AK hitting the mud. He then yelled something to his comrade that I took to mean,

"Imbecile, what the hell you doing? Pick up that rifle."

That was when I yelled back at him and said,

"Now *you* drop *your* weapon!" But, he didn't. Instead, he brought it up in our direction. He was going to spray me *and* his buddy. I had no choice but to plant two rounds in his chest. The suppressor did its job as the bullets spat out, sounding something like clicks. Immediately, the guard's body dropped and splatted into a large mud puddle.

I jammed the muzzle of my Glock a little harder into the back of smoking man's head. "Do you speak English, Mohammed?"

The man shook as though he was freezing to death. "A...a little. Will you kill me too?"

"No. But, it's time you went to bed for the night." I then placed my forearm around his neck and clamped my hand onto his shoulder to apply a sleep hold. He struggled a bit and I told him,

"Don't fight it." After he became limp, I let his body drop into the muck as well. As I had already taken the other sentry's life in addition to the two at the observation point, I told myself *that* was enough people to die tonight. Tomorrow would be different. If the blast did not kill smoking man the next day, he would die anyway in about twenty years of lung cancer.

Taking a little extra time before entering the bunker, I dragged the carcasses of the two men to one of the cargo trucks, slid open the rear door and dumped them and their AKs onto the floor. I then slid the door back down and placed a large D link from my pistol belt onto the hasp where a lock would go. Even if smoking man woke up from his sleep sometime in the next eight hours, he wouldn't be able to get out. *And* I doubted anyone could hear him yelling unless the person was in close proximity to the truck. I was further betting that the dead guard was the sentry's replacement who was scheduled to be on shift for the next eight hours. I also hoped no one would be missing them. A lot of speculating on my part. But it was what it was.

It was now time to get down to business. Hopefully, there would be no further interruptions. From one of the Velcro pockets on my field pack I then pulled out my handy-dandy lock gun. The *dandy* part about it was that once I stuck the sharp muzzle into the key hole of the people door and pulled the trigger, like magic it spun the lock cylinder...and *voila*. Fortunately, there was also a lock cylinder on the dead bolt as well. Ripping the door-facing off with my K bar would obviously compute to breaking and entering. And I *certainly* didn't want to break any laws. That would also raise an eyebrow or two if somebody came by looking for the missing sentries.

And that was a significant part of my concern in the success of this mission. The fact that now *four* guards would be missing roll call in the morning and their camp leader hadn't shown up for the past week and a half, had to be alarming to *somebody*. All of this missing-in-action might just be reported to al-Massoud through ul-Fuqra messaging, and that may convince him not to show at all. But, for now, my focus was on setting charges.

Both the deadbolt and the knob lock on the pedestrian door cooperated with my lock gun and I was in. Since I encountered no alarm the first time I was in the bunker, I banked on the fact that one hadn't been installed within the *last* couple of weeks. Although I didn't have any problem remembering what was located where, I still canvassed the bunker again with my flashlight in case something got shuffled around or removed. After that, I began breaking down the Semtex and placing it onto crates, boxes and shelves that contained the ammonium nitrate, drums of fertilizer and weapons and ammunition. I then stuck one each M6 blasting cap into the Semtex and wired everything to the Type A receivers. I figured it didn't matter much where I strategically placed the devices because everything would pretty much go up at the same time. And what *didn't*, would do so within seconds of the initial detonation. Hopefully, I had set up my target correctly where there would be no glitches. If a Bedouin tribesman still living like his ancestors did in the 12th Century can set up an IED, why the hell couldn't I do it?

It took me only about a half hour to complete the mission. Still, I rechecked my handiwork to assure everything was connected and ready to go. But just in case I would accidentally mash the triggering device on the transmitter while I was preparing the explosives, I had decided to leave it back on the hilltop at the O.P. I was hoping Steed would not either become curious about the device to see how it worked or accidentally roll over onto it. If so, in merely a split second St. Peter would be issuing me my harp. Or the devil, my accordion.

After taking one last look around, I twisted the doorknob lock and then once outside, reversed my lock gun to engage the deadbolt. With the exception of the missing sentries and the addition of a few more explosives to their collection, everything was returned to the condition in which I found it.

# CHAPTER 26

Retracing my steps, I combed my way back along the edge of the woods a few feet from the road until I came to the long, steep and slippery slope I had to climb to get back to the perch. When the rain had stopped and the air began to clear, the front that had produced the squall line had also brought an atmospheric cooling. I was now wet *and* cold. And to my alarm, I arrived on the rock to find Steed shaking. Worse than ever.

"You okay, Atticus?"

"Yeah. I just can't shake the shakes."

"You might have hypothermia. Here, take my poncho."

"No. I'm all right. When the sun comes up, I'll get warm," he said.

"I'm going to make that shot," I said.

"No. I was hired to do this job and I'll do it. I'll be fine. You'll see."

"You came back too soon from that accident. You should've stayed in that hospital on bed rest. Nobody would have faulted you for that."

He didn't respond. He just wrapped himself tighter in his poncho and stared out over the dark camp. Nothing to see, but I think he was imagining what he *would* see come daybreak. I had to admire the fact he wanted desperately to stay in the game. But he had a lot riding on that shot. However, as contrary as he was being, I wasn't sure if I was going to let him pull it off.

I sat those remaining six hours of darkness, wrapped in my poncho, watching in vigil...watching for any other roving guards that may happen on our perch and keeping an eye on Steed. Steed finally dropped off to sleep somewhere around 0250 almost in a fetal position. I also dropped my head back a few times to watch the stars. On this night of radiational cooling after the rain, they peeked occasionally through the remaining clouds. But that was short-lived. By 0330, a thick fog had begun to settle in. By 0430, it was so dense, I couldn't see beyond the rocks. Even if someone *did* walk upon us, he'd have to *step* on us to know we were there.

However, I ultimately dosed off as well and it wasn't but a few seconds before the dream visited me again. But it ended almost as quickly as it had begun. The explosion of the M79 grenade in my head sounded so real, I awoke with a jolt. It compelled me to think the boom came from down below. In reflex, I snatched up my sniper rifle and pointed it down into the compound. My sudden movement caused Steed to stir and he sat up.

"Are you alright?" he asked.

I then laid my weapon down and turned over on my back. My body was cold and clammy and I couldn't tell if it was from last night's rain or the perspiration that always ensued along with the nightmares.

"Yeah. Sorry to alarm you. I just thought I heard something, that's all."

It was a bad place to have the dream. As I lay there, I closed my eyes once again and uttered under my breath as I often did after waking from that dream,

'Leave me the hell alone, Satan?' I had to blame something or some*body*. The devil was as good to blame as anyone.

The morning sun was doing its best to burn off the fog; however, although it wasn't like pea soup anymore, there was still a slight haze that covered the compound below. Sometimes you just can't figure on all the pieces falling into place. Steed, however, who had been sighting in his scope, had been able to make out every head moving around in the compound, especially those exiting the vehicles coming in. None appeared to be the head we were looking for. I then performed a radio check with Collins.

"Yankee 6, Scorpion, over."

There was no immediate response.

"Yankee 6, are you still asleep?"

"Good morning, Scorpion. Sorry about that. I was just grabbing some coffee from the mess tent."

"You boys are a bunch of wusses, if I must say so."

"Just kidding, Scorpion. Did you make the scene last night?"

"All set. Now we wait for the main attraction."

"I've noted several vehicles coming in. Have you been able to fully see them on your end?"

"Yes. Nobody of importance yet as far as I can tell."

"Just to let you know, we're on the springboard and ready to vault anytime."

"As we discussed, your signal to move in will be earth-shattering."

"Understood."

"Nothing further...Scorpion out."

Steed had been sitting up since BMNT (Beginning Morning Nautical Twilight) when the first scintilla of light began taking away the darkness. Still covered in his poncho, he at least appeared to be warming up. The ever climbing sun would hopefully work its magic within the next hour or so.

"Here," I said.

"Have a breakfast bar." I had found one made of peanut butter and oatmeal which would give him some protein.

"Thanks. I think part of the reason I was shaking was that we had no supper last night. What kind of a host are you, anyway?"

I smiled at that. Maybe he *was* getting better. He had developed a sense of humor.

"We need to be watching the reverse slope of this hill as well," I said.

"If I were running things in that camp, knowing I was soon to get a visit from a VIP like al-Massoud, I'd post security everywhere. If you keep your eyes peeled on people coming in, I'll watch our rear. I *need* some target practice."

0930. The fog had now fully lifted. It was like waiting for the other shoe to drop. As we had no idea when the guest of honor would be arriving, with the nail-biting anticipation, the checking of watches every five minutes and the silence all around us, I was sure I heard the Jeopardy theme song playing inside my head. There had been signs down in the compound that al-Massoud or *somebody* important was expected. From time to time, anywhere from a half-dozen to twenty-five hostiles kept milling around almost nervously with nothing going on...no training, no business, no monkey-business. I did notice that more of the men were wearing dishdashas and kurtas or the long gown-looking garb with colorful shoulder scarves, rather than the plain shirts and trousers. They were obviously dressed in their Sunday best for their esteemed visitor.

But then at twenty past ten, someone down below gave some loud commands and perhaps seventy-five more men came running out of the barracks and concrete mosque to join the others already assembling. Quickly, they formed up and stood at attention with their AKs at port arms. And just as we heard the drone of a motor vehicle coming up the hill of the entry road, Collins' voice was in my ear.

"Heads up. Could be who we were expecting."

"Got it," I replied, as the silver car came into view.

"Mr. Steed, I believe it is soon to be your moment of truth."

Steed was already set up in the prone position, having performed his final weapons check...suppressor attached, round in chamber, safety off and rifle cradled comfortably between chin and shoulder. Most importantly, I saw that his hands were steady.

"Everything's ready, Bruce. I'm a go."

It was a Range Rover...a genuine symbol of Muslim oppression. The driver was likely either an ul-Fuqra kingpin from the headquarters that al-Massoud was supposed to have visited or one of the more impoverished Imams from Detroit. As the vehicle then came to a stop in the middle of the compound in front of the assembly of men versus going on to the parking lot to join the other vehicles, I was now dead sure this was our target. For a long moment, our suspense continued, which added to the drama. No one had exited the car. While Steed was watching through his scope, I had my field glasses zeroed in as well. Beside me lay the transmitter, armed and ready.

"What do you think, Atticus? I've got 960 yards on my field glasses."

"962 to be exact," he said.

"Any problem with the distance?" I was concerned more about his physical condition than his skilled ability to make the kill from that range.

Suddenly, all four doors opened. First, the driver got out and stood at attention like a good general's aide does. We knew he was not of target value. But then three others exited and began walking with a grandiose sense of self-importance toward the leader of the formation.

"They all look similar, Bruce. All wearing turbans, all with dark beards and all in their 40s. I can't tell which one might be the Viper."

"Take them *all* down, Mr. Steed," I said.

No sooner had I said that did the first of three bullets spit from Steed's rifle. He had fired all three rounds, including sliding the bolt twice, in less than six seconds. Through my binoculars I saw three heads explode in succession like ripe watermelons.

All I could say was

"Ho-ly crap."

And that's when the Fuqra assembly fell into pandemonium.  Some began running to the four winds while others began pointing up in our direction. I then picked up the transmitter and pressed all triggers. And to my horror...nothing.

"*Son-of-bitch!*" I yelled. I pressed the triggers again and still nothing.

Finally, Steed said rather calmly as bullets began pinging the rocks around us,

"We have them right where they want us, Bruce. I think we need to bug out"

Disgusted and angry with myself at the thought that I had committed some kind of snafu in rigging the charges, it then hit me. Collins was probably right. The bunker was beyond the transmitter range of 400 yards. I yelled to Steed,

"I'm not giving this up. Cover me. Pick off as many as you can."

"What are you doing?" he yelled back.

"I'm going down to the bottom to set this off. *I'm too damn far away!*"

As some of the hostiles were still firing, a half dozen others began running toward our position. Steed began nailing them one by one. I then jumped off a larger rock and started half-running half-sliding down the slope, unfortunately in full view of more advancing hostiles. With my Glock in my right hand and transmitter in the left, I jumped behind a series of rocks and knocked off two men who had by now made it nearly a quarter way up the hill. While stopped there, I tried pressing the triggers on the transmitter again, finding I *still* had to get closer in.

In my ear bud, I then heard Collins say,

"I hear firing, Scorpion. What's happening? Are we set to come in?"

"Negative. Negative. I can't get the bunker to blow! I'm going to get closer. Stay back until...

" Unfortunately, considering I was shooting and talking at the same time, I dropped the transmitter and it slid further down the slope.

"I'll get back to you."

Even though there were still rounds ricocheting around me, I had to get down to the transmitter. I could see that Steed was still doing his part by taking down one hostile after the other. All I could do was pick up my ass and run. I was within about ten feet of the transmitter when I suddenly slipped on the slick, barren rocks and fell forward, rolling until my body landed squarely on the detonation device.

Suddenly, it seemed like the entire world had exploded. The blast was deafening, and the ground shuddered like a 9.9 earthquake. It was good that I was lying face down in between two large rocks, because the bone-jarring shock wave from the eruption of the bunker would have knocked me thirty feet. Still, my entire body felt like it had been stung and hammered from a close-in shotgun blast. When I looked down into the compound, all I could see was a mushroom-like cloud with debris and fiery ash still floating down. Quickly, I pulled my protective mask from its hip holster and placed it over my head.

After I had gotten to a point where I could breathe through the mask, I took a look around. None of the buildings were left standing and bodies were strewn a hundred yards in every direction. Collins and company should have very little to mop up. Did my body landing on the detonation device blow the bunker or was it Maslam's man? Didn't matter at this point.

"We're coming in, Scorpion," I heard Collins say. Overhead I then saw the AH-6c circling the compound, mini-guns ready.

"You okay down there, Bruce?" Steed called.

"What a show. I thought these rocks were going to crumble."

"I'm all right. Can hardly hear though. My head hurts like a son-of-a-bitch."

I heard him laugh through his gas mask. I was glad he thought to put it on.

"I'm coming your way, Steed."

"What?"

We were now apparently having trouble hearing one another through our masks.

"Never mind!" I yelled.

As I had run, jumped and slid more than halfway down the rocky slope, I had the same amount of distance to recover. But no sooner had I reached the apex to where Steed was still in prone, than a hail of bullets began pinging around us again. At least four of the enemy had apparently taken off after the fun started and enveloped our position. A classic fire and movement assault technique appeared to be going on. Two men were laying down a base of fire at the bottom of the reverse slope while two were jack-rabbiting up the hill.

I quickly snatched up my Winchester and popped one of the attackers in the chest while Steed dropped another with a nice head shot. We were doing pretty well hitting our targets considering the lens in our masks were steaming up. However, one of the other hostiles then decided to put his AK on full automatic and began spraying our position. Pieces of rock shattered by the hail of bullets peppered us, stinging and lacerating our faces.

But suddenly we heard two foreign shots coming from the tree line at the bottom of the hill and then everything was quiet. As it appeared that Collins' people had cordoned off the camp, two of his sharpshooters that had worked their way around to the rear of the compound had taken care of business. The remaining two attackers had gone down quickly.

Steed and I then stood and I popped the sharpshooters a salute. To the front and eastern side of the compound somewhere in the woods, we could hear small arms fire which told me some skirmishes were still going on between Collins' people and the few hostiles that were still trying to escape.

In my ear again was Mike Collins.

"We have locked down the perimeter, Scorpion. Are you and Steed alive up there?"

"We're fine. Are you serving lunch back there in your mess tent? Some of us didn't have breakfast. By the way, how do you like the big hole I made?"

"It'll make a nice big swimming hole for the kids from around the county."

"Do you think I broke any windows in Richmond?"

"I know you probably broke a few in Goshen."

"If you will have a few of your boys and girls pick up three bodies with big pieces of their heads missing down in the center of the compound, I'd appreciate it. I don't know which of the three is al-Massoud, but he will be one of them."

"Wilco. We'll then cart 'em back to Quantico for identification. Good hunting, McGowan."

"We'll be down in a few minutes to personally thank a couple of your people for saving our bacon up here. Ciao."

# CHAPTER 27

*You can hold back the rain, bring on the wind*

*Knock us right down, we'll get up again*

*We've dug in deep, made our stand*

*This is our homeland*

**Keith Miles and Jack Sundrud**

**Kenny Rogers**

Before we began our descent from the hill, we flung off our protective masks. Collins had radioed us that all was clear on the radiation front. His detection devices had confirmed that. I then turned and thrust out my hand to the quiet, stoic man beside me. "There's nobody I have ever seen who could make those three kill shots as fast and cleanly as you did. Especially someone with a concussion *and* has just experienced a bout with hypothermia. And especially at that distance. Here's my hand, Atticus." He nodded, shook my hand and gave me a half smile. But in his eyes, I found neither a look of accomplishment *or* celebration. All I saw was weakness. There was no doubt in my mind, Steed was still ailing. I then picked up his field pack along with mine. "Let's go down and join the party."

"You're bleeding, Bruce."

I knew that I had picked up some rock shrapnel and could feel the tickle of the blood oozing down my neck, but I was in no pain.

"I'm okay. Come on. I see Collins signaling."

When we reached the compound, I met Collins at the edge of the hole in the ground. However, we made sure there were no more secondary explosions occurring before standing on the rim. There was nothing that was not either blown to bits or still smoldering. One of the fire units that Collins had waiting in the wings was allowed into the compound to check for sure. The State Police and county sheriff's department were also on the scene of the blast within minutes after it occurred. Collins did let them in for collaboration purposes and traffic control on Highway 42, but gave them only general information about what went down. Because it was their turf, he was compelled to extend them that courtesy. However, he made it clear that the Bureau would maintain control over the scene. He also asked them to call in as many EMT and coroner's units as could be summoned in a three-county area.

The FBI Red Team had apparently scoured the compound very thoroughly for casualties and those who might still be running in the woods. Perhaps a couple of hostiles *had* escaped after al-Massoud and friends bought the farm, but the team had still taken about thirty-five into custody. After the body count, forty-one hostiles met their end as a result of the explosion, and twenty-seven more of them died from bullets, either pumped into them by Collins' people or through the courtesy of Steed and McGowan. Sixteen of the prisoners had some degree of injury...three, serious. They were being treated by FBI medics until the EMTs arrived.

Many of the bodies blown away by the bunker eruption were badly mangled. Some were actually smoldering and there were a few open body cavities, all of which served to bring back memories of my war forty-some years ago. The compound carnage wasn't quite as horrific, however, as several of the post-battle scenes that I had experienced in that war which included bodies that had been melted down by napalm. My olfactory memories of the stench have never left me. It's a wonder as I surveyed the grisly Goshen scene that I didn't have a PTSD flashback that caused me to go into convulsions and piss myself.

Collins continued. "When we came upon one of the box trucks behind that bunker that got blown about twenty feet, we heard somebody yelling inside it. Although his bell got rung pretty good, he was alive. He just couldn't remember the past twenty-four hours. There was a body in there, however, with a couple of rounds in his chest. You wouldn't know anything about that, of course."

"Of course," I repeated.

"By the way," continued Collins.

"One of my men who remained in the staging area said a bear of a man in coveralls came charging out of the woods with a shotgun right after the blast. Says he appeared to be a local who might live nearby. We've detained him just in case."

"That would be Cletus, Mike."

"Cletus?"

"Yeah. He was sort of unofficially working with us."

"I don't understand."

"He lives in a house just off your staging area. That field is his property, so I had to quasi engage him. When we were here a few days ago, he was smart enough to figure out we were planning something. I told him come crunch time we'd like him to just stand by and guard his premises. Okay to let him go. Man's a patriot and please convey to him the government's appreciation. And mine."

"Will do, Bruce."

A young woman in SWAT garb then walked up to us along with a male.

"These are my two sharpshooters that took the heat off you two up there," Collins said.

Steed and I both shook their hands.

"Thanks, kids. We owe you big time," I said.

"All in a day's work, sir," the lass replied.

The bodies of al-Massoud and his two companions were segregated so that they would not be mixed up with the others. Two of them did have identification on them, and one did not. It was assumed *that* individual was the Viper. Forensics would bear that out, however.

In wrapping up our conversation, Collins said,

"You guys need to steer clear of the police. They won't know that you and Steed aren't FBI; nor will they know you blew the bunker and took down a world-class terrorist. *Nobody* will, per Hickcock's instructions. I basically told them we just had this place under surveillance and apparently one or more of the bad guys found out we were ready to move on them; ergo, *they* blew the bunker. They apparently didn't realize it would kill nearly a third of them when it went off. I told the trooper in charge that the Bureau would ultimately get out an official report through federal-to-state channels. I also asked them to keep the press away as it needs to remain a crime scene until further notice. You two probably need to go ahead and de-ass the area. By the way, Bruce, you have a nasty gash on the side of your neck. Looks like a bullet graze. I'll get one of my medics to look at it."

I hadn't even noticed, although when I took my protective mask off, I found that it obviously protected me in a way I didn't expect. There was also a chunk of rock lodged between the eye lenses. But, sure enough, when I touched my neck just below my right ear, I drew my hand back and found a mass of blood.

"Not to worry," I said.

"I'll fix it." From my first aid pack on my pistol belt I then pulled out a pad of gauze and applied it firmly against my skin. It was the first real time I felt any pain. After applying some ointment, I pressed the gauze back into my skin a little harder until the bleeding stopped.

"Good as new."

"But it looks bad, Bruce. Missed your carotid by a few centimeters. Maybe you should wait for a paramedic. You need some stitches."

"Naw. I'll take care of it when I get back."

"Suit yourself. Well anyway, great results, guys. I'll work with you two anytime." Collins then shoved his fist in the air. "Army strong."

"Hooah!" I grunted in return.

*****

Steed slid onto the passenger's seat of my Suburban, placed his noggin against the head rest and closed his eyes. I was even more sure that the past eighteen hours on that rock in the pouring rain, in hypothermia conditions and without nourishment, had indeed taken its toll on him.

"Let's get some lunch," I said after cranking up my engine.

He nodded, but didn't otherwise respond.

In Clifton Forge, just off the interstate, we stopped at a Hardees. I had something I hardly ever get...a big, fat gobby cheeseburger. But as hungry as I knew Steed was, he merely munched on a few fries and drank about half of a Diet Coke.

It was well past time that I called Hickcock. I hadn't forgotten about it, but first things first...like lunch.

"Hello, John," I greeted.

"About *time* you called me with the news. At least I got the results from Collins."

"I was going to get around to it. Mission accomplished, however."

"You and Steed did good work. Mr. Johns will be pleased. The Viper is history, and the first blow has been struck against Jamaat ul-Fuqra. Once it is learned what you found in that munitions bunker and that al-Massoud was planning to use ul-Fuqra to attack our country, perhaps the justice system and the liberal organizations that are protecting them will re-assess their positions. Of course, most Americans, when they hear the news, won't realize how close the country came to something worse than another 9-11, times ten."

"Hopefully, our mission won't have been in vain," I said.

"And hopefully, no civilians will wander into that compound and step on any unexploded ordnance that might have been spun out by the blast."

"Collins said he will have his EOD expert and other members of his team sweep every meter of that compound before they leave it to assure it's cleared. Our Public Affairs Office will handle any media inquiries about al-Massoud, ul-Fuqra activities and what happened in the Goshen compound. Basically, I will write the press release. If there's further inquiry, such as from a special committee, Mr. Johns and I will put our heads together on it. As for you guys? *What* guys? You're retired. And Steed? Well, the last I checked, Mr. Steed was living happily ever after on his fortune somewhere in the Caribbean with his new bride."

"You forgot to mention our bonus, of course. I guess you'll be paying us with captured drug money, eh?"

"How did you find *that* out?"

"Hey, this country's broke. Where else can you cough up that much change?"

"Enough about where the money comes from. Anyway, I'd like you and Steed to be here at my office the day after tomorrow for a debrief, if you can fit me into your busy social calendar. Maggie and I would also like to take you out for a celebratory dinner at a Waffle House of your choice."

"Funny, John. But, I like my waitresses to have full sets of teeth when they smile at me. What time do you want us there?"

"Noon will be fine."

"See you then. By the way, when you're kissing on Maggie, also give her a kiss for me."

And then I heard nothing but dead space on the other end of my phone.

I did check myself out in the mirror before going home and Collins was right...the gash on my neck did need stitches. I was bleeding again. So on the way back, I stopped by a Doc in the Box to get sewn up. It took nine stitches. And Collins was right a second time; a couple of centimeters and the bullet would have severed my carotid.

I didn't think we looked any worse for wear when we dragged our bodies in the front door. A little tired-looking, muddy and wrinkled up, maybe. But, Adriana noticed the bandage on my neck first thing.

"Who shot you *this* time?"

"You won't believe this, but..."

"You're right. I won't...so don't bother," she said rather curtly.

"And was that *it*? End of mission this time?"

I nodded. "End of mission. We will go to Washington, DC in a couple of days to brief the Bureau on our findings and then Atticus is on his way back to Dallas. And me? Back to being your house husband."

I thought I'd get a scolding because of my newest wound...or at least a lecture. But that was all she had to say. Maybe she was just being nice since Steed was standing nearby. I'd catch it later.

Speaking of Steed...he still didn't look so hot. A couple of times in those early morning hours I thought for sure he was down and out. But he had performed magnificently in spite of his malady. I think he would have walked into hell to gain his freedom. It was his one shot. Pardon the pun, but actually, it took three. Three bullets. Three heads. Five seconds. Now it was up to Hickcock to come through for him.

As I headed for the shower, Steed merely threw up his hand and said he was going to lie down. In spite of his daunting effort that afternoon to regain his strength and vigor, he was fading. He said he didn't want anything more to eat or drink...just needed some sack time.

The birds outside our window woke me the next morning, all cheerful and singing praises to the Almighty like they were. I laid there also thinking about how the Almighty got us through that very difficult eighteen or nineteen hours over there in that compound. I thought maybe *I* should be singing as well. And it was the first night in weeks that the dream had not invaded my sleep.

"You must have been tired last night," Adriana commented while I was stumbling toward the bathroom. "You were sound asleep in less than a minute and it was the first time ever that you came home from fun and games that you didn't hit on me."

"Okay, then, what are you doing right now?"

"Not messing around with *you*. Now get dressed and go downstairs to check on Atticus. He looked frail when you came in yesterday afternoon. And we didn't see him the rest of the day."

"He shouldn't have left that hospital," I agreed. "What was so all-fired important that he just had to get back here?"

I dodged the question by saying, "I'll get my clothes on and go check with him."

It was a few minutes past eight when I rapped on his door. There was no response.

"Atticus, you still asleep?" I called.

Still no answer.

I thought he might be in the bathroom showering, so I wasn't getting worried yet. I then decided to grab a cup of the java Adriana had made earlier and go sit on the veranda a while to see the kind of morning the birds were singing about. I'd give Steed fifteen minutes and then knock on his door again. If he didn't answer this time, I'd get the pass key and go in. But when I stepped out onto the porch, to my amazement, there he sat, drinking coffee from my favorite cup...with a more refreshed, even ebullient look on his face. The swelling was also fully gone from his temple.

"I hope you don't mind, but I helped myself to some coffee," he said. Then I realized too late that this is the cup *you* always drink out of. Sorry."

"No need to be sorry. I'm just glad you're okay. How long have you been up?"

"Since about six-thirty. I didn't see either of you stirring, so I went out and took a walk. When I got back, I smelled the coffee. But I *am* a little hungry, so I thought I'd ask Adriana for her van and go out for some toast and eggs."

"Naw, I'll fix you up some. How do you like your eggs?"

"Scrambled...with Tabasco sauce."

"Tabasco? You're kidding of course," I said.

"Remember, I grew up in Louisiana. I put hot sauce on everything. Too bad you don't have any crawfish to go with the eggs. You don't, do you?"

"Now you're grossing me out. But, hey, I'm glad you're feeling better. I was wondering if you were actually going to make it yesterday afternoon."

"I admit I felt pretty rough. Then I woke up about five this morning thinking about those million bucks. But the money will mean nothing if the pardon doesn't materialize for some reason. I'd hate to be looking over my shoulder the rest of my life."

"Hickcock was firm on that. I'm sure you can trust him to come through on the deal."

"And I trust you're *right*. But for now, I want to take you up on those eggs. You sure Adriana doesn't have any crawdaddies laying around?"

# CHAPTER 28

We did nothing but kick back that day, ate our three squares and relaxed. Adrianna made a nice dinner for us of roasted chicken, corn soufflé and of course a salad...the staple around Wolf Laurel. After we helped her clean up, she left to go to her book club and we sat on the veranda each putting down a carafe of wine. For some reason, he liked the light, sweet stuff like White Zinfandel, but I broke out a bottle of Merlot. As we sat there, Steed then spent about a half an hour on the phone with Maria. Following their conversation, he told me she couldn't wait until they returned to Antigua. Not only was her family grating on her, practically demanding she, at least, stay in the Dallas area to help care for them, she was looking forward to going back to their Caribbean bungalow to start planning the details of their wedding.

"Are you ready for that, Atticus?"

"For what?"

"You know...marriage. You seem like the kind of guy that's just good being by himself. Ever been married?"

"No. I guess I was just too busy killing people." I caught his wry smile.

"Don't remind me. I might just go back to disliking you."

"How about you? Adriana told us she was married before and her husband had died, but was she your first or second wife?" he asked.

"Second. My first wife and I were happy for twenty or so years."

"So what happened?"

"Then we met."

He laughed.

"I guess I did love Darlene in my own way, but I don't believe I ever *really* experienced love until Adriana. Just remember something, pal; be sure it's love you're feeling and not an over-active libido. With my ex, I first thought love was just one sweet dream. But marriage was the alarm clock."

He grinned and shook his head. "I can't figure you, McGowan. Here you are a ruthless, tough guy who would drop a man without batting an eye, yet you sit here like one of the housewives of Hollywood talking about love and marriage."

"Just showing you my soft, sensitive side, Billy Joe."

Steed leaned his head back against the rocker. "Billy Joe. No one's called me that for years. I do kind of miss it."

"What did they call you before you took the alias

Atticus Steed?"

"Bill...or just Cavanaugh. I think I liked the title 'Lance Corporal Bill Cavanaugh' better than anything."

"Why don't you go back to the name?" I asked.

"I wanted to, but Atticus Steed is the only name Maria has ever known me by and she likes it."

"There you go, Steed. Already compromising. One thing you have to remember, kid...you gotta let 'em know who wears the pants right up front or you'll find yourself in a marriage where one person is always right, and the other is the husband."

"You should've been a comedian, McGowan. I actually believe you're trying to talk me *out* of getting married. Don't concern yourself, though. I'm ready for this and know what I'm doing. I love Maria and want to spend all my remaining years with her. This is a chance at a new life for me, all the way around. And I'm not going to screw it up this time."

"That's what I was looking for, man. A little fire. Something that broadcasts the fact that you *want* this marriage."

"So, you were just kind of testing me, huh? Seeing if it was something I really wanted. Bruce McGowan... a comedian *and* a psychologist."

"Just having a little fun with ya, man, that's all. Glad you're feeling better."

*****

At eight-thirty the next morning, I kissed wife number two goodbye and then Steed and I walked down the front steps into the rain and fog toward the Suburban. Considering the inclement weather, we were actually leaving about twenty minutes later than I wanted, but Adriana insisted that we have breakfast before we left. And I wasn't going to disappoint the Mrs. Not *this* Mrs. I figured we could still make it to the Hoover Building in good order by noon.

Things were going pretty well for the first couple hours of our trip, but sometimes when I'm in deep thought or deeply engaged in conversation with my passenger, I tend to press down on the accelerator. And I *was* probably doing a few miles over the speed limit, when my rear view mirror was suddenly filled up with a flashing blue light. Of course it also had to be near one of the Harrisonburg exits. I pulled over to the shoulder and stopped. Deja vu *again*. I didn't even *have* to see his face to recognize the two-hundred seventy-five pound frame walking toward me.

"Oh, *hell* no," I said.

"What?" Steed asked.

"Deputy M. Seibert."

"You know him?"

"Unfortunately. I got a speeding ticket from this guy a few weeks ago on my way up to meet with Hickcock."

And then I heard the familiar rap on my back glass.

"Drop your window glass, sir," he ordered.

I did so and it immediately began to rain inside my vehicle. I was glad the fat bastard was getting soaked out there.

He let out a sigh.

"You again. Do you remember me?"

I *wanted* to take it back as soon as I said it.

I never forget a face, officer. But in your case, I've tried to make an exception."

"And I remember your smart mouth. License and registration and then follow me back to my cruiser."

I glanced at Steed and saw that he was trying to stifle a grin.

"Damn," I said. I thought of a couple of worse words, but kept them to myself.

After trotting back to the cruiser in the monsoon rain, I quickly opened the passenger door, jumped in and slammed it. Hard. I not only had to endure watching the deputy write up a ticket in his second grade penmanship, but had to listen to his lecture about "keeping it under the sound barrier, especially on the wet interstate." He then handed my registration back to me along with the ticket. "I oughta *keep* that license, you know." Without word, I then got out of his car and jogged back to mine. But then, I realized that he *did* keep my license. So, I dropped my window and motioned for him to come back to my door. I just wanted to see him get soaked all the way to the bone this time.

"What is it, Mr. McGowan?"

"You kept my license."

Checking his clipboard, he found he still had it stuck up under the metal clip. He then put it between two fingers and stuck it under my nose.

"Now, do the good people of Virginia a favor and slow this hoss down."

I then looked at him and smiled.

"Can I also ask you to do the good people of Virginia a favor as well?"

"What?" he said gruffly.

"Would you please either comb or braid that nostril hair? The way it hangs down makes you look like you have one of those Hitler mustaches."

He then squinted his eyes and formed his mouth into an astringent curl.

"Goodbye, McGowan." If he could have pulled his gun out and shot me, I'd be a dead man.

Through the mirror I watched as he waddled back to his cruiser and then plopped his carcass down in the driver's seat. I could have sworn I saw him checking his nostrils out in his mirror.

I thought Steed had come unglued he was laughing so hard. That's when I knew the putz had obviously nearly fully recovered from his accident.

*****

The fifteen-minute delay on I-81 didn't do much in getting us behind. It did, however, cost me another hundred dollars and four more points. My insurance agent was not going to like this.

After stashing ol' Diablo in the Hoover underground parking garage, we took the elevator to the 5th floor. Hickcock's office was the second door on the left after the elevator. His assistant, whose name I found out was Tessie, the one with the smoker's cough, took us into his office in the adjoining room. When she opened the door for us, we found Hickcock behind his desk, Maggie in a side chair and Preston Johns sitting on one corner of Hickcock's desk.

Johns walked directly to us and shook both of our hands. "Heroes of the day, gentlemen. You made it happen. Congratulations."

Hickcock then sprung from his chair and walked over to shake our hands as well.

"Ditto, fellows. We definitely had the right team on this. By the way, Bruce, I see the bandage on your neck. Collins told me you had been wounded."

"You call this a wound? I've had mosquito bites worse than this."

Johns chuckled.

"As I remember him, Agent Hickcock, he takes a bullet very well. Anyway, gentlemen, I want you to know that the President is extremely pleased. Your actions in Operation Firestorm will not only damage the al-Qaeda hierarchy but its overall infrastructure as well. It will finally prove to the State Department, which has refused to shut these camps down, that Mubarak Gilani and the Jamaat ul-Fuqra terror cells are out to destroy America. The evidence we obtained will show that al-Massoud collaborated with one Mohammed Shahaz at the Hancock headquarters and masterminded the plot by utilizing one of its eastern regional terrorist cells to carry out the attacks. Fortunately, and thanks to you, they did not succeed. Two of the people that you killed, Mr. Steed, had some form of ID on them. One *was* Shahaz, and he was identified by his driver's license. The second was a notorious radical extremist Imam from the Detroit mosque, the largest in the U.S. He had poured a hell of a lot of money into the ul-Fuqra operations throughout. The third had a passport on him with the name Abdul Maajid."

Steed looked at Hickcock and then back at Johns.

"You mean I didn't nail al-Massoud after all?"

Hickcock replied,

"The man's passport photo was matched up with others we had of Massoud and after running it through the facial recognition system, there is a 98.7% assuredness that the man *was* al-Massoud. The Medical Examiner at Quantico, who performed his autopsy just this morning, found on his back a large tattoo...that of a Viper. Al-Massoud had an ego the size of Iraq. It flattered him, even *glorified* him for others, especially his enemies, to refer to him as *The Viper*...one who strikes quickly and kills in a matter of seconds. He was all about power within the terrorist community. As he demanded that he be exalted in stature by his brotherhood, he would then ultimately rise above the imminence of even bin-Laden. Have no doubt, Mr. Steed, that you killed the number one terrorist threat in the world."

"You had me there for a moment," Steed said.

"Anyway," continued Johns,

"you proved that you are not only one of the best marksmen in the world, if not *the* best, you proved your commitment to this mission. And your country appreciates it."

Larsen, who had not been a major player in the day-to-day mission discussions, then stood and walked up to Steed to shake his hand.

"You know, Mr. Steed, a few months ago, even though you saved our skin by knocking off the bad guys who were after us and earlier refusing the hit on Hickcock and me, I still wanted to nail you worse than anyone on our Ten Most Wanted list. When the planning began on this mission, I saw absolutely no value in engaging you; but

Agent Hickcock talked me into it." She then looked over at John.

"And I think he's still ridiculously taken with you. But, it was his idea to take you off the wanted list and seek a pardon for you. Me? I told him he was nuts." She then stopped there for a moment and Steed just stared at her, waiting for the 'but.'

"But," she continued. "You proved me wrong. I now find that there *are* a few redeeming qualities about you after all and that's why I'm pleased to be the one to give you these two pieces of paper. The first is a Letter of Pardon for all crimes committed by you prior to 10 August of this year. As you can see, it is signed by none other than the President himself. And as promised, here is a certified check issued by the Department of the Treasury for the amount agreed upon. The good thing is, it's tax-free. Congratulations, Atticus Steed. You are hereby a free man." And then she added, "And so is Billy Joe Cavanaugh." I thought I caught a slight smile.

Tears formed in Steed's eyes, and he gave her a slight head bow. "Thank you, Agent Larsen."

Johns and Hickcock again shook his hand as well.

"Does that mean I'm no longer partnered with a criminal?' I asked.

That evoked smiles from *everyone*.

"There is one thing, gentlemen," said Johns. "No one outside of this room, except the President and the FBI

SWAT element, will ever know of your involvement. If the press begins to look for people to crucify over this mission because of all the casualties, the FBI takes the hit."

"Suits me," I said.

"And by the way, Bruce," added Hickcock.

"Here's a little something for *your* services, as agreed. Just know that you are not now nor were at any time working for the government in regard to this mission."

"I knew that." I then inspected the contents of the envelope and added,

"Is this a great country or what?" A check made out to *me* for a million dollars. I thought my pounding heart would leap clean out of my chest. But then I regained my composure, swallowed, and asked,

"Is this tax-free?"

"It is."

So, I was right about where it came from. Drug money is not taxable.

For the remainder of the afternoon, Steed and I sat with Hickcock and Larsen, providing them with a briefing of every detail involved in our planning and execution of the Goshen Jamaat ul-Fuqra mission. Basically, it ended up being a moment-by-moment account of everything that occurred from day one. What Hickcock would do with his notes on the mission, even he and Larsen had no clue. It was assumed that the notes and his subsequent report would be locked away in a vault somewhere...some place where other classified documents go only to be de-classified or more likely destroyed in twenty-five years or so.

The story of the FBI's raid on the Goshen compound had already hit the media and Hickcock read us the AP early report that *"a total of sixty-eight ul-Fuqra members, mostly Middle Eastern, and a few American jihadists, were killed at a Goshen, Virginia training camp. Twenty-seven others were wounded and taken to local hospitals. The sixteen who were captured were temporarily incarcerated in the federal prison in Richmond, Virginia. It was also believed that al-Qaeda chieftain and radical leader, Asahim al-Massoud, AKA The Viper, was killed in the raid. The FBI is in possession of intelligence photos taken by the jihadists of federal and commerce buildings, bridges and monuments in Washington, D.C., and New York City, that were targeted by the ul-Fuqra organization. It is believed that al-Massoud was the planner of the tentative attack on the above cities. Confiscated from the camp as well were photos (actually my photos) of crates containing small arms weapons, rocket launchers, and weapons of mass destruction...C4, drums of fertilizer and ammonium nitrate that would be used in a planned terrorist attack on the above cities on September 11th. At this time there is no information on the validity of the intelligence that precipitated the FBI's raid."*

At 1630, the agents terminated the de-brief.

"Okay, gentlemen," began Hickcock,

"we promised dinner and let's make it early. Not only do you need to get back to West Virginia this evening, but Maggie and I have other plans." He then reviewed how that sounded.

"Not together, however."

I then cocked my head and gave him one of those 'don't lie to me' smiles.

"There is a favorite restaurant of the Washington elite. Casual, like you're wearing, is okay."

"O'Malley's," I said.

"Not O'Malley's, Bruce, although I know you can't wait to go back there. This place has Louisiana fare, which we know you'll like."

"Just what I've had a hankering for," Steed said.

I shook my head.

"Crawfish. Let's see now. You take a bottom-feeding roach-looking critter that is not really a fish, bite the tail off and then suck the brains out of the head. And then you have to eat a thousand of them to have a meal. Sounds appetizing. I assume they serve steak or chicken."

We did have a very nice dinner at Maison Deux. After a bit of coaxing from my table mates, I had a pasta dish in a spicy sauce that did contain crawfish. The difference was, the tiny pieces of meat had already been pulled from the carcasses of the little red bugs, and I had no problem putting them down. They were actually pretty dang succulent.

We were done by seven and just about all that needed to be said *had* been said. After we stepped out on the sidewalk and handed our tickets to the valet, Hickcock put out his hand and said,

"The government thanks you both for your service. I guess we won't have reason to come across one another again. But, good luck to you."

Steed replied,

"That grieves me, John. I thought after all we had been through, we had become kind of like family."

"Family?" quipped Maggie.

"Yeah, come to think of it, I do have an uncle who reminds me of you. He still has about six years left on his sentence."

Steed laughed and then his face turned serious.

"You gave me back my life, you know. And you didn't have to. You could have kept me out there on the Most Wanted list. I won't forget that. If you ever need me for anything, you know where I'll be."

Larsen said

"If we ever need you for your talents, Atticus, that means Hickcock and I will be in serious trouble."

"Goodbye, John...Maggie," I said.

"If the new breed of Special Agents are anything like you two, federal law enforcement is in pretty damn good shape."

On the way back to Wolf Laurel, from out of the blue, Steed said,

"She called me *Atticus*, Maggie did. She had never done that before. I think she likes me, Bruce."

I just nodded and smiled.

# CHAPTER 29

It's always an exhausting ordeal when I drive up to Washington and back on the same day. I haven't done that many times, but I can vividly remember the days that I did. It was after eleven-thirty when we came through the door at Wolf Laurel. There were two reasons, however, I was not particularly feeling the fatigue that usually accompanied such road-weary days: first, the long, arduous mission was over and I didn't have to think about it anymore; and secondly, I was a little richer than I was this morning. I just hoped my bank didn't reject the government's check.

"Well, I'm hitting the sack," I said. "There's an angel upstairs who I'm sure is waiting for me to fondle her wings. Are you turning in as well?"

"I think I'll just sit out on your veranda in the night air for a while and smoke this cigar the restaurant gave me. I haven't smoked one in years, but doing so tonight will be my celebration...like a new papa savoring the birth of his new baby. In *my* case, however, it's a new birth of *freedom*."

"I can understand that," I replied. "But please do Adriana and me a favor. Just don't burn the damn house down. Good night."

When I arose the next morning, dressed and poured a cup of coffee from the pot in our upstairs kitchen, I then stepped outside and again found Steed sitting in one of the rockers.

"You been out here all night?"

He chuckled. "No. I took about three puffs of that cigar and quickly remembered why I never smoked. I then tamped it out and went inside. Even after brushing my teeth and gargling with mouthwash, the taste of that El Ropo Supremo laid in my mouth all night like a dead mouse. I can *still* taste it."

I sat down in the rocker beside him and took a deep breath of the tart morning air. Neither of us uttered a word for a while.

Finally, he said, "Yeah, I can see Maria and I living in a setting and a town like this. This West Virginia is a pretty nice place. Maybe we'll come back here some time for a visit. Maybe to Wolf Laurel. Would you be all right with that?"

"We'd welcome you back anytime."

"I have to admit I had reservations about partnering with you on this deal, Bruce."

"Ditto, man. I felt the same about you."

"But I will tell you that seeing you in action, I was downright mesmerized at times. The way you handle yourself is nothing short of amazing. I consider myself privileged to have worked with you."

Trying to respond as humbly as I could, I said,

"Well, I *have* lost a step or two, but appreciate you saying that. I thought my days of action were long behind me. Maybe now they will be." I paused a moment and then turned my head toward him.

"But, it was fun while it lasted, wasn't it?"

"Your idea of fun is not exactly my idea of mirth and merriment, old boy," he said.

"So, will you stay in Antigua now that you don't have to hole up?"

"I'm going to leave it up to Maria. We talked a little about it on the phone before my brain passed out last night. I know she's concerned about her parents, but she wants us to have a good life together. And she doesn't want it to be in Dallas. Neither do I. Nice place, but hotter than hell in the summer."

"Well, if you're serious about returning here, the good old Dubya Vee is a darnn good place to live. A million bucks will buy you a hell of a nice place. And then there's the two million you have in that Swiss account that the government had unfrozen."

"I haven't forgotten about it, believe me," he replied.

"But money is not what drives me. Something else does at this point in my life."

"Yeah. I think it was your Trekkie hero James Kirk who said, 'Money is money, but women...are better.'"

Steed swept his eyes over the flock of pink rhododendrons just off the south side of the veranda, deeply rich in their splendor. There was a slight chill in the air and an early hint of autumn gold and crimson faintly visible in the trees on the distant mountain. He smiled and nodded.

"Yeah. Not a bad place at all." He then glanced at his watch.

"Well, I guess I need to get to the airport in a few minutes, if you would be so kind to take me."

"Be glad to," I said.

Adriana, apparently still struck by Atticus Steed's good looks and manners, gave him a long hug and told him,

"It was wonderful having you and Maria here...although she had to leave on such sorrowful terms. And of course most of the time, you were out playing super spy with my husband."

"Thank you, Adriana. You're a beautiful woman and a gracious hostess. Maria and I felt comfortable here." He then turned and looked at me.

"*Not* so comfortable in the land of Goshen, however."

She then gave him another hug.

"You will have to come back someday soon."

Any further body contact and I was going to have to throw a bucket of water on them. She's mine, Steed. You have one of your own. Now go get her. I'm usually not the jealous type, but this was ridiculous.

*****

The Bureau jet was already waiting for Steed on the tarmac. Hickcock had extended just one more courtesy to him by offering to fly him to Dallas on the Bureau's nickel. Damn nice of him.

After Steed pulled his bag from the cargo area of the Suburban, we began walking toward the terminal. I then saw him draw in a deep breath allowing his lungs to digest the sweet mountain air. It would be a three plus hour flight to the Dallas-Fort Worth Airport and then he would be in the arms of his fiancée. There was just a hint of a smile on his face and I took it to be one of not only relief, but anticipation.

"How does it feel to have your life handed back to you?" I asked him.

"Like an anvil has been lifted from around my neck. Like I've been born again."

"You've got an opportunity here, Atticus. Don't backslide. Don't screw it up. No guns, no hits, no errors."

His smile then widened into a grin.

"I won't. That is if I can just keep the government away from my door..."

"I'm with you, Mr. Steed." I then glanced over at the large American flag on a nearby pole flowing lazily in the morning breeze.

"Yeah, Uncle Sam, I appreciate the money and you thinking about me; but the next time you call, your favorite nephew is telling you to go to hell. I will now only be my *wife's* Action Man."

Steed laughed heartily, but didn't reply. From the look in his eyes, I could sense the wheels turning in his head. I think what I said reminded him that with his now unfrozen assets and his latest financial boon, he would soon be living as a worry-free man in the lap of luxury with his new wife. A *rich*, worry-free man.

I couldn't go through security, of course, so I shook his hand just before he approached the TSA agent.

"Give Maria my best," I said.

"Take care, old man. Careful not to let the rust set in." He then smiled again and turned away. Just as he was about to enter the screening area, he set his bag down, turned around and popped me a salute.

I returned it with one of my own. But mine was the *Vulcan* salute. The one where I just held up my hand with the second and third fingers spread apart. I then nodded and yelled to my Trekky new friend standing across the terminal,

*"Live long and prosper, Mr. Steed!"*

## <u>Praises for Col. Lee Martin's Mystery Novels</u>

### The Third Moon is Blue

Exciting and thrilling, this is a marvelous mix of psychodrama, romance and loss. Lee Martin really paints a picture well.

———————————————————————— Readers Favorite

The Third Moon is Blue took me back to a time in early adulthood in a way no other book has ever done, partly due to the locale, but also because of the way in which he relates the story in vivid detail.

———————————————————————— Glenna Fisher

The Third Moon is Blue is a great read! Lee Martin has given us a little of something for everyone…an air of intrigue and mystery, a riveting, emotional story of heartache and fear, a life-like depiction of courage in war…and in life. It's all woven together with a love story for the ages…

———————————————————————— James C. Crutchfield

# Wolf Laurel

First of a great trilogy. Lee Martin introduces us to Bruce McGowan in this first of three wonderfully-intriguing books with McGowan as the protagonist. Once you meet McGowan, you won't stop reading until you've finished the third book (A Hateful Wind) and beg for a sequel.

— Andy Black

The main character in this novel, Bruce McGowan, is truly a "John Wayne meets Clint Eastwood" cowboy. I love this character! This is a great read for anyone who enjoys reading about patriotic heroes, intrigue, espionage and covert action. Lee Martin is a true master of fantastic storytelling and "suspension of disbelief". In fact, I would not doubt that some of the features in this tale hold quite a bit of truth. I could not put this book down and I have read all of the sequels since.

— J.C. Laurie

## The Six Mile Inn

Lee Martin is a master story-teller, making Lavinia's story a compelling page turner. If you enjoy stories woven around actual events, and like a little romance, murder and suspense with a great cast of characters, give this book a try. Definitely worth reading.

———————————————————— Reader's Choice

## The Valiant

Mystery novelist COL Lee Martin continues to excite his audience with his latest release of "The Valiant". I have read most of his books, but "The Valiant" is by far my favorite. In baseball terms, Lee Martin has hit a standup homerun. "The Valiant" is an intriguing mystery novel that includes a silent hero, a spunky, blonde librarian, and a cop that doesn't quit until he gets answers to his questions. The Valiant will keep you on the edge of your seat to the very end. This is a book you'll find hard to put down.

————————————————Marc Morris The Talmadge Group

I could not put the book down. You'll keep trying to anticipate the next twist. If you're my age, it might even conger up some memories of the past.

—————————————————————————— Bill Deck

The novel is a work of a mature author, well in control of plot and structure. Clues are distributed carefully to keep the reader alert and interested throughout. In terms of characterization, the main protagonist is well-defined and believable. The crime story aspect is particularly successful, keeping the reader guessing until late in the work regarding the identity of the culprit. The 'happy ending' is pleasing and emotionally satisfying. It was nice to encounter what many Europeans would consider a positive-minded American finish. Such a denouement is rarer here.

—Dr. Sharon Fuller/ Dr. Roy Fuller
— Angers, France

## Ten Minutes till Midnight

Lee Martin, normally a writer of mystery novels, documents the most hideous murder case in Colorado's history in "Ten Minutes Till Midnight". This true crime story is a must read, fabulous book. It is required reading for those who wish to influence the culture for good by understanding what turns so many human beings into murderers, and also, by understanding the brokenness of America's criminal justice system.

— Bob Enyart
—Denver Radio Personality's